Praise for

"A fun, lighthearted paranormal romance that will keep readers entertained. Ms. Cassidy fills the pages of her book with nonstop banter, ghostly activity, and steamy romance." *—Darque Reviews*

"Delaney, with her amusing sarcastic asides, makes for an entertaining romantic fantasy with a wonderful mystery subplot . . . Readers will relish this lighthearted jocular frolic." *—Genre Go Round Reviews*

"Cassidy has created a hilarious lead in Delaney Markham. Readers will run through all types of emotions while enjoying laugh-out-loud moments, desperate passion, wacky and fun characters, pop-culture references, and one intense mystery. The book's charm is apparent from the first page, but the twisted mystery tangled throughout will keep the pages turning." *—Romantic Times*

The Accidental Human

"I highly enjoyed every moment of Dakota Cassidy's *The Accidental Human* . . . A paranormal romance with a strong dose of humor." *—Errant Dreams*

"A delightful, at times droll, contemporary tale starring a decidedly human heroine . . . Dakota Cassidy provides a fitting twisted ending to this amusingly warm urban romantic fantasy." *—Genre Go Round Reviews*

"The final member of Cassidy's trio of decidedly offbeat friends faces her toughest challenge, but that doesn't mean there isn't humor to spare! With emotion, laughter, and some pathos, Cassidy serves up another winner!" *—Romantic Times*

continued . . .

Accidentally Dead

"A laugh-out-loud follow-up to *The Accidental Werewolf*, and it's a winner . . . Ms. Cassidy is an up-and-comer in the world of paranormal romance." —*Fresh Fiction*

"An enjoyable, humorous satire that takes a bite out of the vampire romance subgenre . . . Fans will appreciate the nonstop hilarity." —*Genre Go Round Reviews*

The Accidental Werewolf

"Cassidy, a prolific author of erotica, has ventured into MaryJanice Davidson territory with a humorous, sexy tale." —*Booklist*

"If Bridget Jones became a lycanthrope, she might be Marty. Fun and flirty humor is cleverly interspersed with dramatic mystery and action. It's hard to know which character to love best, though: Keegan or Muffin, the toy poodle that steals more than one scene." —*The Eternal Night*

"A riot! Marty's internal dialogue will have you howling, and her antics will keep the laughs coming. If you love paranormal with a comedic twist, you'll love this book." —*Romance Junkies*

"A lighthearted romp . . . [An] entertaining tale with an alpha twist." —*Midwest Book Review*

More praise for the novels of Dakota Cassidy

"The fictional equivalent of the little black dress—every reader should have one!"
—Michele Bardsley

"Serious, laugh-out-loud humor with heart, the kind of love story that leaves you rooting for the heroine, sighing for the hero, and looking for your own significant other at the same time."
—Kate Douglas

"Expect great things from Cassidy."
—*Romantic Times*

"Very fun, sexy. Five stars!"
—*Affaire de Coeur*

"Dakota Cassidy is going on my must-read list!"
—*Joyfully Reviewed*

"If you're looking for some steamy romance with something that will have you smiling, you have to read [Dakota Cassidy]."
—*The Best Reviews*

Berkley Sensation titles by Dakota Cassidy

YOU DROPPED A BLONDE ON ME

KISS & HELL

MY WAY TO HELL

THE ACCIDENTAL WEREWOLF

ACCIDENTALLY DEAD

THE ACCIDENTAL HUMAN

ACCIDENTALLY DEMONIC

You Dropped a
Blonde on Me

DAKOTA CASSIDY

B

BERKLEY SENSATION, NEW YORK

THE BERKLEY PUBLISHING GROUP
Published by the Penguin Group
Penguin Group (USA) Inc.
375 Hudson Street, New York, New York 10014, USA
Penguin Group (Canada), 90 Eglinton Avenue East, Suite 700, Toronto, Ontario M4P 2Y3, Canada
(a division of Pearson Penguin Canada Inc.)
Penguin Books Ltd., 80 Strand, London WC2R 0RL, England
Penguin Group Ireland, 25 St. Stephen's Green, Dublin 2, Ireland (a division of Penguin Books Ltd.)
Penguin Group (Australia), 250 Camberwell Road, Camberwell, Victoria 3124, Australia
(a division of Pearson Australia Group Pty. Ltd.)
Penguin Books India Pvt. Ltd., 11 Community Centre, Panchsheel Park, New Delhi—110 017, India
Penguin Group (NZ), 67 Apollo Drive, Rosedale, North Shore 0632, New Zealand
(a division of Pearson New Zealand Ltd.)
Penguin Books (South Africa) (Pty.) Ltd., 24 Sturdee Avenue, Rosebank, Johannesburg 2196,
South Africa

Penguin Books Ltd., Registered Offices: 80 Strand, London WC2R 0RL, England

This book is an original publication of The Berkley Publishing Group.

This is a work of fiction. Names, characters, places, and incidents either are the product of the author's imagination or are used fictitiously, and any resemblance to actual persons, living or dead, business establishments, events, or locales is entirely coincidental. The publisher does not have any control over and does not assume any responsibility for author or third-party websites or their content.

PRINTING HISTORY
Berkley Sensation trade paperback edition / December 2010

Library of Congress Cataloging-in-Publication Data

Cassidy, Dakota.
   You dropped a blonde on me / Dakota Cassidy.—Berkley Sensation trade pbk., ed.
      p.   cm.
   ISBN 978-0-425-23699-4
   1. Single mothers—Fiction.   2. Middle-aged women—Fiction.   3. New Jersey—Fiction.
I. Title
   PS3603.A8685Y68 2010
   813'.6—dc22
                                                                                              2010032481

PRINTED IN THE UNITED STATES OF AMERICA

10 9 8 7 6 5 4 3 2 1

ACKNOWLEDGMENTS

This book is for and because of some empowered, determined women who just wouldn't get off my back and let me give up. They are Kate Douglas, Karen Woods, Sheri Fogarty, Angela Knight, Margaret Riley, Ann Jacobs, Treva Harte, Sahara Kelly, Maryam Salim, Diane Whiteside, Laura McHale, and MT. The power of their encouraging words, their late-night e-mails, their phone calls and instant messages during the darkest, freakiest time of my life kept me clinging to the edge of the cliff. The "Suck it up, Princess" rule comes from them. For that, and so much more, I'm one grateful woman.

To Pam and Don at *A Romance Review*, who let me read and review books until my eyeballs warbled. Look what you created . . .

My parents, Robert and Eleanor, who, for the grace of God, still love me after cramming myself and my two sons into their eight hundred and twenty square-foot retirement village home.

To the real ladies of Leisure Village East—Mary DeWitt, Gail Kniffen, Gail Hammond, and Mary S. Or the Gail-Marys, as I lovingly once called them. You are treasured and priceless to me—*always*.

My agent, Elaine Spencer, who believed in this project and helped me flesh it out in a grocery store while we bought roast chicken. You da bomb diggity, chica!

Most especially to Rob—you were unexpected, and I was unprepared, but it's been unbelievable. I'm so glad you didn't give up. I love you.

Also, for anyone who has experienced or is experiencing the heartbreak of divorce, the fear and the anxiety this journey may have brought: Hold on. Don't lose hope—even if you're clinging to the last thread in a rope that's frayed and worn. I know where you are. I also know where you can go if you don't let go. *Don't. Let. Go.*

And last, but so definitely not least, this is for the very patient but firm night manager at the 7-Eleven in Jersey who, on a rainy, dismal night told me he wouldn't hire me for the midnight shift—which led to my mini-nervous breakdown of public, desperate sobbing and begging whilst I shared my tale of unemployable woe and divorce doom.

Dude, turning me down for that job (like my eleventy-billionth rejection. Surely you can see how that led me to public displays of histrionics, yes?) was the best thing you could have ever done for me. It was humiliation and degradation at its finest—but you handled me like an amateur psychologist who had a minor in soothing "broke divorcing women gone wild." That night was a major turning point for me. The one where I realized if I didn't grab the wheel of this runaway freight train, I'd lose control forever. Or become a pathetic candy-ass with a backbone made of Jell-O. It was my first lesson in the "suck it up" theory. I'm glad I opted to go Jell-O free.

So thanks—and thanks for the free cold Pepsi, too. All that crying and pleading makes for a dry mouth and sore throat.

Dakota Cassidy ☺

AUTHOR'S NOTE

The town of Riverbend is purely fictional, just in case you folks off the Jersey Turnpike take exception to me messing with your exits. But booyah to the fine people of Brick—exit 91 off the Garden State. You rule! And a quick note about New Jersey state laws on divorce. I've taken a smidge of artistic license, but not nearly as much as you'd think. In keeping with the idea that this is fiction, do note, any and all mistakes are mine.

PROLOGUE

The first rule of the Ex-Princess Club? Suck. It. Up.

What a difference one year, six months, eight hours, four minutes, ten seconds, and total empowerment makes. Today is the anniversary and a half of the official end of my trophy-wife days. Well, they didn't officially end that day, but it was the catalyst to a slew of things that helped make the end. It's when "Suck it up, Princess" found a whole new meaning for me, and the defining moment when I decided it was high time I traded in my frilly girl panties for a set of steel clangers.

And Jesus, it was butt ugly.

I was in the Cluck-Cluck Palace (yeah, that's right. Fast food chicken, ladies), and my mouth was moving a mile a millisecond while I applied—okay, begged—the day manager for a job, accosted a teenager, and ran into someone who reminded me I hadn't always been candy for someone's sweet tooth.

Ironically, eight months prior to that day I could've owned the Cluck-Cluck Palace and everything in it. Okay, maybe I personally couldn't have, but my soon to be ex-husband, Finley Cambridge, and all his lovely money could. But on that particular day, I had zilch. No money, no job, and no hope for future employment because I'd been nothing more than someone's pretty toy for over twenty years. That is, until I wasn't so pretty anymore. My ass was sagging, and so were the "girls" (which, if you ask me, should be called boys. If they were girls, they'd be team players and stay where they belong.), and I was visiting my swanky salon a whole lot more for touch-ups than ever before. Total harsh to my life buzz.

Anyway, it was on this day I realized I'd fallen and had forgotten to get the hell back up. There's nothing like humiliating clarity, stark and in your face, to spur you into action. Or make you want to slink back to your dark, dank hole of depression.

It's a choice.

Oh, and Christ, did I ever slink for a while after I was downsized from my cushy position as Mistress Of All Things Arranged In Glass Vases And Decorated In Silk. I cried. I didn't shower. (I know. I know. Don't judge.) I wore gray sweats. If you knew me, you'd understand the true depth of my despair when I resorted to the color gray. I moped. I whined. I cursed men with my fist raised to the sky. I cursed the universe with *two* fists. I listened to crappy love songs and boozed it up. I didn't eat. I didn't sleep much either. I, in general, behaved like a candy-ass.

And then one day, I didn't slink or whine anymore. That kind of sissified crap wasn't going to pay the bills—or support my son—or give me a reason to get up in the morning.

Because here's the thing—if you're anything remotely like me, you are where you are because you held the hand of your sugar daddy who skipped *with* you down the path of the totally sheltered, and you did squat to stop it. He wasn't alone, friend, and you obviously weren't paying close enough attention to where that path was going, 'cause it left you high and dry.

But I'm here to tell you, you can turn this mutha around. I did.

Though a word of caution—gird your loins.

CHAPTER ONE

Note from Maxine Cambridge to all ex-trophy wives on the art of sucking it up and how *not* to get a job after never having been in the workplace to begin with: Sometimes less really is more. While you, the unemployed, may find it therapeutic to spill your guts, or even foolishly believe rambling your woes to your potential employer will create sympathy and help you nab that much-needed job, news flash, sistah. In your quest for gainful employment, shut up. A lot.

"Welcome to the Cluck-Cluck Palace, where we speak beak. May I take your order?"

Leaning over the service counter, Maxine Cambridge kept her voice low. "I need to see the manager, please." She gave a covert glance around the fast food restaurant's dining area, checking to see if anyone she knew was maybe having a secret liaison with a double Cluck-Cluck combo meal. As humiliating as it would be to be discovered here, it wouldn't be nearly as horrific as being caught eating in a batter-dipped Nirvana, all up in a Cluck-Cluck Palace's triple chicken-nator's business.

The all-natural juice bar this was not.

A worried frown formed on the young boy's forehead, as yet smooth and unwrinkled by life's little travesties. Hah. What did a kid like him know about worry? Worrying was filled with shameful events like digging for change in your mother's old Jennifer Convertibles sofa so your kid could have frickin' milk for breakfast. Or selling every pricey designer outfit you owned to an upper-end thrift store for a shitty twenty bucks, then walking away feeling like you'd just renegotiated the Geneva Conventions single-handedly and had come up a winner.

Worrying was being forced to move back to your small hometown in New Jersey, and seeing the people you'd known all your life look at you with pity.

Worrying was eyeball-rolling dissertations on a division of assets, losing your sole form of transportation, i.e., your snazzy red sports car, and being beaten weekly with glee to a frothy frenzy by an opposing divorce attorney who loved nothing more than to watch you while your panties wadded as you sifted through so much paper a tree had surely lost its life for the endeavor.

Worry was the pending end of your connubial bliss—a bliss you had no idea wouldn't always be connubial. How could this sweet, sweet young boy know the half of what worrying was all about?

"Is there a problem?" he croaked, interrupting her favorite mental game of "stare poverty in the face."

Maxine shot him a reassuring smile and kept her response light, even though her intestines were tied up in knots and her head throbbed. "Oh, no. No problem. I filled out an application here a week ago, and I'm just doing a quick follow-up." *You know, before I head to the pawn shop to see if they'll take my breast implants for cash.*

"*You* filled out an application?" he asked, his fresh, alert eyes scanning her from head to toe, taking in the only pair of designer shoes she hadn't sold to the thrift store. Yet.

A deep breath later, she said with a smile, "Yep. So can I see the manager?"

"To work *here*? Why?"

Apparently, incredulous was the name of the game today. "Well, yeah. Because there's nothing I want more than to wear that red gingham-checked apron and a hat with a big yellow beak. I probably don't want to breathe as much as I want to wear that outfit. It's a long-ing I can't quite describe, but one that I absolutely have to pursue in order to find total fulfillment."

The look he gave her was blank. Astonished, too, but mostly blank. "I'll see if Mr. Herrera's in."

"Thanks," she looked at his name tag, "Carlo. I'll wait over by the condiments."

Ducking out of the short line, Maxine backed away from the counter to give herself a good view of the private offices through the kitchen. Mr. Herrera wasn't getting away today. Not if she had to tie him down with the strings of his gingham apron and make him hire her.

By all that was minimum wage, come the time when she left this fast food joint of batter-dipped sin and fried iniquity, she'd have a job, and she'd wear the ridiculous uniform, hat and all, with pride—because she needed the money.

Needed.

From the corner of her eye, Maxine caught Mr. Herrera, day manager of the Cluck-Cluck Palace in small-town Riverbend, New Jersey, exit 98 off the Garden State Parkway, attempting escape via the rear door. Silly man. He'd never be quick enough for her and her desperation, not even with her in three-inch stilettos. The clack of her frantic heels resonated on the tiled floor when she made a break through the lunch crowd to head him off at the pass.

She caught him just as he was about to push his way out the door and into the humid heat of the day by placing a non-confrontational hand on his bicep. "Mr. Herrera. I'm so disappointed. All I want to do is make nice with you so you'll hire me, and you run away at every opportunity like I'm the reincarnation of Jeffrey Dahmer. Why is that?"

He winced, toying with his gingham-checked necktie. "Because you've been in here every day for the last week, and if I've told you once, I've told you a million times—your application has to be processed through headquarters."

Maxine gave him a glossy-lipped pout. That used to work on almost everyone who had testosterone and walked upright. Or it had. Okay, so it wasn't the glossy-lipped pout of twenty, but these lips, the forty-year-old ones, still totally untouched by Botox, were in damn fine shape for their age.

Thus, she willed them to bedazzle her prey. "Oh, c'mon. You know that's not true. Gabriella over there filled out an application on the same day I did. I know she did because she liked my bracelet and I told her if she had some cold hard cash, *any* cash, I'd fork it over free and clear. All this while she was in the process of filling out the same application I did. You hired her. Now look, she's a chicken-frying engineer, and I still haven't been called for an interview."

He grunted with a grimace.

"So did she have to go through the same process as I do, or am I being discriminated against because I'm *forty* and you don't think I'd be willing to work the hours these poor kids do for minimum wage?" She played the "forty" card extra loud, making several heads in the dining area turn. "Because you'd be wrong." Way wrong.

He blustered, frowning so that his bushy eyebrows scrunched together. "That's not it at all, Ms. Cambridge."

Max fought for a centered calm. Her hysteria would only incite anxiousness that, in turn, would evoke rambling sentences she couldn't control once she got wound up. "Then what *is* it? Look, I'm willing to work any hours you'll give me. I'm willing to do all the dirty work you need done. I'll scrub toilets, sinks, refill ketchup bottles, shred lettuce—"

"Our lettuce comes already shredded."

How helpful. "Whatever. The point is, I'm all in. Just give me a chance," she begged, her hand suddenly around his arm. Before she knew it, what was originally planned as a subtle, dignified nudge for employment became a hostage situation, if the way she was gripping his arm with firm fingers was any indication. Desperation had its blatant nuances. *"Please."*

Rolling his shoulders in discomfort, he pulled away from her grip like she was The Claw. "I can't help you. We don't have a position available right now." He stood his ground, for which she'd show admiration by way of a polite golf clap if it wasn't for the fact that she and Connor would end up drinking her mother's till dry very shortly if she didn't find some kind of steady paycheck.

One deep cleansing breath later, Max's eyes searched his behind his oval frames. She could do this. Whatever it took. "Please. Look, I'm begging you, okay? I need a job. I'm sure you hear a hundred sob stories a day with the economy in the shitty state it's in, but I'm not kidding when I tell you I just need one person to give me a chance. Just a little break. I know I'm not sixteen anymore, and if I needed reminding, I'd just have to ask the hundred other places like this that I've applied to to tell me so. I get it. I know I have no experience in fast food. Believe me, *I know.* I have no experience in selling condoms either, but you can bet I'd do it if it meant I could earn a buck hawking ribbed ticklers. Well, that is, if the manager at Condoms on the Go-Go would have let me. But he said I had no *experience* in condoms. I say, hah! What does he know? I know condoms. I've used them plenty in my time. But that's beside the point. So tell me something, because you seem like a guy who's in the know—how the flip can I get some of this experience if no one will hire me?" Her voice had risen, pitchy and anxious, and her hand was right back at desperation, clinging to poor deer-in-the-headlights Mr. Herrera.

There was a long pause before he spoke. Clearly, he sought to measure his response to her impassioned request. "Ms. Cambridge, can I ask you something? I mean, if it's not too personal."

She automatically looked down at her perky breasts, floating just beneath her open-collared silk shirt. "You want to know if these are real, don't you?" Everybody did, and she'd answer if it meant a job.

He cleared his throat, giving a stern shake of his head, looking anywhere but at her frisky décolletage. "Oh, no. No, no, no. I would never . . . I'm just curious about your—well, why someone like you needs a job here? Aren't you the lady who used to do the commercials for Cambridge Automobiles? You know, 'Put your seat—'"

"'In something sweet,'" Maxine finished. Her face flushed a hundred shades of deep red. Why, why, why had she jumped straight to the boob question? "Yeah, that was me." And now it wasn't. Because she wasn't twenty-five anymore, and her husband didn't want her anymore, and she'd been traded in.

"And you drive a fancy car, and you wear fancy clothes . . ."

It was always like this when she showed up in Connor's car or someone recognized her. Max plucked at her white suit jacket. "I'm dressed like this because I just left my lawyer's office—which, FYI, was a complete waste of gas money I didn't have, and the car's my kid's. I borrowed it from him so I could go see my 1-800-dial-divorce lawyer for him to tell me I'm defining broke in a whole new way, then swing by here so you could tell me you won't hire me. My son's car's one of the few things my soon-to-be ex didn't take from us, but don't hold your breath for me, because I'm sure he'll want that back, too." She finished by clamping her mouth shut. Truly, it was the only way to stop the train wreck her big mouth had become.

Yet for a mere moment, Maxine found the sympathy she'd hoped to tap into written on his chubby, moon-shaped face. He was waffling. Perfect. "Ah, messy divorce?"

Messy had levels. Her divorce was at DEFCON 5. "You're understating it. That's very kind. I don't want to get too personal and scare you off by divulging too much so you'll only end up uncomfortable, but here's where I'm at. You in?" If she could just make one person understand how close she was to welfare by telling them how she'd been bamboozled, then pride could go eff itself.

Mr. Herrera nodded his reluctant consent. "Do I have a choice?"

"Not if you hope to leave here unscarred." Maxine clutched his arm again, pushing her back into the glass exit door for leverage.

He scanned the top of the dining area over the top of her head. "Then of course. Do divulge." He sighed.

So she did. "Okay, so in a nutshell, this is the skinny, and I'm telling you this because I want you to really understand why I harass you every day. It's a lot. Sure you're up to it?"

His feet shuffled.

Shit, she'd given him an out.

"Forget I asked. Just listen. I *am* going through a divorce. It's been hell. No, it's worse than hell—it's hell times eight gotrillion. I was married to a very wealthy man who's redefined the phrase 'ironclad prenuptial.' I had no idea anything was wrong with my marriage until I found out, quite by accident and by some jackass's mistake in the society pages, that I was soon going to be anything but Mrs. Finley Cambridge. Okay, that's not one hundred percent true. There were indiscretions . . . But I thought we were back on track. Wait, maybe I did have a suspicion or two—make that ten, but that wasn't really clear until I had some distance and hindsight. Oh, if I could only tell you the kind of hindsight I've been blessed with." Maxine paused, sucking in some chicken-fried air and clenching her jaw so she wouldn't burst out into big, fat, girlie tears.

"Anyway, I have no money. None. Nothing. I know you're probably thinking, nothing? Yeah, sure. A major player like Finley Cambridge left his wife of twenty years with nothing. C'mon. You must have *something.* Like a severance package for time served. Hush money, maybe? That's exactly what you're thinking, right?"

Mr. Herrera winced his agreement with a slow nod.

Maxine clucked her tongue. "Yeah, that's what everyone thinks. But I swear to you, Mr. Herrera, I have squat. When I found out about my husband's wandering wanker, I left. I just didn't know I'd left-left. *Everything*. I also didn't know when I left that I'd never see my house, my car, my personal Pilates instructor again, forever. Those ridiculous luxuries aside, I thought we'd get a normal divorce. The one where you and your kid have a place to live and food on the table, because your pending ex is rich and owns half of New York, New Jersey, and parts of Connecticut. So he has cash to spare, and even if it meant downsizing our lifestyle, and me going back to school to get a decent job because I'm no slacker, I still believed he'd do the right thing. I was, according to my dial-a-lawyer, delusional. If you were me, wouldn't you have made the same crazy assumption?"

Mr. Herrera's brow furrowed. "Assumptions can be troublesome."

"If you only knew the half of it. So since this nightmare began eight months, four days, and thirty-six hours ago, I've been trying to get on my feet. I've applied for forty-two and a half jobs. I say half because I'll do almost anything to earn a living, but there'll be no mechanically separating chickens for this girl. I left that interview halfway through it in defense of chickens everywhere. I've been turned down for every single position I've applied for in the town of Riverbend—which, if you were wondering, doesn't have a whole lot in the way of industry. So here I am. Penniless. Jobless. Pride-less. And that's why I come in here every day, Mr. Herrera, because I need a job. I need just one person to give me a chance. Kids come and go in these places when a taste for a change and a position at Hot Topic comes along. I can promise you that's not me. I'm reliable, honest, and hardworking. I'll work whatever hours you have—I'll work the graveyard shift. There were two positions available last week. Gabriella got one. That means one's still up for grabs. I just need you to please reconsider hiring me. *Please*."

The manager's face changed, and her rising anxiety gave way to the tiniest bit of hope. If she could just get her foot in the door . . .

But hope, much like her dye job, was fleeting.

A loud bang on the door behind her made them both jump, thus freeing Mr. Herrera from her WrestleMania-like grip.

Maxine gasped when she caught a familiar face pressed against the glass door with a head that wore the prized Cluck-Cluck Palace's beak hat. "You hired *him*? He's who got my job, isn't he?" she accused, her eyes flashing in the manager's direction.

Be it frustration, exhaustion, or maybe utter and complete loss of all rationale, her nut officially flipped. It'd been a long time coming, filled with endless hours of poring over the want ads, being rejected time after time for jobs even her own kid wouldn't apply for. The sheer terror she felt each and every time she realized that she and Connor had far less than a pot to piss in.

The anxiety-riddled nights spent sleeping upright in her mother's armchair while she hatched and re-hatched ways to find work. The moments of startling clarity when she was constantly walloped over the head with her stupidity and the fact that she was nothing more than a dried-up ex-beauty queen who'd gone almost directly from high school and the Miss Riverbend Auto and Glass pageant to marriage and a man who was twenty years older than her.

For sure, she was long overdue for a breakdown. That it was a beaked hat and a gingham-checked apron that sent her into the abyss would surely be cause for some major regret.

Later.

Maxine gripped the door's handle and stuck her tongue out at Phillip—the other kid who'd filled out an application with her and Gabriella, daring him to fight his way into the store *she* should be working in.

Phillip yanked back, his freckled face confused and red from the cloying heat.

"Mrs. Cambridge! You can't keep a customer from entering the store. If you don't leave, I'm going to have to call the authorities!" Mr. Herrera whisper-yelled, trying to pry her fingers from the handle.

Oh, no, brotha. No way was this kid—this child who needed a job like he needed an eyelift—getting her job. Goddamn it, he didn't need a job. But by all that was holy, she did. Mental flashes of her and Connor staple-gunning boxes together on the side of the road to create living space sent her panic into four-wheel drive.

Gritting her teeth, Max flapped one hand at Mr. Herrera and flattened herself against the door. "He's not a customer. He's an employee! An employee who has *my* job!" Swatting at his large hands, Maxine clung to the handle while Phillip yanked harder. She dug her heels in, wild-eyed and panting. "Noooooooooooooooo!"

But as a tag team, Mr. Herrera and Phillip were a force she couldn't reckon with. The door buckled, ripping from her sweaty fingers as Phillip gave one last tug, rocketing her out onto the manicured grass by the sidewalk, and him right where he wanted to be. Inside the Cluck-Cluck Palace. Her nylons caught on a neatly trimmed boxwood hedge, tearing a long line from her ankle to her thigh.

Both Phillip and Mr. Herrera burst out behind her, grunting and panting.

The humidity was thick, clinging to her stupid suit and plastering her silk shirt to her clammy skin. The blazing sun beat down on the top of her head, leaving her dizzy and almost breathless. Almost. She wasn't done. Not yet. "*You,*" she pointed a shaking finger at Phillip. "You stole my job and my damned hat. You Cluck-Cluck Palace—"

"Max? Max Henderson?"

The air from her seething bubble of anger deflated with a metaphorical hiss. She'd been made. *Oh, Jesus. Please, please, please, God, if you're good, and gracious enough to forgive my complete lack of socially acceptable behavior, when I turn around, don't let it be an associate of Finley's. Or worse a parent of one of Connor's classmates.* But hold on. Maybe there was salvation. No one from her once elite lifestyle called her Max . . .

Maxine swung around and squinted into the glare of the mid-afternoon sun. She cocked her head in the direction of a tall man wearing low-slung jeans and an exceptionally white T-shirt.

"Campbell. Campbell Barker. Remember? We graduated together. Class of 1987."

She teetered on her heels, gathering her purse tight to her chest as he moved closer. Campbell . . . She couldn't recall a Campbell.

Mr. Herrera tapped her on the shoulder. "I think I'm going to have to ask you to leave the Cluck-Cluck Palace's premises now, Mrs. Cambridge, and please, do us all a favor. Stay. Away. Or I'll be forced to call the authorities after today." The irony of him asking a *Cambridge* to leave the premises might have had her in a fit of slaphappy giggles, if not for the fact that a hunky man in sun-washed jeans that molded to hard thighs was upon her.

Campbell's tall, bulky frame covered the distance between them in two strides, and he looked to Mr. Herrera and that wee suck-up Phillip with a question in his blue eyes. "Everything okay?"

Catching sight of him up close, Maxine swooned a little. Not only was he blessedly blocking the sun from frying her eyeballs but the scent of his freshly laundered T-shirt invaded her nostrils, so comforting and clean it brought hot tears to her tired eyes.

His eyes, deep blue and thickly fringed with short lashes, were laced with concern and caught hers. "Max? Is everything all right?"

Weary from battle, Maxine finally found her voice. "Everything's . . . it's fine. I'm sorry, Mr. Herrera—for my behavior." And she was, but not so contrite that she didn't have a little fight left in her. Especially considering the fact that she was leaving yet another fast food restaurant sans employment. "But I'm telling you, you'll regret hiring him." She narrowed her eyes in the skinny, undeserving Phillip's direction. "And not me."

"Now, Mrs. Cambridge—"

But Campbell cut him off with a raised eyebrow. "Are you telling me he wouldn't hire you? *You*? Max Henderson—prom queen, voted most popular, and head cheerleader of the Riverbend Rams?"

Well, when it was put like that . . . But she got the playful irony in his husky tone and decided to go along. Giving Campbell her best sad face, she nodded. "Yeah. I'm too *old* for the Cluck-Cluck Palace."

"I said nothing of the sort," Mr. Herrera's face, dotted with sweat, puffed out in indignation.

"No, that's true," Maxine defended him. "Not in so many words, but it was implied when you hired him and not me." *So, huh on you.*

Campbell rolled his tongue along the inside of his cheek, casting Mr. Herrera a disappointed expression. The lines on either side of his full mouth deepening when he pursed his lips. "Wow. That sucks. I was so up for a Cluck-Cluck chicken patty melt with curly fries, too. Love those fries. But seeing as you discriminate against the elderly here, I think I'll take my business to, say, The Beef Barn. C'mon, Max. There's a cattle combo with my name on it. Bet they'd hire an old lady like you there." He nodded to Mr. Herrera and Phillip. "You two have a good day, you senior-citizen haters."

She couldn't help it. Her head fell back on her shoulders with a long snort of laughter as she let Campbell lead her down the stretch of sidewalk toward the parking lot and away from, by far, the most humiliating display of disgruntled, unemployed ex-trophy wife ever.

With his hand at the small of her back, he paused when they were out of Mr. Herrera's sight. This time, when he looked down at her, his deep blue eyes held amusement. "You don't remember me, do you?"

Not even a little. Maxine wiped her wispy bangs out of her face, now stuck to her forehead with perspiration. "Of course I do."

His chuckle was resonant and deep. "Nah. You have no clue who

I am. But if it helps at all, I was the one who kept you from setting yourself on fire in chemistry with Mr. McGillicuddy. We were lab partners for a semester our senior year."

Her eyes opened wide. Shut. Up. This was that Campbell Barker? Tall and lanky with an Adam's apple so pronounced you would've sworn he'd swallowed a golf ball Campbell Barker?

He grinned, showing a flash of white teeth that sported neither braces nor the once huge gap in the front of his smile. "It's my hair, right? But the feathered look was so eighties. It had to go. Otherwise, I'm confident you would have recognized me. I was too cute to be that forgettable," he joked.

Holy to the outermost limits in makeovers. She was speechless. This couldn't be the Campbell she remembered from high school. He was too thickly muscled, his waist was too lean, and his stomach was too ripply. Really ripply, if the way the cotton of his shirt clung to his mid-section was any indication.

And Shazam, his badonkadonk hadn't filled out a pair of jeans then like it did now. Neither had his long legs with thighs that had their own ripple effect. She was stunned.

Campbell gave his flat abs a smack with a full palm when her eyes found his again and nodded with a knowing grin. "Growth spurt. A big one."

Indeed. "You look . . . so . . ."

"Big and manly?"

A giggle spilled from her lips. "Yeah. That and completely different."

"Twenty years'll do that. So what brings Max Henderson, er, Cambridge to the Cluck-Cluck Palace for a job?"

Poverty.

That was when shame set in. The shame that forced her to look anywhere but at him. Of all the places and all the times to reunite with someone you'd gone to high school with. When you were applying for a job at the Cluck-Cluck Palace, while destitution nipped at your heels.

Oh, how far the once vibrant, fun-loving Maxine Henderson had fallen. She wasn't Miss Riverbend Auto and Glass anymore. There were so many things she wasn't anymore; it hurt her head to ponder it. Exiting stage left before the questions got too deep was prudent. "Long story, and I don't have time to tell it." Glancing at her watch, Maxine made like she had somewhere important to get to. "It was really nice seeing you again, Campbell, but I have to run. And thanks for saving my hide back there." Shooting him a distracted smile, she hooded her eyes, trying to locate her car.

"Bet it's that one," Campbell said, leaning over her shoulder, his hair tickling her cheek. His finger pointed out her son's car. A Lotus Elise in a sea of practical SUVs and compact cars.

Her head moved just enough that his breath, minty-fresh and warm, caressed her cheek. His reassuring presence behind her back, the shelter of his wide chest, left her stomach weak with an emotion she couldn't describe, but was probably closely related to the now extinct dinosaur known as "Male Attention." "How'd you know?"

"Cambridge Automobiles—'Put your seat in something sweet.' You did the commercials, I heard. Besides, it says it on the license plate."

Fuckall if she wasn't tired of being remembered for a series of badly written, even more badly acted commercials for a car dealership.

She let her head hang lower, stepping off the curb to leave Campbell Barker's beefcakeyness and the reminders he stirred up about the innocent, naïve path she'd taken. Those tears, tears that threatened to fall far too often these days, reared their salty heads.

But Campbell caught up with her, gripping her arm with nonthreatening fingers. "You know, I was serious about lunch. Let me buy you some, and you can catch me up on what Max Henderson's doing these days."

Max—*Maxine* Henderson is a Cambridge now, but she won't be for much longer, and she's buck-assed broke, living with her son and her mother in a senior citizens' retirement village.

And she isn't doing a whole lot more than she was doing twenty years ago. Her pom-poms have long since frayed, and her tiaras aren't so shiny these days. What she thought was once a perfect world is now a beautiful disaster.

Squeezing the bridge of her nose, Maxine hoped it would keep the tears at bay long enough for her to make a dignified exit. "I can't, but thanks anyway. I have to pick up my son. But really, it was nice seeing you."

"Here." He shoved a business card at her. "Call me—maybe we could grab some coffee. I'm a good listener."

Maxine reached out to take it from him, more politeness than anything else. When their fingers grazed, a weird assault of sensations traveled along her arm. "Thanks, Campbell. Maybe I will."

Stuffing the card in her purse, she knew she wouldn't.

Maxine Lou Anne Henderson Cambridge wasn't anything like the girl her old lab partner had once known.

Catching up with Campbell, who was astonishingly different than he'd once been in the best of ways, would only be like opening her wounds of regret with a dull butter knife and dumping vinegar on them.

It would only remind her of the other path she hadn't taken.

The path of self-sufficiency and independence.

The path that would have left her with a career that would have provided for her and Connor during a shitwreck of a divorce.

The path where she could tell Finley Cambridge and all of his lovely moolah to kiss her still untouched by a plastic surgeon's knife ass.

The path that had led her to become Maxine—because Finley had said her full name was much less garish—instead of just staying plain old Max.

CHAPTER TWO

Note from Maxine Cambridge to all ex-trophy wives on the business of sucking it up, divorce, and sparing the children the gory details of poverty and infidelity: While divorcing the sugar daddy who left your bucket bone-dry, try not to allow your resentments to become an issue with your kid. Be the better person. Instead, to release pent-up rage, seek out a hunky man-boy and wonk him until your eyeballs roll and he slams the rage right outta ya. That was a joke. Don't really do that. Chew gum. Or your tongue. Whatever's easier on your fillings.

Maxine pushed her way through the screen door to her mother's retirement-village one-level ranch in Leisure Village South, where the motto was "the end of your life is just the beginning." It was a great place for her mother to live out her retirement years while she aged with more grace and agility at seventy than Maxine felt at almost forty-one. Her mother'd found a circle of friends in the ten years since she'd moved in. They had tons of activities in the village to keep her motivated. Most importantly, she had her own little space and her own things surrounding her.

Mona Henderson was big on her tchotchkes. There wasn't a birdhouse or garden gnome her mother didn't love.

Maxine threw her purse on the speckled counter in disgust. Jesus Christ in a miniskirt, her behavior had been beyond deplorable today.

She'd forgotten what boundaries were. Boundaries sucked.

Publicly beating down a teenager because he'd joined the land of the employed was heinously unforgivable.

A teenager.

And she'd done it in front of a former classmate who'd probably yuck the experience up at the next reunion at the Holiday Inn Express with everyone who thought Max Henderson would make it big—or at least end up Miss Universe. Today, it was going to take a lot more than reminding herself there was no shame in clawing your way out of unemployment to keep from pitching herself off the roof of her mother's house.

Her mother looked at her over the top of her magnifying reading glasses. "So how goes the chicken business?"

Maxine kissed her on the top of her dyed strawberry blonde head before slinking down into a chair at the kitchen table. "It doesn't."

"Doesn't what?"

"Doesn't go. They hired someone else." Instead of looking directly at her mother, she allowed her humiliation to drive her eyes to the rooster clock on the wall above her mother's head. "But before I found that out, I shared every pathetic detail of my life with the poor manager. And I babbled . . . endlessly."

"Well done. Pity's always a hallmark to every successful job interview. So we concur that the Cluck-Cluck Palace sucks weenies?"

God love her mother and her sharp tongue. Never afraid to say what she felt, it had sometimes embarrassed the shit out of Maxine, and sometimes it had been what kept her hanging on. She only wished she had at least half of the set of balls her mother did. "We concur." Blowing out a puff of air, she rested her head in her hands. A loud clanging from the far end of the house made her head throb. The heat and Campbell Barker had left her with a headache.

Her mother pinched the back of her daughter's hand with affection. "Doesn't matter. That hat would have looked stupid on you anyway. Your neck's not long enough for all that beak. You'll find something, dear. I know it."

Maxine's laughter was colored with a million shades of bitter. "If only I had a hundred bucks for every time you've said that after another failed attempt to find some kind of employment, Mona Marie Henderson, I could at least afford to put some food on your table. Maybe buy toilet paper in bulk."

Mona dropped her crocheting to the table, waving a hand at her daughter. "Don't be silly. I don't need your money, and I don't need nearly the amount of toilet paper I once did before I started that bladder-control medication. Besides, we have plenty of food."

Did creamed tuna on toast really constitute food? "Ma, you say that every time I don't get the job, too. But Connor and I can't keep sucking you dry. The money you keep spending on every little thing we need, not to mention feeding us, is trashing your retirement fund."

Money she wouldn't need if she hadn't made the most naïve mistake of her life. That very mistake was at least on par with Chernobyl.

"Nonsense. I don't feel sucked anywhere, and the only credit card you had when you left that egomaniac is maxed out on lawyer fees for that nimrod attorney who bills you for these imaginary hours he claims he's worked. You have nothing, but I don't have nothing. So stop worrying, Maxie. My finances are in fine shape."

"Says who?"

"Says that Elmer Roy over there on Gladiola Avenue."

Maxine's head shot upward, hoping to catch a glimpse of the emotion her mother's light blue eyes held when she spoke Elmer's name, but she came up dry. Her mother remained a total rock of deadpan. But Maxine had seen her mother giggle like she was at the prom on more than one occasion where Elmer was concerned. "So when did you see Elmer?" She cooed his name, teasing and light.

Mona shot Maxine an exaggerated look of disinterest with a shrug of her slender shoulders. "Bingo—or was it Waltzing with Sherry on

Wednesday? I can't remember. So it couldn't have been much of a hoopla. Doesn't matter, he told me I'm solid. He should know, retired accountant that he is. Your father, God rest his cantankerous soul, left me in tip-top shape. Now stop worrying your pretty head about it. I won't hear about sucking and things that're dry. We'll be fine."

More tears stung her eyes. Her mother said that every time they had the unemployed conversation, too. If it hadn't been for her mother on that long-ago, tear-filled, agonizingly ugly night when she'd left Fin, she and Connor really would be at the local homeless shelter.

Another loud clash of metal against metal reverberated through her mother's small house. The humid air, combined with her lack of sustenance, left her feeling like whoever was swinging that tool was all up in her head, knocking around her brain matter. "What do you have against an air conditioner, Mom? It's eight billion degrees outside, and what is going on back there?"

"But there's a nice breeze coming in from the shore, and that noise is me finally getting that leaky pipe fixed in the guest bathroom. 'Bout time, too. Only took three phone calls and an association meeting to get it done. Though I hear poor Garner's been backed up since his valve replacement. But he got himself some help this week." Her mother frowned. "There was something I was supposed to tell you . . . Oh, I know. The Talleywhacker called. Wants to see Connor."

The Talleywhacker, aka Finley. Connor's age didn't help in trying to keep Finley's infidelity a secret. Neither had the leak in the society pages. Connor understood far more than she would have liked him to. As a result, he not only got the ugliness that had gone down between his parents, but he was so angry with his father, he refused to see him.

He'd left his Xbox 360, among other things, behind to prove his point, too. She couldn't decide whether to beat her chest with pride that she'd managed to instill morals in him or give him a good spanking for being so frickin' difficult. Maxine sighed, knowing the answer and the sneer that would follow, but asking because it was her job as Connor's parent to do it. "Did you tell him he'd have to talk to Connor?"

"I told him I'd have Connor call him back from the pay phone down at the 7-Eleven, seeing as you can't afford a cell phone for him. I also told him he'd better hope we could take the drunk homeless guy who sleeps on the side of the building, because we'll have to steal his change to make the call."

Sneer on cue. Unbuttoning her jacket, Maxine laughed. "Don't taunt Finley, Mom. It'll only result in me maybe losing my kidneys in the next round of this reincarnation of World War Two."

"Finley Cambridge can bite my old, wrinkled ass. He's a dead-beat, and don't think, unlike you, I'm afraid to say so. If my memory serves me, that's what I called him just before I threw the phone at the wall." She tilted her sharp jaw upward. Her hair, fresh from cushioned pink curlers, shook when she gave Maxine a defiant flash of her eyes.

Maxine slid closer to the wall, fiddling with the rip in the fading flowered wallpaper of her mother's kitchen. "Ma, there has to come a time when Connor sees his father again. Fin cheating on me doesn't mean he cheated on Connor." Sooooo PC. Sooooo much bullshit. Fin may not have fornicated around on Connor, but he'd definitely cheated him.

Connor should be planning his graduation next year, attending the college he'd dreamed about since he was little, hanging out with his friends. Instead, he was living in a retirement village, driving twenty minutes each way to school five days a week so he could graduate with the same classmates he'd had since kindergarten, and walking little old ladies' dogs night after night to afford the gas money to do it.

Her mother grunted, smoothing a hand down the front of her Day-Glo green, nylon sweat suit. "Really? I disagree, Missy. When Fin decided to take his crotch elsewhere, he also took his money, and his son's home, and left you with nothing. I say that's cheating his kid out of all the things he deserves just so he can stick it to you. Is Finley going to raise him?" Mona scowled. "Not likely. All the things that boy had before Finley went off and did the humpty-hump with that tramp, and now he has nothing? That's cheating by proxy, girlie."

Technically, that wasn't totally true. "Fin did give Connor the option to come back and live with him and Lacey." Maxine cringed. It tore a hole in her heart just thinking of not having Connor with her. Almost as bad, when she said her husband's new fiancée's name, even eight months later, it still gouged another hole in her heart—albeit a much smaller one than possibly losing Connor. They weren't even divorced yet and Fin already had a fiancée.

Lacey, Lacey, Lacey. The pain of Fin's infidelity didn't hurt nearly as much as it had at the start of this, but what did hurt was the idea that now Lacey was sleeping in Maxine's California King, eating her freshly flown-in lobster, and didn't have a single care in the world, while Maxine and Connor lived near impoverishment.

And all because she was a total fuckwit.

Yet none of the outrageous luxuries or lack thereof mattered much anymore. They were all like a hazy dream. What mattered was survival. Something she had no clue how to go about, but strived for every waking moment anyway.

"Yeahhhh—big of him to offer his *son* a place to live. Connor's a smart boy. Too smart for his own good sometimes. He knows what Fin's doing to you by hiding all of his money, and swindling you out of his millions. Like that jackass would miss a couple million, never mind a couple hundred bucks. He had some kinda gall, leaving you a buck ninety-nine in your joint accounts and canceling all those credit cards just before you found out about that Jezebel. He knew damned well what he was doing, and he didn't leave you any ammunition to fight back. Finley didn't get where he is by not knowing how to protect himself."

Maxine's nod was a tired one. That much was true. The very second Finley got wind of the fact that she'd found out about Lacey, he'd cleaned out their joint accounts and canceled their credit cards, leaving her with just one with an eight-thousand-dollar limit to pay a lawyer who did nothing but collect a twenty-five-hundred-dollar retainer, ignore her pleading phone calls, and stall.

Fin knew once she'd wrapped her head around his infidelity, she'd freak. But he'd made sure her freak was nothing more than a whimper, and it was all perfectly legal. That he'd planned this so diabolically behind her back made it that much harder to swallow.

"Connor knows you can't afford a *real* lawyer, and that's why you're where you are—because that creepy shyster who has a basement office doesn't know his arse from his Mr. Peabody. If you would just let me dip into the till, we could get you a *real* lawyer—"

Maxine's hand was instantly in the air, palm forward. "*No*, Mom. No more money. I have the lawyer I have because my credit card could only afford so much before it broke. I don't even care about the money anymore. I just want out. Do you have any idea how much it'd cost to hire someone capable of handling Fin's lawyers? A whole lot more than even you have. And if I didn't get anything out of his tight ass so I could pay you back—then we'd really be screwed. So forget it. And before you get crazy, I have a confession to make. I discovered something today on the ride back from my interview. I'm where I am because I didn't do anything to stop myself from getting here. I can't totally blame Fin for this mess. I think it's time for me to take some responsibility for this shitwreck."

That was the ugly truth of it. Not only had she trusted her lesser half blindly, but she'd listened to Fin's SAHM bullshit about staying home with Connor and raising him the way a mother should, being party planner and all-round entertainer of the millennium. She should have insisted he let her go to school when the longing had hit her. But Fin had liked her at his disposal—until he'd disposed of her.

Not that she'd pushed to go back to school. Pushing Fin was akin to walks along eggshell-lined streets. You had to take those strolls very carefully.

Seeing Campbell Barker today had reminded her that somewhere between graduation and this very second, she hadn't just lost twenty years of marriage, money, and some stupid-ass weekly trips to the day spa, she'd lost her cubes. Her opinion. Her desires. *Max*, as Campbell had called her, couldn't have been talked out of anything she wanted way back when. In fact, that was how she'd ended up married to Finley to begin with.

Her mother's smile was bitter. "Yep, that's partially true, but it doesn't mean you shouldn't get some kind of severance for time served with that control freak. You raised a good boy, virtually on your own, while Fin swung from every female's chandelier in the tri-state. Connor knows how you've suffered. And I'm not talking about suffering because you can't slip on a fancy-schmancy designer dress or sit in the back of a chauffeur-driven car. I'm talking about the essentials here, kiddo. Food, shelter, a Goddamn cell phone. I'm seventy, and even I have a cell phone. Connor's making a stand, and I'm proud of him. He's sticking by his mama. Makes for a fine man."

"Yeah," Connor agreed, pushing his way through the door and dropping his binder on the chipped Formica table. "I'm a fine man."

Mona whacked him playfully with her crocheting book. "Don't get too far ahead of yourself, buster. You're no man yet," she teased, smiling when Connor leaned in to give her a quick pinch on her wrinkled cheek.

"So how's Geezer Village, er, I mean, Leisure Village treating you today, Grams?" Connor chuckled.

Mona's smile was warm, her pride in Connor evident. She didn't let just anyone call the retirement village she lived in "geezer." "Just fine, buddy. Got somebody back there right now, fixing my leaky pipes. And he ain't no geezer."

Max decided to broach the subject of Fin with kid gloves. "Your dad called, honey."

Connor shrugged his broad, ever-widening shoulders deep in the door of her mother's aging avocado refrigerator. "So? He can dial a phone."

Despite what Fin had done to her personally, Maxine made the effort to do the right thing where their son was concerned. Do what all the school psychologists and *Divorce for Dummies* books preached were healthy for children of marital woe. Keep the slander about the kind of bottom-feeding fuck Finley was to herself. But if Connor had inherited anything from the Henderson lineage, it was stubborn pride. "Don't be that way, Connor. He's still your dad, and he loves you."

Popping a grape into his mouth, Connor snorted. "Not as much as he loves his money. If he really loved me, he'd stop trying to force me to choose him over you by taking all my stuff away from me. He thinks if he pushes hard enough, I'll go crying back to him because I miss having a big-screen TV and surround sound in my bedroom. I bet he'll want my car back soon, too. I'd sell it for the money and use it for us if he didn't hold the title to it. At the last visitation hearing, the judge said I was old enough to make my own decisions, and I decided I don't want to see Dad."

Such jaded words from such a young kid. Maxine's heart clenched. Her mother was right. Fin was using his money and all of Connor's "things" to woo him back home. That Connor hadn't caved in eight months was a testament to how hard he'd dug his heels in.

But if she knew how to do anything at all, she knew how to play nice. Christ knew she'd done that for a very long time. "Maybe you could just try, Connor. For your poor, tired, jobless mother. Your dad off my back about visitation would be huge. I get what you're trying to prove, and it's noble. I'm about as honored as if I'd been crowned Miss USA, but you have college to think of. Somehow, I get the feeling the pay at the Cluck-Cluck Palace isn't going to make your collegiate dreams come true."

Her biggest fear at this point was that Fin would find some way to weasel out of paying for Connor's education if their son didn't bend to his will. The bastard had found every loophole known to man so far to keep her from getting anything he deemed his. He'd also managed to duck paying her much in child support, and the near future wasn't going to require shades, from what her lawyer told her today. Fin had bloody, chum-loving sharks for attorneys. Whatever he was doling out to them per hour was paying off.

Connor tipped his chestnut brown head in Maxine's direction, a question in his thickly fringed eyes. "So you did get the job at the Cluck-Cluck Palace, Mom?"

Oh, the degradation of having to tell your sixteen-year-old you were a Cluck-Cluck Palace reject. "No. It was just a figure of speech. Or basically what any salary I end up making will boil down to. I just meant that our horizons ain't so pretty. I can't afford to buy a six-pack of Pepsi—and college costs more than four ninety-eight."

Connor leaned his back against the fridge, his dark eyes, so much like Fin's, gazing into hers. "So what you're saying is I should let him blackmail me so his *son* can have a college degree?"

Yep. That was what she was saying. Harsh. "I think I'm just saying that re-establishing your relationship with your father wouldn't be a bad idea with graduation a year away. It's a big time in your life, and he should share it with you."

"Yeah. Him and Laceeeeyy."

Maxine gripped the edge of the table before she spoke. This was where decency and holding your tongue were like getting a Brazilian wax. "I'm sure he'll bring Lacey. She is going to be his wife. Don't judge Lacey. You don't even know her, and you could fix that if you'd just see your dad."

Connor's eyes narrowed at her, his body language screaming "end

convo." They'd been down this road and it always ended at the same
dead end. "I have to do my homework, and then I have to walk
Mrs. O'Brien's dog." He grabbed his binder with a final dark glance in
her general vicinity and headed to the guest bedroom where he slept.

Maxine groaned, slipping off her heels to let them clunk beneath
the table. "He's gonna kill me, Ma. I don't know what to do to get
through to him."

"Let him be. Sometimes you have to let the little shits make their
own choices and hope it all works out."

"Like you did with me when you told me marrying Fin was the
stupidest thing you'd heard of since Paul Newman asked Joanne
Woodward to marry him?"

Mona raised a silvery eyebrow. "Just like that."

"Do you want to hear me say I should've listened to you? That
instead of marrying Fin I should have gone to college so that I'd have
something of my own to fall back on in my time of need?" Because
that was true, too. She'd let Fin handle everything, never thinking
he'd leave her with absolutely nothing and tie everything else up for
an eternity.

Even when her marriage had faltered, when Fin had been the
unfaithful piece of shit he was on two prior occasions, had she
crawled out from under her cashmere blankets and maybe considered her marriage wasn't going according to plan? Nay. Instead, she'd
glossed over his wandering dick. She'd made promises to herself to
be more attentive to his every need. To stay in shape, she'd worked
the elliptical like a whore at a singles' convention seven days a week.
She'd gotten bigger hooters. She'd justified Fin's cheating by blaming
herself and her imperfections, for having the audacity to grow older.

"Nope. I want to hear you say you're not going to let that dead-
beat whip your keister. Stop letting him intimidate you. He owes you,
honey. Can't change what's done, Maxie. There's no going back. But
you can change what's happening to you right now."

Right. Like she could ever change what she'd done.

The heat, her anxiety, and her helplessness made her rise to the bait her mother dangled in her face each time she was rejected by a potential employer. "I'm not sure how else you'd like me to change what's happening to us. I've applied for more jobs than all of us combined have fingers and toes. I've begged. I've pleaded. I've humiliated myself on more than one occasion—today being the mack daddy of 'em all. So, got any tidbits of inspirational change for me, Mom? I'm all ears."

Her mother's crocheting hook clacked on the scarred tabletop when she made "the face" with the wave of an arthritically gnarled finger. "Don't you get huffy with me, young lady. You remember who slaves over a hot stove to make you creamed tuna on toast. All I'm saying is, instead of leaving your fate in someone else's hands, make your own."

Oh. Okay. Yeah. That was the answer. "You wait here while I get my magic wand, oh Guru of Fate."

Mona snorted. "You're a real comedienne. Can the funny. I'll say this one more time. You let that deadbeat intimidate you and take everything without so much as a puff of indignant air. You took care of all his needs for twenty years. You were at his beck and call while he made big deals and you hosted fancy dinner parties. But in the end you get nothing? There has to be some way around it. Stop pulling the covers up over your head and fight back, Maxie. Where's your gumption? What kind of judge is going to declare that even if you don't deserve something, my grandson doesn't either? Bah! That's garbage, and if you started threatening that walking penis instead of hiding from him, you'd find out he's not so big and bad after all."

Maxine clenched her fists, and her jaw, throwing in her thighs for good measure. Admitting her mother was right, that she was indeed afraid of all of Finley's money and connections, was the hardest thing she had to do every day when she looked at her reflection while she primped for another interview for a job she wouldn't get. "No, here's how it'll go. If I start threatening, he's going to whip out that damned prenup he had me sign. You remember the one, right, Mom? The one I didn't even know I was signing that said I leave with what I came into the marriage with? Which was nothing more than some tiaras and a pair of pom-poms. So it does me no good to threaten the walking penis!" Of all the mistakes she'd made in her life, blindly signing something she didn't even read made her a tard to the nth degree.

"Whose penis walks?" Gail Lumley, one of her mother's crew of four friends, asked from outside the screen door. Her shortly cropped hair, sharp onyx eyes, and quick step never failed to make Maxine remind herself this mob of women were all in their seventies.

With an upward tilt of her eyes, Maxine rolled her neck on her shoulders, and gave Gail the warmest smile she could summon while pulling out a chair for her to sit in. "No one's penis walks, Gail. Mom and I were discussing Fin. Again."

Gail let the door slam shut behind her and nodded affirmation, plunking down with a groan of the old vinyl seat. "Right. The Peckerhead."

Mona cackled, slapping Gail on her thigh. "That's the one."

Her mother's friends had dubbed Fin "The Peckerhead" one night at bingo, among other things. Since then, thinking up new and innovative nicknames for her wayward husband had become an endless source of amusement, all of them involving his nether parts—especially if they were drinking malt liquor. "Shhhhh, ladies. You're like second graders who just found a new game," Maxine scolded with a grin she fought. "Connor'll hear you."

Gail leaned into her with a saucy smile. "I'm sure Connor knows Penis-less is a peckerhead."

Maxine's mother, head thrown back, began to cackle. "Penis-less. You crack me up, Gail Lumley."

"Penis-less? Aw, girls, are you trash-talking me behind my back?"

A shiver, long and thready, slithered up her spine.

For the second time today, Maxine found herself silently calling upon the Lord's help. Again she prayed. If *He* were a good and gracious God, *He'd* never let that be the silken tones of Campbell Barker coming from behind her, sliding into her ear like melting vanilla ice cream over warm apple pie.

Gail snickered. "Nobody'd ever say a thing like that about *you*, Campbell Barker."

Okay, so today God wasn't feeling particularly good or gracious.

Clearly, she'd used her quota of pardons.

CHAPTER THREE

Note from Maxine Cambridge to all ex-trophy wives on the art of sucking it up, Princess: No job is too menial when you're broke. When someone offers you money for services rendered and you're broke—despite the fact that the service you'll provide sucks testicles that are big and hairy—don't look a gift horse in the mouth, Princess. Set aside your inflated opinion of what's beneath you, and run like hell for that light at the end of the tunnel. Colored paper awaits you. The green kind. You know, the kind you haven't seen since you were relieved of your wifely duties? Even if it smells like dog poop and mothballs. Money's money. Suck it up. This is your new life. Welcome.

A sun-browned hand came to rest on her shoulder, warm and delicious. The comfort it brought made her close her eyes for a moment and inhale before even realizing she had. "Max Henderson twice in one day. It's like Christmas without the annoying blinking lights," Campbell joked, making Maxine's mother giggle and Gail cluck her tongue with a wink.

God really did have a hard-on for her today. Maxine straightened in her chair, her spine stiff, her lips compressed. "Yeah, imagine your crazy luck. So what are you doing in my mother's house?"

He held up a wrench that gleamed silver in the bright afternoon sun spilling from the window above her mother's kitchen sink. "Fixing her leaky faucet, and FYI, I didn't make the connection. I didn't know Mona was your mother."

Campbell Barker plumbed leaky faucets? Not the whiz she'd known in high school. But who was she to pound the gavel of judgment? That meant at least one of them had an honest to God, paying job. She swung around on the rollers of her mother's dining room chair to face him. "You're a plumber? I thought you'd gone off to college to get a business degree—or something."

He nodded with a grin that left deep grooves on either side of his lean cheeks. "Yep, but I decided a business degree was boring and way beneath me. So I bought a plunger and some PVC pipe. Look at me now, huh?"

"Campbell is Garner's son. He works helping his dad now, Maxie. He's a good boy," her mother said with a doting smile in Campbell's direction.

"He's a good-lookin' boy, too," Gail added with a devilish glint in her eyes. Because stating the obvious was so essential. "Don't you think so, Maxine?"

She cringed.

"Yeah, don't you think so, Max?" Campbell encouraged with a chuckle and a nudge.

Yeah. She thought so. After eight months of not finding anyone or anything remotely interesting while she rode the train to poverty, today she suddenly thought Campbell Barker was good-looking. Funny that.

Thankfully, her mother's phone rang, saving her from having to answer Campbell's smug question. Maxine lunged for it, following the ear-splitting jingle her mother'd set on the highest volume, digging beneath a pile of *Good Housekeeping* magazines to get to it. Looking at the caller ID, she didn't recognize the number.

She'd hoped it was Lenore. The one and only friend Maxine had left on planet Earth, seeing as the still employed trophy wives didn't much commune with the commoner she'd recently become. Len didn't give a shit that she wasn't rich anymore. She didn't give a flying fuck that the women they'd once socialized with stuck their surgically tweaked pert noses up at her. She didn't even care that practically all of her close-knit family wasn't speaking to her because she'd defended Maxine.

Instead of her little sister.

Lacey.

Pressing the "talk" button, she ignored the pang of regret that it wasn't Lenore calling to let her live vicariously through her, and answered the phone. "Hello?"

"Maxine Cambridge?"

"Speaking."

"This is Joe Hodge. I got one of your fliers today over at the rec center. You still walkin' dogs?"

She'd walk saber-toothed tigers if cash were the reward. Her heart began to race. It was Connor's idea to place fliers all around the village, advertising dog walking. When they'd done it, the original intent was for him to offer his services, noting how many of the elderly had pets but in some cases were semi-homebound by the occasional aches and pains, leaving them unable to take their dogs on long walks or bathe them. Desperate times and the fact that she was supposed to support her kid, not the other way around, made her decide she'd give it a shot.

At that point, she'd have slept with the devil for cash. So two days ago, she'd made up some fliers on her mother's antiquated computer and hung them up all over Leisure Village. And now look—she had a taker. Which meant the forces of the universe hadn't totally abandoned her—they were just slacking off for happy hour appletinis.

"You still there?"

Maxine cleared her throat, taking the phone down the small stretch of hallway to the guest bathroom. Stepping over the debris of scattered tools, she planted herself on the closed toilet seat. "I am. So, uh, Mr. Hodge, right? You need your dog walked."

"Well, I'm not callin' for a date, that's for sure. We haven't even met."

Maxine giggled. She'd discovered that when you reached a certain golden age, you didn't much care about protocol, or in the case of her mother's other cohort in chaos, Mary Delouise, modesty and manners. Something she had to admire. Their time here on Earth was limited. Why waste it on bullshit and sucking someone's ass? "What kind of a dog do you have, Mr. Hodge?"

"You got rules about what kind a dog you'll walk?"

"No, no, of course not. I just want to be sure I have all the details."

"He's a mutt. A big ole mutt, and he shits like a horse. Big stinkin' piles of shit I can't pick up no more 'cause of the fact that I have arthritis in my knees. Hurts to bend down, you know. Doc says I gotta take baths to relieve the pain. I say, who the hell's gonna pull me outta the tub after I get in there?"

Who indeed? A finger went directly between her eyes to massage the bridge of her nose. Sometimes, when she wasn't hiding in her mother's house and she actually chatted with the occasional village resident, she found it was hard to keep them on task. Much like herself when she rambled in nervous bouts. Jesus, she'd be a handful at seventy. "I understand completely. So how often do you need someone to walk your mutt?"

"As often as he has to shit. And his name's Jake, not Mutt."

The heat of the bathroom was becoming sauna-ish. She struggled to pull off her suit jacket, draping it over the yellow vanity. "Why don't we set up a time so I can meet Jake and we'll discuss it then?"

"You busy now?"

Busy? Hah. Cold hard cash had just called her via AT&T. Though it was probably only Happy Meal money, it was money, and even a meeting and the promise of some hot lovin' with John Cusack wouldn't keep her from it. "What's your address? I'll be right there." Forgetting the door was open, forgetting there was a man present,

Max unzipped the back of her skirt and shimmied it off as she memo-rized Joe Hodge's address, clicking the "off" button on the phone.

"We haven't even had that cup of coffee and already you're get-ting naked. Who'd have figured Chuck Norris actually knew what he was talking about when he infomercialed me into buying that Total Gym. He had that look in his eye like he knew if I worked out enough, hot women would just throw their clothes at me."

Maxine let her head hang low.

To look at the skirt she'd been wearing, now almost at her ankles. Nice. God was clearly back to shunning her again.

Instead of hiding, she turned to face him full on. What differ-ence did it make if Campbell Barker saw her in her panties and silk shirt? Nowadays, this could be considered haute couture—sort of. "Did that twinkle in his eye tell you they'd be old chicks with lumpy asses and thickening waists? If I were you, I'd ask for my money back. You were raped." She reached for the only towel in the bathroom—a hand towel, holding it up in front of her while she slid her skirt back upward with her free hand.

Campbell stepped into the bathroom, laying his lean fingers on her waist to help her zip up her skirt. His deep chestnut brown hair, thick and tucked behind his ears, was shiny and silken under the light in her mother's bathroom. "Who says you're old? Have you looked in the mirror, Max Henderson? You look just as good as you did in high school."

Her eyes met his in the big mirror over the sink, her heart skit-tered with his broad hands at her waist. Not for over twenty years had she thought another man would ever touch her, and now here she was, in her mother's bathroom, being touched in a way so personal she was uncomfortable and excited and . . . uncomfortably excited. Simultaneously. She couldn't meet her own eyes, let alone his, in the mirror. Though she had just enough time to note that she was no lon-ger a Vanilla Pudding blonde. The stripe of medium brown hair along her scalp, her natural color, said so. The corners of her fading green eyes with the beginnings of crow's-feet said it, too, and the small but rapidly growing lines around her mouth—lines that sure as shit weren't from busting a gut laughing.

"So who says you're old, Max?"

Everyone who owns a Ferrari and has a personal trainer.

The close quarters, the scent of Campbell's clean shirt, and his hard good looks flushed her with sudden irritation. "No one has to say it. Where I've been you don't say it. You just know it. *I* know it. And stop calling me Max. It's *Maxine*." Neener, neener, neener. Like high-handedly reminding him her name wasn't shortened anymore was going to help her retain some of her wayward pride.

"Were all the people blind where you've been?"

No. They were young, tight of skin, free of cellulite, with 20/20 vision. "Where I've been doesn't matter. I'm here now." Here. Here. Here. In her mother's throwback-to-the-seventies bathroom with the brown swirly wallpaper and yellow vanity top.

"Yep. You sure are. And I'm here, too. I wouldn't call you unlucky today, *Max*."

Her knees went watery and soft when he said her name, and she couldn't think. "I have to change."

"I wouldn't dream of stopping you."

"Alone."

"Damn. Maybe you're not as much fun as Christmas after all."

Slipping from his light but mind-bending grasp, Maxine snorted. "I'm nowhere near as fun as Christmas. I'm not even bordering the excitement of Groundhog Day. And now I have to go walk a dog. Really, Campbell, it was nice seeing you again. In my underwear."

He laughed, backing away. "It won't be the last time I see you."

"In my underwear?"

"Not that a guy can't hope, but I meant around. You know, the village. Because I work here now."

No. It *would* be the last time he saw her if she had anything to say about it. The fluttery belly dances and weak knees were something she was never going to fall for again. They led to clenches of your intestines and irritable bowel syndrome. Add in the not-so-sweet fist up your ass, and she was so out.

Gliding past him, Maxine ignored the tingle the contact of their arms brought, hers smooth, his rough with dark hair.

Dog shit. That's where her focus had to be. Scooping Jake's shit. And money. Not Campbell Barker. "Yeah. Around. I'll see you." Maxine hurried down the hall to head to her mother's room to change, closing the door and turning the lock.

Sitting on the edge of her mother's green and burgundy floral bedspread, she gripped her knees to stop them from shaking before she changed.

Campbell Barker had scared the bejesus out of her. He looked at her in a way that was as distinctly unfamiliar to her as Hanes underwear. Like he'd consume her and spit out little pieces of Maxine when he was done, then pick his teeth with the fingernails from her very own hand. Finley had never looked at her like that—especially not in the last ten years or so.

And she'd been in her underwear.

The last pair of frilly, girlie panties she owned.

But brighter horizons were on the way. She had a job. A job scooping shit, but it was a job.

Throwing on her gray sweats, she piled her hair, unseen by her stylist Gerard in nine long months, up into a ponytail with a scrunchie, not bothering to look in the mirror before she left. There'd been a time if she'd gone out looking like this, half of the Jersey shore would've had apoplexy. There was a time she wouldn't have dreamed of going to the mailbox without at least some makeup. Nowadays, there wasn't much point to it.

She didn't have a mailbox.

It dawned on her how utterly out of this realm her life had become. The day had come to pass when Maxine Cambridge couldn't even summon the energy to care about what she looked like. Surely the Rapture was upon them.

But what was the point?

She'd never look in a mirror and see whatever it was Campbell Barker thought he saw, and what she used to see had become so distorted she didn't want to chance even a mere glimpse at it.

$\sim\!\ell\!\sim$

"Mr. Hodge?"

"Yup."

"I'm Maxine Cambridge." She stuck out her hand, smiling at him through the small opening he'd made in his rather ratty screen door.

"So you're Mona Henderson's little girl." Joe Hodge said it, rather than asked it, and he stated it with the hint of a knowing, yet wistful, smile.

"Yes, sir. That's me." All forty-one years, body parts heading for her southern locales.

His chuckle was deep and raspy, his bushy eyebrow rose in a sort of begrudging admiration. "That Mona, I like 'er. She's a firecracker."

Yeah. Mona was a real bad mamma jamma. If her mother was nothing else, she was definitely an exploding fire hazard, and apparently, she got around the village. "No doubt that's my mother."

He cocked his head, thick with sprouts of bushy gray and white hair, and squinted. "You know, you look a little bit like that girl who used to do commercials for that snazzy car dealership. Damn. Can't remember the name—"

Jesus. Was there no one who didn't remember those fucking commercials? Did everyone watch the Goddamned TV? It was like a knife in the gut every time someone pointed out her once local claim to fame.

"Cambridge Automobiles," Maxine supplied with an almost smile. Take that, Finley Cambridge. When Fin had suggested that maybe she was tired of doing the dealership's commercials and it was time to give her a break, Maxine had let herself believe he was nurturing her. She'd also wanted to believe it was because he was being generous of spirit and had finally realized she was tired of being the face of Cambridge Auto. She'd wanted to believe. End of.

Of course, now Maxine realized there was only so much soft lighting and Spanx to go around before you couldn't hold it, suck it, or girdle it in anymore. Fin hadn't been trying to spare her feelings at all. He'd been keeping the home fires burning until he found the next sacrificial, twentysomething, goo-goo-eyed over him blonde.

Joe nodded with an eager grunt and a shake of his finger. "Yeah, that's it. But lookin' at you up close, I see you're too old."

Smack. Down. Ouch. "Actually, you're right, Mr. Hodge. I was that girl for fifteen years. Then I was put out to pasture because old cows make for some chewy, tough eye candy."

"But they make right fine purses, if you'd asked my dearly departed Millie." He rocked back on his heels with a cluck of his tongue.

Maxine's chuckle was soft. Her eyes weary with gratitude. "Nice save."

"I was married for forty-two years. I could save the government, if they'd let me."

A "woof" in the octave of big and baritone came from somewhere in the back of the dark interior of Mr. Hodge's ranch. "So anyways, nice to meet ya. C'mon in." He took her hand in his and gave it a brisk up-and-down motion before curling his stubby fingers around the inside of his suspenders.

As she stepped into his screened-in porch, the distinct odor of mothballs and spaghetti sauce wafted to her nostrils.

As did the odor of big dog. Really big dog.

The dog bounded from the back of the house with the thump

of immense paws and snorting gulps for air. He stopped when he reached Joe, standing almost to the top of his thigh. "And this is my Jake."

Maxine bent at the waist to reach out and give a scratch to his long, floppy ear. Jake pulled back, showing her his teeth with a low growl. Snatching her hand back, Maxine looked to the elderly man with a question. "He's not good with strangers?"

"He's grumpy sometimes. But I figure, if he's gotta take a shit, he won't care who's holding the other end of the leash." He held up Jake's black leash, palming it to her.

"Uh, does he bite?"

"Not hard."

Money. Think money, Maxine. And the fact that you're an animal lover. You need to make this work. Besides, it's not like you don't have bandages and Neosporin, candy-ass. Taking the leash, she clutched it, lost for what to say next. Details for this gig hadn't been high on her priority list when she'd fled her mother's and Campbell.

"So I suppose you want to talk money?"

Oh, Jesus Christ and all twelve apostles. Yes! Yes. She wanted to talk money. "I think we better before I take Jake."

"So whaddya charge?"

Duh. Money. "Uh, well . . . Jake's pretty big . . ."

"And he shits big, too." Joe shrugged his burly shoulders, his craggy face sheepish. "I'm just bein' honest."

"How often do you want him walked?"

"Twice a day. You charge by the walk or the time it takes?"

Math. She sucked at it. "Um . . ."

"Suggestion?"

"Shoot."

"I say you charge a flat fee. This way, you're not obligated to spend any more time with the little bastards than it takes for them to shit, and you don't have to keep track of minutes. And like I said, Jake—"

"Shits big," Maxine finished, grinning at him. "Okay, so what do you think is fair? I mean, seeing as Jake's not likely going to want to take me out for kibble and candlelight right now, maybe this should be a trial run?"

Joe gave Jake an affectionate slap on his backside. "Nah. He'll warm up to ya. I'm on a fixed income, but I figure some money's better than no money in your case. I'll give you forty bucks a week to walk him twice a day. Oh, and clean up his—"

"Shit."

Joe grinned, his dentures ultra white in the fading sun. "Yeah. You provide the baggies."

"Baggies?"

"Yep, big ones, too. We got an ordinance around here. No dog crap just left layin' around. Gotta clean it up. You got one of them shit scoopers?"

No. But wouldn't that be helpful in light of the fact that she'd had more than her fair share of shit dumped on her lately. Maybe then she could shovel her way out. "No. I wasn't thinking that far in advance."

Joe reached over her shoulder and yanked a pooper-scooper from behind her. "You'd best invest in one then. You can use mine for now. So we got a deal?"

Maxine smiled at Joe, then down at Jake.

Who growled.

Perfect. But Maxine ignored that in light of the fact that forty bucks was riding on the line here. That was milk money, baby. Maybe a box of granola bars, too. The chocolate-covered ones. "Yes. It's a deal. What time should I be here every day?"

"Nine and six. Jake here only shits twice a day."

Alrighty. "Okay, then. We're off." Kneeling beside Jake, she hooked her finger under his collar, but he growled again, low and rumbly. "Help a girl out, would ya?" she whispered close to Jake's

ear. "I'm not going to let you eff up my first job, buddy. I need cash."
With a quick snap, Maxine latched the leash to his chain-link collar
and rose.

Jake didn't.

She gave him a hard tug. He dug his large paws into the porch
floor and pulled back with a snarling grunt.

Maxine looked to Joe.

Joe winced. "C'mon now, Jake. Be nice to the lady." He fished
around in a brown paper bag he pulled out of his pants pocket, digging out a green bone before handing the sack to her. "Treats," he
said as way of explanation. "To get his carcass in gear. Now do yourself a favor. Hold on," he said, just before throwing open the screen
door and lobbing the bone out onto the grass.

Upon reflection, Maxine realized her right arm might always be
just an inch shy of her left forever because Jake had launched himself
out the door after that bone like the bichon frise of his pound-dog
dreams was in heat and waiting just for him.

And she could live with that. Forty bucks *was* involved.

Huffing in ragged gulps of humid air from the back of Jake's hind-
quarters, Maxine also noted there was no walking involved here. It
was all about Jake darting willy-nilly in and out of the thorny bushes
lining the sidewalk, stopping for a mere nanosecond to mark his territory, only to take off again with loping strides she couldn't keep up
with.

And still he had no interest in evacuating his bowels. "Jake! Stop
yanking me around and do your thing already." Was there a command for taking a shit she needed to use? Her hands and wrists were
raw from being dragged, and her Pilates core was clearly out of order.
"C'mon, dude. There's a cookie in it for youuuu," she cajoled. Yet Jake
wasn't having it. He continued to tear ass down the slight slope of the
winding hill, dragging her along the sidewalk as they went.

Without warning, he stopped as suddenly as he'd begun, sniffing the ground with rapid, snorting whiffs. His enormous rusty brown head cocked upward just as she slammed into his back end. Gasping for breath, grateful for the reprieve, Maxine squeezed her eyes shut to thwart the dizzy reeling at her temples. She hadn't eaten all day, and the cloying heat wasn't helping.

Bracing her palms on her knees, she was taking slow, wheezing breaths when she noticed the shift in Jake's body. He wriggled in her grasp, but he wasn't trying to escape.

Popping one eye open, Maxine groaned, but she refrained from asking for help from above. If today was any indication, her hotline to heaven was obviously on the blink.

"Hey, Jake. How are ya, buddy?" Wet slurps from Jake's tongue were muffled by someone's hand.

Forcing herself to open both eyes, she managed to stifle her moan. Rearing upward, she eyeballed Campbell. Freshly showered, smelling of soap and herbal shampoo, his damp hair clinging to the sides of his neck in enticing waves. Oh, and look. Jake loved him. Old ladies, dogs, he had everyone lining up to fan him with palm fronds and feed him grapes.

Sweat trickled between her breasts. "Jake likes you." Why that left her irritated was a mystery to her.

He grinned, ruffling the top of Jake's head. "Who wouldn't? I'm a likeable guy. So what brings you to my neck of the senior citizens' woods?"

If he noticed the roll of her eyes, he didn't comment on it. "I didn't know it was your woods."

Campbell thumbed over his broad shoulder. "Yep. This is my dad's place."

Out of the two hundred units on this side of the village she could have randomly chosen to land in front of, why wouldn't it be Campbell Barker's? "I have to finish walking Jake."

"I'll help."

"I don't need help."

"Really? The way you were gasping for breath while you ran after Jake didn't exactly suggest some hidden strength for the ten-K or your skills as an alpha pack leader. So I'd beg to differ."

Maxine ignored the calming influence Campbell had on Jake. Ignoring his beefcakeyness proved more taxing. Her eyes darted to the black paved sidewalk. "We just need to get to know one another." She looked down at the dog with a half smile. "Right, Jake?"

He took her in with one droopy eye and snarled.

"How's that working out? You know, the getting to know each other thing?"

She sighed. "Fine. Walk." While she knew she was irrationally angry for a multitude of reasons that Jake liked Campbell, it didn't stop her from being so.

Campbell took the leash from her raw, red hand and gave it a firm tug. Jake responded by taking his place beside his strong thigh, popping the squat she could have never elicited from him if Mr. Barker hadn't shown up and turned everything all magical and shiny. "You just have to let him know you're in charge or he'll run rampant."

Maxine's eyes widened. Wow. Mr. Hodge hadn't been kidding. Jake shit big. She stooped to shovel his aromatic essence into the baggie and said out of the side of her mouth, "Thank you, Dog Whisperer."

He chuckled silky smooth like she hadn't insulted him, maneuvering Jake into a steady pace. "Hey, I'm just trying to help make this big career switch from the Cluck-Cluck Palace to dog walking a successful one for you."

"Thank God for career counselors."

Campbell stopped, halting Jake and looming over her, blocking her view of anything else but him. "You know I have to ask."

Maxine's chin lifted. "Knock yourself out."

"What's up your ass, Max?"

That took her by surprise. And, yeah. What the hell was up her ass? Aside from Finley's fist. "I have no idea what you mean."

"You know exactly what I mean."

"Do not."

"Yeah, you do. You're one cranky lady, and you know what I think this is about?"

"So you don't just fix broken pipes and soothe savage beasts, you have the psychoanalysis thing wrapped up, too?"

"Just call me Dr. Campbell."

"So what's my diagnosis?"

"You have a severe case of Campbell-itis. You like me. I'd venture to say you find me pretty attractive. You don't much like that. It burns your britches."

So? "I don't like anything or anyone at this point in my life. I don't much like me. How could I possibly like *you*?" Maxine bit her tongue. *TMI, Maxine.*

The soft purr of a car engine brought her respite from his answer—which she was more than positive would've been cocky and riddled with Campbell-itis.

The fading sun glinted off the hood of a sleek, midnight blue sedan as it crawled up the hill and slowed to a stop right beside them. A quick glance at the vehicle's owner told her that, definitely, whoever was in charge upstairs was grudgin' and she was at the top of that list.

"Maxine," Finley drawled out of the open window, but only after he'd scanned the length of her sweat-suit-clad body, eyes filled with distaste.

Instantly, her stomach lurched and her intestines kinked up. Finley had never come here in the eight months since she'd flown his coop. In fact, she hadn't laid eyes on him since he'd confirmed what the society pages had prematurely announced. Laying eyes on him now didn't garner the reaction she'd given so much thought to in all this time. There was no longing for what might have been, no emotional connection. The sort of connection that was usually a lingering residual effect of sharing so many years together. Not even a twinge.

There was just fear of Finley and the intimidation factor he wielded like Conan the Barbarian. Fuckall if that shouldn't make her pissed as all hell. Instead, she found her knees shaking at a possible confrontation while her mind raced with a million different answers to the question of why he'd finally shown up. "Why are you here, Finley?" she croaked, clinging to the baggie housing Jake's monstrous contribution. Oh, Jesus. Had she croaked? Yeah. She'd croaked the words.

While she held a bag of dog poop. So sad.

He popped open the door and slid out of the car with ease. Dressed immaculately, his black suit with the sharp creases in the pants and bright red tie made her cringe at her own appearance. Like wearing a Dior original would make her any less of a candy-ass anyway.

Jake gifted Finley with the same low growl he'd given her. Campbell gave his leash another firm tug, placing a palm at his snout to quiet him. His next move was subtle, but meant for visibility, when he placed his free hand at Maxine's waist.

"I'm here to see my son. I figure if you're going to prevent him from seeing me, then I'll just come see him."

Right. In all this time it had been the scary Maxine who'd kept him from Connor. It was always someone else's fault Fin wasn't getting what he wanted. When he'd stuck his shank of love up any available vajajay, it was her fault. She wasn't attentive enough. She didn't make him feel like he was a man enough. Her thighs were too jiggly. There was never any owning up with Finley. Maxine's cheeks flushed in indignation. Yet, her protest to his false accusation came out weak and downright sissified. "I did not—"

Finley held up a hand to quiet her, the twenty-four-carat gold of his pinky ring flashing its brilliance. Just another of the many baubles he used to show off his financial stature. There was nothing he loved more than flaunting his goodies. But the thin line of his lips still had the bloody power to make her wince. "I'm not up to your bullshit today, Maxine. Just tell me where your mother's house is and I'll go find him myself."

Campbell rolled his tongue in his cheek, taking a step closer to her ex-husband. "You don't know where your own kid's been living?"

"Leave Connor alone, Finley," she crowed, summoning the will to defy him on her son's behalf. He could manipulate her all he wanted, but the fuck she'd let him beat Connor down, too. "He's obviously not ready to see you."

Finley's cheeks grew sharply pronounced when his mouth puckered. Oh, she knew that look. It was the "You're pushing my buttons, Maxine" look, and it immediately made her rethink her words. "He's not ready because you won't let him be ready. You've brainwashed the shit out of him, you and that crazy mother of yours. Now where's your mother's house? You can't keep him from me, Maxine. I have a right to see him."

She caught the questioning glance Campbell shot her. The one that said, "Why don't you pony up and defend yourself, chickenshit?" But her throat was thick, her tongue sluggish, and her functioning brain matter uncooperative. "Talk to the judge, Finley," she said, meaning for it to sound like a demand, but it turned out to be nothing more than a pathetic order.

And Finley was all over that shit like fried on chicken. He fed off the power he'd convinced her he had. The only thing that had changed in eight months was that she was no longer going to be married to him. Pitiful. "I'd be very careful if I were you, Maxine. You can't afford to lose anything else." The narrowed slant of his eyes, the imposing feel to his stance, the twisted confidence in knowing he held all the cards, infuriated her. Yet the gurgling bubble of anger she so wanted to nurture just wouldn't pop.

However, Campbell didn't seem to feel the same way. He wasn't at all intimidated. Of course, he hadn't lost his cute shoes and a place to live either. His posture was rigid, hovering a good three inches over Finley when he placed himself between them. "I think you'd better cool it, pal, and lay off the threats." Campbell's angular face was tense, his jaw muscles working overtime. The tight clench of his square fist around Jake's leash flexed with a twitch.

"And who the fuck are you?" was her soon to be ex-husband's arrogant question. His shoulders squared, and his wide chest puffed out like he was looking for a good throwdown.

Hoo boy. Finley felt threatened. No one threatened Finley Cambridge. When he became this confrontational, it was time to step in. She'd done it all of her adult life on his behalf.

Some habits died hard, slow, agonizing deaths.

Wonder of wonders, her vocal cords decided they'd cut her some slack, and her response to Finley's question flew from her lips like a bullet from a gun. "He's my boyfriend."

Niiice.

Superfly, Maxine.

CHAPTER FOUR

Note from Maxine Cambridge to all ex-trophy wives on sucking it up: When attempting to put on airs for your soon to be ex-husband, quite possibly one should do so when not in a dingy gray sweat suit, holding a Ziploc bag full of dog poo. It carries just a wee bit less in the way of impact. Okay. It carries *a lot less*. In fact, it's unseemly. In other words, don't let your douche-bag husband see you sweat. Wear deodorant at all times.

"So look who's got a boy toy," Finley taunted, cocking a silvery eyebrow in a manner that dripped with lewd suggestion. The sly innuendo that Campbell was nothing more than a man-whore irked her. Alas, because he was a douche bag, it was only natural he'd assume everyone else was, too.

Maxine cringed, clenching her teeth, wishing she had the clangers to hurl Jake's poop at him and watch it slide down the front of his immaculate suit.

Campbell crossed his brawny arms over his torso, puffing his chest out, too. The nice thing about it was, his chest puffed farther than Fin's. "I think it was a good move on Max's part. You got Preteen Barbie, and she got me, and while I'm not a preteen, I'm definitely not *sixty*."

Score!

As quickly as she inwardly cheered Campbell calling Fin out, she winced. Oh, sweet Jesus. Fin was going to run him over with his big fancy car. Her heart crashed, but she wasn't sure if it was because she was afraid the two men were going to come to blows, or because Campbell had defended her.

A tingle in her stomach began with a small clench and blossomed into a fistful of butterflies, taking flight in her gullet.

Okay, okay. It was because Campbell had defended her. Duly noted.

Finley's foot scraped the pavement when he rounded on them, jamming his hands into the pockets of his expensive trousers. "And what do you know about our affairs?"

Campbell gave him a distinct look of disinterest, shrugging his shoulders with indifference. "I don't know anything about Max's affairs. I just know about *your* affair," he drawled with lazy syllables, moving his body in slow increments in order to fully cover Maxine's. "Or was it affairs, as in multiples, honey?" he asked over his shoulder.

Christ on a crapper. He'd gone *there*. Without any help from her. How had he known where *there* was? God, if he knew, she'd never be able to look him in the eye again.

But that was okay. Who needed to look in his dreamy blue eyes?

He had a nice chest.

This had to stop before Campbell took Finley out. Stepping around Campbell, Maxine put a hand up, but she couldn't make her eyes meet her ex-husband's. They ended up fixating on the crisp collar of his shirt. "Look, Finley, what I do or who I do it with is none of your business anymore. This is about our son, and I don't know if Connor will see you or not. In fact, I doubt it, but the judge did make it clear you had to call first if you wanted to see him, and I don't remember getting a message that your receptionist called on your behalf." So, hah. *Hah, shit. That was weak, weak, weak, Maxine.*

Finley's lips rippled his displeasure. "If you and your hag of a mother would stop filling his head with lies, there'd be no question about whether he wants to see me or not!" he shouted.

Jake wiggled his back end, lowering the upper half of his long, lumbering body to display his discontent. A drop of saliva fell from the corner of his big, slobbery mouth. Campbell gave him a tug upward, pulling Jake behind him until he completely shielded Maxine from Finley. "I can't believe you blame a cute little old lady for your crappy parenting. I think it's time you roll, buddy."

"Was that a threat?"

"Did it feel like one?"

Fin's eyes narrowed. "I think it did."

"I thought cars were your thing. Seems like maybe it's rocket science." Though Campbell's face remained impassive and outwardly unimpressed, she felt his tension, saw the muscles in his back flex. That she took a moment to note there were two very different sides to Campbell Barker was a testament to how he'd affected her in just the matter of a day. He'd thrown a gauntlet down on her behalf, and it left her all atwitter.

However, it was so on if the look on Finley's face was on point. Maxine knew she had to step in and step in fast. It came naturally, saving the man she'd been married to for twenty years from all forms of kerfuffles. Finley's temper was legend. She was keeper of the legend.

She'd been smoothing things over to keep peace with anyone who got Fin's goat for a very long time, and the habit was hard to break. "Campbell?" She wrapped her fingers around his upper arm, noting the bulk, fighting the urge to revel in its smooth texture. "I think we have to go. Isn't *Dog the Bounty Hunter* on tonight? We don't want to miss that. I mean," she gave him a pointed look, "it's *Dog*."

In an instant, Campbell was once again the man she'd been reunited with in the parking lot of the Cluck-Cluck Palace. His eyes cleared from the haze of anger, and his broad shoulders relaxed. With his free hand, he used an index finger to trail a gentle line down her nose. "You're right. I'd be so disappointed if we missed *Dog*." Turning to Fin, he smiled and said, "So I guess we're out. I assume you know the way back to the gatehouse. And if not, I bet that fancy GPS can tell you." Entwining his fingers with Maxine's, they left a frustrated, red-faced Finley in their wake.

While they plodded back up the hill to the tune of Fin's car going in the other direction, Maxine had to fight to keep from sighing in girlish bliss. Campbell's hand, callused, tanned, swallowing hers up whole, offered a security she was pretty sure she'd never quite experienced in this way.

And she had to remind herself she wasn't up for any more experiences just now. "You can let go now," she said with a quick glance over her shoulder. "He's gone."

But Campbell's grip became tighter. "He's an ass."

"Yeah. He's an ass." She showed her solidarity, quiet in tone, completely unconvincing, but solidifying nonetheless.

"Any reason in particular you're so afraid of him?" He asked the question with a ring of protectiveness to his voice.

"I'm not . . . afraid." Not at all. *I'm careful.*

"You're not exactly not afraid."

Her sigh was jagged and embarrassed. How could she possibly explain the kind of Vulcan mind meld her soon to be ex had on her? It made no sense to rational human beings of sound mind and body. She knew that, yet she couldn't begin to describe the kind of uproar Fin left her stomach in every time she had to deal with him, during their marriage and in its current aftermath. "Finley's imposing. He—I—"

"Imposing isn't the word I'd use. Showing his ass is."

"That's more than a word."

"He's more than a word, Max. He's a lot of words. Some I probably shouldn't repeat in front of a lady."

She giggled. "It's okay. I say them in my head about him all the time." If only she could use her outdoor voice when she thought them.

Still holding her hand, Campbell stopped when they reached

Mr. Hodge's, handing over Jake's leash. Dusk had begun to settle, the pink and orange sky reflecting in his blue eyes. "Then why don't you say them out loud and *to* him? He needs a good verbal assault."

Looking down at her sneakers, Maxine fidgeted in his grasp. "You don't know Finley."

"And I don't think I want to. So why do you let him talk to you like that?"

Because each and every time she thought she just might have the market cornered on giving him a piece of her mind, her tongue stuck to the roof of her mouth like it had been freshly tarred there. Factor in her lack of quick retorts for the circles Fin was so good at talking, and she always stumbled. "What good does it do to argue with him? It's better if I just leave well enough alone."

"Better for who?"

Me, me, me. "Well, Connor, primarily. How would it look if his father and I got into a fistfight in the middle of a senior citizens' village? If word got out, and if you know these women in the village, it would, how can I possibly preach to him that fighting isn't the answer?"

"Nobody said anything about fists. I'm just talking about standing up for yourself. He talks to you like he owns you. Like he has every right to be in your business, but you have absolutely no rights at all to his."

She held up a hand to correct him, then let it fall to her side with a slap of her thigh. Campbell was right. Her entire marriage had been based on Fin having all the rights, and her having none. How that had come to be deserved at least a little research.

Tipping her chin up, his blue eyes settled on hers. "The way I see it, he was your husband for a long time, but he isn't anymore—or he won't be soon. He's Connor's father. Sure, that entitles him to certain things, though he definitely doesn't behave as though he deserves any rights to his kid at all. But *you're* Connor's mother, not just the vessel he deemed important enough to procreate with. You have just as many rights as he does. Big money or not. You can give him hell right back, and you shouldn't have to fear retribution if you do. He can't take anything else away from you, right? He's got all the money. He's got all the power. As far as I can see, speaking your mind is all you have left."

Ouch. Maxine winced, lifting her chin up and out of his strong hand. "I just have trouble expressing myself." But only with Fin. He steamrolled her with his slew of words and fast and furious potshots.

"Having an opinion about how he's treated you is more than fair, if you ask me. If I were you, I'd be pretty pissed off at what he's done. Yet, I watched you shrink a couple of inches in height when he went into demand mode. This is 2010, Max. You don't have to walk ten paces behind him."

She didn't. Okay, maybe she walked five or so, but definitely not ten. That was an exaggeration. *Wasn't it?* Shaking her head, Maxine decided to change course again. "Why are you getting so worked up about it? Why do you care how my ex-husband talks to me?"

"Almost ex-husband," he corrected with a half smile, "and the Max I knew would have run up one side of him and back down the other. I guess I was just surprised at how you jumped at the chance to pacify him instead of telling him to take his shitty attitude back to his mini-mansion and barely-beyond-jailbait girlfriend. The Max I knew once gave a bully a thorough tongue-lashing in front of a whole gymnasium of students because he had the 'nads to call Mindy Weirtz flat-chested in front of you."

Maxine's head cocked to the left, calling up the memory. She had read Leon Matheson the riot act, hadn't she? Like she'd written it herself. A small smile lifted her lips upward. "I liked Mindy. She was always nice to me. She helped me with my algebra. I sucked at math."

"So you don't like 'you' enough to at least have even a small, angry protest on your behalf? I wonder what the old Max would have to say about that?" he pondered out loud, giving her a questioning glance that held a challenge.

Oh, fuck the old Max. The old Max had that kind of energy. The new, now older, far less firm, sans pom-poms and rhinestone-bedecked tiara *Maxine* didn't. Instead of reacting, she chose to change tactics. Divert, distract, defuse. The three "Ds" to winning any battle successfully. You didn't need an opinion or a quick retort to do that. "Want to share how you know so much about me and my pending divorce?"

Campbell smiled, deeply grooved dimples popping up on either side of his mouth. "It's like you said, the women here talk. That I happen to be in their space when they do is merely coincidence. And in case you're wondering, they all think your almost ex is a—"

"Penis-less wonder." Maxine chuckled, breaking the tension beginning to creep between them. "Well, thanks for sticking up for me. I promise in the future I'll work on being a big girl and sticking up for myself."

"I'd say you owe me that cup of coffee for beating that jackass about the head and shoulders with my sharp tongue and pithy wit."

Her tongue darted over her parched lips in nervousness. "Thank you isn't enough?"

Campbell let her hand go, but his smile didn't leave his face. Shoving his hands into the pockets of his jeans, he said, "Nah. I gave your almost ex a verbal lickin'. That's worth at least a cup of coffee."

If she said anything right now, Maxine knew she would stammer—knew it. Yet she opted to open her mouth anyway. "I—well, I'm—busy. I mean—I can't—because I'm busy and—"

The space between them diminished before she knew what was happening—his face, handsome and hovering, quite suddenly directly in front of hers, cutting off her babble. The graze of Campbell's lips on hers, shocking and wonderful all at once, left her startled and overheated. They were firm but soft, and so hot she found herself wanting more, leaning into him, forgetting Jake and feeling only the gut-deep reaction his mouth evoked.

The moan that almost slipped from her mouth into his was stifled when Campbell began to back away, still smiling. "I didn't invite you for a night of floggers and ball gags, Max, just a cup of coffee. I'll call you," he said with a deep chuckle, turning and heading back down the road before she could say no.

Maxine looked down at Jake, her heart crashing so loud, she heard it in her ears. "Whaddya think a ball gag is, Jake?"

Jake growled up at her.

"Yeah, I feel the same way," she agreed with his assessment of the situation, shrugging her shoulders. "Some things you're just better off not knowing, eh, pal?" Duplicating the sharp tug Campbell had given him, she tried to pull Jake back down the hill.

Instead of following merrily behind her like she was the Pied Piper of all things big, four-legged, and drooling, Jake flopped down on the pavement, put his nose between his paws, and groaned.

Wrapping the leash around her wrist, Maxine gave a gentle yank. "Aw, c'mon, Jake! It's hot. I'm tired. I'm hungry. So hungry I swear I'll eat your dog biscuits if you don't cooperate. Now move it, buddy!"

Jake sighed.

She put her hands behind her back, placing the leash between them and pulled with a grunt as sweat trickled between her breasts. "Jake, you beast. Get up!"

A whistle came from the distance, sharp and clear, and then someone called out, "Jake! Get a move on, boy!"

She sighed. Campbell.

Jake was on his feet in a half second flat, moving toward Max at breakneck speed. She squinted into the fading sunlight to see Campbell's broad back becoming a distant dot just before she was dragged back down the hill.

What did a girl have to do to get a little respect?

Be Campbell Barker . . . You know. Your booooyfriend who kisses like a dream?

Oh, shut it, would you?

～ ℓ ～

Lenore Erickson eyed the caller ID on her phone and blew out a breath of angry air. She thrummed her fingers on the base of the phone, wondering where her receptionist, Delores, was. A glance at the clock on the wall told her. Lunch. Delores never missed lunch.

She ran a hand through her hair, shaking off the stray dark strands with disgust when they pulled from her scalp.

And the phone continued to ring.

Clearly her sister Lacey wasn't giving up.

Not that Lacey ever gave up when she wanted something. Like, for instance, *someone else's husband.*

With a clench of her teeth, she yanked the phone to her ear and spat, "Belle's Will Be Ringing. This is Lenore Erickson. How can I help you?"

"Oh, stop, Len. It's Lacey and you darn well know it," Lacey grated with her whirring whine.

"Lacey, Lacey, Lacey. Hmmmm . . ." She let her voice wander as though she was puzzled by who exactly Lacey was. Then she smacked her lips. "Wait! Is this Lacey Gleason? The one who's marrying that slimy prick Finley Cambridge before he's even paid the blood money to his attorneys for a divorce from my best friend Maxine—you know, his *wife?* Is that the Lacey I'm talking to?"

A hiss of irritated air swirled from the other end of the line. "It's not like that, Len."

Her eyebrow rose in disdain. "Reeeally? So you mean you're not planning a wedding to a man who's not even divorced yet? Wow. Guess you're back in my will. You know what that means? You, yes, *you,* the Lacey who's no longer an adulteress, get the gravy boat shaped like a pig. Festive, right? And pink. Very pink." Len didn't even attempt to hide her fury with her baby sister—her pampered, overindulged, lazy, husband-stealing sister. Each time she thought of the pain Lacey had caused, it made her gut clench into a hard knot.

Lacey sniffed, resorting to tear tactics. "Please, Lenore. Can't we try and get past this? What's done is done."

Len scoffed in response. Loud. "Done? Is that old mule that's almost three times your age divorced yet? No. No, I don't think he is. Done implies that all those nagging loose ends like marriage vows have been tied up. Severed, I believe is what they call it these days. And last I checked, Lace, my best friend Maxine was still married to your rich fiancé, all while she lives in a retirement village with her mother and can't even afford a gallon of milk because her husband—your *fiancé*—is a cheap fuck and won't throw her a bone. So as far as I'm concerned, nothing's done, lamb chop. I haven't heard the fat lady sing. Not one note."

"I swear I didn't mean for it to happen the way it did, Lenore! If Mason hadn't screwed up—"

"Mason? You're blaming Mason? Please. Stop. It was you who wrote that engagement announcement, wasn't it?" That Lacey still didn't get the kind of damage she'd created, the kind of pain she'd inflicted, meant she had no conscience as far as Len was concerned.

Lenore braced herself for her sister's defense by gripping the edge of her walnut-stained desk with a white-knuckled hand. The defense that had absolutely no personal accountability and a whole bunch of pathetic justifications for some truly despicable bad behavior.

"Yes, but I told him—"

"Right," she snarled, cutting her off again. "You told Mason not to print it for a month, and because it ended up in the wrong pile, or whatever the hell happens at a newspaper when glitches like this go down, and instead ended up in the society pages a month early, *he* screwed up?" Lenore gave the earpiece a hard knock with her knuckle. "Hey in there, brainiac! You should have never, ever written it to begin with, Lacey! Don't you think it was just a little premature, dare I say, presumptuous, to do something like that, seeing as Finley hadn't even told Maxine he wanted a divorce yet? Did you know that the man you're engaged to, that teenybopper airhead dabbler, called the paper and almost had Mason fired? He's our cousin, a cousin with two kids and a wife and no sugar daddy with a blanket of cash to cover up with if he loses his job." Spittle had formed at the corner of her mouth. She wiped it away with an angry thumb.

"But he didn't lose his job," Lacey cried in protest, her voice holding that familiar plea, the one that was supposed to bring the house down. "I made sure Finley took care of it."

"That was real sporting of you, Lace. But you forgot to ask him to take care of his kid—who read that announcement right along with Maxine—in a *newspaper*. What do you suppose it felt like to find out your husband and the father of your child was leaving you for the friggin' receptionist at an automobile dealership?"

"If you would just listen to me!"

The sobbing.

Lacey was a whiz at sobbing, with big, wide, tear-filled blue eyes while she wrung her dainty hands, all put-upon. Lenore's own eyes rolled upward as her fingers flipped through swatches of tablecloth samples. "Listen to what? Listen to you tell me how your panties just fell off your pert backside when you hopped into bed with another woman's husband? If that's what I'm listening to, I'd rather listen to oh, I dunno, someone's skin being peeled from their living body. So save it."

Not an inch. She refused to give Lacey an inch. All of her short life she'd been treated like someone had stamped "Fragile" on her forehead. If Lacey's lower lip trembled in displeasure even a little, their parents were assholes and elbows to rectify and pacify. When Lacey wanted something, no matter the cost financially or emotionally, their parents provided. Lacey never went without.

Well, not this time. Maybe, had she not been so spoiled, had she been required to pay even the slightest consequence, she'd have thought twice before she wonked Lenore's best friend's husband. Like maybe a whole two minutes after said best friend had kindly secured a job for Lacey at Finley's dealership. The job Lenore had begged Maxine to give her sister who had no purpose and no plans for the future other than to hook up with geriatrics that had fat bank accounts and belonged to someone else.

How she hadn't seen the dalliance coming could officially be filed under the Seven Wonders of the World. Never would she have thought Lacey would cross a boundary so un-crossable—so sacred. Her sister'd done some shady things in her time. She'd weaseled, manipulated, used her beauty and body to garner whatever it was that she wanted at the time, but this, in Lenore's mind, was unforgivable.

So unforgivable Lenore had finally put her foot down and refused to help with a single wedding plan, thus creating the biggest family brawl at Sunday dinner six months ago, making World War Two look like nothing but a wee spat.

"Lenore, you're my sister. How could you not be involved in my wedding?" Her tone took on that of a petulant child, which wasn't any huge surprise. Lacey was almost twenty-two years younger. A surprise gift from God, as her parents had put it. It was as though her parents had forgotten how to parent when Lacey came along, or maybe they were just too tired to put the kind of effort into disciplining her that was required to teach a child the entire world didn't tip on its axis just because you made the "pouty face."

"You plan weddings for a living. What'll it look like if you don't plan mine?"

Ah. She was busting out the familial card. Nice. Len scowled. "It'll look just like what it is. It'll look like I think what you've done to Maxine and her son is disgusting. It'll look like I just can't support planning a wedding before a divorce has even happened. It'll look like I'm ashamed that my own sister would slink off with a pig of a man while my best friend and her kid are penniless!"

The raspy sigh of Lacey's aggravation that the not quite ex-wife of the man she was marrying had the audacity to inconvenience her plans grated in Len's ear. "God, I'm so sick of hearing about Maxine and how broke she is. She's not your sister. I am! And if she needs money, why doesn't she just get a job?"

"That's a good question, Lace. One you might ask yourself. But you don't apply for jobs, do you? At least not the ones that require you do much more than spread those firm thighs, right?" Slamming the phone down, Lenore had to lean forward and clutch her belly with both hands to keep from projectile hurling.

Fury on Maxine's behalf rippled along her spine in waves of heat. Grief that her sister was making the biggest mistake of her life while trashing someone else's, with their parents' support, jabbed her like a hot poker in the gut. Nothing else had gotten through Lacey's thick skull; maybe being as crude as possible, laying it all on the line, would get the message across.

Tears of her own stung Len's eyes. She'd been so relieved when Maxine had finally left Fin—when she'd finally seen the light about his cheating.

When she'd found out it was her sister he was leaving Maxine for, the guilt she'd experienced that she'd had a hand in his infidelity, even if it was only by relation, made Len sick. Maxine was never anything but good to Lacey when she'd talked Fin into giving her the job at the dealership. In return, she'd had that kindness thrown right in her face.

Letting her head drop to her hands, she put her elbows on her desk, ignoring the calls from frantic bridezillas, shoving the pictures of ridiculously overdone wedding cakes to the far side of her work space. It was days like this, times like this when she missed Gerald so much that a hollow ache, one that came and went in painful fits and starts, sprouted deep in her soul.

Gerald would have understood. He would have had her back when her parents had taken Lacey's side in this fiasco. He would have listened to Len rant when she'd concluded that Lacey's marrying Finley meant her parents could breathe a sigh of relief because their beautiful but helpless daughter would have someone to take care of her instead of making her take care of herself.

And Lacey would end up just like Maxine if Fin managed to live another twenty years. She'd devote her life to him just like Maxine had, and he'd leave her with nothing for her efforts. Clearly, it was going to take a two-by-four to her head before she realized it.

Lenore's finger traced the heavy silver picture frame on her desk that housed a smiling Gerald, making her smile back at him. She did it often, as though he could still see the warmth her eyes held, feel the comfort and love just his presence in a room once brought her. Though that smile turned to sad longing when she remembered everything Gerald had purposely left behind.

Her.

Their life.

Their world.

Whoa. Stopping now, she chided herself. Pity was a bottomless vat she had no time to indulge even a quick swim in.

There were brides who needed her. Floral arrangements to approve. Doves to find.

Shaking off her anger with Lacey, she swung around in her office chair to look out the window. The view of Saint Ignatius across the street from her basement business always soothed her.

However, the tall man looking directly at her, a fine specimen of bomb diggity doing his best to be covert while under cover of a tree trunk, was anything but soothing.

CHAPTER FIVE

Note from Maxine Cambridge to all ex-trophy wives who are struggling through the painful process of sucking it up: Look, cash is cash. If in your forced independence you find you must participate in events that bring heightened color to your cheeks, creating the urge to crawl under a table and curl into the fetal position while you rock yourself into a forgetful state, remember this. Be brave, she-warrior. Do note you're fighting the good fight on behalf of all ex-trophy wives everywhere who are struggling to assert their right to be in the workplace! Hold your head high when humiliation rears its ugly head. And should you doubt this noble cause, I reiterate: Cash is cash. That means sometimes, into everyone's life, a little troll-tossing must fall.

"That you, kiddo?"

From the kitchen entryway, Campbell poked his head around the corner of his father's small, musty garage. "None other than."

Garner Barker tinkered with a battered toaster oven sitting under a small tabletop lamp on his workbench. He pushed his glasses up to give Campbell a gruff smile. "How'd it go at Mona's? She can be pretty testy. Sharp tongue, that woman."

Sharp daughter, that woman. He fought a smile and a fond memory of Max half-dressed in Mona's bathroom. A memory that might have brought him to full arousal if not for the watchful eye his father had on him. "Mona's fine. No trouble at all." He came to stand by Garner, placing a hand on his shoulder. "It's hot in here, Pop, too hot for you to be tinkering with some old toaster oven when we can just as easily buy you a new one."

Garner waved a screwdriver at him with a deep chuckle. "No need to waste good money. Even when you got plenty of it, Richie Rich," he teased.

Campbell shoved his thumbs under his armpits, rocking back on his heels. "You won't be wasting any money if you don't listen to what Dr. Klein said, because you'll be too dead to waste anything. As I recall, he said you were supposed to take it easy, especially in this heat. So why don't you hand over that screwdriver before things get ugly and I have to dirty my lily-white hands by taking you out." Campbell shoved his palm under his father's nose with a warm smile.

Garner sighed, slapping the tool into his palm with irritated reluctance. "That bloody doctor and all his rules. He's like the gestapo with a stethoscope. I like to tinker. I miss tinkering. What's the world coming to if a man can't tinker in his own damned garage?"

Slapping his dad on the back, Campbell chuckled. "Not an unsightly, heatstroke-induced end, at least not for you. Not on my watch anyway. Now c'mon. Don't you wanna watch *Wheel of Fortune*?"

"That Vanna, she's just not as cute as she used to be." He clucked his tongue at the shame of it all.

With a shove of his elbow, Campbell pushed the door to the kitchen open, the waft of cool air a welcome respite after the heat of the day, and the heat of Max Henderson. *Wait, 'scuse me. Maxine Cambridge.* "Okay, how about some dinner?"

"Bah," Garner muttered, waving a hand at him as he headed to his favorite recliner, slumping down in the buttery-colored leather to dig around the seat for the remote. "You're a crappy cook."

"Wow. Who's got his grumpy on tonight?"

"I'm going crazy here, kiddo. I need something to do."

He shot a sympathetic look at his father. Garner was always an active man. If it wasn't hobbies, like woodworking or tinkering with some electrical appliance, it was Campbell's little league games or Cub Scouts. He'd never been much of a TV watcher—he'd never been one to allow himself to be sidelined. This heart attack had put him on the bench, and it was killing him as sure as it was keeping him alive.

"I know you are, Dad, but you're not doing anything until Dr. Klein gives the okay. That's why I'm here. Remember? To help you after your *heart attack*—which, in case you're wondering, nearly gave me one. You don't seriously think I'm doing this just so I can spend my days with all these slammin' silver-haired seniors, do you?"

His dad's laughter was from deep in his chest. "I'm being an ungrateful old curmudgeon, ain't I?"

The nod Campbell gave him was sharp, but his smile was affectionate. "You betcha. But if you'd just let me, I'd—"

"Uh, uh, uh," Garner admonished, instantly quieting Campbell's protest. "I won't hear it. What you're doin' now is all the help I need. Got that, palie?"

Pride. His father had much. Campbell threw up his hands in mock defeat and headed toward the kitchen. "I hear you. But if I have to hear you, you have to hear me. So hear me when I tell you, I'm The Enforcer. If you want me to help you in the village, I hold the keys to the kingdom until you're better."

"Fine, Prince Charming," he grumbled back.

Campbell chuckled into the interior of the new stainless steel fridge he'd talked Garner into buying and dug around to find the bag of broccoli florets and the bag of carrots for steaming, or maybe a salad. "How do you feel about a salad, Dad?" he called over his shoulder. "I don't have to cook that."

Christ, he really was a crappy cook. He needed to look up some heart-healthy recipes online for fish and chicken. They couldn't go on eating raw vegetables and prunes forever. Though, it was what had led him to the Cluck-Cluck Palace today. So he could eat fat and salt without the guilt his father bestowed upon him in the way of puppy-dog eyes and beads of saliva forming at the corners of his mouth.

"I feel the same way about a salad as I do about that crappy yogurt you told me was gonna taste just like key lime pie."

Campbell stuck his head back around the kitchen doorway and frowned in his father's direction. "Hey, cranky pants. It was on the list of approved dietary suggestions. How can you blame me for fall-ing for it? It *was* pie . . ."

"It was shit for shinola. Can't we order a pizza? C'mon, son. What's one little slice of Giuseppe's with extra cheese? Wait. No. I'll make you a deal. No extra cheese. Just plain old pizza. Whaddya say?"

Holding up the bag of broccoli florets, Campbell shook his head in the negative. "Oh, no, Papa-San. One little slice of pizza's what put you in that hospital. All that crap you were eating on the fly was clog-ging your arteries." It was all Campbell could do not to visibly shud-der when he remembered seeing his father ashen and gasping for breath behind an oxygen mask on that hospital bed. "You'll harden your arteries right up with all that gooey cheese, and then where will we be? You'll never get a date with that Ramona over on Petunia if you can't move your arms and legs. She likes to do the Watusi. That dance looks like work and a lot of heavy breathing. You don't want to blow that, do you?"

Garner's face went from sour to curiously cheerful at the mention of the cute little Ramona. "She's a card, huh? Don't get me wrong, she's not your mother, but she's one to watch." He winked.

There was a slight pause in his ongoing battle to keep his father on the straight and narrow path to righteous good health. No one was his mother. He missed her as much as his father did. All the more reason to hang on to his father for as long as he could.

"Speaking of cute gals, you shouldn't be here feeding me tri-colored vegetables I only want to stick my finger down my throat and throw up. You oughta be out findin' your own cutie-pie, not hangin' around your old man."

His father's suggestion made Campbell's expression instantly guarded. "Who needs women when you can hang out with an old man who wears Bengay for cologne and support hose socks *with* his sandals?" He jokingly pointed to Garner's knee-high pressure tights.

Garner lifted off the recliner, giving his leg a jiggle. "Sporty look, don't you think?" Making his way to the kitchen dinette, he plopped down in one of the striped cushioned chairs while Campbell set about his anything-but-proficient vegetable chopping. "Hey, you met Mona's daughter yet? I hear she used to be a real looker."

His head popped up. "Used to be?" The defensive tone to his voice made him regret his words, so much so that he wanted to slice his tongue off with the knife. Garner knew him well. Too well, and he always knew when Campbell had something to hide.

His father's grin was tinted with lasciviousness. "So you did meet her."

With a noncommittal shrug of his shoulders, he mumbled, "Yep."

"She as purty in real life as she was in those commercials she used to do?"

Campbell had never seen the commercials, but yeah, she was, in his father's words, damned purty. Gray sweat suit, Ziploc bag of dog excrement, hot lips, and all. "I didn't pay a lot of attention."

"Yes, ya did."

"Did not."

"You did, too. Mona told me you did. I called to see if you needed any help over there. Mona said you were in the bathroom wooing her daughter. She said it looked like you two were doing just fine."

He heard the teasing laughter in his dad's voice. It made him grind his teeth. "Is nothing sacred in this village?"

"Nope. Not with the bunch of gossips we got runnin' around here.

'Sides, what's the big deal? You like Mona's girl. I think it's good that
you finally like *someone*."

Someone. Yeah. He noted the innuendo in Garner's tone. The
innuendo that once had a stern sentiment attached to it. *"It's time to
get on with the business of living, son,"* were the words his dad had
muttered over and over for two years. Campbell had resented those
words—words everyone said when they didn't know how else to help
you get past your grief. Meaningless and empty, but meant to comfort.

Today, in the here and now, his outlook was different, less resentful, and far more open to the possibility of the business of living.

Because he'd been reunited with Max Henderson. That's who
she'd always be in his mind—no matter how many rich, almost ex-
husbands she collected. Outwardly, she was still as hot as she'd been
in high school. She just didn't see it quite the way he did. She was also
a neurotic mess waiting to happen.

It was fantastic. Intriguing. Multilayered.

He liked.

For the first time in a very long time, Campbell found he had
more than just a passing interest in the opposite sex. Unfortunately,
Max was far from interested in anyone who had dangly bits at this
point in her life. He completely understood why after his run-in
with her snarling, seething, holier-than-thou husband. She virtually
cringed at the idea of any kind of confrontation with him, leaving
Campbell pissed off for her and beating his chest like some new age
Neanderthal.

What a screwed up emotion to have on her behalf so early on in
the mating game.

That's what this is, he silently acknowledged. *A mating game.*

One he planned to win.

Especially after that kiss. Brief, alluring, sweet, shy.

Hot.

"You're awful quiet in there, bucko," Garner taunted from the dinette. "So you like Mona's daughter. Whaddya gonna do about it?"

Dumping the broccoli and carrots into a bowl, Campbell fished in the fridge for some lettuce. "She's a mess, Dad."

"Who isn't? Doesn't that Dr. Phil say everyone's got baggage? You know what being a mess is all about. Maybe you can be double the mess together."

The grin he couldn't prevent spread across his lips. "I mean that she's not divorced yet. She needs time to heal, figure out what she's going to do with the second half of her life. I'm thinkin' she's not ready for a relationship."

"I hear tell she wants to be divorced, but that husband of hers, the girls call him Penis-less, is bein' a real jackass about it. Took all of his fancy money and left her and the boy with nothin'."

Pulling a measuring cup from a drawer, he slammed it shut with his hip, incredibly angry once more. Gripping the handle of the cup, he took hold of his irrational reaction and set about measuring the exact amount of salad dressing his father was allotted. "What the girls say is true. As a matter of fact, I met her husband purely by chance today, and he's definitely jackass material. She's scared spitless of him."

His father was silent for a moment. "You don't think he raised his hand to her, do ya? Son of a bitch oughta have his Twinkies hacksawed off."

Campbell figured that statement deserved a moment's thought. Max had been afraid to speak up—she'd shrunk right before his eyes. At the first hint of discord, she'd been right in there with whatever it took to cool things off. It had left him wanting to coach her in the art of giving someone hell, and angry. Very angry. "Can't say for sure, Dad. So maybe even you, playa that you are, can see why turning on the Casanova might be bad timing just yet."

His father shook his head, the thick strands of his silvery white hair falling across his forehead. "Nope. I say strike while the iron's hot. You're a good boy. You sure ain't no wife-beater. You like her. That's enough for me."

"Uh, Pop, she has to be a willing participant."

"Says who?"

"Law enforcement." Campbell plunked down the brightly colored salad on the table along with half a turkey sandwich on whole wheat with mustard.

Garner eyed him from across the small, round table, the corners of his blue eyes wrinkling with amusement. "So you gonna go get her?"

Campbell grinned back. "Yep."

"Atta boy."

~⦗~

"You ready, Maxie?"

Tightening her ponytail, Maxine nodded into the bathroom mirror. "Be right there," she called to her mother just as Connor came in to stand behind her.

"You're going like that?"

She frowned back at him. "What does 'like that' mean?"

His dark brown head, which topped her by at least six inches these days, cocked to the left. "It means you don't have any makeup on, and you're wearing Gram's really bright sweats. It hurts my eyes to look at you." He squinted for dramatic effect, placing a broad hand on her shoulder. "I think you're in a slump, Mom."

With a drop of her shoulders, she realized Connor was right. What a shock to his system to see her looking so downtrodden.

And in neon yellow with black piping, no less.

He still hadn't gotten over her less than glam-wow appearance these days. Who could blame him when he'd almost never seen her looking anything less than fabulous even when she was doing nothing more than staying in.

But things changed. Priorities changed. She needed a gallon of milk more than she needed to coordinate her eye shadow with the color of her shoes.

The half of her that was exhausted and rebelling against anything remotely adorned or primped to impress, protested. "I think this is a good color for me."

"Yellow sucks, Mom. Nobody should wear it," he said with a solemn tone and a facetious grin.

A roll of her eyes signaled her discontent. "Look, I'm not going to Bingo Madness to get a hot date. I'm going because the village is paying me good money to call the numbers as a stand-in for Midge Carter. Her psoriasis is acting up. So lay off your old mother, would you? This isn't a beauty pageant." Thank Jesus, too. On a day like today, for sure, Teona Wilcox would have no trouble stealing that much-desired crown she'd spent twelve pageants chasing after Maxine for.

A stab of self-consciousness niggled her. The will to summon up some longing for pretty clothes and mani-pedis escaped her. It had run away just like she had.

If she wasn't careful, she and her "will" would end up on the back of a carton of milk. What did it matter what she looked like anyway? It was just a bunch of little old men and women playing bingo. Besides, it took a whole lot less effort and goop to slap your hair in a ponytail and put on some sweats. She'd get an "A" for time management if someone were giving them out.

Connor scoffed at her with an impatient grunt. "You're not old, Mom. You're *seasoned*."

Or way overmarinated. "Yeah? Is that your new vocabulary word for the week?" she teased.

"Maxie! Get a move on, would ya? If we don't shake a leg, that damn Deloris Griswald's gonna steal up all the good bingo mojo seats. That woman makes me want to pull every last hair out of her lucky troll doll's head."

Maxine let her chin fall to her chest while she massaged her

temples and asked the man upstairs to keep her from purposely falling on a sharp Ginsu in front of her unsuspecting son. When she
looked up, Connor was covering his mouth with his forearm to keep
from laughing. "Do your homework, okay? And try to restrain yourself from eating your grandmother's sardines. I know what a temptation greasy fish in a can can be."

He grinned at her, shoving his hands in the pockets of his low-
slung jeans. "I've sworn off fish in a can—it binds me."

Maxine pressed a kiss to his cheek with a giggle. She was so
grateful for her baby boy. Connor was a shiny penny in a puddle of
piss. "I'll see you around ten. Oh, and if Mrs. Dewit calls about that
cracked-out poodle of hers needing a 'walkie,' tell her I died. Love
you." Sweeping out of the bathroom, she grabbed her purse off the
kitchen table and stopped just shy of where her mother stood rooted
to the kitchen floor.

"What?"

Mona pursed her lips. "You're wearing *that*?"

Maxine looked down at her outfit once more. Was it really as bad
as everyone was making it out to be? "Yeah. What's wrong with it?"

Mona tucked her suitcase-sized patchwork purse under her breasts,
crossing her arms over it. "Would it hurt you to gussie up a little,
Maxine?"

"Why?" Maxine's response was lifeless and flat.

Her mother's sigh was ragged. "Because it's good for the soul,
young lady. I remember a Maxine who didn't leave the house without
at least a carat's worth of diamonds somewhere on her body."

A hand went to her hip in a defiant gesture. "If Maxine had a
carat's worth of diamonds this minute, she'd have hocked them for
cash at Chester's Tchotchkes. I don't have diamonds, and I don't have
a whole lot of bingo-appropriate attire. I don't have a whole lot of
attire, period, remember? When I left Fin, I packed very little, fully
expecting he'd let me get my clothes once I was over the initial shock

that he was boinking my best friend's sister. And I borrowed this from *your* closet."

"Does that mean you can't brush your hair and put on some lipstick?"

Maxine's hand flew to her ponytail. "I did brush my hair, and I don't want to wear lipstick. It's bingo, Mom, not *The Bachelorette.*"

"What about maybe plucking your eyebrows? They look like a Siberian husky's taken up residence on your forehead."

"I couldn't find the tweezers . . ." she mumbled.

"Rumor has it, *Campbell* might be there." Mona used her enticing motherly voice to try and coax the will into her to glam up.

The mention of Campbell brought back the memory of his kiss. A kiss she wasn't able to leave alone since it happened. She'd relived it twice daily for the last nine days—all right, sometimes hourly. An excited butterfly swirled in her stomach, but it was only one, so she mentally stomped on it and crushed its fluttering wings. All that talk of coffee and more than a week had passed since they'd last seen each other, and not so much as a phone call to have even a bottle of water. "So?"

There was a snort of disgust and the shuffle of orthopedic-shoe-wearing feet as Mona, clearly not making the impact she'd hoped for, pushed open the screen door and stomped off to her car.

Maxine rolled her head on her neck, taking a deep breath, then threw her purse over her shoulder to head out and get in her mother's conservative Kia Rio. They drove in silence to the rec center where Bingo Madness was aglow. Twinkling lights adorned the neatly trimmed bushes, and colorful lantern-shaped globes were strung across the low roofline.

When word had gotten around that Maxine was for hire, her mother's phone had begun to ring. In the days since she'd walked Jake for Mr. Hodge, she'd acquired four more dog-walking positions and one weekly hair-rolling session with Maude Grandowski, who suffered from tendinitis in her neck and shoulders. Maude made her macaroon cookies and served her milk when Maxine was done washing and setting her hair. Plus, she'd tipped her five bucks.

When she'd gotten the call to replace Midge, she'd been hesitant. A lot hesitant. She'd been to Bingo Madness once with her mother, and to say these women got hinky about their bingo was to diminish their capacity to be ninja quiet when going in for the kill.

Bingo was serious business at Leisure Village. But when Midge told her it was fifty dollars, there'd been no stopping her from greasing her vocal cords and shining up her best hair scrunchie. Fifty bucks on top of her dog-walking money was a windfall.

Truly, she could now be considered a high roller.

Making their way along the decorative stone pavers to the front door, Mona stopped her just before entering. "You listen to your mother, Maxie. You watch that crazy Deloris Griswald. If she hits the same number as someone else, and doesn't speak up fast enough, things get dicey."

Maxine's eyebrows scrunched together. "Dicey?"

Her mother's nod was solemn. "She throws trolls."

"The dolls with the crazy hair in different colors?"

Mona's nod was crisp. "Yep. Damn well nearly took off someone's head with it, too."

Oh. With a finger, she made an "X" over her heart. "I promise to watch for flying trolls, Mom."

"Don't you mock me, girlie, and see that you do. Louise Clements got hit with one a few months back, and she's holding a grudge. Who knows what could happen if Louise and Deloris go head to head. It could be an all-out troll war."

Maxine shook her head and reminded herself, it was fifty bucks. Fifty. Bucks. Opening the door for her mother, she motioned her in.

Rows of tables, lined with good-luck charms like the aforementioned troll dolls and small statues of the Virgin Mary, were almost full to capacity. The low rumble of excited voices turned to total silence upon their entry.

Maybe she should have plucked her eyebrows . . .

What seemed like hundreds of pairs of eyes, hidden behind assorted thick reading glasses, scanned her from head to toe, and not in a friendly milk-and-cookies kinda way.

Weee doggie. Hostile much? The vibe was that she was an interloper. One who was thirty-some years their junior.

Mona's eyes narrowed. "I told you you should've brushed your hair," she accused.

Maxine leaned down to whisper in her ear, "Oh, hush. If there's only one thing in the world I know how to do it's entertain. Watch and learn from the master."

Maxine dropped her purse on the front table and turned to the still-silent crowd. A sea of silver heads, eyes expectant, focused in on her. She slapped a wide grin across her lips when she picked up the microphone. "Hi, everyone! I'm Maxine Cambridge, and I'm replacing Midge for the night. Well, let me re-phrase that. *No one* could *ever* replace Midge. She's irreplaceable, but I hope you'll accept my humble efforts to help the show go on. I know you'll all join me in thinking a good thought for poor Midge and her psoriasis, won't you?"

Instantly, the tremor of unwanted gatecrasher turned to pity for the ailing Midge, and a gruff welcome for Maxine. "Wonderful," she placated with a delighted clap of her hands. "Now, if you'll all just give me a minute to get myself situated, we'll begin." She set the microphone back down with a puff of breath.

Her mother nodded a grudging affirmation for her coup. "Nicely played—the 'humble yourself for the masses' card. Good choice. I'm going to go find Gail and Mary. They'd better have saved me a seat." Mona swept past the swarm of seniors who arranged and rearranged their lucky bingo charms, stopping at the edge of the third table from the front, which Maxine suspected housed Deloris

Griswald. The narrow-eyed glare her mother shot at the pleasantly padded woman with raven-black hair so stiff with hairspray it had to pack some crunch was the clincher.

From where she stood, there were at least eight small troll dolls with brightly colored hair and two statues of the Virgin Mary lined precisely on top of Deloris's bingo sheets. In front of each troll were the bulbous colored heads of daubers, the official markers they used to check off numbers called. Each dauber matched the hair color of each doll, making this superstitious ritual nothing short of hardcore.

And she just couldn't let herself harp on the OCD of it all a second longer.

"Hey, Maxine!" a woman bellowed from the back of the room, making her turn to face forward. "Esther here says you're the girl who did those car commercials, but I told her no way could you be the same girl. That girl had to be a good ten years younger than you."

If it was the last thing she did, she was going to blow up every television set in the village. A hard swallow and a warning glare to her mother's protective stance later, Maxine answered into the microphone, "Actually, that girl was *fifteen* years younger than I am now—if you're looking for honesty. So yes, I was that girl. And yes, now I'm much older." *Thank you for voicing your uncanny ability to "name that age" in public.*

In front of a hundred or so villagers.

Go, you.

The woman's cheeks sported two bright spots when she slid down in her chair, bringing Maxine sick satisfaction, be it brief and petty.

Turning to the table, Maxine eyeballed the whir of the numbered balls in the cage and took a deep breath. Watchful eyes heated her back. The air became uncomfortably warm inside the rec center, her mother's neon yellow sweat suit clinging to her like a second skin.

Out of the clear blue, she wanted to crawl under the table. What had she been thinking when she'd said yes to hosting a roomful of clearly resentful bingo-lovers who wanted Midge and Midge alone to call their numbers? Not some has-been ex-beauty queen who was so pathetic and so without pride, she was snarfing up senior-citizen cash left and right, doing menial work because she couldn't get a decent job. Poor, sad, helpless Maxine.

The sick feeling that everyone in the room knew how truly pitiful Mona Henderson's daughter was left her inwardly fighting a good outward cringe. She wasn't just an embarrassment to herself, but to Connor and her mother. Ridiculous tears stung her eyes.

Her legs began to tremble. Despite the warmth of the room, her fingers were icy, uncooperative talons. The race of her heart, like frantic wings of a hummingbird, battered her chest.

Oh. Good. An anxiety attack.

"Uh, hey!" someone yelled from the back, his words like nails being pounded into her skull. "Could we get this party started, lady? *America's Most Wanted's* on tonight at eleven, and the way you're going, we're gonna bleed right into *Seinfeld.*"

"Hey, Mr. Fishbein! Cut the lady some slack. It's her first night," a deep, undeniably sex-on-a-stick voice chided with laughter in its tone.

Okay, when she turned around, if Campbell Barker was standing somewhere in the crowd, it was imperative she and the man upstairs have a good sit-down. But not until she was done ignoring the fact that just the sound of his voice had taken her anxious, unwarranted fear down at least three notches.

Why should it matter if Campbell's here, Maxine?

Because I look like a bag lady fresh from a long day of Dumpster diving?

Wasn't it you who just told your mother this wasn't The Bachelorette? *Who cares that you're wearing the most unflattering color on Earth and your hair resembles a Texas tumbleweed? Surely not you . . .*

Her shoulders instantly squared. Right. That wasn't her. She didn't care. In the interest of not caring, Maxine rounded the table like it owed her money, slapping her ass in the chair, and picking up the microphone as though it were a weapon of mass destruction.

She placed it in front of her lips, a glint of a view to kill in her eyes. "So, ladies and gentlemen, are we ready?"

Buttloads of eyeballs rolled upward. If she were counting right, five people yawned.

Yet Campbell didn't. Way in the back, sitting near two elderly gentlemen and one lone woman with hair so teased it was stratospheric, he gave her the thumbs-up sign, followed by his deliciously yummy grin.

That grin, one she hadn't seen in over a week, brought such welcome relief. If she weren't already sitting down, she'd need to. It was true. Men aged much better than women. Not only had Campbell filled out since high school, he'd acquired a gaunt, chiseled look to him that exuded a hard-edged appeal. The way his shirt stretched at his wide shoulders, the ruddy tone of his skin against it, the planes of his muscular arms, made her face hot. A shiver rolled over her arms in response to something as feeble and nonsexual as a sign of Campbell Barker's approval.

A mental shift accompanied that notation, prompting her fair-weather pride to rush through her veins in wavy gushes of celebratory return. Confidence securely back in place, Maxine called the first number.

~ℓ~

"Bingooooo, bitch!" a coarse voice screeched just seconds behind someone else's declaration of bingo, lifting Maxine's eyes to the spot where Deloris Griswald sat.

A petite woman in tailored slacks and a floral shirt rose from her seat one table in front of Deloris's. Her knobby finger waved in fierce admonishment. "Oh, the hell you say, Deloris! I called it first, and you know it!"

Deloris, an imposing, big-boned girl, clutched one of her beloved troll dolls to her chest, the loud green hair seeping between her fingers. She leaned forward over the flimsy table, her mint green and white housecoat gaping at her breasts. "You did not, Glenda! I beat you fair and square." She slammed a thick-fingered, liver-spotted hand down on the table to emphasize "square," making all her poor troll dolls tremble—probably in inanimate-object fear. A plastic Virgin Mary statue toppled over and fell to the ground.

Maxine dropped the microphone to the table in surprise. It let out a piercing screech of protest, making her wince. She jumped up from her chair and pushed her way through the crowd of folks who had also risen from their folding chairs to get a front-row seat to bingo brawl.

Glenda stood on tippy-toe, jamming her face into Deloris's. "Put your hearing aids in, Deloris. I called it first, you cheater!"

Deloris's tree-trunk-sized chest expanded before she opened her mouth so wide, Maxine saw her tonsils from all the way across the room. "I don't need those damn hearing aids to know I called it first—*liar*!"

Hoo boy. Harsh. She'd used the "L" word. Good gravy. It was just bingo. The top prize was only a hundred bucks. Wait. A hundred bucks . . . In the midst of the beginnings of chaos, an odd thought struck her. A hundred dollars was at one time maybe—*maybe*—a pair of silk panties. Now it would buy enough food to feed at least two people for a week.

Huh, maybe instead of calling the numbers she should be playing the game.

Heated words flew back and forth between Deloris and Glenda, their wagging fingers and flailing arms becoming a blur as Maxine made her way to the middle of the ruckus.

She slipped into the fray with the idea she'd bring order. Surely Midge didn't allow this kind of gangsta-esque behavior on her watch.

What was the world coming to when a bunch of over-sixty seniors couldn't play a peaceable game of bingo?

With as gentle a hand as she could, so as not to create the need for some poor soul's hip replacement or worse, activate brittle bone disease, Maxine parted the gathering crowd, placing herself almost directly between the geriatric reenactment of the Sharks and Jets.

Just as Deloris made the windup that was aimed at Glenda, but missed her by a country mile.

Hitting Maxine instead.

Square in the nose.

How many people could own the fact that they'd been clunked in the face at a game of seemingly harmless bingo with a plastic doll that had bushy green hair?

She'd been trolled.

Atonement was due.

CHAPTER SIX

Note from Maxine Cambridge to all ex-trophy wives: When a knight in shining armor offers you a cold pack and a hot dog, do us each a favor; don't play like you don't dig it. You'd only be lying to yourself and the people around you who still have the gift of sight. Better still; keep your new independent, overempowered nuttiness to a minimum. Sometimes, when your nose is gushing blood, help in the name of pity is okay—it's definitely okay from a hot guy. Just don't book a chapel in Vegas for the Silver Elvis wedding package, especially if you were considering the fancy fog machine.

Len slid from her car onto the pavement of the parking lot in Leisure Village with silent feet, her fingers clutching the illegal can of mace she carried with her no matter where she went.

Whoever this joker was, popping up everywhere she'd been for the last week, behaving as though he was some cheesy rip-off of James Bond, he was in for a ration of her special brand of shit. She rolled her eyes at the idea that he was delusional enough to think she hadn't noticed him each time he ducked under a store awning while she grocery shopped or made some half-assed attempt to hide behind a bush when she left her office.

Ridiculous.

She'd spent a week wondering why a man as divine, as tall, as delish in a suit as this one happened to be was dogging her every step. Another question she might ask herself was why, in all of hell, she had the wherewithal to think he was attractive when he could well be a murderer? Hard up was one thing—lonely and in need of male companionship were, too—but to entertain a potential menace's lickability factor was just plain disturbing.

She'd considered calling the police, but to what point? What would she say? A man who looked remarkably like an advertisement, albeit a decadent one, for the *Wall Street Journal* was trailing her. And no, officer, he's never once made a single threat, physical or verbal. They'd label her batshit and order 911 to ignore all calls from her.

Lenore snuck up behind him without a hint of awareness on his part, in heels, no less. He was easy prey, seeing as he really sucked at the covert. She held up the can of mace, finger on the pump, ready to fire, her eyes narrowed, and yelled, "Who the hell are you, and why are you following me?"

When he swung around, the scent of his cologne, by no stretch of the imagination cheap, swished in her nose on the air of the humid evening. He looked as surprised as she was, though her surprise was very different. The distance she'd seen him from since he'd begun stalking her had done him no justice.

His lickability factor, at least in the lanterns' glow from the rec center, was boatloads bigger than she'd first estimated. Her breath caught in her throat. But then she reminded herself—those who engaged in the act of manslaughter weren't necessarily heinous to lay one's eyes upon.

It wasn't a mandatory prereq that killers have warts and bad teeth. Some were probably equally into hygiene. Just because he wore chichifroufrou cologne didn't mean he wasn't capable of band-sawing her legs off and stuffing them in a tub full of muriatic acid.

Just because his hair, the color of the night that surrounded them, was shiny and well-groomed didn't make him less capable of dumping her somewhere in the woods. The slate gray suit he wore, an expensive label she knew well, didn't mean he hadn't spent the better part of his pimply pubescence pulling wings off innocent flies.

"Lenore Erickson?" His delicious lips said her name, warm silk threaded in the asking, totally interrupting her completely out-of-line assessment of him. He took a step closer, making Len take a quick one back.

"Who's asking? And"—she waved her hand in the space between them—"you back up or I'll take your eyes out. So unless braille was something you planned on taking up, back off!" She flashed the can of mace at him in a threatening arc.

Hands wide like a football player's, but lean and tan, went up, mimicking a pair of white flags. He grinned, his long legs moving him away from her. "Backing up."

Len's eyes narrowed. "Who are you, and why are you following me all over town like some bad spy movie?"

His grin grew wider. "Adam Baylor." Sticking his hand out, he nodded his dark head. "Pleasure. You are Lenore Erickson, aren't you? Lenore the wedding planner for Belle's Will Be Ringing?"

Suspicion flared in her eyes. "Maybe, maybe not. What do you want?"

His tongue rolled in his lean cheek, giving her the impression he was a wee bit short on patience. His eyes, gorgeous and chocolaty, were veiled, screaming he had a secret. "A bit of your time."

Len's head cocked to the left. Her time? "For?"

"Us to get to know one another." His answer was seductively evasive, his thickly fringed eyes equally so.

"How the hell do you know my name?"

"It was a rather easy cross-reference to achieve when I looked up the name of your business. You know, that place you go every day called your office with the sign that says 'Belle's Will Be Ringing'?"

He was mocking her . . . And then it hit her. This was one of Fin's lackeys. Probably some two-bit P.I. who'd taken that pig's money under the table to make a quick buck. He'd sent this Adam to try and get something on Maxine so he'd be able to prove she was Attila the Mother or something.

When Maxine had called last week, more upset than she'd been since this whole mess had started, to tell her that Fin planned to speak to his attorneys about the "conditions" Maxine allowed Connor to live in, her mouth had fallen open in disgust.

It shouldn't come as a big surprise Finley had decided the gloves were off, and at all costs he was going to get Connor to come back to the mini-mansion, even if it meant trashing Maxine in the process.

That rat bastard.

Like she'd ever give her friend up, even if there were something to actually give up. "Finley sent you, didn't he? That scum-sucking piece of shit," she spat, swinging the can of mace around in an arc. "You have some set of balls, skulking around his wife's best friend, trying to dredge up dirt on her. Finley Cambridge has some nerve, trying to make like my best friend's a bad parent when he's the dirtiest of them all!" she shouted, shrill and brittle. "How dare that lowlife infidel have the nerve to try and take Connor when he wasn't even divorced before he was engaged! How much did he pay you to make Maxine look bad, you—you—*jerk*?" *Oh, such harsh name-calling. Show 'em you know how to make 'em bleed with your fierce tongue, Len.*

The typically quiet village heightened the echo of her snarling threat.

Instead of sneering back at her, instead of becoming defensive, he shoved his hands into the pockets of his trousers and smiled again, flashing his gorgeous white teeth. "I'm not exactly sure what that diatribe meant, but maybe you can share its meaning with me when I drop by your office later this week? I'm late for a dinner meeting, so explanations will have to wait." He stepped around her, the scent of his cologne assaulting her nostrils once more as he simply walked away.

Or at least he made the attempt to leave until she grabbed hold of his arm. Which happened to be very well-muscled. But that was beside the point. Those few words he'd spoken, all cool and cordial, infuriated her, erasing all fear he might slaughter her right here in Geezer Village.

"Hold on there, scumbag!" Len yelped. "Where do you think

you're going? You've been following me around for a solid week! What the hell kind of game are you playing?" Her teeth clenched together in seething fury. The humidity of the evening, coupled with her anger, made beads of sweat pop out along her forehead.

His response was as calm as the last one had been. "No game, but again, as I said, plan on seeing me in the very near future," he drawled, using a gentle force to peel her clinging fingers from his arm. "Good night, Ms. Erickson."

And he was gone, detaching her fingers from his arm with ease and slipping into the night as though he'd never been there.

Len looked down at her shoes. Goddamned heels. She'd chase him down if she had her tennies on and her glasses so she could actually see where he'd slunk off to. She squinted into the velvety darkness, cocking her ear to listen for his footsteps.

Damn. Nothing. All week long he'd had a target as big as a bull's-eye on him and now suddenly he'd mastered the art of skulking.

Stuffing the mace back into her purse, Len stomped off toward the rec center to help out in the kitchen while trying to make sense out of Adam Baylor's cryptic words.

Adam smiled to himself as he slid into his car, parked discreetly near a patch of trees by the golf course, to the tune of Lenore's cry of frustration and her angry feet pounding the pavement. His intention had never been to do anything more than locate Lenore as a way to find Maxine, who was no longer at her old residence.

He found his intentions had suddenly changed.

Blood spewed from Maxine's nose like she'd been stabbed in an attempted homicide instead of just clocked in the nose by a little old lady wielding a troll doll with green hair.

"Mrs. Griswald! Give me the doll, *please*," Campbell ordered in a cajoling but demanding tone. "C'mon now."

Voices from above swarmed about Maxine's head, fading in and out before tuning in like a radio station. She groaned at the sight of her own blood.

"You give that to him right now, Deloris!" Glenda backed Campbell up, peeking around his broad back. "Look what you've done," she scolded. "I wouldn't want to be you if Mona gets her hands on you. You could have broken poor Maxine's nose!"

More raised voices came and went, and apparently, with great protest after handing over her troll, Deloris stomped off in a huff.

Strong hands gripped Maxine under her armpits, hauling her up off the floor where she'd landed in a wussified lump, dragging her to the nearest chair. Campbell—sexy, handsome, brawny—loomed in front of her blurry eyes with concern in his. His hand went to her face, brushing back the stray strands of hair that let loose from her ponytail, creating a shiver along her bare arms in the midst of the stinging pain. "Are you okay? Pinch the bridge of your nose. That'll stop the bleeding."

Maxine winced when he tilted her chin upward, rolling a thumb over her lip. "So you caught the perp?"

He chuckled with that deep, throaty laugh that made her stomach flutter. "Not only has she been detained, but we've confiscated her plastic weapon. The trolls with the green hair are always the most deadly. Though we'd better keep an eye on Mona. If we don't pay her some mind, I think your mother just might, on your behalf, commit a crime of passion with that big purse of hers and take Deloris out."

In the midst of the seniors' loud comments of disgust, disgruntled murmurs of, "That crazy Deloris, ruining a perfectly good game of bingo that had just gotten started," and their general need to nurture her wounded soul with crumb cake and coffee, Maxine still managed to throw her head back on her shoulders and giggle. "Please, whatever you do, don't let Mom swing that thing. She's packing some heavy heat."

Campbell held out an ice pack wrapped in a plaid dishtowel to her. "If it's any consolation, it doesn't look broken."

Yeah, that was consolation for being beat up by a sixty-five-year-old. She put the ice pack to her nose and began to rise from the chair, but Campbell placed a hand on her shoulder. So warm. So big. So inviting. "Sit for a minute."

Maxine brushed his hand off, struggling with not just the pressure to keep her in place, but the tingle she felt clear through her borrowed neon yellow sweat suit. "No. I'm good, really. I can't afford to lose fifty bucks because I'm too old and slow to duck," she half joked. "I have to finish or there'll be an uprising. Who knows what else they might dig up to lob at me?"

"Then let me help you." Campbell offered his hand with a warm smile. Warm and seemingly genuine. The interest she'd thought she'd seen in his eyes each time they crossed each other's paths was evident.

And booyah for him. If he could find himself even a little interested in the shitwreck she'd become, he was a better man than she'd ever given him credit for.

Oh, that was so an unwanted thought to have about Campbell. No matter how warm. No matter how easygoing and sensitive he appeared, she wasn't falling for it.

Nuh-uh. If she ever went for a second ride on the relationship merry-go-round, cautious and careful were going to be her new bunkmates until proven otherwise.

Maxine's free hand waved him off. "I'm fine, really." *I'd be finer if you'd stop touching me and making my heart do half gainers in my chest.* With a lean forward at the waist, she shoved off the chair, only to find her head swimming and her eyes blurred again.

Campbell was at her side with a lightning-fast response. He

draped a thick arm around her waist. "Sit back down," he ordered with a tight demand.

"Oh, listen to the man, honey," someone uttered from behind her. "If I was you, I'd let him do whatever he wanted to do to me," the faceless voice snickered.

Maxine's deep breath shuddered from between her lips in an effort to keep from exhaling a breathy sigh. It was as if she'd forgotten what it was like to have a man's arm around her and Campbell's was the only limb left on planet Earth.

Maxine shrugged him off. "I have to finish, Campbell. Unlike you, I don't have a job, okay? I *need* the money. It's just a bloody nose. I can take care of myself." Her irritation, more in part an irrational reaction to the feelings he conjured up with his touch, came out sharper than she'd intended.

Campbell's eyebrow cocked upward. He jammed his hands into the pockets of his well-worn blue jeans. "Okay, Ms. Independent, have it your way. But if you fall and crack your head open from the loss of blood, Dr. Barker's off duty." With an infuriating grin, he left, making his way to address the small cliques of men and women who waited to see what would happen next.

Jeez, Maxine. He was just offering you a little help. Was now the time to reinstate your womanly roar?

Two bright red spots assaulted her cheeks while she wended her way through the crowd, heading back to the table. Okay. So she'd gotten on her high horse and gone all Oprah-empowered. It was stupid. It was petty.

A half smile flitted across her lips. But it was true. She *could* take care of herself. Sort of.

And you've proven just that by denying the warmth and security of a hunkylicious man's arm. Bravo.

"Maxie!" Her mother put a hand on her hip from behind. "I told you, didn't I? That Deloris should be docked or something. Maybe take away her bingo privileges for a year. She's a flamin' nut! Now turn around and lemme look at your nose."

She dropped the ice pack on the table and turned to face her mother. "It's okay, Mom. I'm fine."

Mona's expression was skeptical, her nose wrinkling. "That's gonna bruise."

"Good. Everyone'll be so busy looking at my nose, they won't notice the Siberian husky on my forehead."

"*Maxine*?"

Relief flooded Maxine's face when her best friend hurried across the rec center floor. "Hey, you." She smiled at Len and the reassurance her beautiful outfit and supermodel good looks brought. Always fresh and vibrant, her clothes, low-cut jeans and a wispy turquoise top, were a reflection of the kind of woman Len was. Strong, smart, confident, and classy, from the sharp angle of her cheekbones to the curvy slope of her hips.

Len's purse dangled from her arm when she held up her manicured hands in question. "What the hell?"

Mona nodded in Len's direction with a glint of fury in her eyes. "It was that damned Deloris Griswald. She's a viper!"

Len's glossed, berry-colored lips pursed. She looked from Mona to Maxine. "*Who*?"

Maxine shook her head, folding her arms across her chest. "Never mind. It was just a misunderstanding. I'm fine."

"No, honey." Len shook her chestnut brown head. "I was talking about your clothes. They're an abomination. Good God, Maxine. You've sunk so low. What are you wearing? And why is it such a heinous color?"

Her comment made Maxine bristle in defense of her wardrobe. "I'm wearing this because if I keep wearing the clothes I had on my back when I left Fin, eventually they'll turn to dust. I'm saving the one good outfit I have left for those special occasions when I see the lawyer who never does anything for me, but charges me out the ass anyway. That okay?"

Instantly, Len was apologetic. Her warm brown eyes sought Maxine's when she rubbed a hand up and down her arm. "I'm sorry, honey. That was insensitive of me. It was just a . . . shock." Then, as though a haze had cleared, she noticed her friend's nose. "Holy Mother! What happened to your nose, Maxine? Are you okay? Was it Fin? That bastard—"

"No!" She grabbed her best friend's hand. "Some of the crew here got a little rowdy. It was just a misunderstanding."

Len tsk-tsked, grabbing her jaw and moving it from side to side. "What kind of misunderstanding leaves you with a nose the size of a basketball on bingo night? And who was the hot tamale holding you up?"

Those bright spots on her cheeks returned with a vengeance. Then an idea struck. An idea she planned to encourage. "He's cute, right?"

Len's eyes twinkled. "I think cute is too mild. Delicious? No, smokin'. Yeah. That works."

Mona cackled, swatting Len's backside. "If I was just twenty years younger . . ."

"You'd be a helluva cougar, Mom," Maxine teased. She sought Len's eyes again. "He's working the kitchen, and he's single. Very single. Go forth. Make nice. Flirt. Stare at his ass. It's time you started living again," Maxine encouraged.

That much was true. Gerald had been gone long enough. The mourning should be over and the living should begin. Added bonus— once Campbell got a good gander at her gorgeous best friend, his testosterone would stop knocking on her door. Problem solved despite the niggle of jealousy her solution brought.

Len and Mona exchanged glances. Glances Maxine couldn't read. "What's his story?"

"I'll tell you all about it and him later. Right now, I need to finish this because I really need the cash. So please, go help Ms. Douglas in the kitchen. Maybe after a hot dog or two, everyone will settle down and we can get back to the business of bingo."

Len dropped her fuchsia purse on the table. "Watch that for me, okay? And when I'm done slaving over a hot Crock-Pot with the dotty Ms. Douglas, it's you and me and the Greek Meets Eat Diner. We'll do something decadent like banana splits while we girl it up. My treat, okay?"

Maxine nodded, shooing her off and picking the microphone back up, summoning the will to be cheerful. "Hey, folks! If you give me just a moment to get it together, we'll get right back to bingo. In the meantime, go enjoy the fruits of the knitting club's labor and buy a hot dog. The proceeds go to benefit this year's Frolic Into Fall dance. So eat up and I'll be back in ten."

With a puff of tired air, Maxine found her chair once more. Her head began to throb, the cloying heat of the room closing in on her. She placed her fingers at her temples to massage the tension and winced again. Deloris Griswald packed a mean troll.

Large tanned hands set a hot dog with spicy brown mustard and relish in front of her, making her look up. Campbell smiled down in his gallingly ever-cheerful way. "Now this in no way constitutes helping you. So don't go thinking we're mated for life or anything. Got that, Max Henderson?"

He was gone before she could respond, but it didn't keep her eyes from straying to the flex of the muscles in his back or the confident stride that carried him back into the kitchen. "It's Maxine," she muttered into her hands. "Maxine, Maxine, Maxiiiine."

~ ℓ ~

Campbell eyed the attractive dark-haired woman from his position at the kitchen sink. Clearly she knew Max, and that meant she could possibly have an answer or two to some questions he had. Seeing as

Max wasn't giving much up, he was willing to risk being told to mind his Ps and Qs if he ruffled her feathers to find out.

Grabbing a pair of tongs, he wound his way through the throng of people milling in the kitchen to where Max's friend laid out hot dog buns and began filling them. When she looked up, he smiled. "Campbell Barker."

She gave him a distracted smile, then returned her focus to the rolls, spreading them on the platter. "Len Erickson. What brings a youngin' like you to Leisure Village?"

"I'm here helping my crotchety father until he gets back on his feet. Heart attack."

"Ah." Her smile was a mixture of sympathy and understanding.

"So you're a friend of Max's?"

The package of hot dog rolls fell to the long countertop with a crumple of plastic. She leaned back against the Formica and gave him a hostile gaze of open suspicion. "And if I am?"

Wow, grrrrrrr. "Then we have something in common," he offered simply.

Len's firm jaw tilted upward, her posture stiff and unyielding. "How's that?"

"Well, you like her, and I like her. That's a commonality."

The hard line of her skeptically glossed lips twitched with amusement. "I get the impression I don't like her the way you like her, though."

"Not unless you're a lesbian, I guess," Campbell returned a lazy response, continuing to smile while he filled the rolls with hot dogs from the steaming Crock-Pot. "Which is totally fine. I'm very urban like that."

She threw her head back and laughed a husky chuckle that was warm. "Nope. Not a lesbian. And yes, Maxine's my friend. My *best* friend."

"Then you're just the person I need to talk to."

Len visibly loosened up just a little, letting the hard line of her shoulders slump a bit. "About?"

"Her ex-husband."

Those slender bronzed shoulders stiffened again. "He's not her ex. Not yet."

Was she a Fin lover? Was anyone a Fin lover? *Now's the time to tread carefully, Barker.* "Do you want him to be?"

"Her ex? Probably more than I want to breathe."

It was Campbell's turn to chuckle. "He's a piece of work."

"He's a piece of shit," she spat under her breath, giving a sideways glance to see if anyone had heard her.

"So you're part of the He-Man Fin-Hater Club?"

"I'm the founder," was her dry response.

Nice. "You need a president?"

Len laughed again. "Look here, Campbell Barker. Spit out whatever it is you want to ask. I'll decide whether to answer or not. How's that?"

Campbell nodded, appreciating the honesty. After everything that had happened to him these last three years, including the end of his marriage, he was all about speaking his piece. He didn't waste time dicking around about much anymore, but he didn't want to screw this Q and A up. "Good enough. This Fin, her husband." He paused, forcing the word between his clenched teeth. "Did he ever hurt her?"

Len's fingers stopped separating hot dog rolls. "You mean like physically hurt her? You mean beat her? I'd have killed him myself." She shook her head, the dangle of her earrings swaying against her sharp jaw. "No. He didn't beat her, but you know, Maxine wondered out loud once if that would have at least been more honest than the kind of covert, emotional manipulation and bullshit he pulled over and over again. At least the pain would have only been momentary. The kind of crap he dealt out lingers much longer than a bruise."

She stopped with an abrupt intake of breath. "Shit. That's more

than I should have said. When it comes to that prick, I lose all objec-
tivity. I want the world to know he's a pig."

Campbell let out a breath, too. One he didn't realize he'd been
holding.

"You sound relieved," she commented.

He was. The notion had bothered him since his father had
brought it up a couple of weeks ago. It was what had kept him from
seeking her out and pushing the issue of coffee, because he didn't
want to frighten her with an aggressive pursuit. If Max'd been physically abused, the dynamics would have changed dramatically, and
he wanted to respect that. "I am. It means I won't serve time for
manslaughter."

Her dark eyebrow rose. "So you like my friend?"

There was no hiding the return of his silly-ass grin. "Yep. I like
your friend."

Len stopped separating rolls once more to look him square in
the eye. Her hand went to the curve of her jean-clad hip. "Then pay
heed. I'm not one for treading lightly. If you're offended easily, you
might want to close your ears."

Campbell made a point of capturing her gaze and holding it. "I
like straight shooting. Have at it."

Her assessment of him was only momentary, but he saw the doubt
her brown eyes flashed. When they cleared, she'd obviously made
the choice to let 'er rip. "Maxine's my best friend. I don't ever want
to see her slaughtered like this again. What's happening to her with
this divorce isn't something that's never happened before. It's time-
honored amongst those who travel in our circles. I'm guessing you
know some of the details because the folks here love a good gossip.
Younger gorgeous woman marries older, rich man, lives her life solely
for him while reaping the bennies of mondo moolah only to end up
dumped by older rich man for newer, younger model. She's pretty
beaten down, especially if that outfit she's got on is any indication.

The old Maxine, outwardly anyway, was a much different ball of wax than she is today. So if you want in, then play it straight, and even then I think you're going to have a hard time getting her to play, too. She's got a lot to figure out. She needs the space to do it without complications. At this point in her pending divorce, even though it's gone on longer than *War and Peace*, she hasn't come to terms with what most would have already at least attempted to begin to deal with."

He wasn't sure he understood what Len was getting at. "Are you saying she's not over him?" Not a good sign, if that was the case. She was a lot further behind in the healing process if that was what Len was alluding to.

"No, I'm saying she's not over what he's done to her. She led a very sheltered life until eight months ago. And that's all I'm saying. I've already said too much as it is." With a shift from one foot to the other, Len clucked her tongue. "Look, she really has no business getting involved with anyone until she's right with herself, but if you're determined . . ."

She'd left the door open for him to wander in or not with proof of his determination. So he did. With ridiculous haste. "I'm determined." His answer was quiet and steady.

Her clear brown eyes held a moment of admiration. "Okay then, with that said, if you still want in, don't muck it up or I can promise you I won't be nearly as restrained as I have been with that good-for-nothing Fin. I'll kill you in your sleep. End rant." Len tacked on an affable smile for good measure.

"Forewarned is forearmed," he murmured.

She placed a hand on his forearm and locked eyes with him. "Oh, I promise. There'll be no warning. You got me?"

Campbell returned her gaze, dead-on and sure. "I think we're golden."

Len's nod was brisk and no-nonsense. "Good. Now, pick up the pace with those hot dogs."

With a roll of his tongue in his cheek, Campbell fought another grin. He'd been cleared for takeoff. Reluctantly, but cleared.

One small step for man.

Now, on to one giant leap for mankind.

~ ℓ ~

On her fifteen-minute break, Maxine tried not to gaze longingly in the direction of the kitchen where Campbell and her best friend looked as though they weren't exactly struggling for conversation. Len's laughter tinkled, drifting to her ears followed thereafter by Campbell's husky growl of a chuckle.

How nice that two lonely people in the world had clearly made a connection.

Now there'd be two less lonely people in the world.

Very Air Supply.

Her teeth clenched. She'd sent Len in with the express purpose of foisting her off on Campbell. That she'd gotten her wish and her best friend was giggling over pork products and carbs while looking like a runway model should make her happy-clappy.

Yes, she nodded to herself, cupping her chin in her hand. She was happy. Len had been mourning a man who was four years gone. A wonderful man she'd loved and tragically lost. She was young and vibrant. It was time to move on. Seeing her smile and chat with Campbell was good.

Okay, it wouldn't upset her if she was smiling and laughing with someone else entirely—in another state—wearing a baggy floral housecoat and open-toed slippers—but she had dangled Len in front of Campbell like a shiny carrot of testosterone. Len was just being Len.

A sting of jealous envy hit her hard in the gut. Totally unfair to Len, but there it was. It settled like a lump in her stomach, leaving her feeling strangely empty.

"What's your boyfriend doing with her?"

Maxine lifted her eyes to find Mr. Hodge, unshaven and scruffy, eyeballing her.

"He's not my boyfriend, Mr. Hodge."

"That's not what you said the first night you walked Jake," he reminded her.

Maxine frowned. "How did you hear—"

"The village has eyes and ears, and you weren't exactly using your indoor voice when you pissed on your tree." Mr. Hodge winked, his face scrunching upward into the fine lines and folds of his leathered skin.

Ah, yes. The night she'd hurled Campbell at Fin like he was a pair of nunchakus. Maxine cringed at the memory. "Well, he's not my boyfriend. That makes him fair game."

"Sure seemed like he was your boyfriend from the way you two were lookin' at each other."

He'd come to the conclusion that intimacy and love had sprung from the offer of an ice pack and a troll doll incident? "Then I guess him flirting with her makes him a cheating loser, huh?"

Mr. Hodge smacked his lips in appreciation. "She's a looker."

Yes. Len was a looker. Maxine? Just a mess. "That she is."

He rocked back on his heels, slipping one thumb under his striped suspenders. "You want me to take her out? I brought my cane with me. Cut her off right at those pretty knees." He mimicked a golf swing.

Maxine snorted, putting a hand to her aching nose. "No! She's my best friend, for gravy's sake."

He snorted back and leaned into her. "Huh. Some best friend, stealing your boyfriend."

"He's not my boyfriend!" She yelped in protest, then lowered her voice when some of the seniors turned to stare at her with guarded gazes. "He's not my boyfriend. *Period.*"

She waved her hands at him, shooing him off in the direction of food. "So be a pal, and stop drawing more attention to me. Wasn't it enough that Mrs. Griswald nearly knocked my nose off my face? Add a boyfriend denial in there and I'll be the talk of the village for weeks. Now go on. Go get a hot dog before they're all gone. I hear Ms. Douglas made her special turkey chili. Very heart friendly. Besides, my break's almost over, and I have one more game to call. A girl's gotta make a living, right?" She gave a surreptitious glance around the room to see if everyone had gone back to the business of bingo. There'd been enough drama involving her for one night.

"Maxine!" a female voice, young and untouched by liposuction, called from the entrance, making her head swivel and her nose throb from turning too quickly.

Shit.

Woo to the hoo.

More drama.

In stilettos and chic size-two clothing.

CHAPTER SEVEN

Note to all ex-trophy wives from Maxine Cambridge: Tip on dating. Should a man ask you to join him for coffee even though your nose is the size of the Ukraine and you're clearly not being all you can be fashion-wise—just suck it up and say yes. First, the coffee's free. Second, if you suspect he only wants to sleep with you, reevaluate. Looking the way you do in your growth process, either he must really like you, or he's certifiable. Both of which shouldn't be ruled out. Beggars can't be choosers.

Maxine wanted to duck under the table or maybe fight her way through the crowd to hide in the bathroom until this newest drama went back to her sloppy seconds of a mini-mansion. Bright spots of red adorned her cheeks, leaving her flushed and hot.

Unfortunately, she just wasn't a quick enough thinker to find an escape route faster than Lacey could skid across the room on her ridiculously high heels to come to a halt in front of her and Mr. Hodge.

Mr. Hodge jammed his fingers under his suspenders and puckered his lips. His gaze caught Maxine's when he whispered, "The boy's girlfriend?"

Maxine fought a snicker. There wasn't much separating Lacey from Connor but a few measly years and a little thing called a law against dating underage minors. "No. She's my husband's girlfriend, um, fiancée."

Mr. Hodge grunted his disapproval. "Can I use my cane on her?"

Placing a hand at her temple, Maxine rubbed gingerly so as not to touch the area near the bridge of her nose, which had ballooned. "Go have a hot dog, Mr. Hodge. Please. I'll see you tomorrow morning for Jake's walk. Okay?" She gave his arm a warm rub to encourage him to let it be.

Her eyes must have said it all. Joe left, but not before he glared at Lacey, edging past her with a defensive stride then turning his back on her with an indignant huff.

Maxine would smile at how endearing it was to be so silently, vehemently defended if not for the fact that it was, simply put, pathetic that she wasn't doing it for herself.

Not helping matters was the idea that she really should have listened to her mother when she'd expressed her displeasure about Maxine's chosen attire. She looked just like the frumpy, hot mess everyone expected a soon to be ex-trophy wife would look.

On the other hand, Lacey was ethereal.

Fabulous.

Lacey gave her a tentative smile, the amber glow of her youthful skin, fresh from Tiny's Tanning Hut, soft and smooth even in the harsh lighting of the rec center. Maxine found herself trying to ignore the tight mid-thigh length white skirt and figure-hugging green silk shirt Lacey wore with the collar turned up to frame her face. Her black heels clattered with purpose. "Hi, Maxine." The long sway of her buttery blonde hair caught the light. Someone had been seeing her old hairdresser, Enrique. Those were *her* old highlights.

Maxine's chest tightened. "Lacey."

Lacey gasped when Maxine met her eyes. "What happened to your nose?"

"I beat up Fin's other girlfriend. If you think I look bad, you should see her," she quipped, sadly enjoying the look of horror that crossed Lacey's face.

But then she let out a nervous giggle. "Oh. I get it. That was a joke. You were always funny, Maxine."

Yeah. Funny. Maxine didn't respond. Instead, she stared Lacey down with blank eyes, the impulsive urge to run far and wide gripping her.

"Can we go outside?" Lacey waved a hand, motioning toward the door, the flash of her ungodly enormous diamond engagement ring momentarily blocking out everyone and everything.

"Why? So we can duke it out by the swings on the playground?" Maxine managed to ask, pleased her tone was cool and dry as a bone when her legs felt quite the opposite.

Lacey's beautiful face flashed confusion. "Huh? There's no playground here, Maxine. Don't be ridiculous. It's a senior citizens' village."

"Which you're now more than eligible to live in with your new fiancé."

Lacey's eyes glittered angry and cold, finally catching Maxine's sarcasm. "Could we please be adults here?"

Nope. As petty and low blow as it was, she needed a pound of flesh. It might as well be Lacey's perky soft tissue. "You're only what, a year or three past the legal age of adulthood? I'm not sure you have as much adult under your belt as I do. Means we're not exactly on equal footing."

Lacey's aggravated sigh lifted her slender shoulders. "I'd really like to talk to you."

About what? Finger painting and glitter glue? "I'm busy here. Working."

She flashed a coquettish smile, one Maxine was sure had led many a man to whip out his wallet and shower her with hundred-dollar bills. "I promise I won't take up much of your time."

Maxine's fingers traced the outline of the ball cage, the whirring of it somehow soothing beneath her fingertips. Standing here in front of the woman-child she'd once attended school plays and dance recitals for never failed to leave her reeling. "We have nothing to talk about, Lacey. Go home to my house where you live with my husband and sleep in my California King."

"Maxine, please!"

The high-pitched tone of her request and the all but stomp of her expensively shod foot made Maxine blanch and, to her mortification, once more had everyone gawking at her.

Midge Carter was going to give her the ax for sure. She let her head drop to her chest, finding it only made her nose hurt more. Turning on her heel, Maxine made an acquiescent beeline for the door with Lacey in tow.

Once outside with the door securely shut, she spun around to glare at Lacey, who looked angelic under the soft glow of the lantern lights. "What could we possibly have to talk about, Lacey?"

Crickets chirped in the unseasonably humid evening, the thrum of Maxine's anger intensified by the heat and the fact that Lacey looked so coolly unfazed by it. "I'd like to talk to you about Connor."

Her mouth fell open, her head cocking to the left as though she hadn't heard Lacey right. "Connor . . ."

Lacey's eyes went gooey and soft. "I just think it's awful that Fin and Connor aren't speaking, and I thought between the two of us we could find a way to rectify that."

"Rectify?" someone crooned from the crack in the door. The heavy metal burst open and out poured her mother, her mother's friend Mary, and Len. It slammed shut with a heavy groan. Mona attacked with a gnarled, arthritic finger aimed at Lacey's petite nose. "Did you just learn that big-girl word in English class today? You go on and get the heck out of here and mind your business, you—you—"

"Mother!" Maxine hissed a warning, taking her mother by the arm, holding her back from Lacey's space. It was enough she herself had given Lacey a once-over and behaved like the teenager she'd earlier accused Lacey of being. Mona didn't need to be in the mix, too.

But Mona brushed her off with a furious snort. "Oh, no, Maxie!

She has no right to interfere. None. She's done enough of that just by spreading her—"

"Mom! Stop. *Now.*" Her eyes sought Len's, pleading with her to help, but Len's eyes, hard and cold, flashed indifference.

Mary, typically gentle and soft-spoken as opposed to her mother's and Gail's loud and proud attitudes, placed a hand on Mona's shoulder. "Mona. Don't go working yourself up over this piece of trash. She's not worth your heart medication, honey."

Hookay. That wasn't so soft-spoken or genteel. "Mary Delouise!" Maxine rasped, shocked by the venom in her outburst.

Mary shook her auburn-dyed head, her gray eyes shooting flames from behind her prescription glasses. She crossed her arms over her thin chest, tugging at the white pearls clasping the front of her shoulder-draped sweater together. "Sorry, Maxine. I'm with your mother on this. This girl's a home wrecker!" She shot a look of disdain at Lacey, and followed it with a fleetingly apologetic one to Len.

Mona moved around her with a speed that surprised Maxine, backing Lacey up against the rickety fence lining the pathway to the door. "You stay away from my grandson! There isn't anything he can learn from you but how to cheat and lie!"

She couldn't have prevented it if she'd wanted to, Maxine told herself. She just wasn't quick enough. Or at least that was what she soothed her guilty conscience with when she reacted too late to keep her mother from leaning in too far, sending Lacey backward with a startled yelp over the old fence and headfirst into the thorny bushes, heeled feet pointing skyward.

Maxine tugged on her mother's arm, moving her out of the way. "Mom! You can't go doing things like that," she chastised with a yelp. "It just makes everything worse. The two of you are behaving like preschoolers."

Mona gave her an unapologetic snort. "I never touched her, and if all she suffers is a couple of thorns in her backside, she'll be far better off than you and that son of yours she so wants to *help*." Her mother, red-faced, eyes spitting fire, reached for Mary's hand. "Let's go back in, Mary, before I take her over my knee and give her the spanking she deserves but never got because she's a spoiled little girl."

Mary leaned over and gave Lacey the old disapproving evil eye before yanking open the door and pushing her way back inside with Mona hot on her heels.

Len reached a hand down to Lacey amidst the mean-spirited cackles from Mona and Mary. She hauled her upward none too gently, giving her sister a scathing look before setting her away from her with a jerk of her hands to Lacey's shoulders. "Don't ever come back here, Lacey," she said between tight lips. "You're never going to be the cooling balm that soothes this mess you've made. Can't you see that? Go back to Finley. Just go away."

Lacey's round eyes welled with tears as she brushed haphazardly at the branches clinging to her perfectly coiffed hair. "How can you say that to me? I'm your sister! I just want everything to be okay for Fin and Connor," she whispered.

And oddly enough, much to her surprise, Maxine believed her. In Lacey's immature mind, she probably did regret that her affair with Fin had torn a father and son apart.

At that very moment, what Maxine wished more was that Fin regretted it as much as Lacey appeared to.

What Lacey couldn't possibly realize, because she wasn't much older than Connor, was that Fin and his son had never had much of a relationship unless Maxine was forcing them to interact. Fin was still too selfish to give himself unconditionally to anyone—even his own son—and Lacey didn't know the first thing about the dynamics of a father and his child. She didn't know herself well enough to grasp her own dynamics, let alone the sort belonging to a sixteen-year-old kid.

Len's hard swallow was visible, her response deadly quiet. "This wasn't the way to make everything okay, Lacey. If you were old enough, mature enough, you'd know you're just throwing what you've done in everyone's face by coming here. The only thing I'm sure you're old enough to understand is that what you did to Maxine was wrong, and that still didn't stop you, did it? Now go get in that uber sports car your fiancé gifted you with and don't come back here. And I mean that. I don't want to see you anywhere in my vicinity— *ever again*."

Maxine knew how hard this had been on her friend—making the choice to stand by her instead of backing Lacey, her own flesh and blood. She hated that it had come to this. What she hated even more was the idea that she felt even a little sorry for Lacey. Yet here she was, taking in her husband's lover with sympathetic eyes. "Len," she said, soft with concern. "Please, don't. It's not necessary. I'm fine."

Len's smile was wry when she patted Maxine on the cheek, her bangle bracelets tinkling against her wrist. "No, honey. That's not true. Nothing's fine with you. None of this is fine, and some days, I just want to crawl under a rock because it was your good heart and my selfish, gold-digging sister who put you in this predicament. I don't know that I'll ever be able to stop saying how sorry I am. But at least one of us," she shot a pointed look at Lacey, "really *is* genuinely sorry."

Lacey caved to her sister's intentional humiliation with a sob, taking flight in an impressive high-heeled sprint to the parking lot. The roar of her car engine and the screech of her tires resounded in the thick night.

Maxine's stomach heaved, her legs heavy and weak. Closing her eyes, she took a ragged breath of stifling air. Len threw an arm around her, giving her shaking shoulders a squeeze of comfort. "I don't want it to be like this, Len. You know that," she said, weary from the night's events.

Len pressed a kiss to the top of her friend's head and sighed with a ragged breath. "I don't want it to be like this either. But it is what it is. I just can't abide a liar and a cheat, especially when it's my own sister. No one was ever going to set Lacey straight about the damage she's caused if I didn't. You know what my folks have been like about this. You already know the score. What I said to her tonight's nothing new."

Maxine nodded, squeezing her eyes shut to ward off tears. "I know. I guess hearing it secondhand up to this point just didn't have the kind of impact as seeing you spit fire in person does. You were really hard on her, Len."

"Someone has to be, Maxine. This time she didn't just rack up a huge credit card bill or scratch the car my parents borrowed from Dad's 401K to pay for. She ruined a *family*."

Maxine shook her head, sad with a realization prompted by her friend's words. "You know, about that family thing. She couldn't ruin something that never was. We were only a family in my mind, Len. *Mine* only. How often was Fin really around unless I'd pressured him to be there?"

"Doesn't change the mess you're in now. Lacey helped with that. We've been best friends for fifteen years. You stuck by me after Gerald's death and never batted a false eyelash when our group of quote-unquote friends snubbed me. Now I'm just returning the favor. Oh, and as an FYI: Not a chance in hell I'm sitting across the dinner table at Christmas from that smarmy pig stuffing turkey between his lying lips."

There was just no budging her firm stance. In tired defeat, Maxine laid her head on her friend's shoulder, inhaling the comforting scent of her perfume. The tears she'd hoped to thwart dripped from her eyes, falling to her feet in big, salty drops. "I think I never want to do this again."

"Play bingo?"

"Leave the house."

"But if you don't leave the house, you can't go out with the luscious Campbell Barker. Niiiice coup, my friend."

Maxine pressed the heels of her hands to her eyes. "Um, I think you made the coup."

"Me?"

Maxine measured her words, fighting to keep any hint of green out of her tone. "Yeah," she offered casually in a no-big-deal kinda way while she stared at her sneakers. "You guys were yucking it up in there. Seemed like you were having a pretty good time." *With all those hot dogs and all that giggling over those hot dogs . . .*

"All he talked about was you, Maxine."

Her head shot up. "Reeeeaaaallly?" She paused. "Wait. Jesus. That sounded all girlie and high school, didn't it?"

"It did." Len grinned her confirmation with a wink.

Bleh. "Forget I said that. Forget he talked to you about me. Just forget it all."

"Why would I forget it? It's the most animated and interested I've seen you in forever."

Maxine slapped her hands on her thighs in disgust. "That's the whole problem, Len. I shouldn't be animated or interested just because of a man. I should be animated about me. I should be interested in me. It should all be about me at this point in my fucked-upness. Me and Connor. I should perk up over *me*-stuff, not man-stuff. I think it's obvious from the way I look, I'm not so animated about me." And she couldn't summon up enough disgust for herself to change that. "I spent way too much of my life catering to someone else's idea of who I should be. Never again."

Len's hand reached out for Maxine's. When she took it, her friend squeezed it affectionately. "Honey, I'm going to say something that might piss you off, but you know me. I'm not afraid to tell you when I think you're being a dipshit."

She showed her affront by way of a snort. "I'm being a dipshit?"

"Red-alert-level dipshit. You can be empowered without being a Nazi about it."

Okay, so maybe empowerment should be utilized in small doses. "Are you saying you think I'm pushing my limits of self-discovery to an all new and dramatic height?" She batted her eyes at her friend and giggled.

Len patted her hand. "What do you think?"

"I think you're answering a question with a question."

"That's because I know you have the answer."

Oh, she had answers. She just had to make sure they were life-style changes instead of just empty words. "It's okay for me to like a man without thinking I'm going to lose myself entirely. Happy?"

"I'm happi*er* . . ." Emphasis on the "er."

Maxine swallowed, letting another one of her fears loose into the universe. "I'm afraid. I'm afraid I'll fall into the same old traps I fell into with Fin. I'm scared witless if I ever become involved again my whole world will end up revolving around pleasing someone else before I find out what pleases me. So just finding someone even a lit-tle attractive has my guard up." *There, have some more dark, deeply rooted paranoia to muck through.*

"I get it. Knowing you don't want to do that again is sort of half the battle, right?"

"I didn't ever want to do it to begin with, Len. I just did."

"But you were like twelve when you got married. Your idea of what a relationship should be was formed while watching *As the World Turns* and *Punky Brewster.* It wasn't by trial and error or life experience. Fin was your *only* experience. You were immature and goo-goo-eyed, but you're not twelve anymore, honey."

If there was one thing she was going to remain firm on, it was not losing herself to an intimate relationship before she had a relation-ship with herself. "I need to find out who I am alone. If I can be inde-pendent, stand on my own two feet—and that has to happen before I consider anything else."

They sat side by side in silence for a moment. The warm breeze sifting between them while Maxine pondered her last statement. Couldn't she do both? The real question was, could she keep herself in check enough to make sure her lines didn't blur while she did both? "Campbell makes my knees a little weak. I thought at first it was just osteoporosis, but I've come to the conclusion he's just nummy."

Len's eyebrow rose. "He's definitely weak-knee worthy."

Just admitting that had her stomach doing a Highland fling. "I can't believe I said that out loud."

Len's throaty laugh filled the air. "It's okay to enjoy the fact that a man finds you attractive without feeling like you've been rendered powerless, Wonder Girl."

Maxine scoffed, frowning and ready to offer up one of her ultimate fears in her defense. "Says you. Do you remember how obsessed I was with making Fin fall back in love with me again after his first affair? Do you remember the Dr. Phil books I read obsessively? Better yet, do you remember the extremes I went to? I had a boob job, for Christ's sake. I gave up so much of myself just to cater to him. I'm never giving up that much of myself again to a man, Len." Not without a fight.

Len's face softened. "Not every man is Fin. I thank Jesus and all twelve for that revelation every night. I'm grateful I know enough to know there're still good men to be had. But answer me this. Do you really think if you become involved with someone someday, you'll curl up and die in some dank, dirty corner if he lets his dick do his thinking for him again?"

"Don't be ridiculous."

"Point made." Len smiled.

"I don't get it."

Len's lips thinned in disgust. "Do you remember Fin's first affair? Do you remember telling me you didn't know who you were if you weren't his wife? Do you remember telling me you just wanted to curl up and die if you had to live without him, despite the fact that he'd been unfaithful?"

God. Yes. She remembered. It had been the darkest, loneliest, most pitiful admission she'd ever made. She wasn't ever going back to that black void of empty fear. Ever. "I remember. Those were some dark moments, huh?"

She massaged the back of Maxine's hand with soothing fingers. "The darkest, and through the entire thing I kept thinking, 'Why the hell doesn't she get mad? Why doesn't she insist he go to counseling with her to help her deal with the kind of insecurity and pain an affair creates in a marriage? And if Fin refuses, just like he did, why doesn't Maxine just leave his ass flat? Why is his infidelity only her burden to bear when she didn't do anything wrong? And why, why, *why* does she think just because Fin owned up to it he deserves some kind of Medal of Honor for bravery in the line of marriage?' It made me want to throttle you, my friend. Instead of dealing with that head-on, you stuffed all of those emotions way deep down and set about making everything perfect for Fin. The *last* person on Earth who deserved that kind of treatment. If anyone should've been making nice, it was him."

Hearing Len's thoughts about her archaic behavior from that time in her life made Maxine cringe with a shudder. That she couldn't see then how Fin had manipulated his admission of infidelity into doing her some kind of favor because he'd confessed it made her want to claw his eyes out now.

As ashamed as Maxine was to admit it, there'd been many long hours to fill while Fin was off at work or some business dinner when she'd wished he'd never told her in the first place. Who did it really benefit when you confessed an affair? It relieved the guilty party, but it brought a wealth of residual pain for the one who'd been deceived. "My self-esteem was at an all-time low."

"Ya think, Maxine?"

Oh, yes. She thought. "I admit my views on relationships were skewed."

"The skewedest I've personally ever borne witness to," Len joked.

"I've been thinking . . ."

"You want a drum roll?"

Maxine smiled. Hearing Len point out some of her old habits made the desire to create healthier habits more clear. "I know what I don't want in a relationship—if, and that's a big if, I ever set sail on the relationship boat of love again, I have a list."

"I love self-revelation. It's all deep and shiny. So share," Len encouraged with a smile and a nudge.

"I don't want to feel like my entire world's coming to an end because a man doesn't love me or want me or decides he wants to trade in his older model Lamborghini for a newer Ferrari. I want to fill my life, Connor's life, with more self-worth than that."

"Know what I think, Maxine Cambridge?"

Maxine chuckled. "I'm all atwitter with anticipation, friend."

"Just your admission that you're afraid of giving up too much of who you're becoming to be in a relationship that isn't exactly what you want is a clear sign you'll be on the lookout for the red flags."

A lost piece of the Maxine puzzle resurfaced and clicked into place. She wanted a life full and rich with the things she loved, so if she ended up sans man forever, she'd still have a soft place to fall.

"Look at me all growing. Though I'm not ashamed to say I would have rather grown with a checking-account balance," Maxine joked, meeting her friend's gaze.

"You are, and thank God. You're not defining yourself by the attention and praise of a man anymore. I swear to you, honey, you really can be in love and not have to give up everything you enjoy to do it. *You* define you, Maxine. No one else can or ever will again. So don't go overboard with the 'I'll never touch a man with a ten-foot pole again' where Campbell's concerned. Sharing your life with someone can be a wonderful thing if you remember the key word is *sharing*."

"Who's going overboard here? Campbell and I aren't even remotely involved. We aren't anything." Though maybe being "something" wasn't nearly as offensive as she'd once thought it would be. Not now that she'd shared what hindsight had taught her about her marriage.

"Which means I'm one step ahead of you in the 'don't be a dried-up man-hating shrew for the rest of your life because one man sucked the very soul from you for all of your wasted youth' speech. Enjoy Campbell's interest for what it is. If nothing comes of it, then nothing comes of it. Just breathe."

Maxine's laughter was carefree. For the first time tonight, her lungs felt less like big ten-pound weights in her chest. If only her bruised nose would follow suit. "So . . ."

"So?"

"He asked about me?" She toyed with the zipper on the front of her sweat suit with clammy fingers.

Her friend's eyebrow cocked, her response mockingly solemn. "Oh, he asked."

Maxine shot for an air of indifference when she said, "So tell me what he asked."

"Nope," Len said with a chuckle, putting her hands in the back pockets of her jeans. "He can tell you himself. The only thing I will tell you is he's had the BFF warning. He knows I'll saw off his love sacs if he even considers jerking you around."

"How thoughtful of you," Maxine teased, rising to pull Len up with her. "You won't reconsider telling me just a little bit?"

"Nuh-uh. I've interfered enough. Though, if I were you, I'd maybe consider giving him some kudos for liking the real Maxine."

"Meaning?"

Len's look was critical when she waved her hand up and down the length of her friend. "Honey, you look horrible, and still the man thinks you're a slice of awesome. Think of it this way. If the two of you ever get to the wonking stage of the game, morning breath and smeared mascara won't make him want to chew his arm off."

Maxine threw her head back and laughed. "He's a brave warrior."

"He's a nice one, too. I liked him. And he's pretty brick shithouse to boot."

Yeaahhh. So much brick shithouse Maxine had to fight to take in more air every time she saw him. "I'm not even technically divorced yet. I think it's a little premature to date anyway."

"That stopped Fin? Or have you forgotten he's *engaged*?"

"Doesn't make it right, Len," she murmured. Right sucked. But there was Connor and setting examples to consider.

"Nothing about what Fin's done is right. You don't love him anymore. The married point is moot. The real point is you're in the middle of divorce proceedings. They're just taking an ungodly amount of time to get through. You know you want a divorce. You just don't have one yet. But you will, and in the meantime, it's hurting no one if you date as long as you're honest about where your divorce is at."

Which was nowhere, though she wasn't about to share that with Len. She'd only tell her she needed to find a new, better lawyer with the invisible cash she was supposed to summon. "I have to be *asked* on a date first," she hinted, fighting the flutter of her heart against her rib cage at such a notion. A date. She hadn't been on a date since senior prom.

Len's stare was purposefully blank. "Yep."

Maxine nudged her shoulder. "Oh, c'mon. Just a little hint about what he said."

"Not a chance." She yanked the rec center door open. "Go on, Mistress of All Things Bingo. Finish up in there. You up for the diner afterward? Or do you want to go home and put some more ice on that nose? Your mother told me what happened. Tough crowd, the over-fifty-five set, eh?"

The events of the long evening settled between her shoulders in the way of a sharp ache. "Do you mind if I take a rain check? If I keep scooping enough poop, it might be my treat," she enticed.

"Deal. But promise me something?"

"Anything."

"Don't wear that color ever again, and pluck your eyebrows. They look like hamsters. Love yourself, sweetie. With a pair of tweezers or a jar of hot wax."

Maxine giggled when she flipped her friend the bird, heading back into the rec center, feeling considerably lighter than she had just three hours ago.

~~~

"Miss Wiiiigggllles, c'mon. Make potties for Auntie Maxine," she coaxed the small, fuzzy Pomeranian who stared blankly up at her like she was making demands in a foreign language.

Settling on her haunches, Maxine ran a hand down along Miss Wiggles's fur-coated spine, chucking her under the chin. "Auntie Maxine's beat, punkin', and her nose could really use a frozen T-bone followed by an ibuprofen chaser. So let's make poo and call it a night. Whaddya say?"

Miss Wiggles leaned into her hand for a brief moment then sat back on her haunches, too. Slipping to the ground, Maxine dropped her ass to the pavement with defeat and sighed. Miss Wiggles hopped in her lap to snuggle.

Maxine held up the Ziploc bag. "See this, Miss Wiggles? We have to fill it up. Please?" she whimpered. Her nose whimpered right along with her by way of an angry throb. A quick glance in the rec center bathroom mirror had revealed dark purple bruising and an ugly, mottled yellow blotch on the left side of her cheek.

"Are we experiencing potty malfunction, Miss Wiggles?" a deep voice asked, the speaker stepping into the light of the globed street-lamps lining the sidewalks of Leisure Village.

Her stomach gave a fierce lurch when Campbell offered his hand to help her up. She found her eyes falling to the tight fit of his jeans where his thighs met his hips, and bit her lip. Placing her hand in his, she rose upward, Miss Wiggles securely tucked under her arm. His arm went to her waist when she stumbled, because really, whose legs wouldn't crumble like dry cookies in the presence of all that hottie?

Their bodies met, touching, molding to each other as if they'd always done so. Maxine grimaced when her hips decided they liked Campbell's just fine. His muscled thighs, aligned with hers, left her wondering what they would feel like minus a pair of stonewashed jeans.

Oh.

Nice time for her libido to fire up.

"How's that nose?" he asked with his arm still bracing her.

"Do you think purple and yellow blotches are a good look for me?" she asked back on a hard swallow. His chest. It kept distracting her. Jesus Christ in a miniskirt, his chest was so okay to stay pressed against hers until her death, when rigor mortis set in.

The hand she'd placed on his arm to steady herself persisted, internally begging her to allow its fingers to skim the planes of his pecs. She swayed.

Campbell tightened his grip, his long fingers splaying across her waist. "I think what really gives me goose bumps is the red mixed in with all those blotches. Very appealing."

"So what you're saying is it's not working with my outfit."

He chuckled. "Only if you're Rainbow Brite."

Maxine chuckled, too. Nervously.

And then there was silence again, Miss Wiggles sighing a deep sigh of contentment against Campbell's shoulder, mirroring Maxine's internal sigh.

Campbell's eyes stared into hers directly, unblinking, as though he were taking in every inch of her face and memorizing it.

God. What a sucky memory she must make right now.

The evening pulsed between them. Crickets chirped. The street-lamps hummed.

Expectation came, went, and came again in her stomach full of cartwheeling Olympic gymnasts. She couldn't help but think about Len's mystery conversation with Campbell. Was this man, so smart and funny, kind to the elderly, good with animals, and hot to boot, really interested in her? And if so, why? She didn't have a lot to offer. In fact, had she ever had anything to offer other than her twenty-two-inch waist and a nice rack?

As the silence ticked on, and her mind raced, Maxine decided Len had read too much into Campbell's inquiries.

Her stomach sank again. Why would a man this together, this flippin' good looking, ever ask her out? If he'd asked Len about her, it was out of curiosity because of all of the village gossip. Who wouldn't be curious about the neurosis-laden, almost divorcée who'd gone from riches to neon yellow sweat suits and eyebrows like caterpillars?

When Campbell finally spoke, it was as he was letting her go, stepping backward. "C'mere, Miss Wiggles," he almost cooed, taking the dog from her trembling fingers and setting her on the grass by his feet. "Let's make some magic, young lady," he coaxed the preening Pomeranian.

Disappointment led Maxine's eyes to stray to the ground for a mere second before she lifted them to his, purposely—with resolve. There'd be no lying down and dying because someone didn't ask her out on a date she'd made up in her own mind to begin with.

Her shoulders squared at this mini-milestone. There'd be no weeping and wailing either. Rejection sucked sometimes, but it wasn't the end of the world. Not nabbing a date with a man she probably wasn't ready to date anyway was just fine.

So bummer that.

When she finally unlocked her "I never wanted to go out with you anyway" gaze from his, and her eyes strayed back to the ground, Campbell asked, "So, Max. How about that cup of coffee? Maybe tomorrow night? Seven sound good?"

Yeah, rejection wasn't the end of the world. But acceptance did have a woo to the hoo factor to it. Not a big woo. Just a little hoo. "Where do you want to go?"

"The diner maybe? Wherever we go, I promise it'll be well lit and have plenty of people."

Maxine giggled. "I—I've . . . I haven't been on a date since leg warmers were still popular. I guess I just don't know what to say. I mean, it isn't that I don't know what my answer's going to be. I just mean that you caught me off guard. Sort of. Oh, and not in a bad way. Just off guard, you know?"

Oy.

The smile he flashed was playful with no hint of the dangerous glint he'd had in his eyes earlier. "Just say yes. Yes, Campbell, I'll have a cup of coffee with you. Maybe two if you keep being so damn cute and charming."

Her heart skittered, and her hands searched for something to do other than throw themselves around his neck in high-schoolish gratitude. So silly. It was only coffee.

On a deep breath that made her bangs puff upward, she responded. "Yes, Campbell. I'll have coffee with you at a well-lit place with lots of people around."

She noted his expression never wavered, but his eyes glittered. He handed Miss Wiggles's leash to her with a grin that made his five o'clock shadow appear rakish in the lamplight. "So I'll see you tomorrow at seven, Max."

As she took the leash, their hands brushed, creating an electric current of excitement in the pit of her stomach once more. "O—okay . . . tomorrow."

Campbell caught her chin, caressing it with his thumb. "You ice that nose, okay?" he reminded before capturing her lips, molding them to his with a sweetly hot sizzle of blood rushing to her ears. It lasted maybe only twenty seconds or so, no longer than the last kiss they'd shared, but long enough to awaken those dormant hormones so long overlooked.

This time a sigh did escape her lips, and a sinful chuckle of confidence released from his. When she was able to open her eyes, he'd begun to saunter away. "Don't forget to scoop that poop," he said, laughter threading his words.

Maxine gave a quick glance to where Miss Wiggles sat beside her feet, quiet as a church mouse, a pile of some of her best magic right beside her. She bent to scoop it up and deposit it in the bag, retrieving the dog to give her a quick snuggle. "Is there anything that man can't create with just a wink and a smile?" she asked her.

Setting Miss Wiggles back on the sidewalk, Maxine took her time bringing the Pomeranian home to her owner, Mrs. Kniffen. She needed a moment to absorb the idea that she was going on a date, time to assimilate how she was going to broach the subject to Connor.

She needed to do more than just absorb and talk this over with Connor—she needed a lot of things. First, a much-required fashion intervention. "Miss Wiggles? When you're going on a date for something as casual as coffee, is it acceptable dating etiquette to wear a sweat suit?"

Miss Wiggles snorted her apparent disapproval, trotting happily beside her toward home.

"But it's a festive color. Purple. Don't you like purple?" The Pomeranian let a visible shudder roll down her spine.

Her shoulders slumped. She didn't have a whole lot to choose from except what she borrowed from her mother. Almost all of her wardrobe, accessories, and cute shoes were long gone. Lacey'd probably had a poolside bonfire with them back at the mini-mansion. Right next to those stupid silver saw palmetto trees she'd once babied like she'd given birth to them.

"So tell me, Miss Fashionista, how do you feel about housecoats on a first date? You know, like the ones with the big flowers on them and the snaps down the front?" This time, Miss Wiggles growled low.

Maxine rolled her eyes at the persnickety Miss Wiggles.

Hater.

CHAPTER EIGHT

Note from Maxine Cambridge to all ex-trophy wives on really, really sucking it up: When on a tight budget, Walmart and other various discount chains can be your moth-eaten pocketbook's friend. Yes, *you* must do your own shopping. No, there are no personal shoppers to carry your purchases. No one will offer you beverage and sustenance in the way of wafer-thin crackers with goat cheese whilst you peruse fine outerwear. However, this *is* the place where you'll find affordable foods and two-fer deals, and finally, yes, you must push your own cart. The indignities, eh? Go forth and purchase feminine hygiene products at discount prices. "Welcome to Walmart."

Adam hunched down in his rented car in the Walmart parking lot, observing the woman he'd finally identified as Maxine Cambridge, and forced himself to focus on why he was in Riverbend in the first place.

But his thoughts kept straying to Len—her hot accusation that he was some two-bit PI for Finley Cambridge. Her vehement defense of her friend made him smile.

She was intense, sexy, and devoted to, and protective of Maxine.

Now that he had the information he needed, he should be focused on doing what he came to do and getting out of Dodge.

So why was he pulling out of the Walmart parking lot and driving in the direction of Lenore's office?

~ℓ~

"Okay, Maxie. This," her mother said with widespread arms clad in a plaid button-down shirt, "is *Super Walmart*. It's the best place in town to shop when you're on a budget. Well, sometimes you can get a real bargain at the Stop & Shop on chuck roast, but Walmart has everything, household items, small appliances, clothes. All sorts of bunk."

Maxine's mouth hung open in awe as she perused the vast acres of aisles and aisles of—of *stuff*. So much stuff. Stuff for as far as the eye could see. "Wowwww," was all she had to offer.

Mona shook her head and rolled her eyes in Gail's direction. "I'm almost ashamed to call you my own, toots. You really haven't ever been inside a Walmart? I still can't believe what a princess you are."

The shake of her head was sluggish. "Nuh-uh. Not for a long, long time. Lola did all of the shopping. I just wrote down what I wanted and she provided." Jesus. That sounded so shallow—so diva-esque, even to her own ears. "And I'm not a princess, Mom. Princesses aren't poor. So take a good look"—she pulled at the lining of her pockets to show her mother—"I *am* poor. As a church mouse. The horror, huh? And it wasn't like I wouldn't have been more than willing to go do the shopping and errands, but Finley was adamant about the 'help,' as he called them, doing what they were paid to do."

A wistfully sad smile crossed her face when she remembered how kind Lola had been to her when she'd discovered her crying in the pantry because she couldn't find the can opener.

It had been a situational breakdown just a month after she'd found out about Fin's first affair. One of those "straw that broke the camel's back" deals. Her fears and her overactive imagination had all ganged up on her at once, and she'd taken her frustrations out by openly weeping over her inability to locate a simple can opener.

Lola's sympathetic smile and offer to make her a cake couldn't completely hide the pity in her eyes. That was when Maxine knew that everyone but her was aware of Fin's need to discover if the Fountain of Youth really was inside the vagina of a twenty-year-old.

Everyone Finley employed knew he'd stepped out behind her back. How pathetic she must've appeared. Poor, dim-witted Finley Cambridge's wife. Forgotten head cheerleader of the Riverbend Rams and ex-small-time beauty queen.

But not anymore. A big squee to that.

Maxine's cheeks sprouted two red spots at the recollection, spurring her determination to understand this crazy new world of coupon-clipping and buying ground beef in bulk.

Rubbing her hands together, she eyed Gail and her mother. "Okay, ladies. So my secret's out. I don't know thing one about Walmart, but I've got my list and two weeks' worth of scooping poop in cold hard cash. Let's get it on."

Stomping off down the first aisle that grabbed her attention, she held up her list like it was a she-warrior's guide to the galaxy. Her eyes glazed over with each aisle she traipsed through. This was a Candy Land of gadgets and doodads the likes of which she hadn't seen in a long time.

Oh, sweet Jesus.

They even had Sno Balls.

The pink ones.

In bulk!

Two hours later, Max found herself enraptured, enthralled, enthusiastically sick with the kind of joy she was garnering from ticking items off her list. Items she was purchasing with *her* money.

"Omigod, Ma! Looook!" she squealed, ignoring the inquiring stay-at-home moms turning toward her in clusters of frayed ponytails. "I found tampons. They're the good ones, too. The ones for heavy-flow days. Two boxes for five dollars!" She grinned, pride beaming on her face as she waved the boxes at her mother. They qualified as a necessity, and better still, they fit into her budget. Two boxes of tampons would last her at least four months.

Oh, happy period.

Her mother leaned over the cart and whispered out of the side of her mouth with a harsh snap, "Maxie?"

Distracted by the shiny display of bags and bags of Snickers bars, Maxine muttered, "What?"

"Stop it. You're making a scene. It's *Walmart*, Maxie. Not Diane von Furstaface." Giving her a sideways glance, Mona frowned. "People are giving us funny looks."

"It's Furstenberg, and they're giving us funny looks because you still have a roller in your hair, Mom." Maxine plucked at the pink cushiony curler.

Mona waved her off, snatching the curler from her and dropping it in her suitcase-sized purse. "No. It's because you're behaving like you just found the answer to the meaning of life. It's *Walmart*. Nobody gets excited about Walmart."

Gail shuffled up behind them and snorted. "I do. It's my one chance to get out and commune with discount coupons and cheap lingerie."

Maxine's eyes lit up when she squeezed Gail's arm. "They have lingerie, too?" she gasped with a coo. "Oh, show me!"

"Maxie!" her mother whisper-yelled, grabbing on to the sleeve of her shirt. "Pipe down. It's not the kind of lingerie you're used to. It's made of cheap material, and besides that, you can't afford lingerie. Now stick to the things on your list or you'll never learn how to budget properly." Redirecting the cart, her mother gave it an exasperated shove toward the food section of the store. "We're here for essentials, Maxine. Not frillies," she harrumphed.

Maxine looked at Gail, shoving her hands into the pockets of her jeans with defeat, her shoulders slumping as they trudged behind Mona. "What a killjoy she is, huh?"

"A real harsh to your buzz." Gail cackled at her clever use of the slang Connor'd been teaching her. "But she's right, you know. You have to learn how to shop with limits so you and the boy can survive."

"Yeah," she admitted with stoicism. "Limits suck."

Gail nodded her shortly cropped head. "That they do, but you'll get used to 'em."

Linking her arm with Gail's, she pulled her close and whispered with a covert glance to her mother's plaid back, "Do they *really* have lingerie here?"

"Maxine!" her mother called over her shoulder. "Focus, miss. We're here for lima beans and boneless chicken breast for a dollar ninety-nine a pound. You can't feed Connor jazzy polyester pj's."

Maxine stuck her tongue out at her mother's back.

Gail snorted, lining up behind Mona to unload their purchases.

Maxine jumped ahead to the front of the line, digging through her purse for the cash she'd saved. As the cashier rang each item up, she watched the tally with hawk-like eyes.

A sigh of relief escaped her lips when she realized she'd stuck to her budget.

"Fifty-eight sixty-one," the cashier said, boredom lacing her tone.

Maxine handed her the money, and couldn't help but ask, "Do you like working here?"

The young woman's eyes rolled up into her smooth forehead. "Seriously?"

"Seriously."

"Who actually likes working here?"

Maxine felt a ruffle of one of her feathers. "You get a steady pay-check, don't you?"

"So?" She shrugged with a "big deal" attitude.

So? "So, that's a valuable thing in today's economy, don't you think?"

Her clear green eyes held Maxine's for a moment, very clearly searching for the crazy in them. "Whatever."

Whatever? What-ev-er? How could someone be so nonchalant about something as important as a regular paycheck? "You don't know how lucky you are," Maxine couldn't help but mention, her tone condescending. Worse, she knew it. Heard it, justifying her indignation with the notion that she'd kill to have a job like this one, and someone needed to hear about it.

"Yeah. I feel real *lucky.*" She chewed her gum, stopping only to blow a bubble as she put the money in the register.

What an ungrateful little . . . "Yeah, that's right. I said *lucky.*" Maxine tapped her fingernail on the small ledge housing the debit card machine. "You have no idea how fortunate you are to have a steady income to pay the bills. Do you have any idea how you're taking your youth for granted? You could be like me, you know. Almost forty-one years old, the divorce from hell on your back, and no job at all. So when you roll out of bed tomorrow, count your lucky stars you have a job just like this, young lady!" Spittle flew from Maxine's mouth, she was so infuriated by this youngster's ungrateful arrogance. Heads turned in every which way from the checkout aisles at her righteously indignant speech.

Her mother stuck a tissue under Maxine's nose with a snarl. "Maxie! Wipe your mouth and pipe down. It isn't your job to lecture every teenager from here to Secaucus about their good fortune. Take your change and let's go."

Maxine's haze of anger instantly lifted. She glanced at Gail as they pushed the cart out of the checkout aisle, her mother twenty paces ahead, the angry stomp of her orthopedic shoes slapping against the dirty tile floor. "Too much?" she asked with a hesitant wince.

"Uh, yeah. I think you've gone overboard with the empowered-woman stuff. You don't have to stake your claim everywhere you go, toots. People don't really care that you just bought your own tampons with money you slaved over bingo and poop for. These are people who do that every day and only dream about the kind of money you and the Talleywhacker had. Their joy about earning minimum wage, even with benefits, evaporated when they found out how many doubles they'd have to pull to make ends meet."

"Sorry," Maxine mumbled, running a hand through her mussed hair. "I got carried away. But she's so missing the point, and so ungrateful. I just wanted to—"

Gail held up a hand to halt her protest. "I get it, kiddo. But in this particular case, less is more."

She shoved her change into the pocket of her jeans with a sheepish apology on her face, looping her arm through Gail's. "I promise to stay on the down low with impassioned speeches to teenaged girls about experiencing life before marrying a talleywhacker."

Gail gave her a critical eye as they made their way out into the hot parking lot. "So I hear tell you got yourself a date with that good-lookin' Campbell."

"It's not really a date. Just coffee." *Oh, it is not, Maxine. It's like an epic event. Like being invited to the Oscars or something, and you know it. Quit downplaying your giddy joy.*

Gail spoke Maxine's very thoughts. "It's okay to be excited about being asked out by a nice-lookin' boy, honey. You can bet your sweet bippy I'd be excited if somebody that handsome asked me out. Now look," she muttered, reaching into her purse to rummage and pulling out a small Walmart bag. "This is for you. So you can get your pretty on tonight for Campbell." She held up a tube of lipstick, shiny-silver in the mid-morning sun.

Tears sprang to Maxine's eyes. It was the lipstick she'd been eye-balling while she'd waffled over whether she could afford it or not. Deciding the extra five dollars wasn't in her budget, she'd regretfully put it back and moved on. "Oh, Gail," she squealed, hugging her. "Thank you. I'm pretty sure Campbell will thank you, too."

She reached up to pat Maxine's cheek with affection. "You wear it well, honey, and have a good time tonight. Try to relax and just be yourself. I used to be quite the looker. Had plenty of dates in my time before I married Lamar. I know what I'm talkin' about."

With a snatch of her fingers, she opened the door for her mother, then Gail, hoping they couldn't see the tremble of her fingers at the mention of her pending date with Campbell. She slid into the backseat, pressing a hand to her nervous belly.

She'd been possessed by an idiot to accept a date with him last night. In the cold light of the early morning, while she'd gagged down coffee and a piece of dry toast, her stomach had reminded her of her idiocy.

In stereo.

The lipstick in her open purse caught her eye, twinkling like a treasure nestled amongst the crumpled tissues.

Well, even if she was an idiot, she'd be an idiot with luscious Baby Boysenberry lips.

~~e~~

Maxine eyed Connor from across the dinner table as they finished up the last of the pot roast her mother had made. Hers still swam in the congealed brown gravy, uneaten due to her anxious stomach. "So you're sure you're okay with this?" she asked in reference to her "just a cup of meaningless coffee" date with Campbell. "Because if you're not, just say the word and it's off."

Mona grunted, wiping her mouth with a yellow paper napkin. "The boy would be a convenient scapegoat, Maxie."

Connor stretched his arms, giving his grandmother a conspiratorial smile. "It's okay, Gram. I watch those talk shows with you. I know it's healthy and encouraged for a woman in her forties to begin to date again after ending a long relationship."

Mona rose, slapping Connor with affection on the back. "You're a good boy. Just like your grandmother, you are." She drifted off, clearing away the mashed potatoes.

Maxine slid closer to Connor on the wheels of her chair. "Seriously, pal. If you feel uncomfortable—not ready, I'll cancel."

"Mom?"

Her ears perked, at the ready to pick up the phone and beg off Campbell because her son wasn't ready for her to date. "Yes?"

"Aren't you the one who needs to be ready? And who's in charge here anyway?" he asked, cocking a smart-ass smile at her. "I already date, in case you've forgotten the 'wrap your willy' speech you gave me at fourteen after Tara Martin got pregnant."

Maxine blanched at the memory. She and Tara's mother Joyce had once served as PTA moms together when the children were in third grade. To think of little Tara, cute, flaxen-haired, and freckled, knocked up left Maxine reeling. She'd sat Connor down the moment she'd found out and drilled the safe sex routine into his head like she was a DeWalt and he was a Sheetrock screw. "I just want you to feel secure in the idea that no matter what, you come first."

Connor rolled his eyes, shoving the last bit of pot roast into his mouth. "It's not me that has to be ready, Mom. It's you. I'm cool with it. I like Campbell. He seems nice. He gave me a ride back from Mrs. Kniffen's the other day after I weeded her garden."

"I can't believe this is so easy for you . . ." Why couldn't it be easier for her?

"It's not a big deal," he said with a shrug, brushing the sweep of his dark hair from his eyes with a shake of his head.

Her eyebrow rose. Her freshly plucked eyebrow, thank you. "Well, if it's not such a big deal, why don't you have coffee with him, and I'll stay home and watch MTV?"

"Because you're just too old for MTV."

"You're funny."

"You're freaked," he teased, bringing his plate to the sink before patting her shoulder on his way out of the kitchen.

Hell to the yeah. Connor's assessment was astute and far more mature than she was prepared for. "This is all new to me. I never dated much," she mumbled to herself.

"And that was the whole problem, Maxie," Mona said from the sink. "You went to the candy store and picked out the first pound of chocolate you laid eyes on instead of tasting a little from each batch before committing to one."

Maxine rose, bringing her plate to the sink, too. "Did you taste test every type of chocolate back in the day, Mom?"

Mona's lips tilted in a secretive smile. "I did my share of dating before I met your father and decided he was who rang my bell. I did a whole lot more'n you did, that's for sure."

"Dad was a great guy." Maxine fought the hitch in her voice. He'd been gone ten years now, but Robert Henderson had been the best of the best. How she'd missed seeing who he was instead of who he wasn't still haunted her today.

Her mother's hands stopped soaping dishes for a moment. "That he was. I wish he could have been here to give that husband of yours the walloping he deserves for doing what he's done. Bob would have wrapped his blue-collar pipe-fitter's hands around that fancy boy's white-collar neck and choked the money outta him. He never liked Finley."

Which was one of the very reasons Maxine had been so drawn to him in the first place. Because he was the exact opposite of her father. Flashy, showy, lavish. Her father, understated, quiet, loyal, was everything Finley would never be. He'd provided the essentials for his family without a qualm, but all of the frills Maxine once so loved as an immature young woman were frivolous to her dad.

She'd been conned into the shiny, never realizing it would end up so tarnished.

Maxine squeezed her mother's shoulders and planted a kiss on her cheek, inhaling the cloying scent of her perfume with relish. "I know he was disappointed in me, in my choice to marry Finley. I wish I could tell him how right he was and how sorry I am."

"He knew you loved him, Maxie. He just wanted what was best for you, and in your father's mind, that didn't mean a big house or fancy cars. It meant hard work, security, deep abiding love, honesty, pride . . . Most of all, it didn't mean Finley's love of your knockers. Your father was a simple man with simple needs. But he was so proud of you and all your beauty pageants. Worked a lot of overtime to see to it you had pretty dresses to compete in. You had a future. In his eyes, you were Miss America."

Yeah, and she'd given all that potential glory up to marry one of the judges who'd participated in her last pageant. "Somehow, Mom, I don't think Miss Riverbend Pizzaghetti qualified me for Miss America."

She soothed herself with self-deprecation often when she was reminded of where she was headed when she'd met Finley. Competing in more beauty pageants with the hope of winning a scholarship to a bigger college than community.

Her father was the one to protest the loudest when she'd become engaged to Finley. Eventually, he'd given his blessing, but it had been begrudging and with a warning that if his princess ever suffered a single moment's grief, he'd kill Finley.

Mona's glistening eyes found hers. "You know what I mean, girlie. No one knows how far you could have gone because you stopped competing and considering college when you met the Talleywhacker. Your father wanted the best of the best for you. He wanted you to be happy and fulfilled."

"Were you fulfilled, Mom?"

Her mother's wistful eyes returned to the sink with a slow nod of her head. "You bet I was. We had everything we needed. We might not have been dripping with diamonds, but the bills were always paid, we always had food on the table, and most of all, we laughed together. Nobody made me laugh like your father."

Maxine's throat convulsed, thick with regret. Yes. They'd laughed. With their daughter and together when they thought no one was watching. How all those critical elements in a loving, equal relationship could have escaped her in the husband-picking department left her bereft, with a wish to see her father one last time, to thank him for the wholesome goodness that was his way of life.

"I can't go back," she said, brushing a tear from her eyes. "But I'm really trying to go forward." Every day she was trying.

Mona dried her hands on the dishtowel, throwing it over her shoulder to cup Maxine's cheek. "Now don't go getting all weepy. You're right. Can't go back, honey. So we go forward. Your father'd be proud of how hard you're working to stand on your own two feet without so much as a dime. You have a second chance to be happy. Really happy. You're finally seeing that happiness can be about the little accomplishments, like the food you bought and put on the table yourself tonight. I know what that's like. Both your father and I wanted that for you, too. Maybe it's time to see what you can see beyond the snazzy."

What was happy? Was she happy to have finally found some air to breathe that wasn't owned by Finley? Yes. God, yes.

There'd been a time when she didn't think she could breathe without him, until she'd hit that wall eight months ago. When the stress of that dramatic flight to her mother's cleared, she'd discovered, even with the financial strain she was under, the pressure of keeping everything together for so long was gone. The relief her revelation brought was priceless.

Was she happy to be impoverished while she was breathing all that un-owned air? Not so much. Was she happy that she didn't get thing one about being on her own, or that if she didn't figure out just how to do that she'd fail her son? Not a lot. She was clinging to the edge of a very precariously crumbling ledge, and her fingers were aching and tired. But she could breathe. The rest would just have to figure itself out. "I'm not sure I understand the fulfilled happy thing, yet. But I'm going to try that, too."

"That's because you don't know what you missed while you were busy being someone's dress-up doll. But you're getting there. Speaking of getting there, I picked you up a little something." Reaching under the kitchen sink, her mother pulled out a Walmart bag and unceremoniously shoved it at her. "It's for your hot date. Go try it on," she encouraged in her usual gruff manner.

A peek inside revealed a light pink blouse with capped sleeves and small opalescent buttons. Maxine's throat clenched shut again.

This reminded her of the times when her mother would surprise her with rhinestones she'd stayed up all night to hand sew on one of her pageant dresses. Or another yard of material that was ghastly expensive to make a shawl to go with her evening-wear gown. "You shouldn't have done this, Mom. I could've worn—"

"Another one of my sweat suits? Even I have to admit, they're all wrong for you. Go try it on and see what it looks like with those jeans you have. I have some pearl earrings you can borrow that'll match those sharp buttons."

Her hands reached out for her mother, squeezing her to hide the tears of gratitude that welled in her eyes. Indeed. It really was the simple things. "Thanks, Mom."

Mona gave her a shove at the waist, waving a dismissive hand in the air. "Go or you'll be late."

With a sniff, Maxine made her way to the bathroom, stripping off the old cotton T-shirt that had once been her father's and slipping into the shell-pink shirt. For the first time in eight months—and in spite of the fact that this shirt was anything but the expensive clothing she'd once worn—she felt pretty.

Sort of.

It wasn't the pretty she'd once spent so much time perfecting. It wasn't the glamorous, bangle-braceleted, high-heeled, pound-of-lip-gloss pretty she'd become accustomed to.

Yet it was lighter. A much different species of pretty. A dialed-down-a-notch pretty. Like stripping away all that glitzy crap and finding the bare minimum had given her a tiny glimpse at who she was struggling to become. Someone who resided somewhere in the middle.

And it was okay. It was more than okay, Maxine thought, brushing her hair to let it fall to her shoulders minus the help of product and hairspray. The brown stripe creeping its way from her scalp to the middle of her head was gone thanks to some hair dye. Those glisten-ing highlights weren't half bad. She wasn't blonde anymore, but a warm shade of ash brown much closer to her natural-born color.

With a pause, she took a final, critical look at herself. A date. She was going on a date. Christ. What would they talk about?

She'd cancel. Call in not ready to take this walk out on a limb wobbly from the weight of her fears.

Maxine reached for the top of the toilet, gripping it to steady her-self as she sat down and took deep breaths, searching for perspective.

Okay, so what if it was awkward? She'd done awkward with a roomful of people as Finley's wife when he went off on a tangent or had too much to drink. So what if it didn't work out? It wasn't like she didn't know what that was like. They'd shake hands like adults and call it a night.

Good. Rising from the toilet, she resolved to take this for what it was. A cup of noncommittal coffee.

A dab of lipstick later and she flipped the light off in the bath-room, knocking on Connor's door before she popped it open. "You doing homework?"

Connor's head swiveled to meet her gaze from his place at the small desk Mona had purchased for him so he could keep up with his studies. "You look nice."

"Ya think? It's not exactly very glamorous."

"What's so special about glamorous?" he muttered from the side of his mouth, gnawing on the tip of his pencil.

Maxine ran a hand over his thick head of hair, pausing in wonder at the maturity his words showed. "You know what? I don't know anymore. Okay, so give me a kiss, buster. I'm going to go purge before Campbell gets here, and I want to be sure I have time to rinse my mouth with mouthwash. Purge breath would definitely mean any hope for date two is out."

Connor chuckled, giving her a quick kiss on the cheek. "Stop getting excited. It's just coffee. You said it yourself."

Yeah. Just coffee. "Get to bed on time, and if you need me, Campbell's cell number's on the fridge. I love you." She slipped out the door and took another breath before making her way to the kitchen to wait for Campbell.

She stopped in the living room, where her mother sat in front of the television, knitting and watching *CSI* reruns. Mona whistled. "You look good, kiddo."

"I want to puke."

"Don't do that. I just had the carpets cleaned."

"Why am I so nervous? I've never been nervous around a man a day in my life."

"Because he's a real man, Maxie. All the others, including Finley, were just fancy-boys. Real men make your stomach warble, and with any luck, those eyes of yours, too."

Maxine's eyes went wide. "You did not just say that to me."

"Yep. I sure did. Might do ya some good." She chuckled the words, her line of vision never leaving the television.

"We hardly know each other, Mom." How could this be the

same mother who'd warned her that if she got pregnant because she couldn't keep her underwear on, she'd lock her high atop a lonely hill in a remote castle with no doors or windows until she was a hundred?

"Sometimes you don't need to know anything other than he's all in working order. I'm pretty sure a stud like your Campbell's got everything required to get the job done."

Her face flushed. "Mom! Are you advocating one-night stands now? *Who are you?*"

"I'm advocating letting loose a little, Maxie. That husband of yours kept you too cloistered. He had all the control," she snorted. "Still does. So why not take some back?"

Maxine's eyes were wide, incredulous. "Take control by sleeping with Campbell?"

"Wow," a deep voice growled. "This is the best date I've ever not even gone on," Campbell quipped, passing by Maxine with a light hand to her hip to give Mona a quick kiss on the cheek.

Mona winked and swatted his arm. "She's a neurotic mess, Campbell. Wish I could be a fly on the wall."

"Don't you worry about a thing, Mona. I love neurotic messes. They're complex and challenging. Right up my alley."

"Good thing, because you're obligated to take my girl out and show her a good time. Now go. I don't want to miss that Horatio clenching his teeth while he's overacting."

Campbell turned to Maxine with a grin that made her knees begin to buckle and her breath halt. As first dates in over twenty years went, she'd hit the jackpot. Freshly shaven, wearing a pec-loving sky blue sweater and low-slung jeans that molded to his strong thighs, he made her mouth dry. And he had all of his hair. A big plus in the over-forty crowd. "Let's go," he said, holding out his hand to her.

No. Oh, shit. She wasn't ready. She was never going to be ready to date. This was ludicrous, a stupendously monumental error in judgment on her part.

Yet she forced herself to place her hand in his and found she relished the warmth of his callused palm and the way his fingers encouraged hers to curl around his.

The realization of the moment startled her.

The feel of Campbell's hand encompassing hers, a hand she'd moments ago been reluctant to give to him, now experienced a flickering ember of an emotion stemming from the category titled "safe."

Yes. That was it. Her hand in his represented safety, and hold on—she could still breathe. Giving her hand to him didn't mean, at least not at this moment, that she was handing over her soul.

What a crazy thought to have. How dramatic and over the top. That holding Campbell's hand somehow represented safety and the conclusion that he didn't want to own it or remind her who owned it or tell other people who owned it wasn't rational. They hardly knew each other.

Yet there it was. She felt it. Knew it like she knew her own shoe size.

Ah, but then there was something else that crept up out of the clear blue. It really was okay to go out and enjoy a cup of coffee without a fear in the world she'd have to come home to a brooding, sulking Finley.

A Finley who'd had a bad day and needed his ego stroked. A Finley who pulled all the strings and damned well knew it. A Finley who'd had his claws in her so deep, every second she spent away from home was spent anxiously waiting for the other shoe to drop.

All while she let guilt, totally self-imposed, eat at her chaotic mind filled to the brim with the potential chaos he could create if she wasn't there to stop it. The worry, the expectation of something to worry about in her marriage, was over.

Forever.

And she hadn't even realized that's how she'd been living until this very second.

So here she was.

Campbell noted her sluggish feet and turned to ask, "You okay?"

Yeah. *Yeah.* She was okay. Her smile was genuine when she gazed up into his blue eyes. "You know what? I think I am. Let's go have coffee."

And she meant it.

She, Maxine Cambridge, was going to have coffee and she was going to do it unfettered.

She was free.

Free.

Every muscle in her body relaxed, leaving her limbs almost buttery soft.

And by hell, she was *still* breathing.

CHAPTER NINE

Note from Maxine Cambridge to all ex-trophy wives: Freeeeedom! Remember the song by George Michael? C'mon—lemme hear ya sing, freeeeeedom! In your fight for survival, though you might be poor, do remember, you are a *free* woman. Celebrate by dancing naked. Or clothed when in public venues. Don't hamper your freedom with nasty fines and possible jail time. Although, three squares and fresh-air time from twelve-fifteen to one forty-five doesn't sound like it completely sucks . . .

Len turned off the small desk lamp and threaded her way through the boxes of champagne glasses that had arrived just ten minutes before she was due to pack in another long day. How she'd ever thought she could run her own business, virtually alone, now escaped her. There weren't enough hours in the day to soothe frazzled brides, handle every minute detail of a wedding, and still catch a couple of hours of sleep before she did it all over again.

But she was making headway, getting bigger weddings, nabbing pricier venues. It could happen if she could just keep it together long enough to create a reputation. She still had contacts from her old trophy-wife days, and she had no qualms about cashing them in.

A shadow by the entryway to her basement office startled her momentarily until Len recognized the large frame that went with it. *This* was not helping her keep it together. "Wow. For Finley's stoolie, you blow at inconspicuous."

"Then it's a good thing I'm not Finley's stoolie," he said, strolling into view, handsome, hard, confident.

Her snort, totally indelicate and rasping loud, filled the small, cluttered space. "Right." The urge to grab her mace should prevail, but unless her Spidey senses had gone askew, she didn't feel the least bit threatened. A notion she still didn't understand.

He leaned against the front of her particleboard desk, crossing his patent-leathered feet at the ankles. His steel gray suit, sky blue shirt, and navy blue tie immaculate. "If you'd kept your mace to yourself, you would have known that much about me."

Facing him, she crossed her arms over her chest, flashing purposefully defiant eyes. He had such an honest look about him, but behind his gorgeously lashed eyes there were secrets. They just didn't feel like they derived from the devious end of the spectrum.

Though, Adam's return only reminded Len she'd continually put off mentioning his sudden, rather suspicious appearance to Maxine. She battled with whether she should mention him at all. Lately, it was just plain too good to see her best friend finally make an effort to pull herself up out of the hole she'd wallowed in to spoil it with the thought that Finley might have hired someone to spy on her.

She wasn't even sure if Adam had anything to do with Finley anyway. He'd never said one way or the other. She'd been the one doing all the accusing that night.

Len had left that meeting with him in the retirement village parking lot wholly unsure if his intentions were devious. Yet guilt now gnawed at her gut. She'd call Maxine the moment she left her office and ask her if she knew an Adam Baylor. Until then, she'd get rid of Mr. Schmexy. "I don't want to know about you, especially if you have anything to do with Finley Cambridge."

His eyebrow cocked upward on an otherwise unperturbed face. A nice face. Too nice. "I have nothing to do with Finley Cambridge."

"Then how about you tell me what you want and go away when you're done."

The firm line of his lips tilted upward in a sensual smile. "I want you."

Those words, seductive, delicious as they slipped from his mouth, sent a hot wave of heat to the place between her thighs. And she had to fight not to stumble on her next words. She kept her face impassive, though her heartbeat clanged in her ears. "That's unfortunate. I'm not available for the wanting." She waved a dismissive finger in the direction of the doorway.

This time his eyebrow rose with a pinch of arrogance, but his lips curved. "What if I told you I never take no for an answer?"

Len's fingers reached into the pocket of her baggy dress, cinched at the waist with a thick, black belt, and dug for her cell phone. "What if I told you I don't care what you want and you'd better go somewhere or I'm calling the police?"

Damn. She was incredible when she was all worked up. The sharp angle of her defiant jaw tilted upward just enough so he could catch a glimpse of the long column of her creamy throat. Dark eyes shone bright with fiery independence and ultra-empowered woman. His quick gaze assessed her small breasts and the lacy bra she wore beneath her low-cut dress. A lacy bra he wanted to tear off with his teeth before dragging his tongue over a pert nipple.

Definitely easy on the eye.

Not so easy on the unmentionables. A fact he was trying to keep to himself by jamming his hands into the pockets of his trousers. This unexpected reaction to her was exactly what had brought him back here. To pursue an answer. To dissect the strong current of electricity that had no rhyme or reason after such a short amount of time doing nothing more than following her like some sick pervert. Which he wasn't, but he had ducks to line up in a row, precautions to take before he revealed anything more to this stunning, easily excited creature. "Why don't we start over?"

Her dark eyebrow slanted, her suspicion clearly ratcheting up a notch. "Start what over?"

Adam Baylor's eyes swept upward, beginning at Lenore's slender ankles and ending with her deep, dark eyes now cloudy with cynicism. "Our acquaintance, so to speak."

Those beautiful, full lips, cherry red today, curled inward. "I can't see a single reason why we need to be acquainted."

Feisty. Mmm-mmm good. Adam pulled his hand out of his pocket, rounding on her if only to take another whiff of the musky perfume she wore. His lips grazed the shell of her ear, and he took note of her visible shiver and the goose bumps lining her arms. A shiver he recognized for what it was, and it had nothing to do with fear. "Meet me at Wendt's for a drink, and we'll see if I can't change your mind about that. If you're not there within the hour, you'll never see me again."

He noted her outraged gasp and the heavy clunk of something Adam figured she wanted to nail him in the back with but had decided against by letting it drop to her desk.

He forced his chuckle to a muffle by placing a fist over his mouth. Hot.

Lenore Erickson virtually smoked.

Maxine climbed into the passenger side of Campbell's old truck, giving it a covert once-over. She hoisted herself inside to navigate a place to sit on the battered red leather seat.

His lean hand grabbed the box of plumbing supplies and hurled them carelessly into the back. Campbell patted the area now cleared of debris, smoothing a tear in the leather. "Not exactly the sweetest thing you've ever put your seat in, huh?"

She wasn't sure if he was poking fun at her for once having the luxury of driving the cream of the crop in automobiles or if he was embarrassed by the condition of his truck. Which wasn't exactly state of the art, judging from the hard jolt and the swoop the chassis took with a lurching creak when they rolled over a speed bump at no more than four miles an hour.

Yet the use it had clearly seen over the years was comfortable. The kind of truck you could roll down the window and throw your bare feet up on the dashboard in while you ate an ice cream cone on a hot summer's day.

Her eyes found her hands, folded primly in her lap, her earlier internal war cry of freedom and all its supposed bennies now but a mere whisper. The metaphoric fist in her head was still raised to the sky, it was just waving in the air with a whole lot less vigor. Instead, she'd begun to veer more toward plain freaked out that she was on a date.

A date. "I like the color of the seats," she offered in a weak attempt to thwart the possible jab at her ex-lifestyle.

"I swear on a Cluck-Cluck Palace combo with curly fries, my other car's a Ferrari."

That made her laugh with a hollow chuckle, no longer as much bitter as it was disgusted with the ridiculousness of a housewife with a Ferrari. "Ironically, so was mine. A Spyder, I think, or some creepy, crawly name like that." She couldn't even remember anymore. More to the point, she didn't care to remember.

He whistled his approval, his full mouth pursing deliciously. "Niiice. Mine's a 308."

Right. Not that the numbers meant anything to her anyway, but right. "So where are we going for coffee?"

"It's a surprise."

Along with her loss of confidence came a hesitant niggle. There was no love lost between her and surprises. She'd had enough surprises for one lifetime. *Surprise—your best friend's sister's sleeping with your husband!* Call her a cling-on for making the comparison between that horrible event and anything Campbell might have to offer, but it was a mind-set she hadn't been able to shake even while she was doing all this growing.

Peace was what she sought, without any invasive ripples. Her silence provoked an insightful response from him, leaving her uncomfortable at how attuned he was to her rather bizarre emotional pendulum. "Not a fan of surprises?"

"I've had a few in these past months and they didn't always have a happy attached to them. I'm sorry. It was just a stupid gut reaction that has nothing to do with you."

And everything to do with the fact that I should absolutely not be dating because I'm a melodramatic, emotional candidate for a therapeutic couch, she wanted to add. Closing her eyes, Maxine analyzed this new territory and decided she was clearly having a ridiculous response to this new attack of nerves.

Campbell stretched his arms out ramrod straight, gripping the steering wheel with an insolent grin. "Promise. No bad surprises, but it stays a surprise."

And somehow, just his word soothed her. Not to mention, her insides became molten mush when he grinned like that after making a statement so clearly meant to let her know he was in charge. *Lighten up, Maxine. This isn't about control. It's coffee, surprise location or not.*

Silence, not uncomfortable or in need of filling up with words, prevailed in the truck. The radio hummed a station low, and if she was hearing correctly, a little Harry Connick Jr. Leaning forward, the tangle of knots in her stomach loosening, she touched the radio's dial. "Do you mind if I turn it up a little?"

Campbell's eyes turned to meet hers with a smile in them. "Not at all. You like Harry Connick?"

Her nod was enthusiastic when she met his smile. "I do. I love Connick, Bennett, Sinatra, Nat King Cole. Oh, and most anything from the Rat Pack era. I was raised on Glen Miller and the Lennon Sisters, Tommy Dorsey, Lawrence Welk. I know it sounds corny, but it's comfort music for me—" She stopped short, curtailing her ramble by biting her wagging tongue.

Campbell barked a laugh, revealing the brown column of his throat, hard with sinew. A place a girl could nuzzle her nose against while watching a DVD or . . .

"Remember all those bubbles they blew around after Lawrence's show?" he asked. "My parents were big fans, too."

"I remember living to see what dresses the dancers would wear. I loved how they puffed out when they twirled. I used to beg my mom to let me stay up and watch for that very reason." The memory warmed her. Her on the floor with her pillow, and her mother and father on the couch in front of their big console TV.

"I'd have never guessed," he teased.

She rolled her eyes with a snort at his presumption. "Okay. So I like a little frilly. What's the harm in that?"

Pulling to a stop in a small clearing overlooking the woods she'd once hung out in as a teenager, Campbell turned in his seat, giving her that direct gaze with a glimmer of twinkle in it she suspected was meant to humor her. "There's absolutely nothing wrong with that. I like that you like frilly things. All girlie-girls do."

Instantly, her eyes fell to her lap again; she was thankful for the music filtering through the truck's interior to serve as a muffler for her sudden intake of breath. A tear stung her eye. She wasn't exactly looking or feeling very girlie. The upward climb her self-esteem had begun in her mother's bathroom took a ridiculous, sudden downward dive. "Have I mentioned how good I am at the touchy emotions lately?" she teased.

Campbell's fingers scraped the underside of her chin, tilting her jaw upward. "Hey, I wasn't picking on you. I really do like girlie-girls. I appreciate a woman who appreciates being a woman."

The sincerity of his tone, and that granite-hard blue gaze, softened only by the laugh lines around his eyes, made her smile. "I'm sorry. I get stupid sometimes for no other reason than just to get stupid. I have all these new triggers that spout off out of the blue, and they make no sense to anyone but me."

His fingers curled around her chin, and using his thumb, Campbell caressed the spot just beneath her lower lip, making it warm and trembly. "That's because you're changing. You've had a helluva ride these last months, I suspect. To be where you were and end up where you are was like culture shock, I'm sure."

Campbell's words made her bristle. "I ended up just fine." Fine had levels. She was still at level two, but whatever. She'd be ticking off levels in no time with all the hair rolling and poop scooping she was doing. She'd made two hundred bucks last week, working from sunup till sundown. So, yeah. She was just fine.

"Ah," he clucked. "Now you're taking offense where there was none to be had. What I mean is, you were married and financially secure. Now you're single and not so financially secure."

Oh. There was that. Wow. *Sensitive much, Maxine?* Blowing out a pent-up breath, she smiled in another apology. "Again, I'm discovering new ways to define sensitive and over-the-top dramatic."

"You're definitely giving them new meaning. But no worries. I get it."

He did not either get it. "You *get* me taking offense to an imagined hint that I'm a shadow of my former self? How could *you* possibly get it?"

"No. I get being over-the-top sensitive about a subject that's become a focus in your life—a sore spot, if you will. It gets blown out of proportion and you become hypersensitive. It'll pass."

Perspective. He had it. In spades. Again, Campbell's words brought the big picture front and center, making her ask her next impulsive question. She found she had to know if he was thinking what everyone in the village was. That she'd married Finley for his money and now she was getting what she deserved.

If so, end date.

And that'd be damned convenient, wouldn't it, Maxine? Then you could skip right over the part where you're supposed to start taking chances and experiencing new things. There isn't a chance in the world for awkward or anything else if you don't stick around long enough to find out.

Maxine placed a hand on his arm, savoring the crisp hairs sprinkled over it. "Can I ask you something? I mean, before this date, or whatever we're calling it, goes any further."

"It'd make me feel all warm on the inside." He used his index finger to make a circle around his hard belly, evoking a shiver from her she had to fight to keep from becoming visible.

"Do you think that I only married Finley for his money? Or just because my husband was rich, I was self-absorbed and selfish? You know, the typical ex-trophy wife stigma? That because my life was pretty damned cushy, I was a snob? Do you think because I once had a maid I can't clean a toilet on my own? I mean, in the interest of honesty and all. And you can tell me the truth. I can take it."

Campbell's pause made her stomach flop. His pensive gaze made her clutch her hands back together again. Shit. It was bound to happen. Everyone else thought simply because she'd married an older man, what she'd really wanted was to sit on her ass surrounded by silk and Dom until he kicked the bucket.

She'd lived with that for a long time with many of Finley's colleagues, employees, and friends due to the fact that she'd been so young when she married him. When she'd left him and moved to the village, she'd heard the gossip about her supposed gold digging getting what it deserved. So why wouldn't Campbell think that, too? She just hadn't realized how disappointed it would make her to hear it. Maxine winced in preparation.

But Campbell placed his big hand over her clenched fingers. "Nope. I think you just never went outside your circle. Never stepped outside the box because it was safer inside. But I think now that someone's stolen your box, you're seeing they come in lots of different sizes, and you're looking to find the right one to pack yourself back up in. You're just trying them on for size."

This sounded much like the candy store reference her mother had made earlier. Another thought to make note of. Campbell was very astute and understanding. Either he was a helluva player, or he innately had an understanding many men wouldn't. "You have no idea what I'd do for a box to call my own."

His chuckle was rich. "Oh, I can imagine. Remember, I live with my dad now, too."

"But that's by choice—to help him out. My situation's much different. I can't choose to not live in my mother's box because as broke as I am, my new residence really will be a box instead of just a metaphoric one. You have job skills. I have ex-wife skills. There's a big difference." So big.

He let his hand drop from her now relaxed fingers, twisting his body to lean back against the window. "I dunno. You seem to be using some of those ex-wife skills to your advantage."

Really? Campbell's complimentary words made her preen. Just a little. "Explain that, would you? How does my ability to match the curtains to a couch equate skills that'll translate to a real job with real money?"

"You're pretty good with people. You definitely took on that crowd of skeptical grouches at bingo like a pro. The seniors loved you."

"Before or after Mrs. Griswald nailed me in the schnoz?" She rubbed her nose for emphasis, still sore and bruised from the night before.

His laughter filled the space between them, revealing his perfectly straight teeth, and easing the coil of tension in her belly once more. "You had them in the palm of your hand before that. Now I think they want to form a gang and call Mrs. Griswald out on your behalf with lead pipes and heavy rocks."

Maxine cringed. Mrs. Griswald was informed she couldn't return to bingo for a month as a cooling-off period. "I don't want them to shun her. Just take away her weapons of mass destruction."

"The point here is working with the elderly as well as you do is a marketable skill. You're really patient, Max. You're always kind even when I know you want to tear your hair out follicle by follicle because you've repeated yourself over and over to Mr. Kowalski when he forgets to put in his hearing aid. You're more than just a pretty face, Max Henderson. You have plenty going on. You just have to figure out what to do with it in the real world."

Yeah. Good thing, too, because her pretty face was rapidly taking a nosedive toward Tampa. Yet, without warning, that was okay. Her shoulders lifted in a sigh that rang forlorn. "I've decided I don't like the real world."

"You liked the fake, plastic one you lived in better?"

Maxine thought before she became excited, and sensed he was teasing her. She decided to take no offense when she replied, "I liked the plastic money to pay the not-so-fake bills."

Campbell turned off the ignition and gave the dashboard a slap of his hand. "Well, not so rich anymore girl, why don't we see if we can take your mind off your troubles for a little while?"

"With coffee?"

He slid out of the truck and leaned back in on the steering wheel with another smile. "Nah. Something much better."

Maxine gripped the door handle with white knuckles. "But you said we were having coffee." How did you have coffee in the woods? Just because everyone liked Campbell didn't mean he wasn't a rapist— or . . . Oh. God.

"And we will," Campbell replied, reaching under the driver's seat and producing a silver and black thermos. "But not before we do something else. So stop gripping the handle on the door like I'm Charlie Manson and c'mon, Chicken Little." He shut the door, walking around to her side of the truck, popping the door open.

Again, as though Campbell knew holding his hand out was offering her the chance to take another step deeper into this mysterious dating pool, he wiggled his fingers at her.

Maxine gazed up at him, shimmying out onto the hard ground, unable to avoid the brush of their thighs when she clasped his hand. "I just want you to remember, if you have serial killer thoughts about me, I wouldn't want to be you if my mother gets her hands on you. She does have that big purse that looks like a Samsonite and feels like she has a ton of bricks in it. She'd render you brain dead in twenty flat."

Campbell's free hand chucked her under the chin. "I've no doubt she can take me."

"Just so we're clear."

"Crystal. Now get it in gear or it's going to be dark and you'll miss my most excellent surprise." With a tug, he was pulling her down a small slope of dirt and fallen leaves and into a clearing with a big shed.

A shed that could probably house a body—or ten.

And no one within screaming distance for at least three miles.

Eek.

CHAPTER TEN

Note from Maxine Cambridge to all ex-trophy wives: When approaching your first date in eons of datelessness, do yourself a solid, put a kibosh on the bitter and overly sensitive crap, okay? You'll never get another date that way, and even if you don't really want one right now, trust me, your desperate libido will come calling with thunderous fists to knock at your hormonal door. Won't you be sorry you hung on to your baggage then? Instead, love yourself enough to leave all excess baggage not directly related to your date on your layover in Boise.

Max clung to Campbell with a giggle of nervous excitement, leaving him feeling ridiculously manly-man. "I've never done this before," she said in his ear.

"Just keep your arms around me. I promise to keep going slow," he reassured her over his shoulder, revving the engine again with a twist of his wrist. Her eyes, wide and green, gleamed back from behind the clear plastic visor of her helmet. A lot like the old Max's once had during a particularly good football game or when she finally understood a concept in chemistry.

If she knew how often he'd pondered those eyes back in high school, alluring with a smoky hint of amber to them, she'd get off this bike right now and never look back. It was probably better she didn't know what he'd thought back in chemistry class at Riverbend High.

Her perfume wafted to his nostrils when they took another slow turn around the track he'd spent so long perfecting. The delicate press of her breasts against his back, the way she fought not to lean into him when they took a corner, all intrigued him.

His father had warned him just before he'd left to pick up Max to take things slow. She was in a fragile state of mind, Garner'd said.

Fragile didn't quite cover where Max was at, and once more, he found himself doubting whether he should go in guns blazing.

But what was life without a blazing gun?

You only went round once. It was a fact that had stared him in the face, vivid and ugly, not too long ago. There'd be no holding back anymore, but after her overreaction to his comment about where she was in her life, Campbell realized maybe he could rein it in for the sake of the long haul.

Max was skittish, unsure, and clearly very vulnerable. All major no-nos when in pursuit of one's wildest passion. Realistically, now that he was back on his feet and in the game, he should be looking for grounded and stable.

Max Henderson had caught him by surprise with her self-deprecating sense of how she thought she appeared, who she really was. She was neither grounded nor stable.

But he liked.

Despite all the warning signs, he still wanted in. Maybe it was the challenge she presented because she was at a point in her life when the pieces needed picking back up, and he identified with that. He knew what the end of a marriage felt like. Though his circumstances had been different than Max's, the end of his marriage to Linda had left him raw and grudging for some time.

Though that sort of understanding was common among the divorced, it didn't explain the return of the tightness in his chest each and every time he saw Maxine.

It didn't explain the desire to protect her from that asshole Finley by way of fist and bones shattering with a satisfying crunch when he punched the shithead in the mouth for being such a dog. Neither did it explain the peculiar sense of coming home he'd felt when she'd finally placed her hand in his. There'd been trust in that gesture— one he didn't want to break. One he also didn't understand.

What needed doing now was to explore this without scaring her off.

So, whoa, Barker, he chided when they came to a stop right back where they'd begun. A swing of his leg later and he was helping Max off the back of his dirt bike.

Her smile from behind the helmet kinked his gut. Max pulled the helmet off, shaking her hair out, the scent of her shampoo, maybe something peachy, drifting on the warm breeze. He liked the new color she'd dyed it. It made her eyes greener, and gave him a little pat on the old ego that she hadn't dyed it until just now. He allowed himself a little smug and assumed she'd done it in honor of their date.

"That was pretty great," Max said on a laugh, which if he wasn't totally clueless, held a hint of carefree.

Good. He wanted her to forget she was broke. Forget she was in the middle of a divorce. Forget the worry he saw lining her eyes when she spoke of Connor, and just enjoy. His smile was Cheshire. "Yeah. I think so. Let's go have that coffee. It should still be warm." They pushed the bike back to the shed, rolling it in and stacking the helmets. He pulled the door shut, clicking the padlock back in place.

Campbell's hand automatically went to her waist to guide her back along the stone-littered path to the very cluster of rocks where he and his high school band buddies used to drink beer they'd snuck from Andy Randall's dad's basement fridge. The swell of her hip against his hand, the indentation where it met her waist, gave him an unfamiliar jolt, almost making him stop in his tracks.

Max swung around and pointed to the smooth rocks under a cluster of pine trees. "Here?" she said with a frown he wasn't sure held distaste or uncertainty.

"I know it's not exactly Tavern on the Green, but I couldn't convince them to boot a paying customer's reservation for little old me. Not even when I threw your name around," he teased.

Her creamy cheeks flushed a pretty red. Those hands went right back to fidgeting. "I wasn't—I mean—I—"

Campbell climbed onto a rock, giving her a tug. "I was joking." He watched her chest rise and fall, heaving a breath.

"Sorry. The ridiculously sensitive thing again." Pulling her legs up to her chin, she wrapped her arms around them in protective mode.

"Coffee'll rid you of all sensitivity. Especially mine. It might rid you of your taste buds and put hair on your chest, too." He splashed the thick, dark liquid into the thermos's cap, handing it to her before taking a swig.

Max waved a dismissive hand. "That's okay. I like it strong, and who couldn't use a little hair on their chest. It's just one more place to shave and adds to my list of fun things that happen to your body when you're pushing forty-one." And then she was blushing again, putting a hand over her mouth with a grin. "I just don't know when to can it. As an FYI, when I'm nervous, I ramble."

There was something to be said for Max and all this blushing. This time, the crimson crept down along her neck to the prim opening of her shirt, encasing her full breasts. Nice. "Do I make you nervous?" he asked, stretching out his legs and crossing his feet at the ankles. He didn't feel nervous at all. Just relaxed. At ease. Totally.

"I guess it's not you as much as this . . ." She spread her arms.

"This?"

"Yes. You know, the dating thing. I haven't been on one in a long time."

"I get it."

"I find it strangely curious how much you get."

Campbell guarded his next words. Despite all the sharing he hoped she'd do, he wasn't ready to return the favor yet. "I get what it is to go out on a date after a long cooling-off period."

Hypocrite, a voice in his head mumbled.

The bob of her head was of complete understanding. "I'm not afraid to admit I almost backed out on you. There was a moment or two earlier when I thought me and my mother's toilet were more likely to have a date than me and you." She grinned that infectious grin, dimples and all, over the rim of the thermos cup.

Honesty was always okay by him. "I'm way more fun than a toilet, but I can see how a big, strapping guy like me might intimidate a woman."

Increment by increment, Max was relaxing, too. It showed in the way she let her legs unfold, the ease in her tight jaw. A jaw he was fighting hard not to nip. The breeze, humid and cloying, lifted her hair from the nape of her neck, giving him an enticing peek of her moist skin. Laughter, easy and light, trickled to his ears as she let her head fall back on her shoulders and took a deep breath of the humid air.

Her shy eyes fell to the thermos cup when she put it to her lips, lips Campbell couldn't take his eyes off. A drop of liquid lingered at the edge of her mouth, and his thumb went automatically to wipe it away, savoring the plump feel of it against his skin.

It was her sigh, lilting, breathy, that did him in. Cupping the back of her head, he took the thermos's cup from her trembling fingers and set it aside, pulling her close. When she didn't resist, neither did he. Forgetting his earlier hesitation, Campbell inhaled her scent, pressing his lips to the shell of her ear.

Max's shiver encouraged him to continue, passing his lips in small nibbles over the silken flesh of her throat. Still, she said nothing. She made no loud protests, she didn't even squirm, but the enticing way she melted into his body left his jeans far too tight, and restraint became an effort.

The picture she presented, her eyes closed, her hands on his shoulders with a light press of her palms was making him crazy. In an effort to keep from frightening her, Campbell made a quick decision. "Max?"

"Campbell?" She shuddered as she said his name.

"I'm going to kiss you. Any objections?"

~ℓ~

How could she object when he was doing that delicious thing to her neck with his yummy lips? Maxine was no longer at one of her old high school hangouts, but a newfound utopia where Campbell's lips weren't just a memory she relived against her pillow every night. She was all Siskel and Ebert two thumbs up for the real thing. "Not at the moment." That was true. Her earlier fears were slip-sliding away in the sensual path Campbell was taking along her jaw, moving with an agonizing pace toward her mouth.

"Then prepare for the best kiss of your life," he said against her lips.

Maxine heard the teasing tone in his voice, but there was no joking when he placed his mouth on hers, drawing her tighter to him by curling his arm around her waist. A wisp of a moan fluttered from her throat as his tongue slipped along her lower lip, drifting across the flesh with a single stroke.

Campbell moaned, too, low and husky, when her arms went up around his neck, curling into his thick hair. His lean into her, pushing her downward as his mouth took full possession of hers, left her glad they were sitting down. The very idea that his body, long, hard, and so muscled, could be flush to hers had her almost gasping with anticipation.

When the moment came, more than a few of her sleeping hormones cried uncle. Nay, they screamed from the endless pleasure Campbell's body tightly fit to hers brought. The ridge of his cock, hard against her thigh, pulsed, making her want to writhe against it.

There was no way to prepare for the kind of need he created deep in her belly. The space between her thighs grew wet, achy while his tongue dipped in and out of her mouth. She drew him closer, not quite conscious that his lips had left her mouth and were now traveling down to the pearl buttons of her shirt. Her breasts ached in anticipation of that hot tongue licking her tight nipple when he captured a button between his lips and popped it open, leaving the tops of her breasts exposed underneath her lacy bra.

Maxine struggled to get closer, to absorb the shivers of delight he gave her when he cupped her ass and drew her leg high around his waist. The clop of her sandal against the rock didn't distract her at all. Campbell's hand at her breast, kneading it through her bra, did. A nipple slipped free of its confinement and he took it in his mouth, tugging sharply on it.

Her eyes clenched shut, her teeth ground together, the heat of his mouth was so pleasurable. Her head fell back on his forearm as she arched into the wet, hot cavern, gripping his shirt for all it was worth from the dizzy need spiraling out of control.

Campbell's hips ground against hers, the strain of the bulge at his zipper a delicious friction against the most intimate place on her body. The pop of the button on her jeans was almost an afterthought when she allowed her hazy, lust-filled mind to dwell on it.

Her heart raced right along with her brain. The fear of such an intimate encounter warred with the unbelievable desire to find satisfaction. When Campbell placed a hot palm against her belly, sliding down inside her jeans, nothing else mattered but his finger, nudging her clit, swollen and needy.

He stroked her, spreading her swollen lips, his mouth never leaving her breast, drawing her closer to fulfillment. White-hot lightning crackled along every nerve ending she owned, raw and waiting. Maxine's breathing was choppy, ragged as she strained against his hand when he cupped her, slipping through the tangle of curls between her thighs, dragging his finger back and forth over her clit in delicious passes.

Shudders wracked her when she arched against him while she climbed higher, driven by the skill of his hand.

The small explosion she'd always related to climax was so much different with Campbell. It wasn't small, and it was more like several bombs were detonated in her aching body. Relief was a crash of her hips against his hand, the buck of them a rapid gyration as she clung to him, almost begging him to never stop touching her.

She came hard and with a mewl of contentment that would have been a scream if her teeth weren't clenched together. The wave after wave of sizzling hot flashes of electricity pulsing through her pulled a final gasp from her throat.

Boneless, she sank into him, fighting for oxygen, sweat beading her forehead.

That was also the moment reality sank in, too.

Oh, God. What had she done?

You flailed around on some rocks with a gorgeous man who gave you more than one orgasm, honey. That's what you done.

Humiliation had become the cornerstone of her life, a basis for which to flog herself regularly. Why should her first almost-divorced orgasm, make that two and a half, be any different?

Bracketing her face with his hands, Campbell forced her to look at him. "Don't freak out, Max."

She let her eyes drift over his shoulder. Was he kidding? "I don't know that I'll be able to help it. I just . . . we just . . ."

His grin was lopsided and teasing. "Yeah, we did. Or more specifically, you did."

More heat shot to her cheeks. Not only had she behaved like she hadn't had sex in over a year—okay, so she hadn't—but Campbell had derived not one ounce of pleasure from it. Yet, what should she say now that the mood had gone all awkward? *Want me to return the favor?*

"Stop," he murmured an order against her flushed cheek, planting a kiss there.

"But—"

"No buts. I know you're embarrassed. Don't be."

"You're joking."

"Not even a little." He lifted himself enough to button her shirt for her. "No regrets for me." With a quick hand, he zipped her pants up, too, smoothing the material of her shirt down over the waistband. "And don't go where you're going in your head. First of all, it's a little too soon for you to commit to that level of intimacy. And trust me when I tell you, Campbell Barker wines and dines his ladies right—"

"Ladies?" she croaked.

He smiled, his blue eyes dancing. "It was a joke. *When* I make love to you, it won't be on some rocks in the woods. Second, I don't have a condom. Third, I got carried away. You're pretty hot, Max Henderson," he said with another teasing grin. "Here." He grabbed her hand and pulled her to a sitting position, smoothing a finger over her dazed expression with the smile still curving his lips. "Catch your breath, but while you do it, don't you dare be embarrassed. It's not allowed. Just relax and we'll talk some more."

It took a moment for her to adjust to Campbell's attitude. First of all, he didn't appear at all disgruntled that he'd gained nothing from her but a backache.

Second of all, to put it tactfully, when Finley didn't get what he thought he deserved from their lovemaking, he'd certainly never said it was okay. And their afterglow damned well didn't include him wanting to talk. In fact, their scheduled Saturday night lovemaking had always ended with Finley, remote in hand, watching TV.

That Campbell didn't want to throw her in his truck as fast as his legs could carry all one hundred and fifty pounds of her left her astounded.

———— ℒ ————

Maxine was avoiding his eyes at all costs. Her embarrassment would be pretty damned cute if he wasn't fully aware he'd jumped the gun. If she hadn't stopped, he would have, only because he knew their time would come. Though he'd meant what he'd said. He wanted to make love to her in a place she felt safe.

He wanted Max to come to him willingly—on her terms. Now what he hoped to accomplish was simple: soothe her obvious guilt. All of it. The guilt she was nurturing because she felt selfishly indulged. The guilt she felt because she so clearly didn't do things like this often—if ever.

Sitting shoulder to shoulder, Campbell nudged her. "So did you come here a lot in high school?"

The nod of her head was quick, though her eyes stayed on her feet. "Didn't everybody? Did you used to come here in high school, too?"

"Yep. We did a lot of underage beer drinking here back in the day."

"I can't believe I never ran into you."

He winked. "I think our social circles were separated by titles like 'popular cheerleaders' and 'band geeks.'"

Max waved him off. "Please. I bet you have no idea who my friends were in high school."

Oh, he'd beg to differ. There wasn't a whole lot he didn't know about Max, but revealing that just yet might be a date ender—so he backed off. "Either way, I think fate was holding off so we'd wait to meet under the right circumstances. You know, when I was hotter and you were in the middle of a nasty divorce."

Completely missing his joke, those pretty green eyes of hers rolled upward, and her berry-glossed lips popped. "I'm not a big believer in fate."

"Really?"

"Really."

"That's so final. Seems to me a girl like you would believe in all that gushy romantic stuff."

"I'm not a girl anymore," Max made a point of reminding him. "And I'm so over the gushy romantic part of fantasies in my life."

Campbell clucked his tongue. Bitter he got. Bitter he'd tasted. Bitter was another step toward healing. He hoped she hurried up and took that next step. "That's too bad."

Max's hand went to her chin, cupping it. No longer embarrassed, her eyes said she had a burr in her saddle. Campbell understood that. If she could focus on something to pick a fight about, it took the focus off her self-flagellation. "I don't think it's bad at all. I think it's realistic."

That's what all bitter people said. "Reality can have some gushy romances," he insisted with a lighthearted grin, fighting to turn her sour expression around.

"That end in messy divorces," she confirmed. "Just ask me."

All righty. They were veering off in a direction he hadn't planned on. They'd already done that once tonight, but she was making it difficult to get back on track.

Yet, she was right. He couldn't argue. He wouldn't even try. Okay, maybe he'd try. "Sometimes they do," Campbell offered, petulance purposefully leaking into his tone. Someone had to defend happily ever after even if it was him—a semi-Neanderthal.

Resistance showed in the sudden stiffening of her posture. "I guess so" was her dismissive response as she stared into the rapid fall of night, still avoiding his eyes. Eyes that willed Max to look at him and *believe*.

Something that clearly wasn't on tonight's agenda.

Silence drew out between them with nothing but the sound of their breathing. Max was shutting down again. Her snippiness was a combination of her unsettling thoughts about what had happened between them, and a reminder to him that crushed dreams left you cynical.

The sun set in all its purple and red-hot glory. With it set his resignation. Tonight wasn't ending quite the way he'd daydreamed it would on his lunch break over a pastrami on rye.

Shit.

Way to keep it light, Barker.

~ ℓ ~

The drive back in the truck was quiet. Maxine was lost in her stupidity for throwing herself at Campbell like a sex-starved vixen and stomping all over an otherwise perfectly fine date by spewing her cynical view on relationships.

Though, it was honest. These days, she'd decided, for all future encounters, male or female, she and honesty were going to skip together through fields of wildflowers. Hand in hand. If she sounded just a little jaded about love and all its rocking horses and rainbows, forgive her. She *was* experiencing a major slump in her life.

Uh-huh, and while you slump, you're latching on to your baggage like it's a life raft. Go on and cling if you want your future to be riddled with whiny.

Campbell pulled his battered truck to a stop in her mother's driveway, leaving the engine rumbling and dimming the lights. "So how long do you suppose you'll hang on to your grudge against romance and the general benefits it reaps? What horrors do you suppose could befall you if you just let go and stopped clinging to your baggage?"

Part of her sudden rush of fury had to do with the fact that she was still feeling raw and exposed from their encounter. Some of her anger was because he'd pressed a hot button about her baggage. But a mere hour ago, she'd mentally agreed—she was clinging. Twenty years was a long time to let go of rote reactions, hurt, lies. Not to mention habits, routines, bizarre behaviors only a man and wife can create in an emotionally manipulative relationship.

But so what? She had a right to them. They were hers. Like small reminder trophies of where she'd been.

The other half of her, the half that hated disruption and conflict, felt like she'd just hurled an innocent puppy from a cliff for having the audacity to believe in something good—something everyone seemed to want. Something everyone joined eHarmony for.

Those were all good things to want. Respectable even. But did anyone ever really find it? Or did they just settle? Did they talk themselves into believing what they were stuck in had turned out to be exactly what they wanted all along?

Unfortunately, the shitty, cynical side of her decided it wanted to come out and play.

Maxine turned to face him, the lights of the dashboard making his handsome face far too appealing for the angry rant she was about to unload on him. Yet she had a need to hurt him for making her feel things she wasn't ready to feel, to strike out and protect her vulnerability by creating discord.

Crossing her arms over her chest, her posture became defensive. "What do you know about an ugly divorce and the kind of baggage that leaves you with? You have a whole lot of presumptions going on, don't you? But I'm here to tell you, you have no idea what it's like to be dumped like so much trash and left with nothing but the clothes on your back, Campbell Barker! So you can just keep your analysis of where me and my baggage are to yourself!"

With a yank, she threw open the creaky passenger door and plowed to the ground with a slap of sandals on blacktop. Maxine stuck her head back in for one last parting shot. "Oh, and thanks for the coffee. It was a little too wimpy for my tastes, but the effort's appreciated."

A slam of the truck door later and she was stomping into her mother's, shutting out Campbell and his assumptions with a final shove. Flopping back against the door, inside the dark interior of the kitchen, she huffed a sigh of utter aggravation before hurling her purse at the countertop.

No more dates. Definitely no more dates with men who wanted her to leave her baggage behind. Her baggage was what was going to make her stronger, tougher, smarter, if there was ever a next time round. Hanging on to it for just a little longer would serve as a not-so-subtle reminder that she was never going back to being owned by anyone again, but it also reminded her soul mates and soap opera romances were all bullshit.

Oh, and fuck fate.

Fate was for dreamers.

Something she most certainly was not.

⌒℮⌒

Campbell flung open the door to his father's with a little too much emphasis on "fling." He had to grab it to keep it from slamming against the wall and waking his dad.

A light flicked on by Garner's favorite recliner. "I see you went all half-cocked and put your pedal to the metal." He shook a finger. "I warned ya, kiddo," he said on a hearty chuckle.

Campbell ran a hand through his hair then let it drift to his tired eyes to give them a rub. "You did. I blew it."

Garner's head bobbed under the lamplight. "So I guess there was no smooch good night for you, eh, pal?"

His snort was derisive. He'd just as soon kiss those lips again as he would kiss an open, pus-filled wound.

Garner rose to make his way toward his bedroom. "Just because you're mad right now, don't try and talk yourself into thinkin' you weren't hoping your date would end with one either, bucko. You'd just be lying to yourself." His dad slapped him on the back. "Night, son."

"Night, Dad," he muttered, flipping the light back off to brood in the dark.

The understanding he'd doled out all night long had limits, and Max's hardcore pessimism had a way of making him forget all the promises he'd made to himself to sort out what was born out of resentment that would eventually fade, and what was unshakable resolve with her.

He was calling it tonight.

His patience had run out.

See if he ever kissed her again.

CHAPTER ELEVEN

Note from Maxine Cambridge to all ex-trophy wives: Everyone needs a good wake-up call once in a while. If you've smartened up and are now surrounding yourself with only honest people in your life, they're not going to be afraid to give you hell, no matter the venue. Open your eyes. Better still, open your ears. *Listen, learn.* And pucker up, buttercup.

The light in the kitchen flipped on, shining bright in Maxine's eyes. Mona went to the fridge, pulling out a gallon of milk. Her quilted baby blue bathrobe rustled when she reached into the lower cabinet for a container to warm her nightly milk in. "So that went well, eh, kiddo?" She busied herself pressing buttons on the microwave.

Fire burned the tips of her ears. "You were eavesdropping!" She didn't have to ask, she knew. Her mother's bedroom window was centered over the driveway, and now she was going to stick her nose in where it didn't belong. She was going to get unwarranted advice from a woman who'd told her to let Campbell make her eyeballs warble—wobble, whatever.

"Catch more flies with honey than vinegar."

"Maybe I don't want to catch this particular fly," she said, meaning every flippant syllable. Just because Campbell was all things handsome, brought her to unknown heights of passion, and was canine appealing to boot, didn't mean he was appealing to her.

Mona snorted into another, higher cabinet, reaching for a coffee cup. "Right. Well, just in case you go hunting down some other fly one day, do yourself a favor. Lay off the 'poor me I had a humdinger of a husband' biz. It's a real turnoff." A plunk of ceramic later, her mother poured the milk into the coffee mug and sauntered out of the kitchen. "Night, Maxie," she said with a smug smile, the billow of her bathrobe leaving a cloud of blue in her wake.

Maxine gritted her teeth, dropping to the kitchen chair. Lights around the cul-de-sac where her mother's unit was situated dotted the landscaped front lawns of the neighbors. Festive gnomes, all the rage with the seniors, eyed her with disgust in all their gnome-ish wisdom. She sat and stared at them for a long time, her chest tight, her hands clenched.

She just wasn't ready to date. That was all there was to it. Yet, riding on the back of Campbell's dirt bike, her chest pressed to his damp back, had been liberating—dare she admit, fun. And okay, pretty arousing, seeing his jeans hug his thighs and his shirt cling to that harder-than-hard stomach.

Just his physical presence brought her such peculiar serenity as they'd ridden around the track he told her he'd made himself with a bulldozer. Despite her rant about his presumptions, there was no denying her definite attraction to him. He had the ability to turn her inner thermometer up while relaxing her mind. His hands and mouth on her were akin to nirvana.

But Campbell believed in things she could no longer cop to. So she'd just keep telling herself her vulnerabilities after that orgasm had nothing to do with finding an excuse to push him away. Any excuse it took to never again find herself so caught up, only to lose everything in the end. All of Len's advice about sharing lives versus owning each other's was bunk.

So it had all worked out for the best.

Yes. Definitely.

Yet . . . if it was so fine, then why, when she rose from the kitchen table to prepare for bed, did her stomach drop to her feet, and her heart chug with sluggish regret for her behavior?

Why did the sinking feeling that Campbell Barker would rather have his skin peeled off at high noon than ask the crazy, almost divor- cée out on another date as long as he lived leave her bereft?

~ℓ~

Len scrolled through her phone book on her cell, hitting Mona's number. It was past time she at least told Maxine about Adam.

Fire lit her cheeks while she listened to the endless ring on the other end, trying to fend off the jitters in her stomach just think- ing that man's name. She just wanted to touch base with Maxine about him—to be sure he wasn't someone she knew by way of Fin- ley. Though, she'd probably leave out the part about naked and hotel rooms, tangled sheets, and booze.

Len's head sank into her hand in shame, but her body tingled— and it wasn't with embarrassment. On the contrary, she was abso- lutely without a shred of indecency. Though every act she and Adam had committed could be considered such.

And they'd committed. Whoa, had they ever. All night long until her muscles ached and her jaw hurt from clenching back her screams of delicious orgasm.

Her low groan filled her office. She wanted to feel remorse for having her first one-night stand ever. She even wanted to feel remorse that it had been with a man she'd originally thought was on Finley's payroll.

But she didn't. Not entirely.

Because it had been brilliant.

Meeting Adam at Wendt's began as curiosity, to decipher his purposefully cryptic parting shot. His bold demands, his refusal to explain his sudden presence all intrigued her. Sliding into a booth in the darkened interior of the bar was a fact-seeking mission. After an appletini or three, he hadn't just intrigued her; he'd left her breathless.

He was funny, powerful, Cracker Jack smart, and shared far too many interests with her. The reassurance that he wasn't in fact stalking her, but in Riverbend on business, and had been in the village the night they'd met to visit a "friend," left her feeling less and less like he had anything to do with Finley.

When Adam flattered her by telling her he'd happened to see her as he drove past the rec center and finally got up the courage, after following her around town, to introduce himself, Len was already halfway to the fantasy their night became. She never bothered to ask the friend's name—by drink three, Len was too lost in the intimacy the booth they sat in created.

Next, they were in the lobby of a Holiday Inn Express, booking a room like some illicit, giggling couple in a movie. Which had all led up to some of the naughtiest, most mind-smashing sex of her entire adult life.

Oh, Jesus. She was such a sinner.

Of course, Len soothed herself, almost all of her adult life was spent married to a man twenty-three years older than her. She'd had two lovers prior to Gerald, in college, before being swept off her feet and voluntarily quitting college to marry him.

Her husband's memory crept in, sweet and with a still sharp hint of the ache his loss had created. Guilt drove her to look his picture in the eye. He'd been a wonderful lover, but it had been a long time since she was held in the arms of a man—much less one as virile as Adam Baylor.

She and Gerald had enjoyed a fulfilling, intimate relationship before his cancer had gotten in the way. Until he'd died, leaving her financially insolvent and more alone than she'd ever felt in her life.

He didn't just die, Lenore, her conscience whispered in painful reminder.

No. He hadn't just died.

Thankful for the reprieve when no one picked up at Mona's, Len slunk down in her chair and let her head fall over the back of the chair, stretching her neck muscles.

"I brought coffee. I figured you'd need it as much as I did after last night," Adam said, throaty and deep, not looking at all like they'd torn up a hotel room bed, sunk-in bathtub, and small balcony. He was as cool, together, and refreshed as if he'd had eight hours of sleep.

The sonofabitch.

Len's eyes snapped shut. Last night had all been a major mistake. She knew no more about him today than she did yesterday. To boot, she'd slept with a complete stranger.

"I know what you're thinking."

"How Amazing Kreskin of you," was her cool reply, though every muscle in her body was coiled with tension.

Adam leaned over her desk, gripping the arms of her office chair to pull her against the fake wood. "You're thinking last night, and early this morning, I might add, was all a big mistake, and it's something you're never going to do again."

Okay, so he did have Amazing Kreskin–like properties. Len kept her lips clamped shut, but her eyes were wide open, soaking up every last inch of his tailored suit and his thick, slicked-back dark hair.

She made an extra effort to continue to keep her eyes open when vividly remembering that hair, mussed and falling over his forehead, while they rolled around some surface or another. When she spoke, it was measured, and meant to puncture his haughty smile into oblivion. "Actually, I wasn't thinking about you at all."

Adam's lips formed an amused upward tilt. "Let's clear something up. First, your friend is safe from me, if that's what's troubling you in the cold light of day. I gave some thought to the accusations you launched at me at the village the other night, and it occurred to me you might have buyer's remorse today. I don't know your friend and

I'm not a spy for this Finley guy. That said, don't kid yourself into believing what we did won't happen again, Len. It will. I'll call and you'll answer," he said with some more amusement and Neanderthal arrogance woven between his words.

Adam's back was almost out the door when she caught her breath enough to get her ass out of the chair and lob something at his big, fat head.

His chuckle because she missed rang in her burning ears.

⁓

Maxine glanced at the laminated sheet with the instructions for each exercise Georgia McHale had given her and frowned. Was that move the ball over your head to the right and bend at the waist, feet spread in line with your shoulders? With a critical eye, she compared Mrs. Lipknicki's motion to the cartoon character on the laminated sheet. "Oh, that's good, Mrs. Lipknicki! Look at you!" she praised with a warm smile. "That's right, keep your feet shoulders' width apart."

"This isn't how Georgia does it," Maude Grandowski complained.

Planting her hands on her hips, Maxine nodded her commiseration, gazing out at the ten swimming-cap-covered heads awaiting her next instruction. "I know I'm no Mrs. Lawrence, but bear with me, will you? I'm only filling in so we don't have to miss watercize altogether."

"Because you're broke," Mrs. Arnold said from the back row.

Broke. Broken. All the same.

Maxine shook her head. Damn it, those negative thoughts had to stop and stop now. She was only as broken as she let herself be. Displays like the one with Campbell last night, and her ridiculous overreaction to her embarrassment after being in such a vulnerable position—okay, a half-naked position—had given her raw, jangled nerves too much outdoor voice. This morning, upon reflection over coffee and a narrow-eyed, clearly disapproving Mona, that point had been driven home.

The moment she left watercize, she was going to call Campbell and apologize. Maybe she'd turn the tables and invite him for coffee. A peaceful cup of joe, minus a touchy date. And if he turned her down, it would serve her optimistic, dream-slashing self right.

Her eyes met Mrs. Arnold's dead-on. "That's exactly right, Mrs. Arnold." Why bother to deny it? There wasn't a soul in the village, housebound and on an iron lung or not, who didn't know the truth about where she stood. "I'm broke, but I'm working hard not to be broke anymore. So help a girl make a buck, would you? If we all work together, I'll figure this out and you'll all get the workout you deserve."

"Give the kid a break, Darla Arnold," Mr. Hodge warned, swishing the lukewarm water of the heated pool with fluid arms. "She's just trying to make ends meet. Plus, she looks better in a bathing suit than you bunch of wrinkled old hags."

Maxine's eye went wide, stifling a gasping chuckle. Intervention. Before these women made the *Titanic*'s sinking look tame. "Now, Mr. Hodge, you behave, and apologize to the lovely ladies. I understand everyone's frustration. I'm not very good at this, but I'm trying. With your help, I'm sure I'll be able to get it right. So everyone pitch in, okay? All suggestions welcome." Looking up, she scanned the small crowd.

Wide-eyed silence prevailed.

"Oh, c'mon now. I *am* trying." She was. Jesus.

"Maxine?" Mrs. Arnold called again from the back.

"Yes, Mrs. Arnold?"

"Turn around, honey." She used two pruny fingers to make a swirling motion.

Maxine swished around in the hip-deep water to find Campbell, standing at the edge of the pool by the wide steps, sharp eyes assessing her.

Oh.

Suddenly, she felt naked, even in her borrowed red, white, and blue bathing suit with the spray of fireworks across the hip. Her hands went self-consciously to the front of the suit, holding the exercise sheet in front of her breasts where the stiff cups gaped because they were too big. Apologies and offers of coffee slipped right out the window. "Uh, is everything okay?"

"Nope."

"What's wrong?"

"You and me, we have a little something to settle, Max Henderson."

The ladies of the group twittered in breathless coos.

If he meant settle their little spat last night by showing up during a chance for her to make money *and* when she had on a bathing suit that looked like it had come from the Esther Williams era, he had another thing coming. Though a moment of grateful passed when Maxine remembered she'd decided to forgo the swim cap with the red foofy flowers on it.

"Settle? Now?"

"Right now," he said, stomping down the pool steps and into the water to tower over her.

Shocked, her mouth fell open. Campbell Barker was standing in the middle of the shallow end of Leisure Village's pool, fully clothed, work boots and all, wanting to settle something. Her hand dropped from her chest, the exercise sheet falling to the water and floating away like a discarded candy wrapper. Her thoughts scattered, then came together in a moment of complete clarity. Apologies were in order. "Wait! You were right last night. I owe you an apology—"

A glimmer of the devil in his eyes came and went before his lips turned back into that stern line. "Apologize later. Right now, we have something else to settle."

"Wha . . . what do we have to . . . to settle?"

"This," he hissed, wrapping a strong arm around her waist and dragging her to him. Placing a hand on her ass, Campbell fitted her to him.

And then, he did it. In front of God and seniors.

He planted the lips she'd waxed poetic about before falling asleep with tears of regret in her eyes on her mouth with a force that sucked the air from her lungs.

Her eyes, wide open at first, her arms dangling limp behind her, Maxine prepared to pound out her outrage on the hard wall of his chest until . . . Well, until she realized the only thing outrageous about this was that she was having the living daylights kissed out of her, and she was still hanging from his arms like a wet noodle instead of throwing her whole body into it with the kind of zeal it so deserved.

You know, Maxine, like you did last night out on that rock you have a knot in your back the size of the Grand Canyon from?

Her nipples tightened, beading against her damp suit, boring holes through it while the warmth he'd stirred in her last night returned tenfold.

A hand she couldn't believe was hers tentatively crept upward, curling into the back of Campbell's neck when he parted her lips and let his tongue caress hers, dipping, stroking until she matched his forceful, delicious passion. Campbell coaxed, wooing her mouth, bending it to his will, creating sharp ripples of undeniable pleasure in places she didn't know were capable of tingling.

Her leg desperately wanted to wrap itself around his waist just like she had last night to feel his hips against hers.

The moment she thought she'd die of a kiss so good her eyes indeed warbled was the very moment he ripped his mouth from hers, dumping her with a splash back into the pool.

Surprise made her pop back up out of the water, sputtering and shoving her hair from her face. The skirt of her bathing suit floated in awkward tufts around her waist.

Campbell's eyes, glossed with amusement, gave her that cocky once-over. He leaned into her and said, "Figured I'd better drop by and show you what you missed by storming off last night. From here on out, when we end a date, I fully expect a kiss good night, not the kind of guff you gave me. Consider that your warning. Oh"—he stopped as though reminding himself of her earlier statement—"all apologies are accepted between the hours of seven and midnight. Don't miss your opportunity."

Stomping back out of the pool, he turned and gave a quick wink to the group and smiled with a salute to every wide-eyed, mouth-hanging-open watercizer. "Bye, ladies. Oh, and you, too, Mr. Hodge." Splotches of water trailed behind him as he sauntered his way across the tile to the exit door. Sexy, confident, wet T-shirt and all.

The pool area exploded with raucous whistles and clapping. Mr. Warren thumped the diving board with his feet as the gentlemen from the other end of the pool slapped their hands against the tiled edges.

"Well, girlie. That was a man staking his claim if I ever saw one," Mr. Hodge said on a gruff laugh. He clamped a hand on her shoulder, giving it a shake while handing her the instruction sheet she'd dropped. "Close your mouth there, Maxine, and let's get this show on the road. I gotta get home before *The Price Is Right*'s on."

Amid the whispers of "how romantic" and "if only I were thirty years younger," Maxine somehow managed to corral the Campbell supporters back into watercize submission.

Focusing on completing the task at hand was difficult at best while she alternately fumed and swooned. His mouth against hers, the wet heat he'd created down low . . . Maxine was thankful for the water holding her up, as her legs went soft just thinking about that kiss.

In front of thirty or so villagers who wouldn't just be calling her broke, but a broke slut.

Goddamn it.

When she got her hands on that presumptuous showboater, she was going to . . .

Something.

Yes, she was going to do *something*—as soon as her head cleared and her heart stopped jumping in her chest like it was attached to strings only Campbell Barker could tug.

Something . . .

~ℓ~

Campbell stripped off his soaking wet shirt, catching a glimpse of himself in the mirror of the men's locker room. He gave his reflection a smug smile that instantly wavered.

Last night the plan was to never go within a hundred feet of the luscious but totally nutty Max Cambridge. And it had been a good, solid, well-thought-out plan. Not to mention probably one of his smarter ones. She was the crusher of hopes and dreams, after all. Not only that, she was a bundle of nerves and irrational trains of thought.

But seeing her in the pool today amidst all the seniors in her outdated bathing suit, hot as the day was long, Campbell was struck by just how not ready he was to give up the chase for the elusive butterfly. He'd known going in Max was a mess, but he'd gone in anyway only to end up angry because she wasn't healing and learning from her mistakes fast enough to suit him.

Foul ball. Some took longer than others to come to terms with their old insecurities.

That was when the choice had become crystal clear—he still wanted her even with her tunnel vision on relationships, and he was determined to change her mind about the way a man should treat a woman.

So he'd set about changing her mind.

In the middle of her watercize class.

No doubt, Barker, he chided his reflection, *you're going to be in for some shit for that little impulsive stunt.*

But that only made his grin wider.

Connor stopped dead in his tracks in the parking lot of his high school. He gave a sideways glance to his left and right then scanned the area.

His gait was slow as he shoved his books under one arm so he could dig out the keys to the car from his pocket. Stopping short, he faced his father in the glare of the late June sun. He held up the keys with a sullen glance down at Finley. Topping his father by two inches helped him to hold his ground—the ground Finley was about to yank out from under him. Yet his height made him feel less like he was helpless and weak.

With a shake, Connor offered the keys to him. "I guess you're here for these?" What else could he want? He'd taken everything else. But wait, his father hadn't taken it, he reminded himself, calling up the memory of their last phone call—Connor'd just refused to accept it.

Right.

Finley jammed his hands into the pockets of his trousers, eyeing his son with that arrogant, bossy look Connor wanted to punch off his face. He knew it was wrong. He knew his mother'd freak out if she knew he'd even thought something violent like that, but it was how he felt. He wasn't as much of a kid as his dad would like to believe. He got what his father was doing to his mother, and he didn't like it so much.

Finley's perfect hair ruffled in the humid breeze. "What makes you say that, son?"

Connor's chin lifted when he jutted it in the direction of his father's Caddy. "Why else would you bring Joey with you if he wasn't going to drive the car back for you?"

"Joey's good company," he said with his infamous "How can I put you in a new car today" smile. The tight, fake one he gave the customers he still occasionally dealt with.

When his father didn't hold out his hand, a sign in his eyes his dad was messing with his head yet again, Connor reacted. Knowing it was disrespectful, knowing his mother would give him shit for doing it, he did it anyway, dumping the keys at Finley's feet. Screw the power struggle. He didn't need his father to hold crap over his head anymore. The car had been on borrowed time anyway. He knew it, and his father got off on letting him know it.

Finley looked down at his feet where the keys lay, his eyes narrowing, but it was his silence, furious and cold, standing between them, that almost made Connor cower.

Almost.

"Take it. Take the stupid car. I don't care anymore!" he yelped, unconcerned if everyone at Crest Creek High heard him. They all already talked smack about him because his mother was broke and they lived in a retirement village. But he just didn't care. He was sick of feeling like he owed his dad something because he'd chosen to stay with his mother.

Finley stooped to pick up the keys, pocketing them. When he rose, his hot eyes zeroed in on Connor. "Is this the kind of respect your mother's teaching you over there, living with that witch of a mother of hers?"

Call it hormonal, call it impulsive, call it whatever you like, but the rage slipping up his spine and making the hairs at the back of his neck stand up exploded at the mention of his grandmother. "You leave Grandma alone! If it wasn't for her, we'd have nowhere to live because you're a cheap piece of shit!" he screamed, the words out of his mouth before he could remember his mom was going to have his balls when she found out. And she'd find out.

A sharp crack to his cheek threw Connor's head backward and had Finley up in his bobbing face quicker than he'd have given his dad credit for. "You watch who you're talking to, young man! I won't tolerate disrespect like that—*ever*!" he ground out between his cosmetically enhanced white teeth.

Connor backed away, his ire now an ugly beast of more than eight months' worth of pent-up frustration. "How can I respect someone who *threatens* me to love him or I'll lose my Xbox and my stupid house, *Dad*?" he sneered, spittle falling from between his lips. "You don't care about me, and you sure don't care about Mom. You took everything away from us because Mom didn't want to be married to a lying cheater, and now because I don't want to come live with you, you're taking the last thing I have left. Take the car—maybe you could give it to Lacey as a *graduation present*! I hate you!" he hollered as he took off running, caring little that half the track team had stopped all motion in the field facing the parking lot.

Sweat dripped down the sides of his face and gathered under his armpits, but he didn't stop running until he hit the corner of the building and stumbled into the back parking lot for juniors and seniors. His breathing was ragged, coming in harsh puffs when he leaned forward to suck air into his lungs.

"Dude?" His one constant friend since seventh grade, Jordon Armstrong, rolled up beside him in his car. "You okay?"

Connor took an angry scuff at the cement with his toe while he paced back and forth, kicking up dirt and loose gravel. "I'm screwed, man."

Jordon shook his head, turning off the ignition and jumping out of the car. "Shit. He took the car, didn't he?"

"You heard?"

Jordon's gaze was solemn but steady. "Dude, *everybody* heard."

Connor's frustration resurfaced again when he spat, "You know what? I don't care. Everybody's talking about my father and Lacey and how poor I am anyway. I don't care."

"Man, your dad sucks."

"Crap. My mother's going to kill me. I said some shitty stuff to him."

The nod of Jordon's shaved blond head was in agreement. "But he's done some pretty shitty stuff to you and your mom."

No kidding. Looking up, he saw a bunch of the crowd he'd once hung out with in a circle, just waiting to pass the word that Connor Cambridge had a fight with his father in the Crest Creek High parking lot. Jordon slapped his back. "Ignore that jerk Nolan." He nodded in the crowd's direction at the biggest instigator of them all. Nolan Ford. "He's a stupid freak with a big mouth. He was always jealous of you because Tabitha liked you first."

Connor shrugged his shoulders. "I don't care anymore." And he didn't. School only had three days left before they broke for summer. Nothing mattered. Not the friends who now made fun of him, not his lack of wheels, nothing.

His friend, loyal from day one, leaned back against his new Mustang, crossing his arms in a nonchalant manner over his chest, and smacked his lips. "If you don't care, I don't care," he said on a conspiratorial grin. "So get in. I'll give ya a ride home. Coo'?"

Connor knocked knuckles with him. "Coo'."

When they drove past Nolan and his posse, Connor sat higher in his seat, refusing to look away, and fighting the temptation to lift both his middle fingers in honor of their shit-a-tude.

No one was ever going to make him feel like he was some loser because he no longer had what they all had.

"Hey, little mermaid," her mother called from the living room. "How'd watercize go?"

Maxine let out a tired sigh, poking her head into the living room doorway. "I'm guessing you don't have to ask how it went. You already heard."

Mona's laughter was deep from within her belly. "Whoo boy, did I ever. Maude called Mary the minute her big ole webbed feet were dry."

She tugged at her loaner bathing suit, wanting to be rid of the damp, sagging material. "And this is funny, how?"

"He laid one on ya right there in the pool, Maxie, with his clothes on and everything—in front of everyone. How is that not funny? And romantic. Pretty darned romantic."

Fine. It had funny attributes. And romantic ones, too, if they were to split hairs. She shook her finger at her mother in warning. "Yeah, well, he's in for one big surprise the next time I see him. I can't afford to have those kinds of shenanigans going on when I'm trying to teach a class. Georgia will never ask me back again."

Her mother's eyes twinkled with maniacal glee. "I heard you didn't exactly say no to those shenanigans," she taunted, slapping her thigh with the morning paper she was reading.

Who'd had the time to say no? It wasn't like she'd been given a chance to say anything. *Like you would have anyway? Hello. Was that not, bar none, the best ever kiss of your entire life? Campbell's lips and yours were like mac and cheese. Chocolate frosting and sprinkles, Sonny and Cher, Peaches and Herb. You know it. He knows it.* "Fine, so I didn't say no. I wasn't exactly given a chance to say anything," she echoed her thoughts out loud.

Her mother's sharp-as-tacks eyes gave her a pointed look. "And you liked it. Don't lie to me, Maxie. You can fool plenty of people, but not your own mother."

Leaning against the doorway, she made a face of utter disgust. With herself or with Campbell, she wasn't sure. "It was *okay*. Okay? Just okay."

"That's not true, Max Henderson, and you know it," Campbell called from the back portion of the house.

Maxine gave her mother a pinched frown of exasperation. Naturally, seeing as the entire force of every senior in the village was on Campbell's side, why wouldn't her mother be, too? "Thanks a lot for the warning," she mouthed before turning to find herself face-to-face with the kissing bandit.

"You did so like it," he accused glibly.

Her mother chuckled in the background, garnering a narrow-gazed warning from Maxine. She let her eyes focus in on Campbell, who hovered over her, daring her to deny their kiss had been anything less than stupendous. "Is it that you like me being the topic of discussion over warm milk and strudel at the sewing circle or that you never want me to get another job in the village again? And to think I was going to apologize for being such a crappy date. You have a lot of nerve."

"I know. It's a skill some don't give nearly the credit it deserves."

She let an exasperated sigh escape her throat. "Why are you here again?"

He thumbed a finger over his shoulder and held up a wrench. "Still having trouble with that leaky pipe," he offered with that easy-going tone he'd perfected. As if nothing bad ever happened in the world.

The heat, her humiliation, her ire that yes, she'd enjoyed Campbell's kiss and he knew it, made her snap. "What kind of plumber are you, anyway, that you can't fix some leak I can't even see?"

Always with an answer, he smiled all affable-like. "The kind who keeps coming back until he gets the job done. I'm no quitter." He gave her a meaningful gaze, the smile never leaving his face.

Was that a covert attempt at letting her know he wasn't giving up? That he wasn't like Finley? Or was her imagination on the run—maybe doing some wishful thinking? Either way, it made her regret over last night sting all over again. "That was a cheap shot I took."

He nodded gravely in response. "You've taken a couple of those."

"Okay, I'm sorry, but—"

"You're still sensitive. I remember," he drawled with a cocked eyebrow. "I bet you're especially sensitive after that kiss, huh? Who could blame you? I am a pretty good kisser."

Heh. Yeah. "How about we call a truce?"

"You mean like you don't get all excited if I say something that rubs you the wrong way because I'm an impatient knuckle dragger, but instead communicate with me all *The View*-ish style?"

Maxine giggled, finding herself leaning into him just so she could sniff his cologne. "So are we going to make up?"

Campbell took a step closer. "Are you conceding that you took excited to a whole new volcanic level?"

Maxine blushed. Maybe that was a little true. No, it was a lot true. She'd acted out because he made her feel things she was afraid to feel—to trust. "Now who's exaggerating?" she joked with a deliberately flirty smile.

Campbell crossed his strong arms over his chest. "Fine. I'm blessed with the anointment of adulthood. I can go first in the game called communication. I moved in too fast. I didn't mean to, but you have your moments of irresistibility. When you're not crushing a man's dreams, that is."

A shiver of warmth began low in her belly. "That was almost nice. My turn. What happened . . . well, last night flustered me and it made me react badly, and I'm sorry I overreacted."

"Don't forget the reason *why* you reacted the way you did. Go on," he prompted with a teasing grin. "Floor's all yours."

God, all this open and honest communication was work. Maxine's glance up at him was sheepish. "I did it to push you away—because it . . . what happened made me feel exposed . . ."

His smile was one of satisfaction. "I'm glad you're able to admit it. You'd be lying to yourself and insulting my intelligence if you didn't.

You also did it because I'm a handsome devil with skills of the carnal variety—ones the likes of which you've never seen." He wiggled his eyebrows.

Her eyes strayed to the shag carpet on her mother's floor. There was that. "And I—I—it—left me sort of raw, and sensitive . . ."

"Sort of?"

Maxine's fingers toyed with a lock of her hair. "Okay. I was a lot sensitive. But I guess that's where I am right now. The fallout my pending divorce has brought keeps surprising even me. So maybe we should just have a standing apology between us, because I can't promise I won't behave ridiculously again. I get a little carried away sometimes. I hate to drag my baggage with me, but my marriage to Fin shaped how I deal with situations. I know you'll be shocked by this, but typically, when I'm stressed or feel cornered, I run for cover. Reasonable doesn't always factor into my behavior."

"No truer words," he agreed, letting his finger run over the landscape of her cheek, leaving her fighting a purr. "But knowing that's where you are, having that knowledge means you're willingly allowing it to own you, versus using it to learn and move on."

Maxine's gulp was audible. Did he have to be so reasonable? So right? So fine-looking when he was? "You know what sucks the most about you, Mr. Barker?"

He cocked an eyebrow at her. "What's that, Max?"

Maxine let her fingers flit over his shirt with a smile. "Not only are you cute, but you're healthy emotionally. It's damned annoying."

He laughed, capturing her fingers. "I can see how that would be a huge deficit on my relationship resume."

Mona stuck her head between the two of them on her way into the kitchen to answer the ringing phone. "I'm not watching that nancy Dr. Phil anymore, buster," she cackled up at Campbell, never ashamed to interfere. "You just come here every day at three and spout off your words of wisdom to my daughter here, who needs someone—anyone—to knock some Godforsaken sense into her. And you," she snapped the strap on Maxine's bathing suit, "quit behaving like some abandoned puppy. The bad part of your life's over. Let's get on with some good. Lord knows, we could use some." Mona strolled into the kitchen to answer the phone without looking back.

"So, in the interest of getting on with the good, you think you might wanna try the dreaded date again? Maybe a little slower this time out of the gate with the woo-hoo?" Campbell inquired with a grin she was sure held a certain amount of satisfaction that her mother, once more, was agreeing with him.

Her stomach gurgled with that unfamiliar battalion of butterflies. She was about to answer when Mona stuck her hand under Maxine's nose. "The phone. It's for you."

Maxine attempted to clear her head. "Who is it?"

"The village president."

Taking the phone from her mother, she covered it to glare at Campbell, butterflies gone, instant blame at the ready. "If I get booted from subbing for people who're sick, I'm going to own your ass, Barker," she threatened, though her threat was followed by a grin. She jammed the phone against her ear. "Hello?"

Words filtered in and out of her eardrums. All positive—complimentary, in fact. Yet she was struggling to put them all together in a cohesive thought. The most she managed was, "You're kidding?" and "It was an unfortunate incident. Yes, I agree one hundred percent. I'd definitely look into making some kind of policy about trolls. My nose wouldn't be opposed either," and finally, "Yes! I'll take it!"

Damp bathing suit and her mother's scorn be damned, she sat on the couch and clicked off the phone, dumbstruck.

"What?" Mona bellowed with a question when she threw her arms up in the air. "What's the matter?"

Campbell placed his strong hand on her shoulder. "Maxine? Everything okay?"

Her nod was slow in answer. It was more than okay. It was awesome with awesome sauce. Relief, slow and steady, thrummed through her veins.

Mona plunked down beside her, concern in her hawk-like eyes. "What's the matter, Maxie?"

And then she couldn't get the words out fast enough. "After almost nine months . . . I—I . . . The village wants to hire me to be social director and continue to sub for the seniors who are sick. That was Leonard Hammond—the village's board president. He said they were flooded with calls about bingo. The seniors said I was more fun than a car full of clowns. It just took them some time to find out if they had funds to pay me a *salary*. Did you hear that, Mom? *Pay me* a full-time salary to organize events for the villagers, and the first event on my agenda is the end-of-summer dance!" It was almost the end of June. That only left her a little less than a month and a half to prepare.

Oh, my God. She had a job.

A j-o-b.

Mona threw her arms around her daughter, planting a sloppy kiss on her cheek. "Whoopee, kiddo!"

Big whoopee. Big and honkin'.

Her good fortune flooded her, overwhelmed her as tears of gratitude stung her eyes. With a shaky hand, she pushed her hair from her face, and had a thought she shared out loud. "So the Cluck-Cluck Palace can stick their triple chicken-ator up their stupid curly fried asses! It's not a lot of money. It won't get me out of your hair just yet, Ma, but it's something to start. Maybe I can tuck some away to take some business courses at Community." Maxine's mind went at warp speed with the endless possibilities a job reaped.

Hopping up off the couch, she clapped her hands and spun around, falling into Campbell. "I did tell you you were good with the seniors, didn't I?"

"You did," she agreed with a coy, nay, a flirtatious smile. "So I propose we celebrate by trying coffee one more time, minus the baggage."

Be it her adrenaline rush of good fortune, or finally admitting she didn't want to miss the chance to know Campbell, she didn't bother to analyze. Yes. She, Maxine Cambridge, had just asked a man out on a date. "My treat, of course." Because she could actually cough up the shekels—*her shekels*—to pay for it.

There was nothing, absolutely nothing in the world like the kind of independence of earning your own living did to your psyche. The eternal fist in her chest unclenched, relaxing just a little.

Her smile beamed, her head whirled. She might not make the Fortune 500 list with the salary they'd offered, but she would at least be able to help her mother out—ending the cycle of the ozone suck she'd become.

She could buy essentials at Walmart for her and Connor. Food, and oh, euphoria! A box of those Sno Balls in bulk. Maybe she'd eventually be able to buy another pair of jeans—a shirt—*underwear*. Sneakers for Connor. If things went well, and the village kept her on, maybe she could take some online courses.

The slam of the screen door snapped her out of the list she was making in her mind. Connor strode in with his best friend, Jordon, both with their heads down. "Connor!" she shouted. "You'll never guess what just happen . . ." Her words slowed when her son raised his head. Maxine gasped.

His left eye sported a razor-thin cut, the edges of it an angry red, his eyelid swelling at an alarming rate. Maxine rushed to him, lifting his chin so she could have a better look with the sunlight streaming in from the picture window overlooking the front of her mother's house. "Honey, what happened?" Looking to Jordon, her eyes questioned his. "Was there a fight with someone at school?"

When Connor jerked his chin from her clutching fingers, Jordon spoke up. "No, Mrs. Cambridge. He didn't have a fight with someone at school."

Connor shook his head with a fierce look at Jordon, but his friend made a disgusted face, his lips curling inward. "Naw, man. If you won't tell her, I will. Just wasn't right. She deserves to know."

A million scenarios raced through her mind as she examined Connor's eye. "One of you better pony up. *Now*," she demanded.

"I'll get ice," her mother said, running a soothing hand over Connor's back when she passed through to the kitchen.

Campbell clamped a hand on Connor's shoulder. "You okay?"

Connor sighed, shooting Jordon a resentful glare. "Yes, sir."

"Took a pretty good shot there, eh? Lemme have a look to be sure there's no real damage," Campbell said, his words calm and collected.

Jordon hopped from foot to foot, his jaw twitching. "It was his dad," he blurted. "Mr. Cambridge hit him. They had a fight because he came to take Connor's car. They said some stuff to each other, and Mr. Cambridge got mad. Really mad."

Maxine's head snapped up. "*Your father* did this to you?" she rasped between teeth clenched so hard they hurt. Surprise raced through her veins, turning them cold as ice. Finley was many things, shitty things, but he'd never hit either of them.

Never.

She rounded on Connor, pushing Campbell out of the way with a palm to his chest. "Your father did this to you, Connor? Answer—me!"

His sullen expression was all the answer she needed. "Yes. But I—"

The pendulum swung.

From joyous relief to enraged, seething, hot, oozing anger.

"I'll damn well kill him!" Maxine screeched, pushing her way to the kitchen and taking the keys to her mother's Rio without even asking. Out the door in a flash, she didn't hear anything but the vibration of adrenaline pulsing in her head. The itch in her fingers to claw the bastard's eyes out.

She definitely didn't hear her mother bark an order at Campbell: "Warm that truck up before she lands herself in the hoosegow!"

CHAPTER TWELVE

Note from Maxine Cambridge to all ex-trophy wives: If you'll recall, earlier advice was given with regard to never letting your pending ex see you sweat. Keeping in mind violence is never advocated, there are extreme circumstances when sweating will be absolutely unavoidable. They involve protecting your child at all costs and a rockin' right hook. Be sure to put your weight into it. Oh, and change into something appropriate first—something that at least dates back to the 1990s. Just trust me.

"I can't believe you talked me into this—*again*," Len purred into Adam's ear, stretching her long limbs beneath the crisp hotel sheets. He'd seduced her into coming back to his hotel room for some early-afternoon frolicking, and she found she had to fight a groan of reluctance at leaving all this luscious man for temperamental brides who couldn't decide what color their guest book pen should be.

Adam chuckled, deep and rumbling against her ear pressed to his chest. "I can be very persuasive."

And totally addictive. But there'd be none of that, Len reassured herself. She was doing that more and more lately—reassuring herself she could keep this about nothing more than sex. "I have a million things to do." She began to slide away from his warm arms, arms she couldn't stop thinking about when she wasn't surrounded by them.

"I can think of a million better things to do than deal with neurotic brides. They all involve this bed." Adam patted the place she'd just left and grinned.

She laughed, hoping to keep the mood light when she felt anything but. "But those *things* won't pay the bills."

Adam rose up on his elbow, eyeing her as she shimmied back into her slim pencil skirt. "Don't you want to know how I pay my bills, Len?"

Yes. No. Yes. Curiosity had eaten at her since the night they'd had their first encounter, and it continued to do so every encounter since then. Yet, there was something that kept her from asking questions about his life, his job, or why, at the drop of a hat, he could show up at her office any time of the day and convince her to come back to his hotel room and make love.

There were moments when she still couldn't believe she was involved in an intimate relationship with a man she knew almost nothing about other than that he was here for business. What kind of business she couldn't guess. Every once in a while, Len heard bits and pieces of Adam's conversations on the phone with someone she'd concluded was his secretary by the way he told her to reschedule client lunches and make sure to conference him on staff meetings.

But what his dealings here in Riverbend were remained unclear.

And she liked it that way.

Mostly.

Clearly he had money, and the proof wasn't just in his clothing or his cultured vocabulary; it was in the respect the hotel staff paid him. Len knew money—Adam didn't blatantly reek of it. He wasn't flashy or gaudy, but judging from the leftover bottles of wine she caught glimpses of during their trysts, and the labels on his clothes, strewn across the floor, he had a decent bank account.

Somewhere.

Somewhere she was better off not knowing about.

There was definitely something to be said for forbidden and mysterious sex with no strings attached. Even if each sexual encounter they shared made it harder and harder for her to leave him.

Adam ran a long-fingered hand along her thigh, driving her skirt upward. "So—don't you want to know how I pay my bills?" he repeated.

"I thought we had a deal." The reminder was meant to come off breezy and light, but even she heard the panic in her voice.

"Deals were made to be broken." His reply was easy, but his eyes were growing hard.

With her back to him as she slid on her shoes, Len sucked in a shaky breath. "Not this one. You get what you want, and I get what I want, no questions asked."

She thought she heard him rasp an aggravated sigh, but chose to ignore it. Fitting a smile on her lips, Len leaned down and gave Adam a quick kiss, moving away before he could coax her into another hour of playtime, but he caught her arm. "Who says I don't want more than just your enormous libido?" He winked playfully, but his question had a hard edge that made her squirm.

"You did when you agreed to, to"—she waved her hand over the bed—"this. Have you changed your mind?" She held her breath.

Adam's eyebrow cocked upward. "Haven't I changed yours?"

If he only knew how close he was to doing just that. Len smiled, making her way toward the door to avoid any more eye contact. Instead, she focused on the peephole at the top of the door. "Nope. But if you've decided this isn't your thing, I'll know by the silence of my cell phone. No harm. No foul. Byyyee, Adam."

Len pulled the door open with as much confidence as she could outwardly muster, keeping her shoulders square and her head high.

When she hit the other side of the door, she jammed a knuckle in her mouth and steadied her shaky legs by leaning back against the corridor wall.

Thinking back to her earlier notion that this thing with Adam was supposed to be fun, she decided fun didn't leave you hoping you hadn't just made one of the stupidest declarations of your life.

~~~⁓~~~

"Finley—where—are—youuuu?" Maxine screamed into the airy, white modern interior of the dealership that had bought and paid for almost everything she'd ever owned.

Snaking her way past the cars on the showroom floor—cars that cost more than most houses in her mother's village—she cracked each one with a fist like something out of a scene in *The Warriors*.

A receptionist, as pretty as, maybe even prettier than, Lacey popped up from the front desk like a toaster strudel. Her perfect makeup and young fresh skin lost their dewy glow when she frowned, giving Maxine a horrified look of disapproval while taking in her bathing suit and flip-flops. "Can I help you?" she squeaked, rocking on her heels and brushing invisible lint from her thin pencil skirt with shaking hands. "Omigod! You're . . . Are you . . ."

"Am I what?" Maxine spat.

"The Cambridge Auto lady . . . oh, but you couldn't be. You're too ol . . ."

Maxine stuck her fingers under the straps of her bathing suit and hiked her breasts up. "There. More familiar? Yes, I was the Cambridge Automobile girl, probably while you were still wrapped in swaddling clothes. And yes, I'm too old to do the commercials anymore. *Now where's Finley?*"

"I'm sorry, but he said he wasn't seeing anyone today," she said with a dismissive tone, her eyes flitting to Finley's door.

Maxine's eyes narrowed, zeroing in on the door proudly displaying Fin's name right behind Barbie's desk. She rushed the receptionist, stalking toward her, her lips in a snarl. "I'm going to give you the heads-up here, eye candy—move the fuck out of the way or I'll tear your hot, firm ass up like a wrecking ball. Got it?"

The young woman, a gorgeous platinum blonde and taller than

Maxine by at least three inches, blanched. "But I told you. Mr. Cambridge said he wasn't seeing—"

Maxine interrupted her by way of half climbing over the chest-level desk area and slapping her hands on top of it with a sharp crack. "He'll see Jesus when I'm done. If I were you, I'd pack my bags for the Rapture, honey."

Her mouth fell open, her beautiful sloe eyes confused. "What's the Rapture?"

"*Move!*" Maxine screeched.

The few sparse late-afternoon Richie Riches, out shopping for trinkets for their overindulged children and underage brides, made shuffling noises with hurried feet.

She had two brief thoughts when she knocked open the waist-high swinging door that led to the area behind Barbie's desk and to Finley's office with her knee.

First, that damned well hurt.

Second, how sad Finley wouldn't be able to make another million bucks he could lord over her head today because his crazy almost ex-wife had shown up and scared off all the customers.

Slapping her hand on Finley's office door, she roared again, "Finley—get out here, nowwwwww!"

A scuffle from behind, and the loud gasping from someone as they burst through the beautiful, ornate glass doors of the dealership sounded like they came from another dimension. She heard it, acknowledged it, then ignored the familiarity of it.

Because she was going to kill Finley today.

Nothing else mattered.

Not the fact that a place that had once seemed like home now felt like a foreign country. Not the fact that employees who used to smile at her now hid their faces behind car magazines. Nothing mattered but grabbing hold of Finley's throat and choking the ever-lovin' shit out of him for laying a brutal hand on Connor.

The door popped open to reveal a condescending Lord Finley. Nothing less than she'd anticipated on the ride over, but infuriating all the same. Her stomach did that crazy jig of fear it did whenever she had to confront her tormentor. But this time? This time he hadn't tormented her, he'd tormented Connor—and he'd pay.

"Did you hit my son?"

His head, not a hair out of place, tilted back to give her his disapproving, barbed gaze. Like she wasn't worth the scum on the bottom of his Gucci shoe. "What the hell are you doing here, Maxine?"

Her head rolled on her neck, her eyes bulged with anger so rife, so ugly, she knew she resembled an escapee from the whacked ward. She just didn't care. She didn't care that so many of the people she'd once entertained at dinner parties were now gawking at her in astonishment. She didn't care that they were judging her fanciful bathing suit and supermarket flip-flops. She just didn't care. "I said," she growled, "*did you hit my son?*"

"Let me tell you a little something about your son, Maxine," he drawled, his anger on a very obviously tight leash. "He's a disrespectful little bastard, and I won't have it. I don't care if he's living with you and that mouthy flake, he can't talk to me like that!"

Standing on tiptoe, Maxine seethed a response. "That's not what I asked. I asked you if you hit—my—son?"

His silver fox eyebrow rose with mocking delight. There was game to be had, and he loved nothing more than to toy with his opponents. "And if I did?"

Whether it was the way he so carelessly brushed off the idea that he could manhandle Connor at whim or the "I dare you to try and stop me" attitude that set her off, she couldn't say. The months of frustration, the penniless dependency on her mother's depleting retirement fund, the lost and confused state of helplessness and fear as she struggled to figure out what to do to take care of Connor exploded like a mushroom cloud of wigged out.

He could take everything from her—he could threaten, bulldoze, and tirade until she cowed right back to her little corner.

But he could *not* lay a hand on her son.

Maxine's arm reared back before rhyme or reason could prevent it. "I'll kill you, you disgusting sonofabitch!"

There was a sharp crack—so sharp it rang with a satisfying vibration in her ears. Her fist connected with his nose, hard and fast, stinging her knuckles upon impact. A sting she relished, licking her lips like she was savoring the finest caviar.

Finley's head snapped back in a quick bob, blood from his nostrils arched through the air in perfect crimson droplets.

And then it was on—Maxine was all over him like some enraged street fighter, clawing at his hair, pummeling him with her fists. "If you ever touch my son again, I'll kill you!" she hollered, gripping the tie around his neck and jerking it back and forth.

Hands she barely noticed were suddenly on her, grabbing her around the waist, dragging her from her mission of annihilating Finley forever. Her feet swung in mad circles, making an attempt to get away until she heard her mother's voice saying, "Get off of me, you lackey! I'll knock your eyeballs sideways from here to Sunday!"

"Max!" A distant, deep voice called to her. "Calm down—stop struggling," it yelled in her ear. The iron grip belonged to the voice, and with slow realization, the two came together.

Campbell.

Her gasps of breath were choppy and harsh as the rush of furious rage she'd experienced seconds ago left her body in a whoosh. She slumped against the hard body behind her, staring in horror at a bloody, disheveled Finley.

"Someone get me a handkerchief, Goddamn it!" he ordered. "Has someone missed the fact that I'm bleeding?" he questioned the few mortified salesmen on the floor. "Joey, call the fucking police!" he demanded.

Maxine's temper shot back up ten notches. He was going to call the police after he'd hit her son? "Campbell," she barked with a squirm. "Let me go! I'll make Jersey's finest busy little bees when they have to look for your limbs to reattach them, you child abuser!"

"I'll tell you one last time, Max, can it or I'll drag you out of here," Campbell threatened with a hiss, gripping her at her waist with one strong hand, and clamping her arms behind her back with the other.

Finley wiped his effusively bleeding nose with a handkerchief. "Listen to your boy toy, Maxine, and get the hell out of here. Go home and wait for the police, you crazy bitch! I'll have you locked up for assault and battery."

"Is that really necessary?" was Campbell's shocked response.

"You bet your ass, boy toy. She came at me like some kind of wild animal. You saw it." He jammed his face in Maxine's. "I think you're unstable, Maxine. How can you possibly take proper care of my boy when you're clearly mentally unfit?"

Campbell set her behind him with a firm drop to the floor. His face, almost always placid and worry-free, was a mask of tight planes and gritting teeth. "Plant your feet, tiger. Do. Not. Move. A. Muscle," he ordered, his tone rough and cold as ice. When his attention returned to Finley, his voice rang with a mixture of emotions. "You'd have the mother of your child arrested after *you* hit your son?"

Finley batted a hand in the air. "She's fucking nuts. You bet I'd have her arrested." He rose on his toes to bark the words into Campbell's face.

The silence frightened Maxine. The tension between the two men simmered like a pot of sauce preparing to boil over. Sanity returned in a resounding moment of clarity. Her old role a rote response. Maxine's hand went to the rigid muscles on Campbell's back. "Campbell, forget it, let's go, please. Let him call the police. It won't be the worst thing he's ever done to me."

But he shoved her back behind him, aligning himself with Finley so he towered over him, making Finley appear smaller than Maxine could ever remember.

His power trip didn't seem quite so ominous with the strength and coiled tension of Campbell glaring down at him. "You really are some piece of shit, *old man*, hitting teenagers like you do. You cut the kid's eye. Next time you want to go a round, give me a call. I'd be happy to show you what happens when you take a cheap shot at a boy toy. You'll be so busy pulling my fist from your ass by way of your throat, you won't have time to call the cops."

Yanking her hand into his, Campbell dragged her out of the dealership, scooping up her mother along with her.

As they hit the hellishly hot blacktop, Campbell stuck his hand out. "Keys," he demanded in Maxine's direction.

"In the car," she muttered.

"Mona, drive home."

For what was probably another first in Maxine's life, her mother didn't speak a word. Her parting shot was a wink at her daughter before she got in her car and drove off.

Campbell pointed to his truck with a stern brook-no-bullshit finger. "In."

Maxine shuffled away like a chastised kindergartner, pulling open the door and grabbing the high handle above the window to drag herself in. A glance at her hand, now swollen and bruised from the shot she'd taken at Finley, made her wince. Exactly what she didn't need—a trip to the emergency room. A flex or two later, and at least it didn't feel like anything was broken.

Campbell hauled himself into the truck, making no effort to hide his anger when he turned the key in the ignition. The rev of the engine rumbled as they left Cambridge Auto in a cloud of gravel and dust.

Her covert glance at him from beneath her eyelashes told her all she needed to know. Someone was in for a ration of shit. Someone named Max.

Campbell surprised her when he pulled off the highway and into a fast food parking lot. Setting the car in park, he swung in his seat to face her. "Hand," was the gruff demand.

"Wait," she protested with a weak mewl. "Let me explain—"

"Hand. In mine. Now."

Oh, he was mad. Maybe one fight for today was enough. Maxine placed her hand in his. He turned it over in his palm, running his fingers along the knuckles and the bones, then placed it back in her lap. "So, is ultimate fighting how you plan to earn your living?"

Something deep inside her teetered then cracked, opening a crevasse of long-overdue emotions. Laughter spilled from her mouth in waves, leaving her gulping for air.

But Campbell wasn't laughing.

Maxine winced. "S-s-s-sooooorry," she snorted, distorting her face to thwart her fit of giggles.

His expression screamed "Shame on Max." "Look, I get defending Connor. Finley really clocked him one, but you do realize he'll most likely have that little boxing round on camera, don't you? The dealership's got them everywhere. What if he uses it against you to take custody of Connor? What if he does call the police?"

If only Finley were that passionate about his son. Connor was a possession. Something Finley owned. He'd never risk the chance that Connor would actually end up in his care by calling the police and filing charges against her. "I do know that, but you know what? I know Finley better than he knows himself. I know he won't call the police. I also know he doesn't really want Connor to live with him. He doesn't want to help him with his homework and take him for physicals. He wants to own him. Connor's a possession I've taken away, and Finley wants him back. But if he had him, he wouldn't know what to do with him." Maxine paused with a shuddering breath at this newest revelation.

Deep. How deep and introspective. Yet it was the truth. In her soul, marrow-deep, Maxine knew it was the truth, and for the first time today, she'd said it out loud. The thing she'd feared the most in her marriage.

She and Connor had been Finley's property.

Finley only cared that she'd taken something he considered his away from him, because that had always been his game. And it hurt. It hurt for Connor, who was probably more aware of it than she'd ever been.

Tears stung Maxine's eyes. Damn Finley Cambridge to a fiery hell for not being the kind of father she wanted him to be. "Okay, so it was wrong to show up like the stereotypical scorned ex-wife and blow a gasket. But if I'd gone the route of calling my lawyer, I'd have gotten the runaround, because, let's face it, my lawyer's not worth the money he bribed his way through Cracker Jack U with. I know it; everyone remotely related to this mess knows it. I can't afford a better attorney. I can't afford the bad one I have now. In light of that, and the realization that Finley would just grease the appropriate palms to keep this on the down low, I punched him. Right in that smug, lying, cheating face of his. I do not regret it. Do. Not. Not right now anyway. He's never hit Connor. Now maybe he won't ever again."

"I get your anger. You deserve it. You just maybe shouldn't express it in a public setting."

Maxine looked down at her thighs with dismay. "And probably not in my mother's borrowed bathing suit, huh?"

"I think the fireworks across the hip give you a crazy-bag-lady look. All you needed was a shopping cart and some voices in your head," he teased. "Kinda blows your credibility."

With a tentative hand, she reached out to touch his, forging ahead with the impulse to feel his skin despite the zing skipping through her veins at their minimal contact. "Thanks for coming to my rescue, and thanks for standing up for me."

Campbell finally smiled, gripping two of her fingers. "He's some piece of work, your almost ex, huh?"

Her heart tugged with lingering sadness for what would always be lost to her son. "I don't know how I never saw that side of him before. Correction, I saw it, but through rose-colored glasses. I guess I just never expected he'd treat Connor and me with such cold calculation. And I've witnessed how cutthroat Finley can be. I saw him do it all the time with business partners, investors. But when he did it to me, it knocked the wind right out of my sails. Like it came out of nowhere. I don't know why I thought we wouldn't be considered 'Nothing personal, it's just business,' like everyone else. Nowadays, I look back and can't figure out how, in my deluded mind, I managed to make him someone he wasn't. How do you suppose I created a person that never existed?"

"Maybe you didn't consider it because you're not his business partner, Max. You were his *wife*. He was who you wanted him to be in your head. That was good enough for a while, I guess. Sometimes, time and distance are all the perspective you need to see the real deal."

She shrugged her shoulders, but her smile was teasing. "Or a good right hook."

"That was some shot. Maybe you really should consider ultimate fighting." Campbell brought her injured hand to his lips, dropping a light kiss on her fingertips. She reached out her other hand to just take a quick skim across his cheek. Yet, she lingered. Right there in broad daylight.

His arm went around her, pulling her to him until their bodies were almost length to length. His mouth covered hers, sweet at first, increasing the pressure of his lips when her hands went to his thick hair. Tongues touched in silken rasps of heat. Maxine moaned into his mouth when he swept a hand along her hip, parting her lips to kiss her more deeply. Her nipples grew tight and uncomfortable in the sloppy top of her bathing suit.

She wanted him to touch her again, in every place imaginable. She wanted to touch him, too, along the hard width of his chest, brush every rung of his abs with her tongue. Maxine allowed herself the luxury of running her hands along his muscled back, her hips beginning a rhythm familiar but new with this luscious man who made her want to just let go. Even if it was just for a little while. Heat raged in her belly, visions of Campbell driving himself into her willing body flashed before her eyes.

Laughter outside his truck broke them apart, jarring them both.

Yet that vision had felt so right.

Meaning it couldn't be trusted.

Obviously, her judgment was askew. She couldn't trust herself to see things for what they really were after what she'd just discovered about Finley's relationship with Connor. Something she should have seen long ago instead of making excuses for him.

Maxine pulled away first, putting her hands back into her own lap, looking away from him and out the window when Campbell turned the key in the ignition to take her home.

The weight of her realization began to sink in, leaving her more determined than ever to avoid that kind of heartbreak.

For right now, that meant avoiding Campbell Barker.

CHAPTER THIRTEEN

Note from Maxine Cambridge to all ex-trophy wives and on more sucking it up: Apologies—get used to them. You'll make many in your journey. So many that you and the majority of people who inhabit the continent of Australia don't have enough fingers and toes to keep track of them all. In fact, for all the apologizing you'll do for your erratic, ridiculous behaviors, why not just write out a generic plea for forgiveness? It's not only useful as a time-saver but easy on your memorization skills.

Max blew her hair from her eyes with a weary sigh as she looked across the table at the row of volunteer seniors on the dance committee, all with their own ideas on exactly how the end-of-summer dance should go down.

They'd spent many an afternoon here at the rec center and in the tiny office the village had given her, ironing out details. Each time Maxine thought she had everything together, one of them threw a glitch in her plans. Today's debate was music. "So how do we feel about Mr. Emmerson's son's band, folks? We have to make a decision today."

Mr. Emmerson, spry and with an uncanny resemblance to Mr. Rogers, looked to his fellow seniors with hopeful eyes.

Maxine cringed on his behalf. After the grumblings she'd heard about Mr. Emmerson and his son's singing, the vote wasn't likely going to go his way.

"I say we go with a DJ. It'll save us money in the long run and

besides, his son's band sucks," Grace Waller said with no evident care
for Mr. Emmerson's feelings.

"Now, Grace," Maxine chided good-naturedly, though at this
point in her working life, she really just wanted to tear her hair out.
Wrangling this bunch had been like trying to corral greased pigs.
"Okay, guys. How about we treat each other more kindly? It's not nice
to hurt a fellow committee member's feelings—even if what we truly
feel isn't especially kind."

Grace harrumphed in Maxine's direction. "Don't you go waving
that psychobabble at me, young lady. I'm too old for nice. We put a lot
of work into this dance on short notice, too much work to be forced to
listen to Palmer's kid screech into a microphone. He's no Tom Jones."

Nora Ledbetter slapped at Grace's shoulder, sending a shy smile
of apology to Mr. Emmerson. "Oh, hush, Grace. He wasn't that bad."

"Hah! I nearly ate my fork when he hit that high note, singing that
Air-eee-oh-smith song at your granddaughter's wedding."

"Aerosmith," Maxine corrected, "and that's enough, Grace. There
are better ways to go about this than the path you've chosen. So let's
move on." Maxine tapped her notepad, full of items that still needed
dealing with. "We're two days away from liftoff, and we have a million
little things to handle. In light of the fact that we haven't been able
to cast a unanimous vote for music, I'm taking matters into my own
hands and making the choice for you." Because she could. Because
if she didn't, they'd drive her right to the funny farm in one of their
efficient Smart cars.

"But that's not fair!" Mr. Emmerson said with a frown.

Grace narrowed her eyes at him. "Fair, schmair, Palmer Emmerson. Your kid can't sing, and like hell all these dues I pay to live in
this village are going to help fund his caterwauling! I was damn near
deaf by the time that wedding was over. As Simon Cowell would say,"
Grace adopted a British accent, "it was like listening to cats dipped
in acid."

Maxine popped up out of her seat, letting the notepad flop to the table to exhibit her exasperation. "All right, ladies and gentleman, I think that's enough for today, don't you? First off, Mr. Emmerson, I really think everyone in your age group would far more enjoy some Mitch Miller to, say, Boy George's 'Karma Chameleon' or 'Safety Dance,' don't you?" she coaxed. "C'mon now, you know it's true. How about we look at it as more of a generation gap than major suckitude?"

Mr. Emmerson pouted.

"Secondly, I have a dinner date, and we're getting nowhere fast, so let's wrap this up. I'll handle the music, and that's that." She waggled her fingers at them in the direction of the rec center door, forcing her umpteenth patient smile of the day. "I'm officially calling an end to this meeting due to cloudy with a chance of crabby. So go grab some dinner, and we'll start fresh in the morning."

Maxine began to herd them toward the door while they grumbled and she soothed hurt feelings.

Nora patted her on the arm. "You're a good girl to put up with us, Maxine. I know we could try the patience of Job himself when we get to going round."

And all twelve apostles, Maxine thought, but then she stopped her disgruntled thoughts short. She was grateful for this job. No amount of surly seniors with difficult dispositions, set in their ways, could ever change how thankful she was to get up every morning at seven sharp, shower, put on some makeup, fluff her hair, and head to the Leisure Village South offices where she spent her days as of late.

The seniors kept her on her toes. They kept her mind busy while she budgeted and researched new programs and activities to keep them energetic participants in life. She loved working with them— even on their most difficult days.

She loved that Jack Gorman, Leisure Village South's answer to the Bon Appetit Channel's *Mitch in the Kitchen*, sexy over-fifty-five grin and all, had baked her cranberry muffins every Thursday for the last three weeks. She loved that Mitzi Mathews had pitched a new yoga class with her left leg wrapped around her neck to demonstrate to Maxine how beneficial it would be for the over-sixty crowd to learn, among other things, the "Eka Pada Sirsasana pose."

She loved them because they made her feel useful, worthy, alive.

She loved them because they kept her thoughts from straying to Campbell, who'd obviously gotten the message and had stopped calling after week two into her vow to remain uninvolved until she was better able to trust her judgment.

She loved them because they'd kept her from dwelling on the possibility that she'd missed out on something great in Campbell with her caution. Caution born out of fear.

Nora nudged her, the heavy odor of her White Diamonds perfume sticking in Maxine's throat. "So is Garner's boy your date? Nice lookin' fella that one."

Her heart still twisted into a knot when Campbell was mentioned. Forcing a smile, she winked at Nora. "Nope. Tonight's girls' night out. Me, Len, and a plate of meatloaf is what's on the agenda."

"That's lovely, dear, but your fancy friend's no stand-in for Campbell," she remarked on her way out the door.

The waning heat of the sun glared in Maxine's eyes as she raised a hand to wave good-bye to Nora. As she locked the rec center up, she closed her eyes and swallowed hard.

No. Len wasn't Campbell.

But she was a whole lot safer.

"Sooooo, tell me all about your yummy man," Len cooed as they shared a meatloaf sandwich and fries with brown gravy. The Greek Meets Eat Diner was all but empty at nine in the evening, bringing much-needed peace to Maxine, who'd heard nothing but the endless warring of seniors with suggestions for sponsored events all day long today. Coupled with the onslaught of preparation she'd been handed for the big end-of-summer dance, and she was fried.

"I don't have a yummy man. I do have a yummy job. Don't you want to hear about that?" Maxine had been successful in her attempts to avoid Campbell for almost three weeks since the incident with Finley, and she'd like to avoid thinking about him, too.

She'd given him a lame excuse about postponing their celebratory dinner due to her injured hand and run for cover. Since then, there wasn't a moment she'd allowed herself to be caught alone with him, and she hadn't returned any of his phone calls.

Yet, there weren't many moments she hadn't thought about him and his kisses either.

Len clinked her fork against Maxine's glass of water. "Hey in there. I thought you'd decided to give Campbell a chance. But I haven't heard one delicious detail about him since the Cambridge versus Cambridge smackdown of the millennium. What gives?"

She wiped her mouth with the napkin, throwing it on the red Formica table to hide her burning cheeks. Len didn't need to know what had happened in the woods or in Campbell's truck. Yet Maxine felt like it was written all over her forehead. She ducked her head to avoid Len's prying eyes. "It's just too soon. I'm really not ready. Really, really not ready."

"Said who?" Len asked, her eyes hot on Maxine's head.

"Says me. I should know if I'm ready or not, shouldn't I?" Shouldn't she?

Her friend's head shook with defeated disappointment. "I don't know what you think you know, Maxine, but I do know you'll never know if you don't give it at least a fair shot."

"I don't want to sound bitter here, friend, but I am in the middle of the messiest divorce since the Alamo. I'm gun-shy. My judgment can't be trusted."

"The Alamo had nothing to do with a divorce, and here's what pisses me off about this—you like Campbell. He likes you. But you're willing to ignore that and hide behind your messy divorce. You'd give up something that could be a really great experience just so you can avoid the slim chance you'll be raked over some coals. Seriously, how much harm could Campbell do in comparison to what Finley's done? Is there anything more anyone can take from you at this point? And I'm not talking pride or self-esteem either."

The bell on the door jingled, saving Maxine from supplying an answer. The couple strolling into the diner, tall and striking together, made her want to lunge under the table. She sank down into the diner's black vinyl seat and cringed.

Len's head swung around to view the counter where the pair seated themselves. Her eyebrow arched when her gaze focused on her friend. "So our man Campbell's got a girlfriend. Good job, Maxine. Now you don't have to worry he'll hurt you. He's too busy hurting another woman."

She made a big show of glancing back at Campbell and the woman at the counter before adding, "Oh, look. They're sharing an ice cream sundae. How sweet. Ohhhhhh, she's licking *his* spoon. In public. How decadent. But you don't really care about that do you—he was only going to hurt you with his ice cream anyway, right?"

Maxine refused to look. She couldn't look. Wait. Why the hell couldn't she look? Because green was a lovely shade of jealous. "Lay off!" she whisper-yelled. "And, BTW, this just proves my point. I clearly have sucky judgment when it comes to men. Not two weeks ago Campbell was asking me out—today he's out with some over-Botoxed, boobed-out blonde. Obviously, I left such an impression he's all broken up," she said with scathing tones.

"Uh-huh," Len agreed in mock delight. "And do you know who that boobed-out blonde is?"

She'd ducked too quickly to get a good look at her face. Now,

with a cursory sideways glance, all she could see was the curve of
her very shapely hip, clad in an expensive pair of jeans, slapped up
against Campbell's. God, how obvious. How cheap. *Yeah. How much
do you wish it was you?* With a shake of her head, she made a face at
Lenore. "I don't care who she is."

Lenore stretched her tanned arms out in front of her with the
grace of a preying cat. "Oh. Okay. So telling you that's Lisa Trainor
he's feeding a cherry to, you know, Lisa of Trainor's Trainers, the
wildly successful exercise guru franchise, will mean nothing. Good."
She gave a brisk nod, grabbing her purse. "Let's blow and find a place
to hang out that isn't filled with scumbags feeding women ice cream."

Maxine's eyes widened. She reached for Len's hand to keep her
from rising. "It is not!" She and Lisa had done many a charity event
together. They'd had lunch. Hosted dinner parties. The whore.

"Oh, it is."

Maxine's eyes narrowed, disgust filtering through her veins like
hot lava. "And there it is in a nutshell. All Campbell's bullshit talk
about what a jerk Finley is, and he's off feeding ice cream to a cheating slut!" She clamped a hand over her mouth to quiet the rise in her
dulcet pipes.

"Well, technically, he's not cheating at all, Maxine. He's not married. She is."

"Oh, bullshit, Lenore Erickson. That's cheating by proxy!" It was
so much better she'd found out now rather than after she'd fallen for
his therapy-like charms and soothing presence. Not to mention his
crazy talented lips and swoon-worthy orgasms. Who needed a man-
made orgasm when you could have an artificial one anyway? Once
they figured out a gadget for taking out the trash, there'd be a day
when men would become obsolete.

Yet it still stung, and Maxine wasn't sure if that sting was over
the fact that she was still attracted to jerk-offs or because it hurt that

Campbell actually was a jerk-off. She might have run away from him
for fear of getting in too deep, but she'd still wanted Campbell to be
a good guy.

The slimy pig.

Len rose, brushing stray crumbs from her trousers, to give her a
dry response. "I couldn't agree more. You want me to go make sure
he heard that, or should we just take it for granted this place has awesome acoustics?"

Maxine's eyes rose with a defiant glance in the direction of the
countertop. Good. They were staring at her. That was exactly how
she'd planned it. She slid from the booth, coughing on her way out.

There was only one thing to do.

Make things worse than they already were.

Impulse gave her feet wings, carrying her to the front of the diner
where that cheating slut and her man-whore dined on ice cream like
it was a forbidden sexual act. The time for retribution on behalf of
every cheated-on spouse was finally here, and Maxine was going to
dole it out two servings at a time.

Lisa caught sight of Maxine making her way toward them first,
jumping up from her chair like she was greeting a long-lost friend.
"Maxine! Oh, my God. It's so good to see you!" Lisa pulled her into
a hug, her perfume enveloping Maxine's nostrils until she almost
choked from the cloyingly sweet scent.

Setting her from her svelte body, Lisa smiled. Kinda warm, but
Maxine decided it was just good acting. She should know, she'd done
it a million times. "You look terrific, honey. So great. I heard about
you and Finley, and I just wanted to tell you, good for you. He's a pig.
I always knew it—what he's done confirms it."

Wasn't that like the pot calling the kettle pitch-black? Maxine
cocked her head at a "Huh" angle. "Hey, pot, quit calling the kettle a
pig!" she reprimanded with a waving finger.

Lisa's face collapsed. "What?"

Campbell, still seated, put a possessive hand to Lisa's waist. The very hand that had visited that exact locale on Maxine's body a time or two. Jealousy streaked a bright and shimmery path through her veins.

By God, he didn't deserve her jealousy. How dare he create that kind of ugly in her—even a little. Jealousy was a powerful emotion, leaving her infuriated with herself. She really hadn't come that far at all if a liar like Campbell evoked such a passionate reaction. Why couldn't she just be indifferent? Why did it hurt to be rejected by a man who wasn't worthy of the poop she scooped?

Even stunned, Lisa's face was still beautiful. "Maxine? I don't understand," she said in a pleading tone.

Campbell popped his lips, his expression wry. "Oh, I do. Let me explain. I think Maxine's calling you a cheating liar, but I'm not one hundred percent sure. She's making fancy euphemisms a simple boy like me just doesn't understand."

Charming. Wasn't he just? Always had an answer for everything. Always with the pretense he wasn't a smooth operator—wooing little old ladies and their dogs when he was really just a poorer version of the playa Finley was.

Maxine's anger at her reaction to seeing Campbell with another woman, combined with the bleak reality that she'd once more fallen for some man's line, erupted like a whistle-blowing teakettle, all hot and steamy. "That's right! I said it. That's exactly what I'm calling you—both of you! How could you do this to Benjamin, Lisa? And *you*," she swung around to rasp in Campbell's face, one that was unruffled, serving only to make her anger swell to new proportions. "You jerk! You're no better than she is. Just because you're not married, doesn't mean you're not cheating by proxy. It's conspiracy to commit infidelity. Ohhhh, am I ever glad I ditched you, or I'd be no better off than I was when I was married to Finley! But I'm not an idiot anymore, Campbell Barker. I see right through you and your crap!"

Campbell didn't move a muscle. His hand remained firmly at Lisa's waist. Nor did he defend himself. And if she had to give a definitive answer one way or the other, she'd call that little move on his part downright galling. The best defense was obviously no defense.

Lisa, on the other hand, was all sound and motion. Her bangle bracelets clanged, while her lying mouth moved. "Maxine, honey, this isn't what you think! I swear to you—"

"Yeahhhhh," Maxine shouted back, letting sarcasm drip from her words. "That's what Finley said about every nubile vagina he encountered." She let her voice go deep in an almost perfect mimic of Finley's. "'This isn't what you think, Maxine.' I have to ask myself, what is someone supposed to *think* when they find out their spouse has willingly taken his clothes off and stuck his you know what in another woman's boy-howdy!'"

Len grabbed her arm. "*Enough*, Maxine," she ordered in her ear with a terse reprimand. "Turn yourself around and march your big mouth out of here while you can still hold your head up."

Campbell rose, shooting Len a stern warning glance. "No, Len. I'll handle this."

Disbelief riddled Maxine's features. "Handle this? *Handle?* How dare you say something like that to me! I'll show you handled!" Her outrage was loud and proud.

Though Campbell's sudden lean into her gave her bravado a run for its money. His next words were tight and filled with unconcealed anger. "Do you remember when I said you were sensitive, Max? That maybe communication was in your best interest before you jumped the gun and started waving around accusations?"

Yeah. She remembered it. So? Yet, that conversation returned, flitting through her memory like the gossamer wings of a butterfly. Fleeting and fast. And then she understood.

Oh. It was like that.

Hoo boy.

Maxine had a sinking feeling one of those stupid post-divorce life lessons was in her near future. Her anger fizzled. She bowed her head, peeking out at him from behind her lashes. Every rage-filled vessel in her body now quivered with submission. She'd gone and done it again with her insecurities and stupid conclusion jumping. There was nothing else to do but own it. "I remember."

Campbell hitched his tight jaw in Lisa's direction. "Good. That conversation applies to the here and now. Lisa is my lying, cheating *cousin*. On my mother's side, if you're looking for specifics. We used to ride bikes together, and when we rode bikes together, we rode them here—to this very diner. Where, as sort of a family tradition between *cousins*, we always shared an ice cream sundae."

Yes indeed. She'd been right on the money.

This here was a life lesson.

Seek impulse-control medication.

In bulk.

CHAPTER FOURTEEN

Note from Maxine Henderson to all ex-trophy wives: Sometimes secrets come back to bite you in your not-so-youthful butt. Better yet, sometimes they're not your secrets doing the biting—which is always a relief, no? Leave no stone unturned in your quest to live in the light. The truth is out there. Or at least that's what Fox Mulder always said.

Humiliation made her legs quiver. Lenore was right behind her, holding her up. "We're going now," Len said briskly. "Lisa, it was terrific to see you. You look fabulous. Say hello to Benjamin for me." She gave Maxine a hard shove toward the diner's doors. "Campbell? Please," Len said, her tone weary. "Find it in your heart to forgive both me and my lunatic friend. I thought I was jokingly pointing out the obvious to Maxine, when in fact, I only added fuel to her fire. I think calling her raw wouldn't be an overstatement, though nonetheless inexcusable." Her friend's parting words stung Maxine's ears as she ushered her out of the diner.

Pine trees surrounded the area, their scent clinging to the hot July air, making Maxine want to gag. Side by side, in total silence, they made their way to the back of the parking lot. The click of Lenore's heels was a sure indicator she was cranked. When they reached her car, Maxine grabbed Len's hand, her eyes filled with sheepish regret. "Too much empowerment again?" She bit her bottom lip while she waited for Len to let her have it.

Len's mouth fell open. "That's an understatement if I ever heard one."

Maxine rubbed the space between her eyes with her thumb. "I'm sorry I embarrassed you."

Her sharp eyes glinted. "You didn't embarrass me, but wow, I bet you feel like shit now, huh? When are you going to get over yourself, Maxine? When are you going to take the hardcore lessons you've learned from being married to a prick like Finley and use them for your greater good?"

Maxine's chin fell to her chest, duly chastised and grateful Len hadn't dragged her out of there by her hair. "Like I said before, my behavior's exactly why I shouldn't date Campbell or anyone."

Len's lips thinned. "That's just an excuse to behave badly."

Was it? *Was. It?* Maybe it was . . . "One minute I'm moving right along, thinking I've got it all together and the next I'm a mouth without censor, taking up the noble sword for all cheated-upon spouses. I don't know what comes over me—it just does."

"I know what's come over you. You've discovered you have an opinion and you're winging it around like a baseball bat. You just don't know how to clamp that pretty mouth shut and keep it to yourself or better still, ask questions first before you lose your mind in a public place. But you're learning—the hard way, but still learning."

Maxine's eyes went skyward in remorse. *It really would be okay if you decided now was my time to meet my maker. I'd go willingly. No questions asked.*

Len brushed Maxine's hair from her face. "Look, I'm not going to indulge this for long, honey. No one will. I love you, but you can't just go screaming 'whore' at the top of your lungs whenever you see some imagined injustice without investigating it first. Did you see Lisa's face? Jesus, she was crushed. She and Benjamin are one of the very few couples from that elite circle we traveled in that really do love each other."

Maxine cringed, running a hand over her grainy eyes. The horror on Lisa's face flashed before her closed eyes. She'd used the phrase boy-howdy in reference to Lisa's hoo-hah. Humiliation bludgeoned her from the inside out. "I'm clearly lacking in the area of social cues. Seeing them together just hit a hot button for me."

"Uh-huh. But here's the thing about hot buttons, if you want to champion their cause, don't do it at the top of your lungs in a public place like you're some superhero who's been given a cape and her own invisible plane."

"I get it. I promise to stop defending truth, justice, and the marital way . . . I'll apologize to both Lisa and Campbell the second I can get them to consider canceling the restraining orders," she joked, hoping to lift the wet blanket of Len's discontent.

But Len wasn't in the slack-cutting mood. "That's fine, Maxine. But eventually, apologies aren't going to cut it anymore. Campbell is none of your business. You made it clear you don't want to take a chance on getting involved with him. So what right do you have to stick your nose in where it doesn't belong with a man who's free to date whoever the hell he wants to date?"

God. She hated hearing Campbell thought about dating anyone but her.

And Jesus. What kind of bullshit was that? Who did she think she was? She'd blown him off out of her fear. She'd avoided him when he was fixing that stupid pipe in her mother's bathroom, and she didn't answer his phone calls. Yet, she wanted him to eat fattening fried foods and wander around in her old shirt while he mourned something that had never even gotten off the ground?

Christ.

The sigh Maxine let go was shaky when she ran a hand over her forehead. "All I could think of was Benjamin and how awful it would be for him to find out his much younger wife had gone AWOL. I know how much it hurts to be blindsided like that." That hurt had once taken over every aspect of her life, kept her guarded, hypersensitive to anything even a little off-kilter.

She'd once awakened with it, eaten with it, shopped with it, slept with it. It was the kind of hurt that never gave you any peace. It jaded you, ate at you, and eventually turned you into a shrieking, self-righteous shrew. Obviously.

Len's hands gripped her shoulders. "I'm sure you thought you were defending Benjamin's honor, Maxine. I shouldn't have teased you, but I was certain you'd come to a place where you'd realize a casual, mature investigation was in order. Like, 'Hey, Campbell and Lisa. What brings you two here—*together*?' Not a complete flip out. I *knew* there had to be an explanation. Campbell's a good guy, whether you want him to be or not."

"I don't know what I want," she admitted in defeat.

"Sure you do. You want to explore Campbell. The problem is you don't trust that you trust Campbell."

"That makes no sense. And you're right. I had no right to stick my nose in where it doesn't belong." Though in the moment, she'd felt like she was championing some great cause for all who'd suffered infidelity.

"You stuck your nose in because you were jealous, Maxine. Just own it."

Her defense mechanism kicked in. "I was not jealous. I was just looking out for an old acquain—"

"Len?" a silky voice said from the dark.

They both whirled around to see a tall man, a very attractive, well-dressed, tall man, come out of the shadows and into the overhead lights of the parking lot. Maxine noted the myriad emotions flitting over her best friend's face, giving her the grateful opportunity to forget her own stupidity for just a moment. Surprise was certainly there, but so was a flicker of warmth mixed with anger at this man's intrusion.

Len's voice was low and definitely irritated when she asked, "What are *you* doing here?"

His voice, on the other hand, was controlled, no-nonsense, and damned sexy. "Eating before our date."

Maxine's eyes went from Len's to the handsome interloper's, searching for the signals they were sending to each other without saying a word.

Len's said, "How dare you show up here unannounced" with a dagger of a death stare.

His said, "Oh, I dare" with arrogantly cocky overtones.

Mere seconds passed, filled with the kind of heat Maxine not only saw, but experienced by way of a proxy shiver. "Len?" Her question wasn't just one, but a hundred. Like who the hell was this long, tall drink of water, this suit-wearing hunk, and why hadn't she been let in on the secret they so blatantly shared?

Len's arms wrapped around Maxine, giving her a squeeze—a distracted squeeze. "You go home, honey. I'll call you tomorrow." Tilting her chin up, her dark eyes focused but a moment on her friend's before skittering away to parts known as yummy man. "And no more public floggings, okay?"

Thankful she was no longer in the hot seat, Maxine shook her head. Uh, no. "No, it's not okay. Don't shuffle me off because you don't want to explain what's going on. Since when do you have a *date*?" she said out of the side of her mouth.

"Since you don't."

"Ohhhhhhhhh, nice comeback, Seinfeld. Who is that?" she asked, none too quietly.

Len's gravy-scented, huffy breath of air wafted under Maxine's nose. "Please don't ask. Just go home."

"Adam Baylor," he interrupted, sticking a hand over Len's shoulder in the direction of Maxine.

She took it and smiled. "Nice to meet you, *Adam*. And how do you know my best friend in the whole wide world, Len?" Len gave her a "knock it off" glare, fueling Maxine's fire and curiosity.

"We're dating," he offered, catching Maxine's playful glance and joining in.

"Reallllly?" Stepping around Len, she leaned into Adam, not quite reaching his broad shoulder. "Tell me something, Adam? Don't you find it funny that Len didn't tell her best friend in the whole wide world she was dating a man? Especially a good-looking man like yourself?"

He made a mock punch to his heart. "It hurts right here. To be hidden away like some dirty little secret."

Oh. She liked. He had a sense of humor, and the way he looked at her friend made Maxine's breath flutter.

Len, however, wasn't enjoying their banter. Her eyes sent the girl-friend signal, the one that said Maxine was going to lose an eyeball if she didn't knock it off. "Isn't Connor waiting for you?"

A roll of her eyes later and she was shaking Adam's hand good-bye. "It was nice meeting you, and Len's right. My son's waiting for me, and my mother gave me a curfew on her car. But don't be a stranger. In fact, if you want my phone number, maybe *you* can call me and fill me in on all the deets my best friend in the whole wide world somehow forgot to share," she taunted in Len's direction, back-ing up again toward her parking space with a grin.

"Go. Home," Len hissed with a finger pointed at Mona's car.

She threw her hands up in resignation before planting a kiss on her friend's cheek with a teasing smile. "I'm going. I'm going, but if I don't hear from you tomorrow about your new stud, mayhem could ensue."

A pop of her car door later, and Maxine was safely inside, taking one last peek at a bent-out-of-shape Len and an amused Adam before she drove away. Seeing them together set off a multitude of her own emotions.

No doubt, it was far past time for Len to move on. She was beau-tiful, interesting, *alive*. But there was disappointment mingled with her happiness for Len. Why hadn't she made a single mention of Adam?

So wrapped up in her own crap, she'd forgotten the word "friend" was a two-way street, and sometimes it really was okay to actually inquire about Len's well-being, was why.

Speaking of her own crap, she had apologies to make.

Her stomach clenched in a tight ball of regret. Once again, she'd read Campbell wrong and in the process scored another point for downtrodden maniacal ex-wives everywhere. Go. Team.

How did you even begin to apologize for calling a perfectly nice man and his *cousin* infidels?

Flowers?

A card? Did Hallmark really have a card for every occasion? What would she say?

Dear Campbell and Lisa,

Please forgive my escapee from the psych ward behavior. I did a bad, bad thing. Cousins should never have to endure that kind of humiliation because cagey lunatics like myself can't control their foolish impulses.

Shamefaced,
Maxine XXOO

~~∞~~

The moment Maxine drove off, Len was on Adam like fried on chicken. "What the hell are you doing here?" Damn it. How dare he follow her around like they had some sort of commitment? The agreement was they'd keep things discreet—no questions asked.

Adam's eyes glittered in the heavy swell of the full moonlight. "Are you embarrassed by me?"

No. Yes. No. She wasn't embarrassed by him. She was embarrassed by her behavior with him. Argh. "You have no right to come skulking around when I'm with my friend!" Righteous indignation was a perfectly acceptable path to follow when you were avoiding the question.

"A man has to eat. Especially when he's dating you and your voracious appetite for all things naughty," he teased, pulling her to him.

Her tension at being found out eased a little. Still, she placed flat palms on his chest to hold him off. "And you had to eat here? There are plenty of places to eat all over the Jersey Turnpike."

"There are, but I hear no one makes meatloaf like the Greek Meets Eat Diner. You made it clear you don't cook, and you won't share a meal with me. So what's a boy to do but fend for himself? I figured I'd grab some takeout while I waited for our illicit rendezvous to begin."

"So this was just a coincidence?"

"Yep. I saw your car parked in the lot and heard your raised voice. I couldn't make out what you were yelling about, so I came to investigate. I was actually concerned about your safety for all the yelling going on. Though I don't know why when you have mace— illegally, mind you. How was I to know you weren't in the middle of a kidnapping?"

He'd thought to see if she needed rescuing after the way she'd been avoiding talk and ignoring his invasive, pestering questions these past weeks? That sentiment did two things. Warmed her in places she didn't wish to have warmed and made her wonder what kind of glutton for punishment he was, considering he didn't really know many personal details about her.

While Len realized all Adam had to do was Google her to find out who she'd been married to, she found she'd rather have him find out via the Internet instead of hushed bedroom conversations after mind-blowing sex. That felt too intimate.

Intimacy was Gerald's—forever.

Sex for now was Adam's, who couldn't be found anywhere on the Internet. The only information she'd dredged up was a long string of names, none of the names with details matching his description.

The mystery surrounding Adam showing up had become something she was reluctant to unravel. It was fun. Exciting, maybe a little dangerous—which, again, made it fun. "Well, I don't need protecting, and I'm finding it hard to believe your showing up here was a coincidence."

The nibble on her lower lip made her forget her accusation. "Believe what you want."

His hard length, fit so close to hers, was a revelation each time Adam pulled her close. He left her swooning, secretly smiling to herself at the oddest of moments. The war between loving or hating that effect on her was an endless mental battle.

Adam let her go without warning, stepping backward. "So I'm going to go get that meatloaf I ordered, and I'll see you at T-minus thirty and counting. Bye, Len." The pivot of his leather heel on the pavement signaled his abrupt departure. He flashed her a playful grin over his shoulder before making his way toward the sidewalk leading to the diner.

Len stumbled to her car on shaking legs, unsure where her anger stemmed from. Adam was playing the game just the way she'd asked him to, and he hadn't balked since the last time she'd shut him down. He hadn't batted an eye when she'd suggested they do nothing more than satisfy each other's voracious sexual whims. At first, it had worked. As long as he wasn't hurting Maxine and he was on the up-and-up about it, the rules were fine.

Yet, lately, when she stared out her window in her office, or went home to her bed to sleep alone, she began to wonder why he didn't care enough to stop playing the game and start pressing her for something more than the color of her underwear.

Her trek to her car stopped cold with that thought. Those sorts of yearnings had to stop, or she just might end up falling . . .

Guilt wove another web of protection over her heart. She wasn't falling into anything.

She was just enjoying the company of a fantastically, incredibly sexual man.

And it was lovely. That was that.

~ℓ~

"Before you go scooting off to your fancy job there, Maxie, you got a letter. It's on the counter," her mother said when she whizzed past her to grab her blouse from the dryer.

Dread came in the way of jelly legs and a squishy stomach. On the upside, maybe it was a letter from her divorce lawyer saying the ink was ready to be set on her divorce papers. Though not likely.

She and Finley were still haggling over visitation for Connor. He refused to sign on the dotted line until Connor agreed to see him. A peculiar request in Maxine's mind. Shouldn't he want to be rid of her so he could marry the fair Lacey ASAP and begin manipulating another young woman's life?

But she couldn't pony up the money to have her lawyer file the final divorce papers, and Connor hadn't just dug his heels in after taking a slug in the eye from Finley, he'd built a moat around himself, eliminating any communication at all.

The envelope on the counter didn't look very official though. It was rather worn and faded pink. Maxine's heart thudded, heavy and hard against her ribs. She recognized that stationery. Her fingers fumbled when she tore it open. Tears stung her eyes, clouding them, keeping her from reading the letter's content.

Her eyes flew to the date on it. *June 24, 2004.* The room tilted for a moment, then righted itself. Ten deep breaths later, she read the elegant scrawl of her dead mother-in-law.

My dearest Maxine,

I write this with a sad heart, but I write it with love for you and for my only grandson, Connor, who makes me so very proud he bears the name Cambridge. You were always too good for my Finley, Maxine. As much as it pains me to write those words, they are the truth. Finley isn't the man I hoped he would be. I've known about his indiscretions for some time now. I've borne witness to the sadness it's brought you, though I know you thought you'd hidden it well. Thank you, my dear, for trying to protect me.

So I turn my eyes to my grandson, Connor, who shows the promise of a fine upbringing, due solely to you. I beg of you to understand why I've done what I've done. Soon enough, you'll know what this letter means.

My love always,
Dorothy

A sob tore from her throat, a sob in memory of Dorothy. If everyone was a product of their environment, then Maxine was at a loss as to how Finley had become such a jerk with Dorothy as a mother.

Her mother-in-law had welcomed her with open arms from the start. They'd shared so many happy times, and she'd adored Connor. Lavished him with love and attention, not to mention trips to exotic places he might not have seen had Finley had his way. Every moment she'd spent with Connor had always felt to Maxine as though Dorothy was trying to make up for something she'd missed out on with Finley.

It wasn't Finley who'd driven two hours each way three times a week to see his mother when she'd finally been placed in a nursing home. It was Maxine and Connor. Recalling the fight she and Finley had about how far away Dorothy was from her only family made Maxine shudder. On that occasion, in defense of Dorothy, she'd managed to find her words, and she'd dumped them all on her husband. Who'd shot her down, reminding her he paid the bills.

"Maxie, honey? You're gonna be late," her mother reminded her.

She held the letter to her nose, hoping to find a remnant of Dorothy's perfume left on it. With a shaky hand, Maxine grabbed her mother's arm. "Sit for a minute, Mom."

Concern wrinkled Mona's face when she slid into a chair beside Maxine. "Did the Talleywhacker finally send you the divorce papers?"

"No." She thrust the letter at her mother. "Read this."

Mona pulled her glasses off the top of her head, her expression marred as her eyes scanned the letter. There was silence broken only by the ticking rooster clock in the kitchen. Her mother laid the letter on the table between them. "What do you think she meant by 'you'll know soon enough what the letter means,' Maxie?"

Maxine's head whirled. "I don't know. I don't understand. The letter's dated June twenty-fourth, 2004, but the postmark is yesterday. The return address is from the nursing home she was in, yet your address is the forward on it. This makes absolutely no sense."

"I always liked Dorothy. She might have raised a total shit, but I liked her anyway," her mother said quietly.

Maxine's fingers ran over her mother-in-law's written words. "This is her handwriting. I've seen it a hundred times on postcards she sent to us when she was abroad, cards for birthdays, anniversaries, whatever the occasion. I have no idea what it means."

"Well, girlie, I say you call up that fancy nursing home her twerp of a son threw her in and ask."

"I will, I will. But I can't right now. I have to get to work. We're hashing out some last-minute details for the dance, and if I'm a millisecond late, your compadres get cranky."

Her mother rose, cupping her chin with a warm, weathered hand. "Dorothy was right, you know. You did good by Connor. All by yourself."

Maxine smiled. A sweet compliment from her mother was as rare as hen's teeth. "I have to get my butt in gear."

"Off to a chapter meeting of Cheat-A-Non?"

The hair on the back of her neck rose. "Campbell," she acknowledged with a somber tone, unable to turn around.

"That's me. The lying, cheating one."

There was nothing to do but turn and face the music. She owed him at least an explanation. Fighting the impulse to beg for his forgiveness by throwing herself into the shelter of his arms, she took a deep breath instead. "I went off half-cocked last night."

His blue eyes were unreadable. "I'll say."

"I'm really sorry. I behaved so badly. I just lost it."

"You'll get no argument from me."

Okay. He wasn't budging. What more could she do than apologize? "So again, I'm sorry. Like super-sorry. The sorriest I've ever been." When Maxine peeked up at him, his glacial expression remained firm. "Still mad?"

Campbell crossed his arms over his chest, the muscles of his tanned arms flexing. "You were really out of line, Max."

Her nod was vehement. "I really was. No question. Way out."

"Lisa didn't even see you coming. You completely blindsided her. And you know what blows about that? She just got through telling me that if she'd known Finley was being such a prick about his money, she'd have hired you even without personal trainer experience. She really likes and admires you, Max."

Crap. Residual remorse for her ugly behavior returned tenfold. "I totally don't deserve her admiration, and believe me, I'm just as disgusted with myself as you both should be with me. I just . . ." What was the point in defending it? There was no defense for shooting and asking questions of the dead bodies later.

"You're *just* a little out of hand. If you're not slugging your ex-husband, you're accusing me of some pretty heinous stuff in the middle of a diner. That sucked."

"Big weenies," Maxine confirmed, contrite.

Campbell finally cracked a half smile. It wasn't the uber grin that made her belly quiver, but it was a start. "The biggest."

A glance at the kitchen clock told her she had to make haste. "I really, really have to go or I'm going to be late, and I can't afford to be late today, but I hope you'll accept my apology. I mean that. Maybe you could drop by the dance Friday night, and I can bow and scrape some more. There'll be lots of Mitch Miller . . ." She enticed him with a smile.

His eyes remained unreadable, his lips unmoving.

"You're still mad."

"I'm still something. I just can't pinpoint what."

Maxine rolled her eyes. "That sounds like something a woman would say."

Campbell's eyebrow cocked upward, but his tight jaw loosened just a bit more. "You should know."

Maxine chuckled, throwing the letter in her purse. "That's fair. I owe you a hissy fit or two."

"Which leads me to a question. Why would I come to a dance *you* invited me to? So you can avoid me like I have the clap? In case you've forgotten, you hadn't returned a single one of my phone calls before that little incident in the diner, and Houdini could have learned a thing or two from you the way you magically disappear whenever I'm even in the same twelve-mile radius. If you weren't interested, you could have just had the balls to say as much. I fully comprehend the word no."

It took effort, but she forced her eyes to capture his, letting her fingers brush his knuckles. "It's not that I'm not interested. I am."

There. The truth. She'd thought about it well into the wee hours of the morning. Either she had to indulge Campbell's interest in her and see what she could see, or she was going to man-up and tell him it was a no-go. When the no-go part of the equation popped up, and her reaction to it was a twinge of deep regret in the depths of her heart, she'd decided things had to change.

"Then what is it, Max? Because the on again, off again thing, the freaking out without any warning, and the avoiding me at all costs will eventually either drive me insane, or drive me to Home Depot where I'll buy a wood chipper to dispose of your body."

Her sigh was shaky. "It's that I'm so used to living my life in total panic mode, I don't know how to find any other gear but high. I panicked after my argument with Finley. It made me realize I'm a shitty judge of character, Campbell. I realized he'd never call the police on me because as much as he'd like to make me out to be some lunatic, he'd never risk the possibility a judge might actually give him full custody of Connor. For all his showy efforts to get Connor to come back home, Finley knew he'd never do it. What's worse is, he doesn't really want Connor to do it. It's always just some big show so he can tell everyone he tried to do the right thing. It's so Fin can tell everyone crazy, unstable Maxine's brainwashed his kid to keep Connor from him. How could I have been so wrong about a man I was married to for almost half my life?"

Campbell's jaw twitched, but he let her curl her fingers around his. "I'm unclear how that applies to me."

"I know this sounds crazy, but if I was so wrong about a man I thought I knew intimately, how could I possibly expect to make sound decisions about one I've only known for a couple of months?"

"And now?"

"Now I think I'd like to find out if my decision-making skills have improved." She fluttered her eyelashes and let her lips lift in a flirtatious smile. The freedom of all this communication had its benefits. She felt lighter already. Even if Campbell opted out, she'd at least taken the chance on not just sharing her fear but making the first move.

Campbell didn't respond, and that was only fair. It had taken her three weeks to come to her senses.

"Anyway, you think about the dance, where I'll humble myself appropriately. Oh," she said, grinning up at him and placing a hand on his chest, remembering the feel of him beneath her fingers, "and there'll be *cake*. Mrs. Lipknicki's making her apple strudel bundt cake. She's a retired caterer, you know. Not a treat to be missed, if you ask me."

"I'm not opposed to bundt cake," Campbell said, making sure she heard the reluctance in his voice.

"I'll save you a piece." Maxine's face grew serious, her heart thudding in her chest. "I really hope you'll come, Campbell," she whispered, experiencing a bit of her own reluctance when she turned to grab her purse and leave before she knocked him down and begged him to give her a second chance.

As Maxine jumped into her mother's car, she caught sight of her reflection in the rearview mirror. Her cheeks were flushed and her eyes were bright.

In those eyes with the beginnings of crow's-feet at the corners was a hint of pride that she'd taken charge of her feelings, owned them, admitted what had scared her off, and had then set about making a move on a man she desperately wanted to experience—full throttle.

A tingle of anticipation fluttered low in her belly, the tingle of new beginnings and independent woman.

Her metaphoric pom-poms shouted a rah-rah-sis-boom-bah.

CHAPTER FIFTEEN

Note from Maxine Cambridge to all ex-trophy wives: The wistful strains of "Moon River" + smokin' hot man can = "Some Enchanted Evening" Sometimes, it's okay to be the captain of your own Love Boat. Taking control of your desires is sexy, ladies. This may require more take charge than you have in you at this point, and that's okay. But if you ever get the chance to steer your own ship—ahoy, matey!

"Thanks for wrapping this up for me, Denise. It's appreciated. Hopefully, I'll have all the pieces of the puzzle in place soon, and I can be done with this." Adam dropped his BlackBerry on the hotel bed and ran his hands through his hair in frustration after his conversation with his secretary. He couldn't concentrate on his original purpose for being in Riverbend to begin with because of a wildly sexy woman with dark eyes and a laugh that made his heart pound like some teenager's.

Damn this woman for making him crazy. He couldn't keep his hands off her. He couldn't keep his thoughts from her. He. Couldn't.

And damn it, he had a fucking cat to let out of the bag. A big one. One that could change everything, and he wanted to share that with Len. He wanted to share a lot of things with Len.

Yet her staunch insistence that they do absolutely nothing more than wring each other dry of all their bodily fluids was so crystal clear, most times, he was almost too hesitant to even ask her something as simple as how her day had gone.

At first, when he'd arrived in Riverbend, he'd been in semi-agreement that they should keep things strictly related to the bedroom. He wasn't typically into that kind of thing, but when their chemistry had exploded over that first drink, Len had managed to change his mind. Little did he know, after that first encounter, she'd leave him with a lingering ache in his gut he'd never experienced in forty-three years.

Besides, most women never really meant they didn't want a commitment—not to the degree the average male looking for no-strings-attached sex did. He'd gone along with it for a time, certain he'd work her out of his system, do what he came to do, and go back to the city. Maybe they'd even end up friends when this all came to pass.

Ironically, that wasn't working out. The more time he spent with Len in the sack, the more he wanted to find out how she lived her life out of it. What her favorite food was. If she liked ketchup or mustard on her hot dogs—if she even liked hot dogs.

Instead, he had a woman who wouldn't share the simplest of details about herself and her life. A woman who was displaying all the signs of preparing to run when he pressed her to allow him to date her rather than just meet him illicitly at his hotel.

But did that stop him from coming back for more? No. Every opportunity he could grab to get away from his office and make a trip to Riverbend he took like some love-starved, abandoned puppy.

Maybe this thing with Len was just a case of his ego and winning. He liked to win.

But that wasn't what his gut was telling him.

Or for that matter, his heart.

～ℓ～

Two days later, after another long day of last-minute details for the dance, Maxine dropped her mother's phone back into its charger with a disappointed grunt.

"No luck?" Connor asked.

"Nope. No one at the nursing home even remembers Grandma Dorothy. The staff's changed hands so many times and they definitely don't remember a pink letter." What Dorothy could have meant in that letter had troubled her all day long. That she'd known about Finley's indiscretions, as she'd called them, made her cringe. Maxine had taken as many precautions as she could to keep their sordid affairs from her, and she'd known all along anyway.

Connor put a hand on her shoulder. "You look really pretty, Mom."

Maxine smiled up at him. Wow, a compliment from Connor was rare. She glanced down at her Target dress, bought on sale for twenty-two bucks, and smiled again. She'd *earned* this dress, and the shiny periwinkle pumps to match it. It felt like it was worth a million bucks. She gave Connor's hand a pat. "Thanks, honey. I guess I'd better go." She rose, smoothing the swirly length of material around her legs and tightening the tie of her halter dress around her neck.

"Do you think we'll ever know what Grandma meant in the letter?"

Maxine paused, a fleeting memory of Dorothy's smiling eyes flashing in front of her. "I don't know, kiddo. But it was so good to get something like that from her when things have been looking so glum. It was kinda like she knew we needed a bit of cheering up, huh?"

Connor smiled with his own fond memory in mind, Maxine was sure. "Yeah. Yeah, it was."

"All right. I'm out," she said, blowing him a kiss. "Wish me a troll-free night, eh?"

Her mother had offered her a ride to the rec center, but Maxine decided to walk. A moment to catch her breath was in order. A silent wish for Campbell's presence was in order, too. She'd had a difficult time focusing today when he came to mind.

What had Len said the other night at the diner? There was only so much she'd put up with before she couldn't put up with any more of her ridiculous behavior. The phrase haunted Maxine. Len loved her—she was willing to go the extra mile. Campbell didn't even like her right now. Why would he bother to even give an extra inch?

Shaking her head, Max tried to put the fear she'd screwed up for good aside in favor of the dance. Her hand fluttered in a nervous gesture over the silky material of her skirt, thankful Grace had offered to man the battle stations just long enough to give Maxine the opportunity to go back to her mother's to shower and change.

This dance was so important. She'd worked day and night for over a month and a half to make every detail as magical as she could within her budget.

If the village board liked her first big event, it would only serve her best interests. Keeping the seniors happy and active, doing things they enjoyed was her first priority, according to the board.

If it flopped . . .

She shook her head as she rounded the corner past the clubhouse. No flopping allowed. Maxine Cambridge knew how to entertain. She'd never thrown a party or charity event that hadn't left her on the society pages. Surely she could manage a small dance for three hundred or so seniors.

She ticked off details in her head in time with the clack of her heels on the pavement, praying her ex-Broadway stage lighting engineer, Sal Antonetti, had arrived an hour early as promised to have the lights ready to greet everyone.

The hill leading to the rec center was steep, making her once more regret not taking that spinning class. Almost ten months without even an attempt at Pilates had left her soft.

A twinkle of lights caught her eye when she reached the top of the rise, and then her breath caught, too.

Lights were strung on each of the ornamental topiary trees leading to the front door of the center, winding around the rich green leaves. They winked in a glow of muted white under the fading purple and orange sun. Each tall oak tree was graced with the same effect, making the front of the center, and the bit of back patio she could see behind it, look like a fairy tale would begin at twilight.

The bubble machines she'd rented and positioned at either end of the building hummed with a low vibration, spewing a soft cluster of milky bubbles every other minute. They floated off into oblivion with magical abandon. Huge white planters, antiqued with a light blue cast, held pink gladiolas, enormous heads of oyster white hydrangeas, and white freesia sprinkled throughout. They lined the path to the door, leaving behind a fresh fragrance mingled with the soft warm breeze of the evening.

Music floated in the wind, the strains of Doris Day's "Secret Love" swirled in her ears. Each song she'd chosen had been carefully picked to meet the rise and fall of the evening, from an excitement-filled beginning to a slow and sentimental end.

Maxine paused for a long moment, holding a hand over her eyes to block the setting sun and soak in the swell of pride her work had produced.

A tall figure blocked her view of the front doors, where the seniors were arriving in droves.

Campbell.

That spark of excitement, coupled with the battalion of butterflies in her stomach, rooted her to the spot.

Campbell wore a suit, tailored, dark, insanely sexy. He'd slicked back his hair, and she was sure he didn't realize how it played up his granite features and blue, blue eyes. He was looking out over the golf course to the right, smiling as each resident passed him, allowing her eyes time to gobble up every divine inch of him without scrutiny from his often intense gaze.

Something inside her shifted so far left, so sharp and powerful, Maxine almost stumbled when she tried to walk the last hundred or so feet to the doors.

And then Campbell turned, as if he knew it was her, leaving her tripping over herself like she hadn't walked a hundred pageant runways in her lifetime.

His glance was cursory until he must have realized who she was, and then his eyes met hers, searching, surprised, gentle, powerful, and approving all in one gaze.

Those blue eyes were like a magnet, pulling her, coaxing her to attach herself to him.

The thrash of her heart pounded in her chest, her surprised gulp intrusive to her ears.

Thunderstruck.

It was the only word to describe how Campbell's gaze affected her.

Thunderstruck.

~ℓ~

Campbell was floored. For the first time in his life, a woman's beauty, so simplified, so pure it radiated from head to toe, left him feeling something he had no identifying emotion for.

His heart crashed around in his chest like he was right back in chemistry class, making him tighten the muscles of his legs just to keep them from going soft.

When Maxine walked up that hill, the warm breeze twirling her blue skirt around her knees in caressing waves of shimmering fabric, the halter top accentuating her breasts with only a hint of their swell peeking through the keyhole at her cleavage, the shine of her hair grazing her lightly tanned shoulders in soft curls left him speechless.

Each step she took toward him, each thrust of her shapely calves ending in sexy high heels, left his mouth bone-dry.

Damn.

That moment, the one where he'd first glimpsed who she must have been once upon a time, made him want her all the more. Not because she was dressed to the nines, but because she'd worked so hard to get back to a semblance of who she once was all on her own.

This Max, the Max who strode along the sidewalk like she owned it, the one who stood two feet away with a hesitant smile, was the Max he wanted to drag to him, make her want him the way he wanted her. She was the Max he knew was hiding behind the neurotic fears and wild conclusion jumping. Seeing her like this made him forget why he was angry with her to begin with. If she only knew how little it would really take to wrap him around her little finger.

Bubbles floated in iridescent hues, picking up the blue and purple of the sky. She laughingly popped them with a painted pink fingernail, playful and easy.

And it held him captivated.

Holding out his hand, Campbell waited, hoping she'd take it again. He understood without knowing why the trust it signified when she let him wrap his fingers around hers. He could only hope she understood what it meant when he made the gesture.

With a flick of his wrist, he twirled Max around, giving him time to reorganize his thoughts. Earlier he'd thought holding out for just a little longer was appropriate. It wouldn't be a lie to say he took just a little pleasure at seeing her squirm. The humiliation Lisa'd suffered had him angrier than he'd been in a long time. And that wasn't even counting the kind of pissed off he'd endured at being labeled a lying cheat.

But he was finding the peachy floral scent of her perfume, the soft flow of her dress curving under her breasts, too damned hard to resist. "You look amazing, Max."

She giggled when they stood face-to-face, her cheeks flushing a pretty shade of pink. "I guess this beats my yellow sweat suit and scrunchie. Oh, and thank you. So do you."

There was nothing that pleased Campbell more than seeing her eyes so full of life, expectation. The only thing that just might top it was seeing her eyes lit up with a very different kind of pleasure when he was buried deep inside her. With the clench of his jaw, he had to jam a hand in his pocket to thwart his decadent thoughts. "I clean up all right."

Her hand went to his tie to straighten the knot, striking him as intimate and so natural it was like she'd done it a thousand times before. "It's the allure of bundt cake, isn't it? Guaranteed to make a man put on a tie," she teased.

"I'll admit the bundt cake held a special appeal." He swung his gaze around in appreciation of her efforts. "Everything looks pretty great. You really know how to get a big bang for your buck. Dad'll be sorry he missed it. He loves big band music."

"Garner's not here?"

"Nope. He's with your latest victim in the city, seeing his heart doctor," he teased, testing the sensitive water.

She winced her regret, but her feathers remained unruffled. "I called Lisa earlier today to apologize. Is everything okay with your father?"

"Just a regular checkup. If everything's a go, he'll be able to do a little work around the village part time." Campbell paused, catching a question in her eyes. "I'll still be here to help until he's on his feet."

If he wasn't mistaken, that was relief lining her glowing features. "So this looks like it's going to be some party."

Max beamed up at him. "If there's something I get, it's how to plan a party. And before you say it, yes, I applied to several event planners before I begged and scraped at the Cluck-Cluck, but it turns out the economy isn't something anyone wants to celebrate."

Mesmerized by the light pink gloss of her lips, he shook his head to lift the haze of lust and admiration he was harboring for her right now. "You ready to go in and enjoy the fruits of your labor?"

"I think so," was her soft, breathless reply. One that made all sorts of crazy things inside him jump around.

Campbell gave her his arm, unable to deny the strange possessive sensation jerking his heart when she clung to his side. That her ex-husband had thrown her away still astounded him. There had been so many things she'd done right in her marriage, he still couldn't comprehend how her skill as a wife had left Finley wanting.

Stepping through those doors into the lighted, flowered, crystallized world Max created for the seniors brought a surge of pride on her behalf.

Eat your heart out, Finley Cambridge.

"Wow," he murmured as he let his eyes inspect her handiwork. Her attention to detail, the care she'd put into creating something magical, was evident in every corner. This was no longer where everyone gathered to play bingo, but a scene right out of a movie.

Round, white papered lights hung from the ceiling, illuminating the dance floor in the center with a dewy, romantic glow. Each table was adorned with a moss green tablecloth, flowing to the floor in graceful folds. In the middle there were centerpieces overflowing with short arrangements of big white flowers and something green in bundles he was sure he'd seen on the Bon Appetit channel with that guy his father liked to watch, *Mitch in the Kitchen.*

Max must have caught the question in his eyes. "Hydrangeas and, of all things, rosemary. I got it in bulk at a huge discount at the farmers market."

"Not only creative but frugal," he said with more of that pride. Watching her see her conception come to life held a pleasure all its own.

Max's chuckle was nervous when she peeked at him with that modest glance, the one uncomfortable accepting compliments. "You like it? Do you think the seniors will?"

He grinned with a nod. "I like it and I'm not really an aesthetics kind of guy. It's perfect. Like right out of a movie perfect. You remember the ones where everyone knew how to do the waltz and women wore heels and pearls even in the kitchen?"

"Are you kidding? I ate movies like those for breakfast when I was a kid, and thank you. It means a lot to me . . . that you . . . came. I'm glad you did."

Nice. She'd finally said it. Now was his chance to hone her sentiment, woo this warm fuzzy they both knew they were sharing. "Me, too, Max. Me, too," he husked, letting her relax into him, leaning toward her to place a kiss on lips that tempted him beyond reason.

A crash of tin and glass screeching to the floor broke them apart.

Flushed once again, Max was instantly in high gear. "That came from the kitchen, didn't it?"

"Yeah. I think so." Damn whoever was trashing his friggin' moment.

"That can't be good," she said. "I'd better go check and see if Mrs. Lipknicki's okay. Do me a favor though, would you?"

At this moment, in this captivating setting, he wouldn't be contrary to doing most anything for her. "If you ask me to dance with Mrs. Fogarty, I'm out. She's mean and cranky."

Her head fell back on her shoulders when she laughed with abandon, the column of her throat sexy and supple. When she recovered, her eyes captured his with a dreamy glaze to them. "Save a dance for me, okay?"

"You bet," was all he could manage around the curious lump in his throat.

"Hey, lovebirds, quit mooning over each other. We have mayhem in the kitchen," Mary chided from behind them.

Max escaped through the gathering crowd, but not before she trailed her hand along his arm, giving it one final squeeze.

Campbell had always had a thing for Max Henderson. As far back as he could remember, and it had reignited when he'd seen her for the first time again in the Cluck-Cluck Palace parking lot.

However, he hadn't always understood what that "thing" was. What it encompassed, why it existed beyond her obvious physical beauty, what it meant.

So who would have thought a gesture as simple as her hand reaching for his would turn that once mysterious "thing" into what he was surer than ever was love?

The corners of his mouth lifted when he caught sight of her flitting through the kitchen, hands flapping, eyes twinkling.

Yep.

Love.

~ ℓ ~

"This is really beautiful, Maxine," Gail said, popping another mini-quiche in her mouth as she swayed to "In the Mood." "That Gilda never put on anything like this. You were lucky if you saw a weenie in a blanket if you got here ten minutes after the doors opened."

Maxine squeezed her shoulders from behind, utterly and unabashedly pleased with herself. "Gilda didn't know the people I know, I guess." Her motto had always been to treat the people who staffed the events she planned well and they'd remember. Thankfully, they'd remembered her and not Finley's tight fist. Between her old contacts and some of the residents' former specialties, she'd been able to pull this off. Her eyes assessed the room with deep pleasure.

Food was flowing from the buffet, nonalcoholic punch filled glasses at regular intervals, and the residents were dancing like teenagers. Laughter mingled with the music, couples flocked to the floor when they heard a familiar tune, and there hadn't been a single complaint she wasn't doing it the way her predecessor Gilda had.

Mona nodded, brushing crumbs from her rose-colored dress. "Gail's right. You hit the nail on the head, kiddo. I can tell ya this much, no one was circling the wagon at last year's hoedown like they are tonight."

"Square dance," Mary corrected before she accepted an offer to dance with Ira Weintraub, whirling away on his arm.

"Hoedown, showdown, square dance. Whatever. All I know is it had hay involved. It wasn't near this nice, Maxie. I'm pretty proud right now. Look at you, would ya? Ten months ago you were a sniveling pansy. Tonight, you're prom queen again. A prom queen with a *job*," Mona added with a cackle. "Who needs the Talleywhacker now?"

Maxine didn't bother to hide her smile. *Yeah. Look at me.*

There'd been a bitter point in her divorce journey where she'd been determined to pay Finley back by getting on her feet to spite him. Tonight, her minor success hadn't produced the kind of victory she'd once thought she'd cheer. An in your face, take that sort of victory.

In fact, Finley hadn't crossed her mind at all. Not once. This was all hers. This, Maxine realized, wasn't about showing Finley anything. She'd become indifferent to him, so far removed from the life she'd once led with him she couldn't even remember what had attracted her to him in the first place.

Her accomplishment was about something entirely different, but just as powerful. It was about getting up off your ass and sucking it up, proving to yourself you could actually dance in the puddles left behind by the monsoon your life had become. It was about owning your mistakes and then letting it go.

It was about finally realizing you didn't need to prove anything to anyone but yourself.

It was about moving forward.

And tonight, it was about Campbell, standing across the dance floor after finishing a clumsy foxtrot with the troll lady, catching her eye with a secret glance as he'd done all evening.

It was about considering letting down her guard and just maybe allowing things to happen as they should. That thought left her with a smile when "Moon River" struck up.

Leaving behind her mother and Gail, Maxine made her way across the dance floor to Campbell. Each step closer, a heart-pounding trek into undiscovered territory.

This time, Maxine held her hand out to him, her smile more confident than it had been in a long time. "Wanna make up?"

"Not if you expect me to do the foxtrot," he said, husky, low, his blue eyes glinting.

"Is that what you call what you were doing out here?"

"Hey, making nice does not mean mocking my two left feet on my trip into the light fantastic," he joked with mock hurt.

She chuckled in return, nervous with jitters. "True that. I take it back, and I promise not to make you foxtrot." Once more, she held her hand out to him, waiting, fighting the tremble of her fingers.

Campbell's fingers finally took hers, wrapping them around his own, and he turned toward the dance floor. He spun Maxine around before pulling her into his arms, the sensual whisper of her dress lifting around her knees when she turned to allow him to press their bodies together. Maxine went willingly, her arms wrapping around his neck as though they'd never wrapped around anyone else's.

Frank Sinatra's haunting rendition left her chest tight, his dulcet tones swelling in her ears while bubbles, glossy and light, floated around them. Lights twinkled with magical promise, the scent of rosemary and freesia danced in her nose.

Everyone else on the dance floor became a muted batch of colors and sound. There was nothing but her and Campbell. There was nothing but his lips resting on top of her head, his heart pounding out a steady, cadent rhythm against her ear. Whatever his cologne, it tantalized her senses with its hearty maleness, creating a shiver of complete awareness.

She tilted her head back, and blue eyes met green.

His arms hardened around her, one hand splayed across her waist, the other between her bare shoulder blades, evoking so many contradictory emotions—decadence to come, security, soul-deep comfort and warmth. So much warmth, she responded by burrowing deeper into him to absorb it, letting her hips meet the slow sway of his.

Maxine couldn't keep her fingers from tracing the outline of his mouth, his full lower lip, the smooth skin on either side of his dimples.

Campbell caught her finger between his teeth, a gentle nip that sent a hard wave of desire to her belly. His eyes grew smoky, glazing over in an all-consuming glance she would never forget.

No one had ever looked at her like this—with so many different levels of intimate emotion she couldn't separate one from the other.

A second later, she found she didn't want to separate anything when Campbell laid his mouth on hers, unmoving, as though he were deciding whether or not to taste her lips.

They inhaled in unison at the contact, taking in each other's breath, and the moment, suspended, poised on the brink of a kiss, was pure magic. A brief second of discovery, a tentative glimpse into what was to come. His hand wrapped around one of hers, bringing it to his chest where Maxine curled it into a fist in his, reassured, alive with humming anticipation.

Campbell's mouth moved against hers in a deliciously slow dance, teasing her lips, skimming them with small hints of promise. His tongue snaked out to dart at hers, stabs of heat rising and falling only to rise again in her breasts, aching and full.

His hard chest heaved against hers when neither of them could keep from deepening the kiss. Unaware of anything but the bend of their bodies and Campbell's mouth demanding and hard, she became lightheaded, dizzy with the awakening of her dull senses.

Every nerve ending she possessed lit with small sparks of desire, growing as he stoked the flames of her need. A moan of the purest pleasure slipped into his mouth from hers as she clung to him, never wanting to leave the shelter of his strong arms. Never wanting to leave so much, Maxine felt the primal tug of it deep, and so stingingly sharp, it might have frightened her if not for the clapping.

Somewhere in her dreamy haze there was clapping.

Which she might attribute to her gaggle of hormones, happy to be utilized again, if she didn't know that was ridiculous.

Both she and Campbell freed their mouths and cocked their heads in confusion.

Every village resident, either on the dance floor or at the surrounding tables, was clapping.

Maxine felt Campbell's chuckle against the cheek she buried in his chest, her cheeks hot red. "I think we shouldn't let them see us sweat," he murmured, amusement threading his voice.

"I don't know what you mean," she muttered, her mortified words muffled against his chest. "I do know I'm willing to try and escape while my red face is still buried in your chest. You think we can make it to the door like this?"

"Follow my lead," he responded, prying her from his body to turn her in a circle she almost lost her footing performing. Campbell bowed at the waist, pulling her down along with him. When they rose to gales of laughter, she took a deep breath and let him lead her off the dance floor.

Mona let out one of her infamous wolf whistles when they reached her, her smug grin making Maxine's face flush with color all over again. Her mother clapped her on the back. "Well, there, girlie, that was some show. I think Mr. Hodge might need some kind of breathing apparatus after that." She chuckled her words. Her sharp gaze took in Campbell's. "So does this mean you're going to do the honorable thing by my girl and court her right and proper, young man?"

Though unsurprised by her mother's forward nature, Maxine rolled her eyes. "Mom!"

Campbell leaned down and dropped a kiss on Mona's forehead.

"I think this means your daughter likes me, and we should go have some bundt cake while she recovers from my awesomeness. She really latched on, huh?"

Mona hooked her arm through his, steering him toward the dessert table. "I'll say. I was getting ready to get the crowbar to pry her off of you if she kept inhaling your lungs like that."

Campbell's deep, resonant laughter was the last she heard of them.

Maxine headed to the kitchen, her head clearing with sluggish chugs. She had things to attend to, and it wouldn't serve her well to allow herself the pleasure of reliving that kiss. She'd only get lost in the absolute rightness of it, lost to the ridiculous unicorns jumping over rainbows in her mind.

Yet the rest of the evening, until the one lingering senior said her good-byes, and right up until the final punch bowl was washed and stored away in the rec center's pantry, Campbell's kiss was all she could think of. He only made things more difficult by refusing to leave until he'd moved the last table back into place for bingo next week.

More often than not, Maxine found her eyes on him when he wasn't looking, soaking up the strain of his muscles under the crisp white shirt he'd rolled to his elbows, her heart skipping beat after beat when he dried the cookie sheets. Thankfully, Campbell had offered to give Mr. Hodge a hand with Jake, telling her to finish up and get some rest.

She flicked the lights off, relishing the quiet when she leaned against the door and gave the room one last scan for debris.

"I'd say you're one lucky girl," a voice from out of the dim light left on in the kitchen said.

"Gail?"

"Just making sure that crazy Edna turned all the burners off. She burned down half her kitchen, leaving her George Foreman plugged in."

Maxine blew a tired breath out from the endless details when dealing with the elderly. "Thanks. I forgot she's forgetful."

"So what're you gonna do about that Campbell?"

She was going to mull this over. She wasn't going to allow the magic of the night to carry her too far out of her comfort zone, that's what she was going to do. "What do you mean?"

"I mean, if I was you, and a man looked at me the way Campbell looks at you, I'd do a fast one-hundred-yard dash right to him. And for sure I know what I *wouldn't* do."

"What's that?"

"Pick that kiss apart. I've been watching you over these last months, Maxine. You're cautious, and you should be. You've had a pretty rough time of it no matter what anyone says about all that money you came from. Nobody deserves a second wind more than you. But you're smart, too, and still you look for things that aren't there. That's not a bad trait unless it keeps you from seeing what *is* there. Campbell's there." Gail rooted in her purse. "Here. He forgot his cell phone. I'd bet my dentures he needs it. *Tonight.* Thanks for one of the best times I've had in a long time," were her last words before she pulled Maxine down to give her a quick kiss on the cheek, planted the phone in her hand, and left.

Tears formed at the corners of her eyes when she was left in the silence. Tonight had been chock full of revelations.

What her heart told her to do next was the biggest revelation of them all.

Campbell pulled off his tie and hung it in the closet, grateful for the peace having his father in the city brought. He wasn't up to an interrogation about Max tonight.

Instead, he wanted to savor the memory of her soft-as-a-pillow lips beneath his, the fullness of her hips, swaying to the tune of "Moon River."

A smile lifted the corners of his mouth. Max felt it, too. He didn't doubt that for a second. What he did doubt was what she'd do about it. He could only chase her for so long until she ran too far for him to catch up.

Either she'd hide under her metaphoric covers again, thinking those dark thoughts about her skewed judgment when it came to the just barely evolved male species, or she'd maybe, just maybe, let the moment be what it was.

Right.

Campbell's fingers went to his lips, calling up the taste of her tongue, the fight he'd had with himself to remember they were in a public place and not cup her breast when it was pressed so enticingly against his chest.

He wanted her tonight more than he'd ever wanted anyone.

Even the woman he'd been married to for eight years.

They'd had their time, and it was good, sometimes even great, but in the end, the vows they'd taken had decidedly different meanings for each of them.

Campbell forced his ex-wife Linda from his mind. She was what had brought him to Leisure Village South two years ago. She was why he knew exactly where Max's head was.

Linda was the reason he understood moving on and knew the word "acceptance" almost as well as he knew how to fix a leaky pipe.

He was way ahead of Max in a healing process he'd almost let ruin his life. Wallowing had become an art form for him until his father had dragged his sorry ass here, fed him in the best way he knew how, spent endless nights reasoning with him, pushing him, and in the end, holding him while he wept like some candy-ass when his dark journey came to a grueling end.

Now if he could just bide his time and wait for Max to come to understand those things, too, maybe they'd find themselves in the same place at the same time.

A knock startled Campbell from his thoughts. He frowned, trying to figure out who would be knocking at one in the morning.

Campbell cracked the door, revealing Max, still in her blue dress, beautiful, and if he was reading her eyes right, uncertain.

When he let the door swing open, inviting her in, it was with the hope that somehow, luck had granted him the one thing he wanted most.

He and Max in the same place at the same time.

CHAPTER SIXTEEN

Note from Maxine Cambridge to all ex-trophy wives: A tip about TMI. Please, please, please, keep your Spanx-wearing to yourself upon your first intimate encounter since parting with your ex. In honor of those who've gone before you, just take my word for it. It will help protect what could have been an otherwise lovely moment to reflect upon one day. I hang my head in shame when I share with you—this is the voice of experience talking.

"You left your phone at the rec center. I—I—well, I figured you'd need it, in case . . ." What *had* she figured? Shit. So much for the high on hormones vixen she'd imagined herself while she'd walked over here full of piss and vinegar. Yeah. No doubt she'd expected to just knock on Campbell's door and demand he quench her burning desires like she knew the first thing about getting a man into bed.

She didn't know seductress from nothin'. But the cell phone had been the perfect excuse.

Now, standing at his door, looking at his shirt unbuttoned, his hair mussed, and his pensive blue eyes, she wasn't above hoping the ground would open up and swallow her.

Campbell caught the phone when she all but hurled it at him like it was on fire and gave her a confused cock of his head. "This isn't mine." He dug in his pocket, pulling out his iPhone to show her.

Oh. Grand. In that case, good deed over. She took a step back, teetering on her heels. "Okay, then. Well I guess I'd better go. It's late. I have to walk dogs tomorrow. So many dogs to walk these days, you know? Lots and lots of poop to scoop. Oh, and I have to water Mrs. Whiteside's lawn. So I'm out. Gone. Going. B—bye."

As she turned to leave, Campbell grabbed her arm in a light hold, swinging her around to face him. "You didn't come to bring me back a cell phone that isn't mine, Max." His accusation was low, seductive, but still an accusation.

Indignant was the perfect response when innocent was what you were striving to portray. "I did, too. Gail gave it to me and said you forgot it." And then it dawned on her. Maxine ran her thumb over the screen, clicking on the icon for the phone's number.

Campbell looked down at the phone and chuckled. "You've been duped, and well played on Gail's part, don't you think?"

Gail. Who else had an app for dancing garden gnomes on their phone? "I'll kill her. I'm going to go over to her house right now and knock down all those stupid gnomes she has frolicking in her garden."

Campbell pulled her close, his stance wide to encompass her legs, his arms warm. "Now don't go getting all excited. I think Gail was trying to tell you something."

Those feelings that had overwhelmed her back at the dance tonight began all over again. "I'm sorry. I didn't know she'd set me up to help me force myself on you."

Campbell leaned down, pressing a soft kiss on the side of her mouth. "She just gave you the perfect excuse to come over here. No force necessary. The rest's up to you."

Her nervous laughter swirled in the warm night air. "Does she have any idea what can happen leaving something like this up to me? It's like leaving a toddler in charge of Watergate."

His finger trailed along the side of her cheek, extracting a purr from her lips she was forced to stifle. "Come inside, Max."

Wasn't that what the evil stepmother said to Cinderella, or was that Snow White? Wait. That was an incident involving an apple. A poison apple. Or was it candy? Either way, Campbell wanted to show her his candy, that much was for sure, but she wasn't totally sure she was ready to show anyone hers. It was old and had stretch marks.

Panic rose and fell in rapid shifts. Oh, Jesus and all twelve.

Yet, when he held his hand out to her and smiled, she couldn't have stopped her hand from reaching for his if someone had chopped it off. Taking his hand just was. That was the only way she could describe it.

His steps back inside were easy, slow. Hers were stilted and clumsy. Blessedly, the interior of his father's house was dark and cool. Campbell's father, unlike her mother, obviously believed in air conditioning, and she was grateful. The flush of heat rising from every pore in her body was like having your insides microwaved on high.

Maxine fell into him due to leg wobble, but Campbell caught her with a shadow of a smile she could only see due to the overhead light on the range hood. His hands were at her waist again, rolling his palms over her hips, easing her toward him until the delicious friction was too much to bear and she allowed herself to be drawn into his embrace.

A sigh of homecoming trickled from her lips. Why he felt so comfortable, or how, was something she would never understand.

Campbell brushed a stray strand of hair from her neck, dipping his head to nibble the sensitive flesh. Her reaction was to melt, and surely, he couldn't be so consummate a neck nibbler as to evoke a reaction like that from her. The thought crossed her mind that she hadn't made love in well over a year now, and possibly this was her unattended libido overreacting.

Yet Finley had nibbled her neck a thousand times, and it was never as tingle inspiring as when Campbell did it. Tracing a path up along her jaw, he touched her lips with his, taking possession of them in a sweep of tongue and delicious mouth.

Her everything throbbed with a pulsing need to slake her desires. But when Campbell's hand cupped her breast, she froze. Not because it didn't feel as good as a bacon cheeseburger with a chocolate shake hitting your stomach in a caloric jubilee of fat and sugar. It wasn't even because she wasn't hearing love songs in her head.

She was.

Air Supply.

Definitely Air Supply.

No. It was due to the fact that she was so nervous, her tongue just had to move. Their last encounter was unplanned. She'd come here with a purpose this time. What she'd forgotten was there'd never been anyone but Fin in her sexual experiences, and no matter how much her loins were screaming for her to put a sock in it, her brain was telling her someone was going to see her naked way faster than she'd had enough time to do crunches for.

Max pressed a hand to his wrist, mumbling from the side of her mouth, "They're fake. Silicone. I had them done five years ago. I hope they hold out. I can't afford to get replacements. That's shallow, right?"

Campbell's lips whispered over hers. "Wow. Really? They're fake?"

"Yeah. So fake they define fake."

Campbell let her hold on to his wrist, but he continued to caress the underside of her breast with his knuckles. *Her fake one.* Oh, God. "They don't feel fake. Do fake boobs feel fake? I've never felt fake boobs before. So if they do under normal circumstances feel fake, big kudos to your plastic surgeon," he teased, walking her backward.

"He was really nice. He made me feel so much better about the process by telling me that my not fake, former boobs had stood up well against the test of time."

"Very complimentary." Campbell let his other hand roam down along the curve of her spine to settle on her ass, cupping her close to him.

"That's not fake. My butt, I mean. But of course you can tell that because you have to reach down to the backs of my knees to hold on to it."

His reply was husky. "I like your knees, Max. I like all of you. Fake or not."

All of her liked all of him, too. But . . . "But you like the Max that has Spanx on underneath her clothes. They smooth out all your unsightly bumps. It's like wearing an iron maiden, only with more give, and thank God I was wearing them the night I left Finley. God knows I couldn't afford them on my salary. But you might not like Max once she spills out of this sausage casing. In fact, we might need the Jaws of Life to get them off me, and I'd hate to rip them. They cost a fortune—in fact, they'd cost three whole weeks of poop-scooping."

"You wanna let me have a go at it and we'll just see?"

Her libido screamed, "Hell to the yeah!" but her fears lobbed roadblocks the size of boulders. She placed a hand at his shoulder. "I think it's time for some extreme honesty here. I'm so turned on I could weep, but I'm also petrified. I'd bet almost all of my next paycheck you're far more experienced than I am at this," she said as he pulled her into his bedroom. Which was nice. Very nautical and beach-ish with primitive wood anchors on the wall and fishing nets across the windows held in place with fake starfish.

"What makes you say that?" he asked, setting her on the edge of his bed with blue and white sailboats floating over the comforter.

"I know what people think about cheerleaders and prom queens. That we put out. I definitely behaved as though I put out that night in the woods, but that wasn't the case back then. My mother whooped the fear of God and Planned Parenthood into me when I was in high school. I never . . . Finley was my only . . ."

"Can I say something here?"

"Yes. Say something. Say anything to shut me up."

"I'll admit I've had more than one lover. When I—how do I put this—you know—outgrew puberty and my body changed, I didn't exactly abstain. But to hear you say I'm only your second lover is a little special."

"Right," Maxine snorted, looking for a reason to create some dissidence. "Even though I may not have put out like it said on the boys' bathroom wall, I know a line when I hear one. I've watched a lot of reality TV. A lot of MTV." Like that made her all in the playa know.

"So what you're saying is even though I chased you all over this village, and continued to do so even after you called me some really offensive names in public, I'm just looking to get laid?"

Well, when he said it out loud and gave her those intense eyeball-singeing glares . . . "The pickin's in the village for a hunk like you are pretty slim. I mean, I can almost see Mrs. Knickerbocker's appeal, she definitely looks pretty hot for sixty, but I just don't get the impression she's your type. I'm sort of the obvious choice. I'm the *only* choice unless some other ex-trophy wife shows up. Or, if you're lucky, my mother's friend Mary's niece. She's gorgeous. I've seen pictures."

Campbell's dark eyebrow rose in clear amusement. "Lemme get this straight. You're just convenient because I'm too lazy to get out of my own way and go outside the village to scope chicks?"

Maybe? No. Everything he said was always so logical. If he'd just let her get carried away with her wild notions, everything would be fine. "I think I'm not sure what I'm saying."

Cupping her face, his eyes captured hers once more. "I think you're creating excuses just to create them. Pay attention, Max, and maybe I can still that spinning head of yours. You're not just some easy lay. Nothing about this has been easy," he teased, his eyes taking on an amused glint. "You're not someone I want to screw and ditch tomorrow so I can say I tapped the one-time head cheerleader from Riverbend High at our next reunion. I'm not going to stop chasing after you even if our lovemaking sucks. If it does, we'll work on it until it's what we both hoped for. I'm not even going to stop chasing you if you say no to me tonight. I'm not in this to bag and tag. I'm not in this because I take a physical commitment lightly. I'm in this because I want *you*—as neurotic and full of crazy notions as you are. I don't care that you've had plastic surgery. I don't care that you wear Spankys—"

"Spanx," she corrected with a more relaxed giggle.

"Whatever. I don't care that you're forty-one—"

"Almost," she corrected.

"Whatever. I don't care about any of the things your free time seems to allow you to concoct in your head. And if that's too much for you to wrap that always-in-motion brain of yours around, say so now, and we'll have a cup of coffee after I take a cold shower."

With his words, something settled in Maxine—clicked. Something solid, something that made sense to the tizzy her head was always in. In that instant, her brain quieted, her fears lifted. Maxine wrapped her hands around his wrists at her jaw and closed her eyes, letting her mouth find his as her answer.

She felt the smile on his lips, the tightening of his hold on her when he laid her back on his bed, pulling her length to meet his. His minty-fresh breath tickled her nose when he asked, "Now, about those Spanx."

About those. "Maybe I should just go take them off. Unless you've done some professional wrestling in your time . . ."

Campbell nuzzled her neck, licking the tender skin with silken rasps of his tongue. "No way I'm letting you go to the bathroom. I don't have a key."

Her nipples tightened when his mouth left her neck, the moist path he'd left on her skin making contact with the air. "Are you implying I'd lock myself in there?"

Campbell rested his chin on hers. "I'm not implying anything. I'm stating a fact."

"That's it," she said with another one of those giggles he was so good at dragging out of her. Maxine slid from the bed, lifting the skirt of her dress and shimmying out of her Spanx with a grunt, tossing them on the bed beside him. "Committed enough for you?" she asked with a whole lot more confidence than she felt.

He patted the bed beside him with a lascivious grin. "We'll see."

Maxine's hands went to the front of her dress, smoothing the silky material as though she could smooth away her not-so-flat belly. Okay. It was now or never.

But what was the rush?

Campbell certainly wouldn't be in such an all-fired rush once he saw what was underneath her dress. A blind man wouldn't be in a rush . . .

"Max," he purred, rising to stand before her. "I've seen parts of you in broad daylight."

"But you haven't seen all of me. I was semi-clothed."

"I'm going to take off your dress."

She closed her eyes with a tight scrunch of eyelids, and lifted her arms toward the ceiling. "Okay."

A chuckle came from the dark. "Maybe you might try not behaving like this is some form of torture. You know, so we don't harsh the romance vibe."

Her eyes remained firmly closed. "Yeah. You say that now. But wait until you see my stomach. Nothing could harsh a buzz faster."

"Look at me, Max." His command was thick, insistent, but no way was she falling for it.

No. She couldn't bear the look on his face she'd created in her mind's eye. Rather like one of those cartoon characters whose eyes bulged in horror with a loud "zoink" written in a bubble over their heads. "Oh, no. This is on you. If you scream and end up fetal, you'll get no help from me."

Campbell untied the halter straps around her neck, letting them fall away. "I haven't screamed in a long time. There isn't much I'm afraid of."

"Spoken like a true warrior. I bet most every warrior says the same thing before he rides his trusty steed off into battle. I'd also bet he isn't singing the same tune when he loses an arm and his entrails are wrapped around a tree."

"I can't tell you how sexy that image sounds. Who needs Viagra with you?" he asked on a laugh, tugging at the top of her dress until cool air drifted over her half-bra.

Maxine clucked her tongue, admonishing his gusto. "You'll need Viagra when you see what I have goin' on under here. So just keep at it, tiger. In no time, you'll be taking one for the team."

His hands skimmed the bottom half of her dress. She heard the rustle of the material against his callused fingertips and winced. "Ready or not . . ."

Not. But if she were always "not," she'd die the crazy cat lady. "Hurry it up. My circulation isn't what it used to be," she half joked, wiggling her numbing fingers.

The whoosh of air when Campbell pulled her dress up bathed her body in shivers. She felt rather than saw him take a step back and cringed. His sharp intake of breath jolted her in her heels. Oh, God. She had heels and a half-bra on and nothing else. "I told you, didn't I? But just like one of those crazy horror movies where you're screaming don't go down in the basement, you just had to go down to the basement. Did you think I was making it up? You have no idea the kinds of tricks I know to hide almost anything unsightly—"

Campbell silenced her by slanting his mouth over hers and hauling her to him, kissing her until she was breathless. He unhooked her bra, running his full palms over her breasts until her nipples ached from the friction. His tongue devoured hers, rasping against it, tugging it with his lips, sipping at her mouth until she thought she'd die from the rush of new sensations he evoked in her.

Maxine groaned when he moved from her mouth to her collarbone, skimming her flesh with hot lips and tongue. Her arms fell from above her head, numb but willing, to allow his broad shoulders to give them support. Pleasure throbbed through her veins as he moved over her shoulder, down along the tops of her breasts, leaving behind his own groan when he cupped her breasts together, laving each turgid nipple.

Hot streaks of electricity shot to the place between her thighs, leaving her swollen and forgetting everything but the feel of his lips and tongue pulling her toward a sensual abyss.

White lights flashed behind her eyelids as his mouth left her nipples, caressing the skin of her midriff, moving lower and lower until she understood where he planned to end up. The thought alone made her grab at Campbell's shoulders to steady her weakening knees. The muscles of her legs burned, tensing and flexing while Campbell moved closer to the most intimate place on her body.

His fingers feathered across the tops of her thighs with a whisper of a touch, testing her reaction, waiting until she adjusted. Maxine gripped at his hair, clenching fistfuls of it, wrapped up in what was to come.

When he parted her swollen lips, laying a tentative tongue over her clit, Maxine nearly screamed from the sharp, sweet sting of desire sitting low in her belly. His mouth was like heaven, his fingers, stroking, plying her, coaxing a building heat, like the closest thing to magic she'd ever experienced.

Her head fell back on her shoulders, no longer mindful of her nakedness or the fact that her high heels were digging into her toes. She wanted this. Wanted Campbell. Wanted.

He dragged his tongue over her clit, swirling it around the swollen nub until she quivered, increasing the pressure until he'd pulled her flush to his mouth, cupping her ass with powerful hands that kneaded her flesh.

Thick tendrils of pleasure swirled along her skin, every nerve in her body crying for satisfaction. An ache, familiar yet bolder than she ever remembered, left a scintillating pressure deep within the farthest reaches of her desire. It grew as Campbell stroked her with his tongue, dragging his fingers over her now slick flesh until her chest became so tight, she couldn't get air to her lungs.

Each pass Campbell took with his heated tongue, each wave of his hot breath, each moan he made from between her thighs made her arch backward, offering herself to him.

The explosion of her senses came when he suckled her clit, nibbling at it with gentle teeth, encompassing it with his lips, bringing a scream Maxine had to fight to keep from escaping her mouth. The mind-bend of pleasure he brought was all she focused on.

Her only need, his tongue and her satisfaction.

A sizzle of fire shot through her, spreading outward until the slow burn turned into a flaming entity. Her gasp of completion was husky to her ears, filled with her hot need. Spirals of pleasure accosted her from every angle, making her hips buck against Campbell's mouth. The frantic need for climax eased as he stroked her hips, letting her rock against him until she slowed with a shudder of a breath.

Her legs, no longer willing to hold her up, crumbled. Campbell caught her, scooping her up and laying her on the bed. She fought for air, her lungs filling and releasing with choppy breaths.

Campbell pulled her to him, letting his hands roam along her heated skin, caressing, soothing her while she wrapped her brain around the utter bliss he'd just brought her.

Maxine's head fell back over his forearm and he leaned in to kiss her, leaving the taste of her most intimate pleasure on her lips. There was nothing to describe what had just transpired. No special word. No particular phrase. Yet it had been one of the single most decadent moments in her life.

Realizing that was when embarrassment caught up with her, making her eyes finally open. Campbell had done all the work. "You—I mean, I—we—"

With a press of his finger to her lips, he smiled, his eyes expressing he understood her dilemma. "Just relax."

"But . . ."

He sighed with a ragged breath. "We have a technical difficulty."

Her groan was of humiliation. "Does it need Viagra?"

Campbell grinned when he barked a laugh. "Uh, no." He took hold of her hand and placed it between his legs. "There's no doubt you do it for me."

Oh, wow. Wow, wow, wow. Everything was in clear working order.

"It has nothing to do with Viagra and everything to do with no condoms. Don't say it. I'll beat myself up plenty tomorrow. But I think this is a testament to my integrity. The fact that I have no condoms says I had no devious intention to accost your woman parts, at least not tonight. I had plans, but you know what they say about those." Campbell shook his head with a wry grin. "No, you can apologize later for your egregious error in judgment. Right now, I think we should just focus on what an idiot I am."

Her giggle began as a snort and built to laughter, leaving her holding her stomach. "Ohhhhhhh, this is priceless. Hold that thought." Maxine burst into another fit of laughter, taking the comforter with her to cover her cooling flesh as she made her way out to the living room for her purse.

~ر~

At the doorway, she held up the gleaming foil package with a smug grin. "You might not have had nefarious intentions, but I did."

His eyebrow rose. "So this was a planned bag and tag?"

Campbell saw the struggle of emotions on her face, noted her avoidance of his eyes. "Sort of. I bought them today at CVS. I don't even know if they're the right size," she confessed with so much red on her cheeks, he wanted to kiss her. "I was uber vixen on the way over here, but the thought of you seeing me naked caught up with me. As evidenced by my babble."

When she was open and honest, there was nothing sweeter than Max. It twisted his guts all up in unfamiliar knots. "C'mere."

Dutifully, she sat at the edge of the bed, clutching the foil packet. "You're beautiful," Campbell said, clear and deep. "Every over-forty inch of you. And never make the mistake of telling yourself otherwise. I don't give a shit about the circles you traveled in that instill the kind of Botoxed crap preoccupations in women over forty. They're all wrong. Everything about you is beautiful."

It was clear to him she didn't believe him, not fully. Once more, he took her hand, placing it at his zipper. "Feel that?"

Max nodded, though her lips didn't move. To her credit, her eyes stayed fastened on his.

"That's how beautiful I think you are, and I've had time to cool off."

When she spoke, her voice was rough, filled with emotion. "Then I guess we'd better do something about that." Her hands went to the front of his shirt, pulling at the buttons until they were undone, slipping her hands over his chest, brushing against his nipples, making them pucker.

The dim moonlight streaming through the window allowed Campbell a view of Max's face, soft, hesitant, determined. She reached for the buckle of his belt, unhinging it, then gave him a small shove to push him flat on the bed.

He went willingly, fascinated by her journey, the small sighs escaping her lips as she trailed her hands over his stomach, reaching for his zipper. It was a fight not to brush her soft hands away in impatience and take control of the situation. Yet he sensed a need for her to explore him on her terms.

Campbell gritted his teeth when Max tugged at his trousers,

pulling them down over his knees. He kicked them off, waiting to see what she'd do next. Caught off guard by the heat of her palm against his cock, he sucked in a hard breath of air, made himself lie still when she enveloped him and began to stroke.

Her hair against his flesh, the soft touch of her lips on his lower abdomen made him groan, dipping his hands into her scalp. He arched up to meet her mouth when she grazed his throbbing shaft, his hips writhing.

No way he'd ever survive much of this kind of treatment. Max's tongue, flicking out over his hard, molten-hot flesh, was his undoing. Grabbing her by the shoulders, Campbell pulled her upward. "It's been a long time, Max. No way I'll be able to stand much more."

The flash of disappointment on her face brought a swell of happiness he was unprepared for. He fumbled for the foil packet by her head, tearing it open and sliding it down over his pulsing cock. Impatient hands rolled Max beneath him. A hiss of held breath escaped his throat when her silken skin blended with his.

Max moaned, too, breathy and with a hint of surprise, if he was hearing right.

Their eyes met in the dark, Campbell questioning her readiness.

Her answer was to wrap her thighs around his waist, scrape her clit against his cock with a motion that almost left him undone.

Campbell measured his entry, paying close attention to her reaction while struggling to keep control of his own. He took possession of her with a slow thrust upward, clenching his teeth at her slick, tight passage.

Their breathing stopped, then let go when their chests crashed together, her nipples scraping his chest, her ankles twining together at his lower back. She was so incredibly tight, like a glove around his cock, that Campbell had to still himself for a moment.

His plan had been to take this slow, but the sexy grind of her hips upward, the way she met him stroke for stroke nearly drove him out of his mind. Hands entwined over Max's head, lifting her breasts higher, arching them, making his mouth water as he took a nipple in his mouth, hoping to slow his release.

Max bucked hard against him when Campbell slithered his tongue over her nipple, relishing the tight bud on his tongue. The thrash of her head against the bed, the tight grip of her fingers, so much smaller than his, served to make his cock harder inside her.

The last coherent thought he had was he'd never survive more than two more strokes inside her silken walls before he lost himself in the insatiable need to come. He battled to be sure her needs were met, and when a shudder passed through her body, vibrating into his, he let go, driving into her hard.

His climax exploded, dragging every last ounce of reserve he had left and forcing it to yield to the powerful current. Each muscle in his body tightened, tensed like coiled springs, then popped loose in a rush, pushing his body to a place he'd rarely been.

Harsh breaths filled the air, Max's chest rising and falling with hard chugs. Campbell rolled from her to ease the weight of his body from hers, pulling her on top of him.

She laid her head on his chest, her legs on either side of him curling into his thighs. That simple act, her head under his chin, her lips pressed to his skin, brought yet another revelation.

This was as close to perfect as he'd ever been.

Lying with her head on Campbell's chest, the palm of his hand stroking her hair, soothing the last vestiges of the most amazing union of man and woman she'd ever experienced, she realized something had changed in her.

Between them.

And Max fought the fear of that change while she absorbed how cherished Campbell made her feel.

"Max?"

"Hmmm," she mumbled against his skin, luxuriating in the clean smell of him, the safe harbor his arms were.

"Do me a favor," he rumbled beneath her cheek. "Tomorrow, when you wake up and you've had a chance to dissect this, try not to freak too big. And if you do freak out, talk to me, because nothing I said earlier has changed. So whatever happens, whatever scares you, just *talk to me*."

So perceptive. Maxine snuggled deeper against him, burying her head in his chest. "Thank you for saying that," she whispered, her eyes stinging.

As she lay next to this man, so strong, so completely confident in who he was, she had no remorse due to the kind of joyful realization he'd brought with his selflessness tonight.

The shift of her heart she'd earlier experienced, the foreign sensation akin to nothing she could pinpoint, returned.

For this moment, for tonight, Max—yes, *Max*—was going to bask in the act of simply being. Max was going to revel in the quiet of her whirring brain and the divine pleasure of having a man as luscious as Campbell beside her.

For tonight.

CHAPTER SEVENTEEN

Note from Maxine Cambridge to all ex-trophy wives: Way to go, guuurrrrll! You got your woo to the hoo on. Here's hoping it was all you'd hoped it would be and more. If so, congratulations! Count yourself among the lucky to have enjoyed a fulfilling encounter with a man other than your ex-spouse. If it was a disaster, don't give up the ship. There are more ships. And take heart, this is the first step in regaining one aspect of a healthier you. Go gain it again. Seriously. Gain it as many times as your brittle bones can take it.

Let the freaking begin.

"I had sex," Max blurted in a nervous twitter of words, unable to finish her lunch. Oh, God, she'd had sex. With a man she wasn't married to. And she'd liked it. Oh, nay, she'd *adored* it. Would do it again in a New York minute, providing the room was dark and Campbell was blindfolded.

Len's head whipped up from the bridal magazine she was scouring while munching on an egg salad sandwich. "Do you mean you've discovered self-love? Like vibrators and doodads?"

Max put her hands to her eyes in mortification. "No. This didn't have anything to do with gadgets called The Sex-i-nator. God, how could you have sent me to that site, Len? Never mind. I mean I had sex." Sex in her high heels and nothing else. The memory made her squirm and smile. How contradictory.

Len's face went wide with surprise. "With Campbell? You made up?"

"Did we ever." By way of tonsil hockey and . . . and stuff. A-mazing stuff.

"How do you feel?" she squealed, her eyes searching Max's when she laid down the magazine.

Her smile could not be thwarted. "It was . . . so . . ."

"Liberating? Empowering? Hot?"

"Yes, yes, and yes." A smile touched her lips. Making love with Campbell had absolutely been hot. She had to fight to breathe, it was so hot. And something else she hadn't quite pinpointed, but was afraid to examine.

Len lifted her glasses to the top of her head. "And today you're going to places in your head only you can go instead of reliving the afterglow, right?"

It was good to have a best friend who understood her crazy rationale when stress and fear took hold of her brain. "Yes, today . . ."

"You're freaking out." Her hands flapped at Max in a dismissive motion. "I understand. Do it again and the freaking lessens."

Speaking of freaking out. "Yeah, I'll just bet you do understand. Care to explain Adam *now*?"

Max observed the glow her friend's face took on, the dreamy look before she caught herself and wiped her lips clean of a fond smile. "Nope." She pulled her glasses back down on her nose and buried her face in her magazine.

"Why? I don't get it. It's clear he makes you happy. It's clear he really likes you. That's terrific. I'm happy for you. Wasn't it you who said it was okay for me to date? And I'm not even divorced yet. If it's okay for me, it's certainly okay for you. Gerald's been—"

"Don't," was Len's stony interruption. "He's not my boyfriend. We're not dating per se. We just sleep together. Nothing more. It's him who wants more. It's me who doesn't want to give it."

Max tried to piece together the flash of emotions in Len's frantic eyes, and the only thing she could be sure of was her guilt over Gerald. It's what kept her from doing anything involving a man.

So for the first time in a very long time, it was time for her to be there for Len instead of the other way around. "Do you want me to say all the things people say when a friend's spouse dies and it's time to move on again? Because I can. I've done it before. I can do it again. I will if it absolves you of the guilt I know you're feeling by sleeping with Adam."

Her lips popped with a sharp smack. "I don't want you to say a Goddamned thing, Maxine. I want you to leave it alone."

Max cupped her chin in her hands when she leaned on Len's desk with her elbows, giving the magazines and garter belts a shove. "No. You know what? You accused me of wallowing in my own stank once. You said I'd never move forward if I didn't let go. Why is it okay for you to say it, and not me?"

"Because Finley didn't deserve you mourning him, your tears. Gerald," she choked, gritting her teeth. "Gerald was nothing like Finley. *Nothing*."

Yes, Gerald had been all things good. Maxine reached a hand out to her friend to console. Gerald's death had been brutal on her with more than one question left unanswered.

It was time Len realized, sometimes, there were no answers. "Gerald's *dead*." There was no other way to put it. "You're not. I won't bother to tell you he'd want you to be happy, because I've said it before. You're not the first person to lose their husband. You can't keep cornering the market on sorrowful widow. Otherwise, you're not doing all that growing you keep telling me I'm supposed to be doing."

Len, always reserved, always so together, crumbled. "I don't want to grow," she sobbed, letting her head drop to the desk.

With sudden clarity, Max understood. She stroked Len's hair. "You like Adam more than you expected?"

She lifted her head, using an angry thumb to swipe at her tears. "Yes."

"And you said he wants more?"

Her sigh was shaky, wracking her shoulders. "Yes. He said if I wasn't willing to go out in public with him soon, he wasn't willing to get naked with me anymore. He feels used. I think my boy toy, who isn't such a boy, has mutinied."

"I'd say that's pretty definitive. Sorta hot, too, don't you think?" Max teased, hoping to lighten the conversation.

"He's very hot. Maybe that's all there is to him."

"So what's keeping you from taking a shot at this and finding out?"

The look her friend fought to hide was guarded. "I don't know."

Max rose, glancing at her watch before saying, "Yes, you do. It's Gerald. You feel guilty for feeling things about Adam you thought were reserved only for Gerald. I hear you can love more than one person in a lifetime, Len. There's some rule somewhere in some big book of love that gives you the thumbs-up on it. So maybe you might want to reconsider just in case Adam's something great you'll miss if you don't stop being such a candy-ass."

Len threw her head back and chuckled, throaty and deep, her mood changing in a flash. "I remember hearing that sage advice from someone not too long ago. Someone beautiful, who still has a great ass."

Max held up her thumb and her pinky. "I have to go or I'll be late, so I won't push you. But you call me if you need me and you want to really talk about this. I've learned a lot from you, Oh Giver of Sage Advice and Rockin' Hot Ass. I haz skills," she joked, sticking her hand in the pocket of the light sweater she wore. "And look," she held up an object with a smile. "I also haz a new cell phone, too. So you can call me anytime, and I bought it all on my own. I'm like a real grown-up now." She reached out to give Len an affectionate hug.

"Hey, wait," Len said, leaning back in their hug, her cloudy face lighter. "We didn't talk about your little rendezvous. You had sex. Was it a well-thought-out venture or spur of the moment?"

"The first time was just sorta sex. This time involved thought, and I bought the condoms." Max gave Len a cocky smile.

"Sorta sex? I don't get it."

"That's because you have all-the-way sex, miss. That tête-à-tête happened a while ago. But last night was sex-sex. Well, after trying to talk Campbell out of having sex with me because I was petrified he was inevitably going to have to see me naked. I almost forgot I'd bought condoms. I bet smart, savvy women like you don't forget important things like that, eh?"

The return smile Len shot Max was vague. "Was it okay for you? Good even? I mean, after the naked hurdle?"

It was so many things Maxine was afraid to list them all. Probably couldn't if someone held a gun to her head. Most of all, it had been a discovery, a reawakening, and just recalling even a tiny bit of it made her blush and yearn for more. "I was my usual babbling wreck," she admitted with a wry grin.

"But Campbell overcame, I'm guessing."

"He did."

"God, that man, he's a rock," she teased.

No kidding. Max's heart warmed and her insides melted just remembering what a rock he was. "He was very patient, and yes, it was pretty spectacular. Now that I've admitted that out loud, I think I feel less freaked. So thank you. And I have to go or this trip to Atlantic City I have to plan with the committee is going to be me driving two hundred seniors in my mother's Kia to gamble in a seedy environment after a buffet dinner. Thanks for lunch. I love you—call me." Max flew out the door of Len's office to avoid saying anything else out loud.

She was back in a good place about last night. If her fears could be kept at bay, and they could do again what they'd done last night, she was in.

All in.

~~e~~

Len thrust her chair back toward the window to gaze out at the mid-afternoon sun after Maxine left. Fall was only a couple of weeks away, putting her, if she was estimating correctly, at an April or May delivery.

Lovely. Spring babies were lovely.

Her hands went to her face to cover the tears she knew were determined to fall.

~~e~~

"Maxie?"

"Mom?"

"More mail," her mother said, waving a manila envelope at her in the doorway of her bathroom.

One last spray of the body perfume she'd picked up at CVS with Campbell in mind, and she glanced at the envelope. Her stomach dipped. "Looks official."

"Oh, you bet it is. It's from the worm."

Max snatched it from her mother's hands and skirted around her to head to the kitchen, dropping the offensive envelope on the counter without looking back.

"You're not going to open it?" Mona's tone was appalled.

"Nope. Not tonight. It'll only screw up a perfectly good mood." She brushed her hands with finality before searching for her purse.

Her mother tightened her quilted bathrobe around her. "Always hidin' under those covers," she accused.

"Yep," she agreed. Whatever Finley wanted, it could wait until tomorrow. Lord knew he'd spent plenty of time making her wait. She had a box of condoms to rip through, and by God, he wasn't going to stop her.

"Don't you at least want to know what he wants?"

"Not at this particular moment. Actually, not at any moment, but I promise I'll look tomorrow. Tonight I have a date I don't want spoiled by Finley and whatever he needs. I spent way too much time anticipating his needs. Tonight's about me." *And my needs.*

Her mother harrumphed. "Look at you and the attitude. What brought this about?"

Sex. Lovely, delicious, Vulcan mind-melding sex. "No attitude, Mom. I just want to enjoy tonight. Whatever Fin wants, even if it's nothing good, would have to wait until tomorrow anyway. It's not like my dial-a-lawyer has a twenty-four-seven hotline."

Mona's eyes went from determined to amused. She gave Max a nudge. "You make sure whatever you enjoy, you enjoy with a condom. Got that?"

Max wrapped her arms around her mother, kissing the top of her head. "You giving me advice like that is just too creepy at my age, Mom. I'm going," she stated, waving her fingers over her shoulder before slipping out the door.

The walk to Campbell's, one she insisted upon rather than him picking her up, gave her stomach a chance to settle. Whatever those papers Fin sent said, it could damned well wait. Fin wasn't going to spoil the excitement she was experiencing about seeing Campbell with what was more than likely more threats and demands.

Instead, she focused on Campbell, the completeness she couldn't help but notice she'd felt when they'd made love. His insistence that she talk to him if she started getting cold feet. He'd been very expressive in his wishes. Almost intense, and Max wanted to understand why.

She wanted to know what happened to Campbell after high school. Where he'd been between then and now, and why he'd left everything to come help his father.

Her knock on his door held no hesitation this time. For the moment, the multitude of uncertainties she was always knee-deep in was quiet.

God save the poor man if there was a sudden uprising.

The grin Campbell greeted her with was mischievous. "I didn't have to come drag you over here by your hair. I'm impressed," he said, chuckling.

"Why would you have to drag me over here? You did say food was involved, didn't you?" she teased, falling into his arms when he enveloped her in them.

"I did. But I thought for sure you'd be so wrapped up in the 'Oh, my God, I had sex with Campbell last night' post-coital freak, you'd forget there was pizza involved."

Her laughter bubbled upward, unhindered and light. "Oh, trust me, pal. I never forget when Giuseppe's with mushrooms and olives is involved. So where's my pizza?"

"I'll show you pizza," he muttered against her mouth, making her melt when his tongue swiped hers before taking possession of her lips.

"Hey." Maxine mock-fought against his effort to drag her toward the bedroom. "You said food. I came. I see no food."

His hands went to her waist, lifting her up to carry her into the bedroom. "I'll show you something way better than food."

Arms wrapped around his neck, she snuggled against his neck and asked, "Is this something better going to provide nutrition, because I have to tell you, I didn't get this ass starving myself. It must be maintained."

"I love your ass," he growled into her ear, sending an army of shivers along her arms and up her spine. "I promise there'll be pizza if you shut up now and let me remind you why you're a brave little soldier for not freaking out."

Max's head fell back on her shoulders, taking him in. "You swear there'll be pizza? You're not just saying that to get in my pants?"

Between small nips of the sensitive spot on her neck, he said, "I'd do pretty much anything to get in your pants. So, yeah, there'll be pizza."

Her giggle was so lighthearted, it almost didn't sound like hers—it was unfettered by anything but the absolute thrill Campbell's words brought. The thrill his desire for her gave her. "Aha. Well, then, commence with the pants thing."

Campbell tipped her onto his bed, eyeing her with a smile. "I have condoms," he stated, as though he deserved a pat on the back.

"And yet you forgot the pizza. Men," she joked when he lay on top of her, fiddling with the buttons on her new blue blouse.

Taking her lips, he made her forget all about pizza when he pushed her shirt aside and cupped her breast, running his fingers over her nipples. She had no hesitation pulling his shirt up over his head, tossing it aside to sink her fingers into his flesh.

Everything about him was hard, planed, hot, and when he tugged at her jeans, she didn't even consider the fact that they were tearing each other's clothes off in broad daylight. It was enthralling, but brief, as her focus was drawn to his fingers parting her flesh and stroking her clit.

Max's moan was low, from deep within, her need usurping everything else but Campbell's hands and mouth on her. Frantic fingers tore at his jeans, shoving them down and away before encompassing his cock in her hands, guiding him to her, spreading her legs so he understood she couldn't wait.

Somewhere between her giggles of delight that he'd forgotten where he put the condoms he'd boasted about and the sweet bliss he brought when he sank into her, she experienced another discovery.

Being with Campbell was more than just sexual. It was easy. Comfortable but exciting. Those notions left her sighing when he pulled her hips flush to his, scraping her clit with the crisp hairs at the base of his cock.

Reason left and only a primal need for fulfillment remained. Each thrust of his hot shaft, each hiss of his breath was so sensual it was all she could do not to scream her pleasure.

The tightening in her belly, the white-hot fissures of pleasure slicing through her, were only made more pleasurable by Campbell above her, his sinewy neck taut, his strong arms tense.

The visual of him, taking her, driving into her, stretching her, his desire for her, sent her tumbling over the edge in a crash of sharply sweet release.

God, he took her breath away.

And once more, she fought the knee-trembling fear she'd find herself consumed by someone again until she was just Maxine Cambridge.

Finley Cambridge's pathetic ex-wife.

~ ℓ ~

"Hmmm," Max cooed. "Pizza."

Campbell wiped a gooey string of cheese from her mouth, pressing a kiss to her sauce-stained lips. "Hmmm, pizza."

They sat on his bed, Max in his shirt, Campbell in just his jeans. When he gazed at her, she found she was less likely to look away, and the panic accosting her earlier once more subsided.

"So you wanna tell me what exactly happened to Max Henderson?" His question was casual, but Max knew he'd made a point of keeping the question light.

"In twenty words or less?"

"In as many words as it takes." He leaned back against the pillows with a smile, patting the space beside him in invitation.

Her shoulders lifted upward. "You know, I've had a lot of time to think about it. Almost eleven solid months of thinking, and crying, and okay, even a little boozing. Yet I can't seem to pinpoint where exactly I lost Max and became Maxine—this woman who, because her husband had money, people instantly thought was shallow and designer-label obsessed. Which was anything but the truth. Were those things nice? Hell, yes. Did they define me the way everyone seems to think they did? No. Because if they did, I'd already be on the hunt for some filthy rich seventy-five-year-old. Who, by the way, would give me back my trophy-wife status." She gave him a quirky smile, closing her eyes to savor her next bite of pizza.

"I get the impression part of what went wrong was Finley just doesn't act like he's much of a team player. As you matured, and your ideas of what a marriage should be changed, his didn't."

Her pause was long, the silence deafening. The muscles of her throat worked while she forced her brain to find the words to accurately describe why she'd let herself become so lost, so consumed by a marriage that had left her unable to care for herself and her son.

Maybe her prior statement wasn't entirely true. She did know when the will to fight had vanished—or maybe, in hindsight anyway, it was just that she'd fought the *wrong* fight. Instead of fighting for her dignity, her pride, *herself*, she'd opted to give all of those things up to pacify a man who'd never once thought his affairs were the result of his wrongdoing. They were always justified by his infamous disclaimers. *"If you had just done this, Maxine . . ."* he'd said, *"I wouldn't have done that . . ."* You could fill in the blanks with whatever adjective Fin could find at the time to prove she'd literally driven him to sleep with someone else.

"The first affair Finley had," Max said, clearing her throat, "I was so clueless it makes me sick, looking back now. All those late nights he was working weren't anything new—I just never believed he'd do something like that to me. I think that's where everything became an out of control SNAFU. I lost sight of everything else but keeping it together. Keeping my commitment to my son, my marriage. Keeping

Finley happy, because for some crazy reason I thought his happiness was all that counted. So once the initial shock passed and the back draft had died down, I was determined to make everything shiny again and forget how much it hurt to know he'd gone elsewhere to . . . you know. Then I went to the extreme of whatever shiny is. I swore I'd be the wife Finley so openly decided I wasn't. I'm pretty sure that's when I lost who I was."

"But I'm guessing somewhere deep inside, that just wasn't working out, stuffing all of your feelings aside in favor of his," Campbell stated rather than asked.

Her laughter might have been bitter if it weren't the truth. "Oh, I stuffed. I set aside all my internal protests and the 'What about mes' to the 'Deal with it' bin in my mind and focused on making everything as perfect as was humanly possible. I worked out seven days a week no matter what. I had my hair lightened. I gushed over every stupid, menial thing he did like he deserved a standing O for just walking through the door every night. I hung on his every word like he was the automobile industry's answer to the Dalai Lama. I had Lola, our maid, make his favorite meals. I was picture-perfect every waking second, and it was exhausting. Each time he'd 'break' our marriage, I'd run behind him with my tube of superglue, pick up the pieces, and glue it all back together as best I knew how."

"And you finally came to the conclusion that somewhere along the way, there were too many pieces lost in the breaking."

"I'm a slow learner," Max joked wryly, resting her head on his shoulder. "When I found out about Lacey, that's his fiancée and my best friend's sister, I hit a wall. I think it had to do with the fact that the other affairs he had were with nameless, faceless women. Lacey . . . Lacey was too close to home. I talked Fin into giving her the job at the dealership to begin with."

Campbell's whistle was sharp. "Your best friend's sister. Ouch."

"But in a way, I'm grateful for Lacey. The night I left Fin was the night I realized nothing was ever going to be enough for him. He'd always want something shinier, faster, prettier. I think the most pathetic thing about my marriage is that I really believed if I kept everything just so, if I re-created whatever Finley found so special in me when I was twenty, I could keep it all together. I just forgot that what he found so special was sagging and in need of a boob job."

Campbell kissed the top of her head. "Is that what you think loving someone is all about? Boobs and butt implants?"

"It's what Finley loving someone is about." Max shook her head with disgust for herself. "I know now my rationale was skewed. I think I even knew it then, but I was willing to sacrifice anything to keep my family whole. I thought that even though the sacrifice involved my integrity, my self-esteem, it was a price I was willing to pay. And before you go there, no, I didn't stay married for the money because I never in eleventy billion years would have believed Finley would cut us off the way he did. I really believed, right up until a month after I left him, he'd help me get on my feet if we ever parted ways. Did I enjoy being rich? Who wouldn't? Would I trade all I've gained since I began this divorce thing? Uh, no." And she wouldn't. Despite poverty, despite the fear of not providing for Connor, she'd never go back to someone thinking they had the right to take everything away from her.

"So he really has left you with nothing. How's that possible in this day and age?"

Her snort was ironic. "Oh, you'll love this. I signed a prenup I was completely unaware was a prenup." Max held up a hand to thwart his inevitable outrage and disbelief. "You don't have to beat me up about it. God knows I've done plenty of that since I saw the copy of it. I remember signing things. I also remember not asking a single question about them, because I trusted Fin. How's that for blind faith in your man?"

It was Campbell's turn to snort. "And there's no legal recourse? That's outrageous. He's a multimillionaire and you're—"

"So close to being homeless I was scouting garbage bins for boxes Connor and I could glue together to make a double-wide. If not for my mother, that's where we'd be. Thank God for the job here in the village, because now, everything's taken a turn for the better. The prenup's ironclad. At least if what my dial-a-divorce lawyer says is true. I can't afford to get a decent lawyer. You know, the reputable kind that calls you back *after* he's charged your credit card for doing nothing more than shuffling papers. But I've finally come to grips with the fact that I did this to myself. I let Finley own me lock, stock, and custom silk draperies from France. I never pursued anything other than being his wife and Connor's mother. He might not have been in love with the idea of me going back to school when I broached the subject, but *I* was the one who let him tell me he didn't think it was a good idea. I was the one who caved. *Me.*"

"But he must, at least according to law, have to give you child support for Connor, right?" Campbell asked, clearly still baffled.

Max looked down at her hands, wringing them together. "He does."

"And you're not pushing that why? At least for Connor. There are laws that say he has to give up a percentage of his yearly income for child support, right? Even if you waived the right to his fortune."

"Yes, that's true." The guilt she felt over not going head-to-head with Finley brought self-loathing of the worst order. "How did you know that?"

Campbell's smile was wicked. "The Internet is a valuable tool, and I'm not ashamed to admit I went searching for an answer after finding out you had absolutely nothing. So explain to me why Connor should suffer because his father can't keep his pants zipped?"

Because it meant taking Finley Cambridge on, and quite frankly, she was afraid. Not to mention, her lawyer seemed a-okay with accepting the paltry amount of money Finley'd first offered. He just wanted Finley to sign the papers so he could get rid of her and her constant calls to complain about his crappy lawyering.

"You're afraid of him," Campbell assessed correctly. "You're afraid if you put up too much of a fight, you'll lose more than you already have."

"Call me a chicken-shit, but yes. I'm afraid of Finley Cambridge, okay? And if I don't fight it, if I agree to what he wants and sign the papers, then it's just done. He gets to keep his money, and I'm divorced."

"So if you're willing to give him everything without a fight, what's the holdup?"

Money, money, money. That's what it was all about, wasn't it? "I can't afford to file the papers. Court fees cost money, but I'm putting some of my paycheck away each week. Maybe next millennium I'll be divorced," she joked, twisting the sheets between her fingers.

Campbell's pause made Maxine wonder if he thought she was holding off for other reasons. "I swear that's the reason. It's the only reason."

"I'm not doubting that. Here's what I'm wondering—if Finley was so into Lacey he asked her to marry him before he'd even told you he was screwing around, why hasn't he filed himself?"

Yeah. Why hadn't he? Surely Lacey must be tired of hanging around, waiting to have that platinum wedding she so wanted. "I don't know. I just know that his money doesn't matter to me. I'll find a way to take care of Connor myself—even if it won't be in a lodge with five-star accommodations and us wrapped in silk. I just want to be free of Finley." With a jut of her chin, she flashed defiant eyes. At the wrong person, but defiant nonetheless.

Campbell cupped her chin, stroking her trembling lower lip. "Don't be defensive, Max. I'm just trying to understand. What I'll never understand is how Finley could allow Connor to pay for his mistakes. That he doesn't want to give you anything for being a good wife for twenty years blows, and I think he's an asshole, but to not want his kid to be secure when he's rich—that's pretty damned sleazy."

She'd be more embarrassed by her stupid fears if Campbell's hand weren't smoothing the muscles of her back in slow circles. "But you know what? It'll be okay. If it weren't for the fact that Connor's suffering the way he is to make his point to his father, I wouldn't care about the money period. Not even a little."

"Really? Even after losing all those vacation homes and luxuries?" he teased.

"I won't lie and say never having to worry about money sucked. It didn't. But replace that worry with the kind that involves never knowing where your husband's hanging his drawers, and I'll take this over that any given day of the week. So, yes, I don't care that I lost all those luxuries," she said with honesty, surprised she really meant it. Well, except maybe for her shoes. She'd be lying if she didn't admit to missing her shoes. "Because all of those luxuries never gave me what I needed most and was just too stupid to see I'd lost to begin with."

"A separate checking account?" he joked with a luscious, teasing grin.

Maxine's eyes fell to the sheets, her voice hoarse when she confessed, "My dignity. My integrity. My opinions. Clearly, as you've witnessed, I'm bordering zealot-like proportions when it comes to my opinions. I let it get out of hand sometimes, but having this new power is like being dubbed queen for a day. Or like being given a lightsaber you have no idea how to use, but choose to battle the Storm-troopers with anyway and ask for directions later."

Campbell chuckled, tucking her closer. "Maybe you might want to hand off the baton every once in a while. Just so people don't start calling you power hungry."

Giggling, Maxine leaned into him. "Know what else? I've found this odd freedom in buying my own gallon of milk with the money *I've* earned. I nearly wet myself when I took Connor to McDonald's the other day and the food I bought was paid for by yours truly. I know to someone like you, someone who's been on his own for a long time, that sounds ludicrous, but for someone like me, it's epic. Who'd have thought some greasy fries could be so empowering?"

Campbell's smile was warm and doting. "Fries can do that to a person."

She chuckled, stretching her legs by pointing her toes and entwining her foot with Campbell's. "I think we should talk about other stuff that isn't about me and the veritable idiot I turned into since high school."

The tip of his finger slid along her cheek in a tender gesture. "You're not an idiot. You married young, way before you were mature enough to grow into who you were supposed to be. So you became what someone told you you should be."

"I think I can be considered an overachiever. So you know almost everything about me. I want to know about you."

The guarded gaze he gave her made her pause. She was coming to know the nuances just one glance from Campbell could create, and this one was, without a doubt, guarded. "What do you want to know?"

"What do you want to tell?" she countered.

It's now or never, Barker.

He forced himself to keep his chuckle light. "Okay, okay. I'm always pounding you for information. It's only fair. I left high school, went to college, and graduated with a degree in economics. Probably the most boring degree to obtain ever. I worked as an HR manager for fifteen years then went back to school to get a degree in computer software. Left my HR position and nabbed a job with a starter company. Loved the change of pace after dealing with employee relations. Not fun, employee relations. Unfortunately, the economy led to layoffs and here I am."

Her finger trailed along his chest in delicious circles. He was enjoying her uninhibited touch. A far cry from the uptight, always-on-guard Max of a month and a half ago. "So you're not just a plumber."

"I'm not just a plumber." *And you're not just an ex-HR/computer software engineer either.*

"I'm going to lay bets you didn't just work all this time since I last saw you in high school."

Pony up, pal. "This is where you want to know about all the women who've experienced the Campbell Barker charm, isn't it?"

"Were there a lot?"

"No. Just some."

"Describe some."

You're stalling . . . "I didn't count."

"You don't want to tell me."

"I was married." There.

Max sat up and swung around to face him, crossing her legs. "I don't want to appear shocked, but I am."

"Shocked that anyone would marry me?"

Max flashed him a smile, one that said she was comfortable, forcing him to tamp down his sigh of relief. "No, I'm shocked anyone would divorce you." Her expression went from teasing to a dark frown. "Hold on. You *are* divorced, right?"

"Yes. I'm divorced. I was married for eight years. Divorced two years ago."

"I'm sorry."

"Don't be. I'm not anymore."

"But you were . . ."

"I definitely was. It's not a time I'd like to repeat." Not even in the next life.

"Tell. Me. About. It. Was yours awful?"

"No. It was pretty amicable."

"There's such a thing?"

"There is when you know there's no going back."

Leaning forward, she gave him a playful poke. "Hey. I spilled. You have to, too. Enough with the cryptic."

"Linda and I were married for eight years. We had a pretty good thing going. At least that's what I thought. We had trouble conceiving, but due to the magic of in vitro fertilization, we got pregnant in our sixth year of marriage." *Only a little more to go, Barker, and you're home free.* But Jesus, it hurt. Like a sharp knife, cutting deeper and deeper, reopening wounds he thought had healed.

"You have children?"

He saw her surprise, registered her drawing back from him. "Had. Our little girl, Gina Marie, died of SIDS at four months old." Gina's small, cherubic face flashed across his mind's eye, toothless grins, baby-powder-scented cuddles, chubby fists lodged against his chest while she slept.

Fuck.

The paling of Max's face, her eyes so full of sympathy, made him physically fight a cringe. "I can't even imagine." Scooting toward him, taking the sheets with her, climbing over the box of pizza, she cradled his head against her shoulder. "I'm so, so sorry. They're just words, pointless, empty to you, I'm sure, but I mean them. You don't have to say anything more."

Campbell lifted his head, setting her from him with just enough distance to keep them touching, but enough to not distract him from just saying it. "I was a wreck. Linda was a wreck. Everything was a shitwreck. After Gina was gone, we functioned, nothing more. I worked, Linda went back to work—we ate, we slept, but we didn't talk. We never talked. I tried over and over until I forgot how to. A few months after Gina died, I caught Linda cheating on me with some guy from her office. Pretty typical as cheating goes, but it was the end for me. Though it didn't really matter. She told me she'd planned to leave me for him anyway. And the kicker to all of this— she said she could talk to him about Gina. *My* little girl. Linda married the office guy and they have a daughter now." How was that for fucking irony? He was done pounding his fist of outrage against his chest, but there was a residual ache always lingering.

"I think it's true what they say," Max responded to his confession with quiet tones.

"What do they say?"

"Someone always has it worse. Count your blessings, et cetera. My divorce has been hell on Earth, but if I lost Connor . . . Shit . . . I want to say the right thing here, but I just don't know what it is, Campbell. I just don't."

He used a thumb to wipe the tears in the corners of her eyes. "I get what it is to be lost and unable to find your way out of the dark. That's why I came here. My father didn't just need my help. I needed help, too. I wallowed a whole lot longer than was good for me. I was angry, and I wanted out. I drank. A lot. I blamed. I bullied. My father finally dragged me to a SIDS bereavement program, and though it took a long time, I finally was able to talk about it."

Max took hold of his hand, pulling it to her cheek, displaying her seemingly endless capacity to console. Much like her behavior with the seniors, she was always quick to make someone else feel better. He found it ironic she didn't do the same for herself.

"So when I tell you I have a fairly good understanding of where you're coming from, give or take a couple of million dollars, I really do."

Max's face held light and dark emotions, fleeing, returning before she appeared to come to terms with something in her head.

She said nothing, but her arms pulled him down to her breast, curling into him with that way she had about her that made him feel all man.

And contentment, deep, abiding, settled in his chest.

CHAPTER EIGHTEEN

Note from Maxine Cambridge to all ex-trophy wives: If your husband has an unfair advantage in your divorce, like say buttloads of money and a gangsta-like attorney, you'll need to be of strong constitution if you choose to face off. So ask yourself this—what kind of precedent do you want to set for not only your children, but your future growth? Are you a worthy opponent? Or are you a chicken-shit?

"You want to tell me what that was about? Or is it too personal?"

Len crawled across the hotel room bed, flopping down with a groan. "Bad tuna for lunch."

"Three days in a row this week?" Adam asked.

She left her head down in her folded arms to avoid meeting his invasive eyes. "Must be some kind of bug."

She felt Adam's weight lift from the bed as his voice became distant. "Is that what they call pregnant nowadays? Lots of things change over time. Especially catchphrases. For instance, my niece would roll her eyes at me if I called someone a doofus because nowadays a doofus is called gay. But kids these days don't mean homosexual gay, they mean gay as in you're stupid. Yet, I don't think they've changed so much that knocked up isn't still just called 'knocked up.'"

Lifting her head was an effort, but she did it in order to take a peek into his eyes. Gazing into them, she wished she'd left her throbbing head buried in her arms. "That's ridiculous," she offered a weak

protest before pressing her closed fists into her eyes to stop the stab-
bing pain in them, and avoid Adam's.

His weight sank onto the edge of the bed fully clothed, and he
lifted her chin, his eyes like chips of ice. "Let me be really clear about
something here, Lenore. You're pregnant. I don't need a test to tell
me so. This has been a real adventure for someone like you, I'll bet.
Married young, widowed, and still fairly young. Rich then poor."

Len fought to keep her gaze steady. So he'd looked her up on the
Internet? She wasn't doing anything wrong.

"And I'm sure I'm making up for the college flings you never had
because you dropped out. But here's the thing, I'm not some fling,
lady. And I'm done unless you want to tell me otherwise."

Adam's silence was deafening, his eyes angry.

Yet, she said nothing.

Nothing to stop him from doing what she'd come to dread would
happen all along if she didn't stop it. That dread was an emotion in the
mix should be a sure sign she didn't want what he was about to lay out.

Still, she kept silent.

Bending toward her, Adam let his face come to sit but inches in
front of hers. His lips thinned, and his eyes narrowed. "I guess I have
my answer then. Now let me make one thing clear. You have no idea
who you're playing with. If I were you, I'd be very careful the next
move I make, Len. *Very careful.* Because if it involves not including
me in something I have every right to know about, no matter what
your decision is, don't think for one second I'll allow it. *I deserve to
know.*" Thrusting her chin away, he rose and strode to the door. "And
one last thing. Gerald's dead. I'm not. I'm here. I'm alive. I wanted
you for more than just sex. I don't get why you just couldn't see that."

The door to the hotel room shut with a hushed whisper against
carpet, grating her nerves to a worn frazzle.

Len reached for her cell phone with cold, lifeless hands and

dialed her gynecologist before she was unable to make the call for
the crying she knew she'd do.

~ℓ~

Adam's lips thinned when he jabbed the "down" button on the eleva-
tor. It was a real effort on his part not to ram his fist through the wall.

He'd held on for too long, hoping for something fruitless.

But the fuck he'd let Lenore Erickson walk all over him if there
was a child involved.

He just had to hang on a little longer until everything was in place.

Then he'd rock Maxine Cambridge's little world and leave Lenore
in his proverbial dust.

~ℓ~

Three weeks later, fury welled up in Max like a pot of boiling water.
That fucking puke. She threw the divorce papers Finley had sent on
her mother's table. Rage rose in her with a swell, leaving bile in her
throat.

Finley was really going to do it. So why was she so stunned?
Because somewhere deep inside her, she'd prayed, hoped Finley
wasn't a total fuck. Yet here it was in black and white.

If she signed these papers, they'd be divorced and he'd get away
with a measly sum of child support, but worse . . . If she agreed to his
terms, which was what everyone did when it came to dealing with
Finley, he wouldn't have to pay a dime for Connor's college education. Everything he owned would still be in a nice, neat little bundle,
all his money still in piles and piles from here to Connecticut intact.

With a fling of her wrist, Max hurled her purse across the room,
watching with satisfaction as the contents scattered on the floor. It
was only a small representation of her rage though. What she really
wanted to do was go all gangsta on Finley and make him scream in

agony, bleed nickels and dimes until she had the money she needed for Connor.

"Hey!" her mother shouted. "I taught you better than that. No purse throwing in the house, young lady."

Pacing, she seethed, ignoring her mother.

"Whassamatter, Maxie? Don't tell me you and Campbell had a fight already? Everything was going so well. I like him. I say we keep him—so don't screw it up by—"

"It's not Campbell," she yelped, struggling for air, dizzy from the effort. She tightened the sweater she was wearing to keep from putting her fist through a wall.

Her mother's sharp eyes fell on the envelope from Finley. "Ah. The Talleywhacker. I should've known. So what does he want now? Your ovaries cryogenically frozen?"

"No," Max gasped from holding her breath.

Mona yanked the paper off the table and scanned it before her eyes narrowed. "The hell we'll let him do this, Maxie!"

She planted a hard fist on the counter out of helpless frustration. Like she could stop him. Like she had the kind of money it would take to find someone who could. Her rage evaporated and defeat settled with a bitter aftertaste in her mouth. Goddamn him for always rising to the top like smarmy cream.

Her mother poked her arm. "Hey. You're not going to let him do this to Connor, are you?"

Tight-lipped, Max responded, fighting to keep her anger on the person who deserved it instead of taking it out on her mother. "And how would you like me to stop him? I have no money left, Mom. I'm just now beginning to be able to meet the payments on my credit card for what I've spent so far on this divorce. I can't afford to pay that ass more money only to lose. Besides that, he said he'd need a bigger retainer," she fumed. The bloodsucking leech.

Mona rolled her eyes. "So we'll get him one. Better yet, we'll get a real lawyer. I've said this a hundred times now, Maxie."

Her hands went up in the air in a gesture of defeat. "How many more times can I give you the same answer, Mom? Jesus, why won't you listen? Your retirement fund can't take any more hits than it already has. Connor and I have been depleting it for going on twelve months. If I get a better lawyer and he at least gets Connor what he's due, it won't pay you back, Mom."

Her chin lifted with typical defiance. "I don't care. Besides, when you win, Connor'll be able to go to that fancy school of his dreams and he'll earn back the money by getting a good job and supporting his old grandmother with a college degree."

Max shook her clenched fists, the blood rushing to her head. "I refuse to risk that. Not. Gonna. Happen. End of!"

"You know what you're doing here, Maxie?"

Her head fell to her hands, weary and throbbing. "*What* am I doing here, Mother?"

"You're throwing it all away because you're afraid of a confrontation with that pissant, and you're doing it at the expense of Connor and the fine education he's worked hard for!"

Oh-hoh. Hold on there. "I'm not doing any such thing. I'm avoiding confrontation *because* of my son. What good will it do for Connor if I chase after his father for money while I scream at the top of my lungs? How is that solving anything?"

Her mother's finger tapped the counter where the divorce papers now lay. "It's showing him you have some pride, kiddo. That when it comes time to keep that disgrace of a father from taking everything from him just because Connor believes what his father did to you is wrong, you've got him covered. Slugging Finley was fine, but it won't pay for Connor to go to college. You're weak, Maxine! Weak and sniveling. I never thought in a million years I'd say that to the fruit of my looms—"

"Loins. It's loins," she took peevish, seething joy in correcting her.

"Your Fruit of the Looms cover your loins. Whatever," Mona shouted back. "I never thought I'd call you weak, but this," she spat, pointing a finger at the paper Maxine was prepared to sign just to get Fin to leave them alone. "*This* is lying down and dying. That child support isn't enough to care for an orphan in Ethiopia, and coming from a man who makes more money than God. It's disgusting," she sneered, her eyes narrowing with blazing flashes of anger. "And you're gonna let him do it, too, knowing Connor wants into a school you'll never be able to afford alone, instead of getting up off your ass and fighting back! What kind of example does *that* set for your son?"

Mona's anger wasn't the worst of what Max heard in her voice. It was her disappointment, so ugly and clear. It was the same kind of disappointment her mother had had in her tone when she'd told her she was marrying Finley in the first place. Her hands gripped the edge of the countertop. "We've gone over this, Mom. I don't have the resources to fight Finley for anything. It takes money to make money, isn't that what they say?"

"They sure do, Miss Answer For Everything. They also say the rich just get richer, and in this case, that no good piece of crap's doing just that. At *Connor's* expense, and you're letting him! I'd give you the resources, if you'd just let me, but noooo—it's so much easier to pull the covers over your head and whine about your life instead of putting on your boxing gloves and going a couple of rounds with the almighty Finley Cambridge!"

If her mother'd slugged her, she couldn't have felt more bruised. Not just because it hurt to be called weak but because she was right. She was afraid to rock the boat. Afraid to take that one last step into the deep end of chaos. A step that would show Finley he couldn't take advantage of her pansy-ass nature anymore.

A step for Connor.

Mona rounded on her, justified anger in her eyes. "You know what you need to do here, Maxine? You need to *suck it up, Princess.* Stop throwing your hands up in the air like the sky's falling, Henny-Penny! Stop letting everyone else do everything for you, and do it for your-self. Did you get so used to Finley doing everything, you've forgotten how to do anything on your own? Find your pride, for Christ's sake. Stop damned well letting everything and everyone roll over you and use that mouth of yours you sure don't mind using when it comes to anyone else *but* Finley Cambridge these days! Suck up your fears. Suck up your notion that that husband of yours can have whatever he wants if he leans on you hard enough. But most of all, suck it up for Connor. He deserves better!"

The stomp of Mona's feet on the kitchen floor left Max with her bitter words ringing in her ears.

Suck it up, Princess.

Like it was that simple.

Princess.

Hah.

~ ❧ ~

"So he's refusing to pay for Connor's college education?"

Each and every time she heard that, she wanted to punch some-thing. "Yep. If I sign those divorce papers, I'm divorced and Connor's never going to see the college of his dreams. Not on my income."

"And if you don't sign the papers?"

"If I know Finley, this will go on and on until I do what he wants."

The hard line of Campbell's jaw tightened. "You're not going to do what he wants."

He didn't question it. He'd clearly already decided she had more of a backbone than she really did. "I don't know what to do," she admitted truthfully. "Could we talk about something else? This is my problem, not yours."

"I want to help, Max."

"*Please*," she said, her eyes weary from the argument with her mother and the battle she'd waged all day in her head about what to do next. "Let's just be together, okay?"

Campbell pulled Max into his embrace, nuzzling her neck, tugging the corners of the flimsy blanket he'd brought tighter around them. "Have it your way, but tomorrow's a new day, and you're only putting off the inevitable."

Her sigh was of relief. "Thank you."

"You know, truck beds are hard on an old man's back." He rubbed his bare flesh for emphasis with the hand that had just driven her insane with lust.

Max giggled, gazing up at the stars in an inky sky. "You should be my ass right now. I think it has 'Chevy' branded on it."

He slid down, nipping at her right ass cheek. "This isn't a Chevy."

Her hands went to his shoulders, reveling in the hard muscle with a squeeze. She hissed when he parted her flesh, swiping at her clit with a hot tongue. "Maybe we should get an air mattress."

"Hmmm," he moaned, vibrating the most intimate part of her. "Or I could just get my own apartment."

Max froze beneath him. "You're leaving the village?"

Acknowledging the obvious panic in her voice, Campbell slid back up along her length. "If I did, we could make love on a real live bed instead of sneaking off to the woods in my truck. I have to laugh at that, you know. Don't you see the irony in both of us, grown adults, mind you, reduced to sneaking away in a truck to be alone?"

A small piece of this new rock she'd found began to crumble. Max had to force a light tone and keep the clingy tucked away. "But what about Garner?" Yeah. That was good. Use one situation to avoid talking about the real issue.

He palmed the back of her head, kissing the tip of her nose. "Honey, my father's getting better and better all the time. And we can't go on like this forever."

Why not? Why couldn't everything just stay like it was? Was there a rule that said anything had to change?

What would her day be like if Campbell didn't pick her up and bring her to the village office for work? What would her day be like if she didn't fill a thermos with coffee made especially for him? What would it be like if he didn't bring her favorite sandwich of bologna and cheese with mustard and mayo on it? What would trips to Home Depot to buy supplies for the office be if Campbell wasn't there to help her choose the best Shop-Vac for the village's money? What would a morning not wondering if Campbell would like her new perfume be like?

And whoaaaaaaa.

Holy shit. What had happened to the woman who wasn't ever going to allow her universe to revolve around a man ever again? Yet, here she was doing it—all over again. *What would it be like if Campbell wasn't her every stupid thing*, she mocked in her head.

"Talk to me, Max," Campbell said, his tone taking a serious edge. "I see the wheels spinning. So say it. We promised we'd talk."

No, no, no. She'd rather die than admit she didn't want him to leave the cozy world they'd created within the confines of the village. She'd rather have her skin peeled off one layer at a time than turn into a jealous shrew.

Jesus. Not once in her marriage had she ever been jealous until Finley started cheating. Then she'd turned into a suspicious lunatic who was always a mess on the inside.

She was *not* going back to that place. She would not be that woman again. That woman was ugly and paranoid. "No, you're right. It would be nice to have some alone time that doesn't include us getting chapped lips." Max forced a cheerful tone, but Campbell wasn't buying it.

"I'd like to think you mean that, honey, but you're a crappy liar."

Grabbing the bottle of wine they'd purchased on the way to their old high school hangout, he offered her a swig.

Max took it without hesitation, taking a huge gulp and wiping her mouth with the back of her arm. She handed the bottle to Campbell for him to dispose of. Cool air blew across her forehead, sending goose bumps along her arms. Composure. It'd be nice if it happened. Like now.

When all else fails, what are you good at, Maxine Cambridge? Hiding. So stow away your misgivings by shoving them under your blankie and fake it. At all costs, keep your stupid to yourself. Summon up the old beauty queen smile and bullshit your way through.

Giving Campbell a nudge, Max shot him a saucy grin. "I am not a liar, Mr. Barker. Now shut up and let's get back to what you started."

Her lips found his, needy, desperate to drown herself in Campbell and forget her never-ending doubts. His arms instantly went around her, placing her on his naked lap.

Max's hands went to his cock, circling the hard shaft with both hands, running them along the satiny skin. Leaving his lips, she skimmed his chest with her mouth, tasting his heated skin, encompassing a nipple, licking at it until the skin was rigid and tight. She found her way along his abs, kissing each hard rung, luxuriating in the crisp hairs that led a trail to his cock.

Campbell's hands wound their way into her hair, groaning when she took her first lick of him. It was purposefully slow, lingering along the hot pulse at the base while she cupped his balls. One thrust of her mouth downward, and she stilled, letting the salty taste of his shaft fill her mouth.

His hips bucked upward at a sharp angle, driving between her lips, groaning as she swirled her tongue around him, sucking, licking, driving him to the edge she now knew by just the feel of him.

"Woman," he muttered with a warning she'd grown familiar with, the mixture of a growl and a husky demand that she stop. Campbell pulled her from him, dragging her upward until she sat on his lap. The crisp hairs on his upper thighs scraped against the backs of hers in delicious friction as she waited for him to slide a condom on.

Campbell's hands went around her waist, planting her directly on his cock. As she sank downward, he controlled her glide, delaying final contact in increments of hot, slick pleasure. Maxine leaned back a bit, thrusting her breasts upward, bracing her hands on his thighs, rocking to the rhythm he'd created.

Her sigh fell into the wind that was no longer cold when he cupped her breasts, tweaking her nipples to fine points. His mouth closed over one. Hot, greedy, he suckled at her until heat rose and fell between her thighs.

Campbell gasped when she rose up then thrust back downward, lifting her hips, gyrating against him until all she could feel was his mouth on her and his cock, hard and hot between her legs.

There was nothing else but this when he made love to her. Nothing distracted her. Nothing stole all of her senses in one breathtaking fell swoop like when Campbell plunged inside of her.

It was all-consuming, deeper than any experience she'd ever had, and it allowed her to lose herself in nothing but her need for him.

When he slipped a finger between her folds, rubbing her clit, Max came with a heave forward against his chest, burying her hands in his hair, clinging to Campbell while he climaxed, too.

Her head rested on top of his for support, her shoulders shook from the effort to take air into her lungs. Campbell smoothed her back, warming her now cooling flesh.

Max shivered, but not from the chilling air. From the fear that one day this would all be over and Campbell would never make love to her again. Never smile with her again. Never share a pizza with her again. Never watch *Yard Crashers* with her again. There were too many nevers involved here.

God.

She wanted to scream her frustration out loud. It was so unfair that she was falling in love yet couldn't trust how she'd begun to feel about this man. She couldn't trust that she trusted him because Max Cambridge shouldn't ever be trusted in the man-picking department.

Oh, Jesus and all twelve. Her mental admission left her panicked, shaky.

No.

It didn't have to be this way if she could just call up all the horrible things Finley'd done to her. If she could just remember what it was to be thrown out like day-old bread, she might manage to keep her fear of losing him at bay.

How could Campbell have made her forget? How could he possibly erase where she'd been and make it seem as though falling in love with him would be just fine?

It didn't work like that.

It couldn't.

"Hey up there. That's my hair you're latched on to, honey. I'm pretty proud it's still my own," Campbell teased.

"Oh!" Max smoothed his hair back, loving the feel of it between her fingers despite herself. "Sorry. I was lost in the moment." And she hoped that statement would suffice.

A glance at his watch and Campbell said, "We've been lost for four hours. I hate to break this up, but we'd better get back. You have an early meeting tomorrow and I have a Jacuzzi to fix at the pool." Kissing her chin, he handed her the sweatshirt he'd brought for her.

Max dressed in silence, accepting Campbell's help when he lifted her from the truck bed and helped her into the cab. The ride back was quiet, though Campbell didn't look as though he suspected where her silence stemmed from.

He held her hand like he always did whenever they were together, caressing it while they drove. Pulling into her mother's driveway, he put the car in park and winked at her. "C'mere," he said, his smile secretive.

She slid across the seat and smiled up at him.

"I have one last thing to say before we say good night. Just because you take me into consideration in your life now does not mean I own you, honey. And don't run scared because I'm considering getting an apartment, Max. The only thing it changes is that we'll have more privacy than we know what to do with. All the small things that have become a routine for us are all of the things I think about, too. You're not alone in that. It makes us a couple, not slaves. Couples do those things, and when they begin as couples, they spend time thinking about each other because the relationship is new."

But what about when it was old and fraying around the edges? What happened then? What happened when one person stopped thinking about the other all the time? What happened when the other person went off and found the cutest big-canned number they could lay their hands on in their swanky new apartment building?

"It also means you way like me. And who can blame you? I am damned cute. Now give me a kiss, woman, and get some sleep. If we keep behaving like teenagers and keeping these late hours, someone's shower's going to end up hooked up to their toilet."

Turning into his arms, Max scrunched her eyes closed to fend off tears. She could never pinpoint if his uncanny perception of her thoughts was a real thread they shared, or if he was just damned good at pretending he understood her, pretending he cared about what she was so afraid of. Instead of giving in to the waterworks, she gave Campbell a warm kiss, filled with all the things she almost wished she didn't feel for him. It would make things so much easier when it was over.

"Night, Max," he said in the tone that always made her fight a girlie sigh.

Calling on her old beauty queen days, she summoned the biggest, toothy smile she could muster. "Night, Campbell," she returned, hopping from the truck and making a beeline for her mother's.

Where she'd live while Campbell went off and got an apartment. And some furniture.

Because all swinging bachelors needed furniture.

~ ~

"You waiting up for me, old man?" Campbell teased Garner upon his arrival home. "You need a good night's rest if you're gonna stop all this slacking you've been doing while I do all your dirty work."

"Hah!" his father guffawed. "I was just catching some of that Craig Ferguson. Sit down and talk to me, son." Garner slapped the couch with the newspaper he held.

"About?"

"About your girlfriend. You two've been pretty hot and heavy for the past few weeks. I haven't asked questions because I don't want to pry."

Campbell raised an eyebrow of skepticism. "You do, too."

"Okay. I wanna pry, but I like seeing you so happy. Can't ever recall that smile on your face before Maxine. So, how's it going?"

His smile was broad, shadowed only by the idea that Max was getting ready to run again. Each bout of her freak-outs had longer periods in between, but she was due—especially after tonight's conversation.

He knew her fear well now. Saw it in her eyes, tagged it for what it was. If anything in their routine changed, she'd concoct some cocka-mamie story to explain it. A story that more than likely had to do with him and women with big breasts. She'd missed her calling. She would've been an incredible writer. "It's goin' pretty good, Dad."

Garner's head bobbed in appreciation for his son's good fortune. "Yep. Means she's due to pitch another one of those fits pretty soon."

He barked a laugh. "That she is. It's uncanny how well you know the female mind."

A wrinkled hand raised in the air. "Bah. I just know she's been through a tough time. Max doesn't trust herself and her instincts yet. She's fallin' for ya and she's afraid she's wrong about you. I don't know what she thinks she's wrong about, but she thinks it all the same. So you ready for it?"

There had to come a time when Max trusted him. Trust took time. He realized that, but if his words and actions weren't enough, what would be?

Yet now, after spending so many hours filled with just her, he couldn't imagine ever walking away.

"I'm sure going to try and be ready, Dad." For now, it was the only answer he had.

Garner patted him on the shoulder with a heavy hand. "Just be sure you make the right decision when that time comes."

Campbell sat for a long time after his father went to bed. The ominous dread he'd toyed with earlier was returning full force.

Try as he might, he just couldn't shake it off.

CHAPTER NINETEEN

Note from Maxine Henderson to all ex-trophy wives on uber sucking it up: Helmet? Check. Chest plate? Check. Sword of justice? Check. The sad fact is, sometimes the mediation of a divorce turns into a battlefield. They say war is hell. Make sure it doesn't end up being your own special hell. Fight for your rights. Fight for your children's rights. Put on your battle gear, ladies. It's. On.

Len dialed Adam's phone number with a smile on her face, frowning when his voice mail answered. "Adam? It's Len. I know we left on—on bad terms, but I owe you an apology. Maybe we could meet, um, for lunch and just talk. Call me."

Lunch was a big step for her. Public dining. Surely Adam would see she was extending an olive branch?

Yet as the hours passed, and he didn't return her call, she became less and less like his lover, and more and more like the stalker she'd once accused him of being after calling him a total of twenty times.

That was when she finally saw the big picture. She'd blown it.

Sky high.

As Len stared at her computer screen long into the night, she toyed with the mouse, scrolling the list of Adam Baylors on Google without a point. Like anything would've changed since she'd last searched for him on the Internet. The only contact she had was his cell phone number. Hell, she didn't even know where he really lived or if he even lived in New Jersey. He'd been the Holiday Inn hottie, and she'd spent a whole lot of time cultivating his role as such, refusing to make small talk, staunchly avoiding any and all personal questions.

And what if she never saw him again? Her stomach lurched. Adam had made it clear, in no uncertain terms, he wanted in on whatever she chose to do about her potential pregnancy, but what if that was all just bullshit and he'd disappeared for good?

The notion didn't sit right with her, though it was certainly a possibility and would definitely absolve her of any guilty feelings she might incur for treating him so callously.

So why couldn't she summon up some relief? This was almost how she'd seen the end with Adam. Well, not quite, but it was an end, something she'd planned on since it began.

So what the hell?

Here's what the hell. You. Blew. It. And now you're sorry and you want to take it all back.

Boo to the hoo, honey.

⁓

"Can I ask you something, kiddo?" Max and Connor sat on her mother's back porch, side by side in rocking chairs, watching the early-autumn sunset.

"You can always ask."

Max nudged his shoulder with hers. She'd been thinking about this question for the last two weeks, while she battled her insecurities over Campbell, and she planned her next move with Finley. "I'm serious."

He grinned while he texted Jordon. "Sure, Mom."

"Do you think I'm weak?"

"Weak? You mean like do I think you eat enough Wheaties?"

"No. That's not what I mean at all. I mean, do you think I'm not doing everything I can to get what's fair for you without creating a bigger gap than already exists between you and your father?"

Connor's mouth twisted at the mention of his father. "Not really. I just think you're doing what you do best."

"And what's that?"

He looked up at her, setting the new cell phone she'd just purchased for him aside. "Am I gonna be grounded if I tell you the truth?"

"Nope. Shoot straight."

Connor didn't look convinced. "You're really sure?"

Max patted his hand for reassurance. "Shoot. What do I do best?"

"Try to keep everyone happy. I think you're doing what you've always done with Dad. Smoothing things over to keep him from freaking out. Letting go of the stuff that bothers you so you won't have to argue. Dad knew you did it, and he used it against you. You used to do it all the time."

Maxine nodded with despair. There was no denying she'd done whatever it took to keep Finley pacified.

"You'd make me clean up my toys so Dad wouldn't trip over one and flip out because his day was always so much longer and harder than everyone else's. You used to give me that 'hush your mouth' sign with your finger over your mouth behind his back to give me a heads-up not to push him too far. You used to distract him when he was mad and ready to fire someone at the dealership over something really lame, like one of the mechanics not calling him 'Mr. Cambridge.' You did stuff like that to keep him happy. But I don't get one thing. Why are you still doing it?"

"Doing what?"

"Keeping him happy. Pretty soon you won't be married to him anymore—it'll be Lacey's job to do it. I don't really care about Dad's money or how much he pays for child support and all the other crap.

I don't care that he's being a jerk and refusing to pay for college. I'll get a scholarship or something. I don't even care if we live here with Grandma until I graduate. But I kinda think you did a lot of things for Dad that if you were someone else, he'd have had to pay for it. That should mean something, shouldn't it?"

A tear stung her eye. Shame washed over her in ugly waves of reality. Not only had she walked on eggshells with Finley, she'd made Connor do it, too. "But those were things I did out of love, Connor. Not because I hoped to be paid for them someday."

"And this is how he pays back that kind of love? That's pretty twisted. If he wanted a divorce because of Lacey, fine, but did he have to treat you like you were garbage when you were always nice to him? Cut you off like he was never married to you?"

If only it were all that simple. It was so classic. The timeless story of a bitter divorce. "I have to admit, I never believed your dad would go this far. I'm sorry, Connor," Max apologized. "I'm sorry I didn't see what I was doing to you while I tried to keep your dad happy."

His broadening shoulders shrugged. "Then don't do it anymore. Even if you go down, go down swinging."

Max absorbed his advice for a moment, still astounded at how astute Connor was. There was so much she wished she could've hidden from him, protected him from. In hindsight, she realized, she hadn't been aware she was making him walk on those eggshells with her because she'd been too busy working at keeping everything together. "And who taught you that motto?"

He smirked before rising to slide open the glass doors that led to the house. "Grandma. She said she taught you that, too."

Yeah. Yeah, she had. "Ever wonder why I don't listen to her?"

"For the same reasons I don't listen to you," he joked. "She's your *Mom*."

Max smiled. Yeah. That she was.

~ℓ~

"Joseph Arwin speaking."

"This is Maxine Cambridge, Mr. Got My Law Degree From A Bubble-Gum Machine U," she said into her cell, smiling when she imagined the look on Joseph Arwin's face at her snipe.

"*Excuse me?*"

"You heard me. It's Maxine Cambridge. I'm calling to fire you."

"Fire *me?*"

She nodded to herself with a smug smile as she turned onto the highway. "Yep. I knooooow. You're so surprised, right? I mean, who would want to fire a lawyer as fine as yourself? One who's fought to the bitter end for me while he ran my credit card up to the max and didn't do a damned thing for me but tell me it was all my fault I was going to be left with no money? Crazy, right?"

His sigh was long and aggravated. "Mrs. Cambridge, is this another frantic call about a situation you created yourself? Something I can do nothing about?" His condescending tone chapped her ass.

Max clucked her tongue into the phone. "You know, funny that. You *can* do something about it. You just want more money to do it. It took me some time, but then I figured it out. If I'd gone to a *real* lawyer in the first place who can, based on his reputation, legitimately charge two hundred and fifty bucks an hour for some actual work, I would have been much better off. But silly me, I went cheap, and you know what they say about champagne wishes on a beer budget, right? Yeah, I got the six-pack, pal. But no more. And just an FYI. If, instead of just shuffling papers for the last year and telling me your hands were tied, you'd have done something more than charge my credit card to pay for your mai tais with the fancy umbrellas at the Tiki Lounge, I might have had more money to pay for an attorney who would have at the very least gotten me some decent child support and fought for my son's college education—which he's entitled to. So hear this! You're fired, and if you see your face on a billboard off the Jersey Turnpike with a big X over it that reads 'Want A Divorce That Doesn't Rip You A New Asshole? Don't Call Him'—you'll know it was me!"

Max clicked off the phone with satisfaction, throwing it to the passenger seat, her cheeks red, her eyes blazing defiance in the rear-view mirror. Wow, when a princess sucked it up, it felt Goddamned good.

Her chat with Connor last night was the final straw in a string of straws that should have broken the camel's back long ago. For all the good she'd taught him, she'd also taught him to be a pacifist.

To sit back and let everyone else rule your kingdom while you pretended everything was okay. While you wrung your hands and relinquished what you could control, leaving the outcome of your life to a man who shouldn't be allowed to control a car radio.

Well, no more. No more sitting quietly in the corner, hiding behind her greasy hair, only peeking out occasionally to see the world pass her by, and letting Finley and anyone else she'd allow take advantage of her.

Not another minute of placating, pacifying, fucking peace-making on Finley Cambridge's behalf.

Cheesy lawyer disposed of?

Check.

Cheap, bloodsucking leech of a husband due for a bashing?

Up next.

And it was only nine o'clock in the morning.

Max Cambridge didn't want to be a Cambridge anymore, but she'd be one for as long as it took to make Fin's marriage to Lacey impossible or until she'd waited so long, Lacey wouldn't be so young and nubile anymore.

Straightening her navy blue blazer, Max pulled into a parking space and marched into Cambridge Auto, heading straight for Barbie in the circular reception area. Her face, blank but beautiful as ever, took on a whole new expression when she caught sight of Max.

Fear.

Max smelled it. As much as it would bring her great pleasure to sink neck deep in it, that wasn't what she was here for. "Tell Finley I'm here," she demanded, ignoring several looks from Cambridge Auto employees. "Oh, and tell him I promise to keep my fists to myself." She winked.

The blonde waffled, her lips moving, but only a stutter coming out. "He—he said he can't be—dis . . ."

"Disturbed. Yeah. He says that whenever he's in there, banging some poor, unsuspecting just-barely-over-the-legal-limit blonde. So press that button on your phone and tell him to put the 'monster'"—she nodded at the memory—"yeah, that's what he used to call it, tell him to put the 'monster' away. The woman who really wants to be his ex-wife is here, and she'd be happy to sign those divorce papers the cheap bastard sent her, but she won't do it until he talks to her."

Bodacious babe headed for Fin's door, knocking on it with worry lining her face and a trembling lower lip. "Mr. Cambridge, you have a visitor who—who . . ."

The door popped open, Fin poked his head out, his line of vision zeroing in on Max. "Maxine."

"Finley," she drawled, stunned at how relaxed she was. She held up the divorce papers, waving them like a white flag. "I think we have to chat."

He straightened his already ramrod straight tie. "Talk to my lawyer."

"But don't you want me to sign these papers?" she cooed, taunting him.

A glimmer of the kill twinkled in his eye. He motioned a hand for her to enter.

She brushed past him, shocked the bottle of Pepto-Bismol she had in her purse wasn't screaming her name. There wasn't an iota of a rumble in her stomach. No acid reflux, no jitters, no cold hands and crashing heart.

Just dead resolve.

Fin closed the door behind her, making his way around his desk. A desk so big, Max had always considered it a phallic symbol of the power he liked to show everyone he had.

And it was a good representation. He *was* a big dick.

Finley eyed her with that cold amusement he'd cultivated over the years. "What do you want, Maxine?"

Her return smile was just as cold. "Out. I want out. If I have to be married to you for one more second, I think I'll crawl right out of my skin."

He tapped an impatient pen on the surface of his desk as though she bored him. "So sign the papers and save your skin."

"May I use your pen?" she asked, syrupy sweet, sitting at the edge of his desk. "I don't have one of my own, but I know how you hate to share, you know, anything. Like houses and furniture and *mon-ey*." Max rubbed her fingers together.

Rolling his tongue in his cheek, Finley handed her the pen without a word, but the tic in his left eye exposed his irritation.

She fanned herself with the papers, putting the pen behind her ear. "You know what, Fin?"

"What, Maxine?"

Ohhhh, his teeth were clenched. Nice. They were at DEFCON level 2 and she'd only asked to borrow his pen. "I've been thinking a lot about what a shitty person you are. What a crappy, lying, cheating pig of a husband you were, too."

Razor-sharp eyes flashed at her. "Have you thought about what a crappy wife you were? If you'd done what good wives do—"

"Oh! Wait. I can finish the sentence for you." Planting her hands

on her hips, she mimicked him. " 'If you'd been a better wife, Maxine, I wouldn't have gone elsewhere. If you'd kept the spark alive, I
wouldn't have had to set fire to half the tri-state area with my useless
dick.' Right? Isn't that how it goes?" She nodded, agreeing with herself. "Yes. That's how I remember it. It was all my fault." Her shoulders shrugged. "Maybe it was. Maybe I didn't do my part. But you
know what?"

His sneer grew. "Get to the point, Maxine."

"I asked a question," she pouted with a coy, flirtatious wink.

"What, Maxine?"

"What if Lacey never gets to do her part?"

Finley rose, leaning over the desk with tense muscles. "What
part?"

"What if I don't sign these papers? I can drag this divorce out forever and Lacey will never get to do her part, stroking your monster
ego as your wife because she won't be able to marry you unless I *let*
her."

His eyes narrowed to ugly pinpoints, but there was something
else there, too. Relief? "So are you saying you're going to hold me
hostage because you're as pathetic as I tell everyone?"

Her smile was sly. "You betcha."

Finley's face cracked, just an inch, but crack it did. "What would
it take to get you to sign them?"

She jabbed a finger into that crack, forcing it open just a little further. "Connor's education. What kind of father are you that you'd let
your own flesh and blood suffer because you want to punish him for
standing up to you? I don't mind telling you, you're disgusting. How I
missed that all these years just goes to show you how far a little cash
and a semi-convincing line will get you. It sure wasn't your brains and
brawn that made me stick around. So, here we are. If you don't draw
up a new agreement that says you'll pay for Connor's every little collegiate need, I'll be Mrs. Finley Cambridge *for-ev-ah*."

Phew. Who was she?

And then she remembered. She was Connor's mother, and she'd squeeze Finley's balls until the Winter Olympics were held in hell before she'd give up the opportunity for Connor to realize his dream.

"You're some fucking bitch, Maxine," he growled.

"Uh-huh. And your vocabulary is still just as original. Stunted, but original. So," Max waved the papers in his face, "do we have a deal?"

"The hell we do," he spat in her face.

"*Bum-mer*," she spat back from somewhere deep and ugly. "I guess Lacey'll just have to wait to change her monogrammed towels, huh?"

"Fin?" A frantic voice barged through the door in clattering high heels and clingy material. "Sweetie? What's going on?"

"Oh, look. It's the never gonna be Mrs. Finley Cambridge number two," Max said on a wicked chuckle. Whatever, whoever possessed her right now was invited to stay. Even if it made her head spin and she ended up yarking pea soup.

Lacey went immediately to Fin's side, concern riddling her face. "What does she mean, Fin?"

He stretched his neck upward, sucking in his cheeks. "Maxine's refusing to sign the divorce papers, pumpkin. I told you she was a bitch."

Lacey flapped a hand as though this were all so silly-willy. "Oh, Maxine, don't be a poop. You know you don't want to be married anymore. You have that new boyfriend. Doesn't he want you to be divorced?" she asked in a tone littered with an appeasing edge.

Seeing Lacey like this, watching her run her hands over Fin's arm to soothe his escalating temper was like a flashback to the early years of her marriage where it was all about keeping Fin calm. "I'm sure he does, but that's not going to happen until I get what I want."

Confusion spread over Lacey's youthful face. "But what could you want? You signed a prenuptial agreement. What else is there? Is it the furniture? I'd give it to you because I'm only going to replace it anyway, but where would you put it at your mother's? Besides, Fin said you didn't want it."

The furniture? With the speed of a fastball to the head, enlightenment smacked right into Max. Jesus Christ on a cracker. Lacey had no idea. None. She was clueless about what Fin was doing. How advantageous to find that out now—right here—at the bargaining table.

Max's smile grew. So did her balls. "Lacey? I don't want the furniture. I don't even want my clothes. That Fin's let you believe those items, *any items*, were ever an option for me makes him a bigger scumbag than even I thought he was."

Her blonde head tilted as if she hadn't heard Max right. "But he said—"

Max's laugh was bitter when she cut her off. "Oh, I can only imagine what *he* said, but here's the truth—"

"Shut your trap, Maxine!" Fin roared.

Max reached over the desk and patted his arm, much the way she did when she was pacifying one of the seniors. Only this time, it wasn't to make his boo-boo all better. "Easy there, big guy. Your cholesterol's pretty high. I know I told you all that whole wheat bread was the only kind Lola could find at the store, but it was really to keep you from having a heart attack. Upon reflection, I should have given you white bread—loaves at a time."

"Get. Out. You. Bitch!"

Hopping off his desk on light feet, Max held up the papers. "Oh, I'm getting, but before I do, pay close attention. I don't know what you've been telling your girlfriend here to make yourself look like you give a damn about your son, but here's the scoop. If you don't have a new agreement drafted, you ain't goin' to the chapel any time this millennium."

Her hands held up the papers in front of her face.

The joy she took in tearing them in half, the sweet sound of paper ripping into confetti-sized pieces was like a symphony of violins playing in her ears. Max threw them up into the air, watching as they drifted to the floor in all their cheapskate glory.

"Fin," Lacey sobbed. "Just do what she wants. Please, honey. So I can finally be your wife. I don't want to wait anymore!"

The shift in Finley's stance, the subtle half an inch or so he moved away from Lacey, brought with it another realization.

He was using both her and Connor.

To avoid ever having to marry Lacey.

Fin could put her off until the cows came home with the excuse that Maxine was behaving like a difficult bitch, and there was nothing he could do but wait. It was free pussy without Lacey having all the Cambridge privileges.

Max's mouth fell open, and then she threw her head back and laughed.

Laughed until tears streamed down her face and she had to hold her stomach to quell the ache. "Ohhhhhhhh, Finley, you crafty old fox, you," she crowed. Clapping her hands, she giggled again, high on this coup she'd stumbled upon. "Lacey? I hope you didn't pay for your wedding dress yet because by the time you get to wear it, *Vogue* will probably have closed its doors."

Max strode to the door, stepping over the shredded paper of her divorce. "And Fin? Just a thought. Maybe you should tell Lacey the only thing keeping her from signing checks as Mrs. Finley Cambridge is your reluctance, nay, your staunch refusal to pay for our son's college education."

With a wiggle of her fingers over her shoulder, Max strutted out the door, bumping into some of the dealership's employees on her way.

Outside, in the crisp autumn air, she indulged in a deep, cleansing breath before getting into her mother's car.

The kind of breath you take when self-confidence fills your lungs so full you can actually taste it.

And it tasted better than any Cristal or Pernod ever had.

Nom-nom.

CHAPTER TWENTY

Note from Maxine Cambridge to all ex-trophy wives: Relationship advice. Jealousy. Such an ugly beast, no? If you're looking for excuses to run and hide from another relationship, the green-eyed monster is a perfect scapegoat. But remember this: In allowing fear to rule your life, happiness will always be an elusive butterfly. So do yourself a skinny. Hunt that bitch down, net in hand, and catch it before it owns you.

Max literally flew from her mother's car into the pool house where Campbell was supposed to be fixing the Jacuzzi. The entire drive back over to the village, all she could think about was telling him what she'd discovered about Fin and all his stalling.

Her joy at finding out Finley's game plan, even if it was still to her and Connor's disadvantage, couldn't be denied its due. She wanted to shout her independence, scream her victory. And in this moment, she wanted to share it with Campbell. To prove to him she wasn't going to be steamrolled.

She stopped short at the sauna, peeking inside to find Campbell wasn't there. Max poked her head into the ladies' locker room to see if someone knew where he was. Hearing Mrs. Riley's nasally voice, Max sighed. Poor Irene probably couldn't hear how loud she was without her hearing aids.

But her next words brought Max to a dead stop.

"You heard me right, Esther. And all this time we thought Campbell was a nice boy. I can't believe he's Garner's son."

A snort filtered to Max's ears. "Well, he's a nice-lookin' boy, that's for sure."

"Not nice-lookin' enough to put up with his kind of crap. The way that poor Maxine's going, he'll just do to her what's already been done."

Max's face flushed over her eavesdropping. *What kind of crap?*

"Are you sure you heard right, Irene? Just doesn't sit well with me. I see the way he looks at Maxine, and I really like Maxine. She's been so good for the village."

"I know what I heard, Esther!" Irene said with vehemence. "He said he was going to dump Maxine for Linda, clear as the day is long. Someone has to tell her, Esther. She's had some time of it."

Everything else drifted away, their voices became muted and muffled by the sound of her crashing heart.

Linda.

Campbell's ex-wife.

Max had to grip the edge of the door to keep her knees from caving.

Breathe.

You've been here before, Max. Breathe.

Breathe and think. But don't think too much before you talk to Campbell.

Coaxing herself to stop and give this rational thought before the snowflakes in her mind became one giant snowball of accusations and unproven innuendo.

Yes, it sounded bad, she reminded herself, but she couldn't get a feel for how bad until she talked to Campbell.

Hookay. She felt the blood rush back into her limbs and her breathing steady.

No more running away. No more pretending bad things didn't happen if you burrowed deep enough under your blankets.

Head-on. That's what she'd do. She'd attack this head-on and give Campbell the chance to explain before she flipped a nut.

She would not fall apart. Her superglue tube was empty.

Good.

Shoving her purse under her arm, she let the door go and headed off with determination to find Campbell.

All mature-like.

～ℓ～

"Mom?"

"Yeah, kiddo?" she replied, distracted by her inability to locate Campbell after two phone calls and a scan of the village in her mother's car.

"Check out what I found," Connor said, plunking down in the kitchen chair beside her and placing his laptop on the table.

Max didn't look up, but muttered, "What did you find?"

"Look. It's Campbell." He held up the screen of his laptop in front of her.

She read the headline on the Yahoo! front page almost with disinterest, skimming the words. That is until she reread it and gazed at the face she was so close to falling in love with. Her response was slow, stilted by the words swimming in front of her eyes. "Yeah. It sure is."

Connor's eyes searched hers. "Mom, what's wrong? This is a good thing, right?"

Max couldn't tear her eyes from the picture of Campbell, excruciatingly handsome, in a tuxedo with some beautiful, more to the point *young*, brunette on his arm.

Jet-setting, according to the article in the top searches on Yahoo!.

"I can't believe Campbell owns Chirped," Connor exclaimed. "That's pretty tight."

Max fought a pent-up scream and tried to focus on not letting her imagination get the best of her. "What is Chirped?"

Connor's fingers flitted over the keyboard, taking her to the official homepage of Chirped. The one owned by Campbell Barker who pretended he was just a humble plumber. "It's a social site, Mom. You know, like Facebook and MySpace? You socialize with other people, and you chirp whatever you want to say in a hundred and fifty words or less. You can network with other people who like the stuff you do. Like if you're into knitting like Grandma, you can search for other people who like to knit, too. Then you follow them so you can keep up with their chirps."

"Do you have an account on Chirped, Connor?"

He shook his head, picking up the laptop. "Nah. Still just the Facebook you said okay to. And yes, it's still locked," he said before she could question him.

So Campbell Barker was rich. Probably richer than Finley.

And he liked younger women, according to the Yahoo! article, toned, tanned, buff younger women who were daughters of rich moguls.

And here he was dating a jacked-up, sagging ex-trophy wife in a senior citizens' village. A poor, old, outdated reproduction of what he dated when he was in Morocco. Or had the article said Saint Moritz?

All that talk about how beautiful she was—Spanx and sagging ass be damned—was nothing but a lie. Every second they'd shared, every moment she'd come to treasure, was about as meaningful as her twenty-year marriage to a man who was just an older replica of Campbell.

Max rested her forehead in her hand, using the heel of it to massage the building tension. What she'd heard today in the locker room might have been relayed inaccurately, but pictures didn't lie.

Idiot, idiot, idiot. *You're no different than the fool you were twenty years ago, Max. Still bowled over by a little attention from a man.*

"Max?" Campbell startled her when he pushed her mother's door open. He came up behind her, squeezing her shoulders and nuzzling her neck. "Hey, honey. Heard you were looking for me."

Her nostrils caught his once welcome scent, her eyes stung with tears of a disappointment so deep, she had trouble breathing. She stiffened on contact, fighting the impulse to haul off and head butt him. "I sure was. All day, as a matter of fact."

Pulling her from the chair, Campbell spun her around to face him, greeting her with his smile. The same smile that was plastered on his face while he escorted some nubile brunette onto some yacht. "I'm sorry. I was tied up at Mr. Morris's. I forgot I never turned on my phone. I came as soon as I heard you were looking for me."

Her heart ached, but she kept her expression stiff, her body unyielding. "Did you forget you're rich, too?" she asked quietly.

Campbell's eyes never wavered when they held hers. They were still just as blue, still just as sincere as always. He glanced around, and nodded his head toward the door. "You want to talk outside?"

In light of the fact that Connor was there, that'd probably be a good idea. Max dragged her coat from the back of the chair, her hands trembling and already cold. "Yep."

He held the door for her, taking her limp hand in his and leading her to the small patio tables and chairs her mother had on her front lawn. "So you know," he said, plunking down in a padded chair like it was no big deal that he was ungodly rich.

Max didn't sit. Instead, she fisted her hands and put them in the pockets of her jacket to fight off a violent shiver. "I know. What I want to know is why you didn't tell me." Did she really, really want to know? Yes, she decided. She was all about the truth, good, bad, and ugly, and though she found she was mentally bracing herself, she also found, she could take it.

Yay.

His smile never wavered. "That part of my life seemed pretty distant here in the village. It's just a number in some bank accounts."

"Was the number on your arm in the picture on Yahoo! just a number in a bank account? You might want to rethink that statement. She was pretty hot."

Campbell ignored her jibe. "The picture on Yahoo!?"

Shades of Finley, playing stupid, slapped Max square in the face. "Yeah. You should be proud. You were number three on Yahoo!'s top searches."

Realization spread across his face. "Must be because of the sale of Chirped."

Max nodded sharply. "Yeah, funny that," she responded, purposely allowing her words to be tinged with sarcasm. "So I guess the joke about the Ferrari being your other car really wasn't such a joke, was it?"

The weary lines around Campbell's eyes had begun to show impatience. "I didn't realize my owning Chirped was that big of a deal, Max."

Her mouth fell open. She held up a hand in disbelief. "Hold on. You didn't think being a multimillionaire was a big deal?" How could he even say such a thing to her?

"It's just money."

"Oh, it's more than money. It's an assload of money. So much money you're probably richer than Finley, and it never occurred to you to tell me. Why is that? Were you afraid I might get a little taste of what I was accustomed to and decide to set my sights on you?"

The smile Campbell wore left his face, replaced with a hard look she'd only seen him give Finley. "Why don't you tell me what you're getting at?"

"You obviously didn't want me to know."

"Shouldn't you be glad I'm rich, Max, and not some poor plumber?"

No! she wanted to scream. When Campbell was a plumber, they were on equal footing. They bagged their lunches together so she could save money. He helped her clip coupons. Campbell Barker didn't have to clip coupons.

This was no different than Fin. Campbell could buy and sell her— he could have anything or anyone he wanted, and eventually, when his money exposed him to something he couldn't resist, if he hadn't already, he'd trash her. Not this time. Money made people angry, and greedy, and spiteful. "You know what's funny about you being rich?"

"Whatever it is, it isn't making you laugh," was his flat reply.

"The funny thing is, you're right, I should be happy. I mean, what girl wouldn't be thrilled to find out her sort-of boyfriend's rich? But not me, Campbell. *Not me.* I know what having that kind of money means. It not only means you lied to me, but it means I'm something you can trade off at whim. It means when the next shiny thing comes along, you know, when you're no longer stuck here in the village with the only woman even close to your age to pass the time with, *sleep* with, you'll be off sailing on yachts with bikini-clad twenty-year-olds. Oh, wait! You've already done that, right? I must pale in comparison to whatshisface's daughter!"

In a second he was off the chair and gathering her by her upper arms, glaring down at her with disgust he didn't bother to hide. "Do you really think I'd do that, Max? What do you suppose my big ulterior motive for not telling you is?"

"I don't know, Campbell. Maybe it's *Linda,*" she taunted up into his face.

"Linda?" he pretended not to know who she meant.

Yeah. Like she was the crazy one here. "Yeah—there's another funny thing. Irene Riley heard you talking on your cell today. The one that was turned off. Remember that?"

"I did turn it off, Max. Jesus Christ, this is ridiculous," he snapped, letting her go to shove a hand through his hair.

"*Really?* I don't know, but Irene said she heard you telling someone you were, and I quote, 'Going to dump Max for Linda'! Isn't your ex-wife's name Linda? So who's ridiculous now?"

Looming over her, he stared her down. "That is exactly what I said—*almost.*"

Max paled. She'd expected denial, a good tall tale, but never the truth.

"What I said was I *can't* just dump Max for *Linda* today because Max and I have a date. Linda's my lawyer, Max. I wasn't talking to my ex-wife. Her secretary called and said she wanted to meet to go over the sale of Chirped, but I told her I couldn't because I had a dinner date with you. Here," he pulled out his cell phone with a harsh yank from his pocket, flipping through pages until he reached Linda's number. "We'll call her up and you can see for yourself. Will that ease your mind, Max? Is that what it'll take to show you I'm nothing like that prick of a husband you can't seem to rid yourself of?"

"You're just like him. Just like him!" she yelled into the cold wind. "You may look better. You might be nicer to little old ladies and has-been beauty queens, but you're just like him. I saw those pictures of you cavorting with plenty of young women, but how ironic there were no pictures of you cavorting on some white sandy beach with middle-aged, sagging, faded prom queens!"

Campbell was quiet for a moment—so calm and eerily still, she wanted to grab him and shake him to make him say something.

The wind blew, frosty and sharp against her heated cheeks.

Wind chimes sounded from all around the cul-de-sac with mournful tones.

Garden gnomes mocked her with painted eyes and cheerful smiles.

When Campbell finally spoke, his voice was almost hoarse and so low, Max had to strain to hear his defense. "You know why there are no pictures of me with women like you? Because there was no *you* until a few months ago."

Her heart shuddered in her chest.

"Know what else, Max? You're right. I should have told you about my money and explained the pictures on the Internet. I'm not a big celebrity. Just a guy who came up with a concept that hit the big time and got lucky. I'm sure the only reason I'm anywhere on the Internet is because of the sale of Chirped. I've kept a pretty low profile until the press got wind of the sale just recently. If you'd given me the chance, I would have told you that. I also would have told you those women, all of *two*, are daughters of good friends of mine whose fathers would hack off my head if I ever considered dating them. I'm betting the brunette you saw online was my friend Hal's daughter. She's seventeen, FYI, and the picture they took of us was from her sweet-sixteen party. But why believe me when you can believe some lowlife journalist who'd love nothing more than to depict some sleazy May-December romance with the teenage daughter of a computer guru?"

Oh.

Oh. Oh. Oh.

She figured he put his index finger to his mouth to keep her from speaking without actually telling her to shut the hell up. "You see, Max, there's this thing called communication, and you blow big chunks at it. You don't ask. You run with some crazy story in your head, and I think tonight I've come to the conclusion you always will."

Cold stabs of fear jabbed her from the inside out. Her feet, frozen in place, ached, her hands numb from clenching them into tight fists. The air seeped from her lungs as she waited to hear what she knew he'd say next.

Campbell's head dropped when he said, "I've been patient, Max. I've let you accuse me of things I'd never even think of doing. And all the time I kept telling myself, 'Campbell, you're getting involved with a woman who's been tragically hurt and brainwashed to believe she's useless aside from her good looks and hot rack. Campbell, you'll have to take it slow. Campbell, don't be too hard on her. She's afraid to trust you. Campbell, you're falling in love with a woman who will always think the worst before she thinks the best.' I've reassured you even when you don't ask me to. I've kept every promise I ever made to you. Hell, I panic if my Bat-watch isn't totally in sync with yours and I call you two minutes past the hour I said I'd call. I don't want to own you, Max. I want to *share* my life with you. I want you to share your life with as many people as you please. I want you to be happy. I want you to find the kind of peace that lets you live out loud. I wanted *you!*" he hollered, clearly unfazed by the porch lights that flipped on in response to his roar.

Max wanted to reach for him, beg him to let her make it right. Len's words came back to haunt her. There was only so much indulgence in her insecurities a person could give, and Campbell had reached his limit.

"So tonight, I'm raising the white flag, because you keep doing the same Goddamned thing, Max, and I've done nothing to warrant the kind of shit you feed me. Tonight, I realized something. You know what that is?"

Her lower lip trembled, yet Max stuck her chest out so she could take it like a man. Because she fucking deserved this. "What?"

"I realized you just can't trust me. You *won't* trust me, and I realized something else, too. Something almost as important as your issues with trust. You're looking for any excuse you can find to get out of this so you don't even have to try. It's much easier to allow fear to control you than it is to fight for control of your life. I expected some doubt on your part, and I was ready to deal with it, but I didn't expect a constant barrage of it. I fully expected you'd get the big picture after spending so much time with me. After I've proven time and again I can be trusted. But this?" He flung his hand up in the space between them. "This kind of suspicion is no way to live. So maybe you were right when you said we were at different places in our lives. I just don't think I believe you'll ever leave that place and migrate to mine."

Campbell reached out a hand, cupping the back of her head. He pulled her to him and planted a quick kiss on her forehead.

She savored the smell of him, the strong feel of his hand when she laid hers against it, only to have him pull away.

"Take care, Max," he said, before taking quick strides to his truck. The engine roared to life.

And Campbell Barker drove out of her life.

Because she was the dumbest ass evah.

Good show, Max.

~ℓ~

"Son?"

"Dad?"

"You wanna talk?" Garner sat opposite Campbell at the dinette table, reaching across to place a soothing hand on his son's arm.

"It's over. I just can't see her ever trusting me, and that's something I can't live without, Dad."

"Yep," Garner clucked. "Trust is the key. It's what kept your mother and me together for forty-six years. So how can I help?"

Campbell couldn't believe it, but letting Max go hurt more than the disintegration of his eight-year marriage. Her face tonight, so beautiful whether she believed it or not, stoic and sad, flashed before his tired eyes. "It'll just take time." He'd have plenty of that in London. And to think he'd been on his way over to her mother's to ask her to go with him.

So they could have time alone. Totally alone.

So he could tell her he loved her like he'd never loved another fucking woman in his life.

His gut churned.

"Can I ask what happened to make Max bolt?"

"Money," he offered glumly.

"The root of all evil, kiddo. So you finally told her you're rich?"

Shit. "No. I didn't tell her. She found out online."

Garner grimaced. "Not good, boy. By not telling her how rich you are, you caught her off guard and scared her. It didn't have to be some big secret, Campbell, and I gotta tell ya, I almost understand her fears. She was married to money, and look what happened there."

His father was right, but rich, poor, or in-between, he doubted Max would ever trust any man.

"You sure you did the right thing, kiddo?"

"She wanted out, Dad. Max was looking for any little excuse she could find not to trust me and run off to her cave and hide. It's easier to hide than it is to take another chance. I guess I just wasn't worth the risk." And that hurt. It hurt like bloody hell.

"Fear can be a powerful thing," Garner agreed gruffly.

"There was never going to be a way to prove myself to her. It would never be enough. She'd always question it. I can't live on pins and needles, waiting for the next shoe to drop, waiting for her to flip out over something she never bothered to ask me about before working up something crazy in her head."

"Do you need some alone time?"

Campbell ran his hands over his face in weary defeat. "It's okay, Dad. You can stay."

"You want to eat a gallon of chocolate-chocolate chip ice cream and play sad love songs? Maybe watch that Oxygen channel for women?" his father asked, his attempt at lightening his son's pain clear in his eyes lined with sadness.

Campbell almost laughed. "You just want to use me as an excuse to eat ice cream."

Garner barked a laugh, slapping his son on his arm. "Any excuse'll do."

Apparently, any excuse would do, Campbell thought, the pain of that revelation tight in his chest. "You go to bed, Dad. Tomorrow's your first big day back on the job. Get some rest."

Garner rose, taking quiet steps out of the kitchen before turning and gathering his son by the shoulders to give him a rare, hard hug. "I love you, kiddo. Even if Max can't."

Even if Max can't.

Won't.

Refuses to.

Fuck.

CHAPTER TWENTY-ONE

Note from Maxine Cambridge to all ex-trophy wives on sucking it the hell up: Do you want to die all alone with the prestigious title Crazy Cat Lady? *Do you?* Get it together, sistah, and show the world the new, self-empowered, smart, independent woman you are by making sound choices fueled by reason—not your insane paranoia. It's either that or you'd better use your newly acquired Walmart skills to find the best deal on that cat litter box with the battery operated thingamajiggy and a coupla cans of Fancy Feast. If I've said it once, I'll say it again. Suck it up, Princess, and take the plunge into the ocean known as sensible and, above all, sane.

"Maxie?"

"Mom?"

"Why are you out here all alone in the dark?"

"Because trolls like me like the dark and I couldn't find a decent bridge," she answered, sniffling into a wad of Kleenex.

"You okay, honey?"

"No. I'm not okay. I will be, but right now, I'm not okay."

"Aw, hell, Maxie—are you gonna start drinkin' again?" Mona plopped down beside her on the porch rocking chair, tucking her bathrobe tight around her neck.

Max let her head fall to her raised knees. "No. No drinking. And I didn't drink that much, so stop making me sound like some raging alcoholic."

"You and Campbell had a fight."

"Yes."

"And it's over."

Max swallowed the lump in her throat. "Yes. You were right about me."

"That's not why I poke at you like I do, Maxie. I poke because I want you to prove me wrong."

Max reached a hand out to squeeze her mother's. "I'm sorry we argued."

"I'm not," Mona responded with an affectionate clap to Max's hand. "You needed to hear it."

"I wish I'd listened much earlier. I had no idea how good it'd feel to have Fin by the balls. Even if it was only for a minute and not signing those papers is really what he wanted anyway. But I've decided I should be more like you."

"Good to know. So you know what *I'd* do in a situation like this?"

"Club Campbell into submission? Harsh."

"But doable," Mona snickered. "So *when* are you going to do something about Campbell?"

Bitter regret tore at her gut. "I get the impression after what he said tonight, nothing would change his mind."

Her mother rocked back and forth, the creak of the chair somehow soothing. "Damn, you did it again." There was no doubt in her statement.

Oh. Yeah. "Yes. I did it again. I compared him to Finley." Christ, just hearing the notion out loud made her want to vomit.

"That's pretty bad."

"Yes. It was pretty bad." So bad. Badder than bad. The baddest.

"Are you gonna cry and whine about it, or are you gonna get up off your keister and at least go out with a knock-down, drag-out? I've seen how he looks at you, girlie. Can't fake that. But you can only do the hot and cold thing for so long before a man gets tired. I think that means it's your turn now. Maybe he just needs to know you're willing to fight for him the way he's been fighting for you."

"I don't think there's any coming back from this, Mom."

Mona rose, pulling a tissue from the box beside Max and cupping her chin. She wiped her tears, smiling a toothless grin down at her. "Won't know unless you try." Kissing her cheek, she whispered, "I love you, Maxie. Love yourself enough to finish this—one way or the other."

She left Max to sit in the frosty gloom of midnight, looking out over the village dotted with the glow of landscaping lights and a buttery moon in a deep purple sky, warring with her constant internal struggle to simply let go. To speak her mind even if painful rejection was the outcome.

Now was a fine time to wonder if she might have been smarter to ask Campbell about the Internet jazz and Linda instead of accusing him.

Yet right now, though she ached deep down in her soul for Campbell and the mess she'd made, she was surprised to find she didn't feel as though there was no reason to get up in the morning.

The kind of desolation and helpless despair she'd once thought would kill her, the immobilizing pain that had kept her frozen when Finley and she were on the rocks, was gone.

Completely.

That eye-opener brought another. Just because she wasn't falling apart at the seams over losing Campbell, didn't mean she didn't love him. Or that she loved him less than she had Finley.

On the contrary, she was crazier about Campbell than she could ever remember being over Fin. But it wasn't an anxious, frenetic kind of crazy, and apparently, that kind of over the moon—the easy, meant-to-be kind—was unfamiliar to her.

How could she not have recognized it was a good kind of crazy?

The kind that didn't keep her up all night long after they parted, creating crazy scenarios involving Campbell and a roomful of strippers. Well, not every night . . . It wasn't the kind of nerve-wracking crazy she'd put herself through when Fin was late calling her.

It was a comfortable kind of crazy. It was the kind of crazy that just was. It just existed between them. The kind that never failed to make her secretly smile for no reason. The kind that, without her even realizing, was secure in letting Campbell go off and do his own thing, secure that he'd make a point to let her know what he was up to. Now, just this moment, she realized he'd made those small, subtle gestures because of her marriage.

And she'd done nothing more tonight than beat him down for it by throwing his efforts right back in his face.

Jesus Christ . . .

Why had she come to that conclusion *now*? How could she have missed all the good with Campbell and found something bad? And *why* wasn't she a hysterical mess because she had?

Sitting forward in her chair, Max smiled, and then she laughed.

Really laughed.

There was no hysteria because she'd learned a potentially painful lesson from her mistake. If she lost Campbell due to her idiocy, she had no one to blame but herself. There was no hiding from that.

Finally.

Maxine Cambridge finally loved herself enough to realize life would move on with or without Campbell Barker, and she'd move with it.

Loving someone who only wanted you to be happy was an addition to your life, not a form of ownership, and when someone loved you, they took care to tread lightly when it came to your painful past. They handled you with care. They respected your battle scars in random acts of understated reassurance. They waited patiently for you to suck it up.

Max smiled, wiping her tear-stained eyes.

Free.

At last.

Heh.

~ℓ~

"Tell her, Lacey, or I swear to you, I'll pluck every fake blonde strand of hair from your head myself!" Len shouted, dragging her sister into Mona's kitchen with a firm grip on her sister's hand.

"I sent you a letter from Dorothy . . ." Lacey sniffled.

The hairs on Maxine's neck rose when she swung around to face Len and her sister. Max threw down the sponge she'd been diligently cleaning an already spotless sink with. "The one from Fin's mother?"

Lacey gulped, her slender neck muscles moving in time with her sobs. "Yes. I didn't know Fin was hiding it from you!" she cried. "I never even looked at the postmark or the return address. I just forwarded it to you at your mother's. But—but—"

"But?" Max demanded.

Tears streamed down her face, creating red paths of salty moisture. "Finley got so mad when he found out I'd taken it from his desk. I was just—just—trying to take care of everything so he wouldn't be so stressed and uptight. With the divorce and him always yelling at me to get it together, I thought I was helping! But he said," she paused, gasping out choppy breaths, "he said if I was more like you, I wouldn't have made such a big mistake. He said I should never have gone through his things, but I swear, it was right on his desk, Maxine. And now—now—"

"He called off the engagement," Len said with disgust, her face filled with unmasked fury. "I did tell you he was a bastard, didn't I, Lacey? I told you you'd end up just like—"

"Don't, Len," Max cut her off. Clear as day, she understood Lacey. Like a glove, she could just as easily slip back on the pain Lacey was suffering. Her identifying with this child, twenty years her junior, knowing she'd been saved from a pain far greater, kept at bay any smug wish to break her like she herself had been broken. "Don't beat her up anymore. I don't think Fin was ever going to marry her anyway. I think using me and my refusal to sign off on the divorce was a perfect excuse to stall her. Fin knew I couldn't fight him on the prenup, but Connor is entitled to an education. He knew I wouldn't sign that away so easily, and it bought him time. Just be glad she got out now and not twenty years down the road."

Lacey's wet gulps were so familiar, so riddled with agony, Maxine almost wanted to wrap her arms around her young nemesis and comfort her. But she didn't know if she could ever be that gracious to a woman, child or not, who'd slept with a married man. "So the letter. It was in Fin's possession? You're sure, Lacey?"

Her face crumpled, her red eyes scrunching closed. "Right on his desk."

Len looked at Maxine with unveiled concern. "And what do you suppose that means?"

"I don't know. But it can't be good." What reason could Fin have for keeping his mother's letter from her? Not for a second did she doubt it was another one of his sneaky ploys.

Lacey sobbed to the point of choking, and that was where Maxine's patience went south. "Take her home. *Please*," she begged Len.

Gathering up Lacey on one arm, Len planted a kiss on her cheek. "Have you talked to Campbell yet?"

"Have you talked to Adam?" Max countered.

"No. But my situation's different. Don't let this go too long. Be strong, grasshopper," she joked with a grin.

Max's response was reasonable and calm and more together than she could ever remember feeling. "I could say the same to you, partner. And it's only been four days since Campbell dumped me. I totally deserved it. I figured I'd better let him cool down before

I whammy him. I have to do this right, Len. I want him to know I mean it. Really, really mean it."

"I can't believe you're not a total immobilized wreck, Maxine Cambridge. I've never seen you so collected. I'd shed a proud tear, but there's enough of that going around." She pointed to Lacey.

Max rubbed Len's shoulders. "True, I'm not falling apart, but it's a miracle my mother has any stainless left on her steel sink," she said wryly, pointing to the sponge. "I'm really okay. I'd rather be great, but I'll settle for okay for now. I think this time, I really get that love doesn't have to consume you to the point of suicide. My life's fuller that it ever was. I replaced all those mani-pedis and spa treatments with some self-worth. Now I just have to convince Campbell I get it. Anyway, you batten down the hatches and go take care of your sister."

"Call me later so we can toss some theories around about that letter, okay?"

Maxine nodded with a faint smile, not taking even an ounce of pleasure when she heard Lacey cry out again on her way out the door, "I love him, Lenore! I can't live without him!"

"Yeah," Len snorted in return. "Ain't love grand?"

Their departure left Max with just her thoughts and the feeling a big chunk of this puzzle Dorothy had created was bringing Finley some serious grief.

She did smile at that. Petty it was, but her smile was shadowed with the sad fact that she might never understand what Dorothy meant.

Not unless she killed Finley for the 411.

Which made her smile again.

~ e ~

Max sucked in a shuddering breath of air. Sick with nerves, her intestines growled in protest.

Her reflection in the mirror made her chant, "You will be strong,

Max. You will go after what you want, and if the answer is no, you'll
go right on doing what you do. Just like you have after you did the
stupidest thing since signing a prenup. You're strong, empowered—
wildly in love. Now go get your man!" She growled into the mirror
then blew herself a kiss. She was going to go get Campbell Barker and
never let him go.

Ever.

The sound of clapping from the bathroom doorway startled her.
"It's about time."

"Ya think?" Max hugged her mother hard.

"I think. But before you go off to war, Joe Hodge is here. Says
Jake's lost."

"Oh, no!" She flew past her mother to run to the front door.
"Mr. Hodge?"

His usually cheerful, moon-shaped face held worry. "I hate to
bother ya, Maxine, but Jake got out on me. I can't find the damn dog
anywhere. I've been callin' him for over an hour. But I see you're
all dressed up. I'm sorry to bring my troubles to your doorstep." He
turned to leave, but Max stuck a finger in his suspenders to stop him.

"It's no trouble, Mr. Hodge. But I worry because Jake's so cranky.
If he corners someone like Mr. Lowell, for sure we'll have complaints
from the association. Let me grab my purse and we'll go hunt him
down." She and Jake had become frenemies of sorts. He tolerated
her as long as she brought him treats and scratched his belly. Over
the past few months, he'd finally come to enjoy his walks with Max.

Purse tucked under her arm, she stepped out of her mother's,
shivering at the purpled, frosty evening. The weather had become
unseasonably cold so early in the fall. "Let's go."

He reached into his pocket. "Hold on. My phone's vibratin'.
Hello? That little shit," he cackled into the phone. "Okay. Thanks
much, Maude." Winking at Max, he held up the phone. "Maude says

she saw him over at the rec center but just a minute ago. Hurry up
and get in the truck so we can catch him."

On the ride to the rec center, Max rolled down the window, calling out Jake's name on the off chance he might have wandered.

As they pulled up, Max wondered aloud at all the cars parked in
the lot. "Do you crazies have some kind of illegal gambling going on
you forgot to share with your village event coordinator?" She shot Joe
a secretive smile, shaking a finger of admonishment. "Because if you
didn't let me in on the chance to make some extra cash, I'd be very,
very hurt."

Joe slid out of his truck, grunting when his knees bent. He made
his way around the front end and opened the door for Max, holding
out his hand. "Nothing illegal going on here. You just go on inside,"
he encouraged with a sly smile.

Her head tilted to the right. "Joe? What's going on?"

Ushering her with a hand to her lower back, Joe gave her a final
push. "Go on in and see."

The doors burst open to the yelps of "Surprise!"

A sea of seniors' faces greeted her. Confetti in colored pieces flew
in the air, landing in Max's hair and her open mouth of surprise.
Noisemakers sounded off in screeching blares. Bunches of multi-
colored balloons that read "Happy Birthday" were tied to chairs. Big
band music screamed from the rec center's speakers, and a table full
of goodies lined the back wall. "What . . ." It wasn't her birthday.

Mary, Gail, Connor, and Mona held a sheet cake between them,
candles lit and glowing. Their smiles were wide and smug. "Blow 'em
out, Maxie, before we drop the whole damned thing on the floor," her
mother shouted over the merriment.

"*How* did you keep this from me?"

"Oh, it wasn't easy—specially with that busybody Esther. But I
still have a trick or two up my sleeve," Mona said, pleased with herself.

"But, Mom. It's not my birthday. You know that," she chided with affection.

"It's your re-birthday, honey," Mary supplied with a wink. "You've been here in the village a whole year, and look at all the things you've accomplished. Some of us in the village thought that was worth celebrating. Now blow the candles out!"

A year.

A year since she'd turned up at her mother's, broken and battered. A year since she'd packed one lowly bag, thrown Connor in the car, and left everything she thought she loved behind. A year filled with more tears than she thought a body could hold in water weight.

Now, a year later, she'd found purpose, and meaning in discovering she didn't need anyone else to help her do that but herself.

"C'mon, Mom. Blow them out," Connor shouted, and everyone else followed suit. "Blow them out! Blow them out!" he chanted.

Max leaned forward with a grin, holding her hair out of the way to let go of a huge breath. Cheers and clapping rang in her ears as she made her way through the room, hugging the people who'd come to mean so much to her.

She grabbed Joe on her way to the table where, she'd been informed, everyone had chipped in to make a potluck dinner in her honor. Max caught Joe on the cheek with a kiss. Two bright red spots appeared on his forehead. "You're a sly one, Mr. Hodge. Thank you. This is wonderful."

"Be better if your young man was here, don't you think? I extended the invite to him, but I don't see him."

He was the last piece to the puzzle of an otherwise terrific night. "He's pretty mad at me, Mr. Hodge, and he should be. I've not been an easy girl to love."

Mr. Hodge pinched her cheek. "But you sure are a purty one. Any smart guy can forgive a pretty girl. Garner's over there, flirtin'

with Leona. Why don't you go ask him where that boy of his is?" He
shooed her away with a craggy hand.

Max attempted to wend her way through the room amidst more
hugs and cheerful well wishes, making a beeline for Garner, but Len
jumped in front of her to give her a hug, paper plate of cake in her
hand. "Happy re-birthday!" She chuckled. "They did some job, huh?"

"You knew, too?"

"Who do you think hooked them up with the cake?"

Max's smile beamed at her friend. "Thank you. You all did a wonderful job. But I'm on a mission. I need to find Campbell. Have you
seen him?"

Len stuffed a bite of chocolate cake in her mouth. "Nope, but his
dad's over there. C'mon. We'll go ask him where he is." Taking her
hand, Len set down her cake and pulled Max toward Garner.

"Maxine?"

She whirled to the tune of a semi-familiar voice and smiled when
she saw whom the voice was attached to. "Adam, right? Adam Baylor.
Len and I were just talking about you." Daring Len to say otherwise,
she took his hand to shake.

His eyebrow rose as he perused Len's face. "Actually, it's Adam
Baylor *Crestwall,* and if I may, I'd like to talk to you. *Privately.*" He
handed her a business card, pointedly giving Len an expression of
unfiltered anger.

Len's face shattered, and Max noted she didn't even bother to
hide it. "You can say whatever you have to say in front of Len, Adam.
We have no secrets."

In what Max would've considered a petty move if Len hadn't
behaved like such an ass toward Adam, he turned his back to her
friend and gazed down at Max. "Your mother-in-law was Dorothy
Cambridge, correct?"

He'd caught her off guard. "She was . . ."

"My father, Wyatt Crestwall, was her attorney. He handled her last will and testament."

Max shot him a confused look. "Okay."

His expression was of shame, but direct and intense as though he was internally battling with something. "Look, there's no other way to say this, and my apologies in advance. My father aided your husband, Finley Cambridge, in stealing a rather large sum of money from you and your son, Connor. Dorothy Cambridge left you a handsome trust fund to be managed by you at your discretion in the event you would need financial security apart from your husband."

The wind was knocked right out of her. Her hand went to her stomach while her head reeled. Dorothy had known. She'd known . . . "I don't understand," was the most in the way of coherence Max could muster.

"Would you like to sit down?"

Leaning against Len, Max shook her head. "No, thank you. Just explain how this happened."

"My father was an unscrupulous man, Maxine. The technicalities of what he did might be difficult to explain to you in terms of the law. The simple answer is my father, Wyatt Crestwall, aided your husband in altering documents that would have left you and your son Connor a good portion of Dorothy's estate. My father's dead now, but just before he passed, he revealed to me he'd been a party to some dealings I can't, even knowing my father as I do, believe he participated in. I've been trying to make some of those wrongs right since his death. And don't misunderstand my father's confession." Adam's voice was bitter but resolute. "This wasn't to ensure his place somewhere divine. It was to pay your husband back for some offense we may never know about or understand. He left me a clue or two, but I've been here in Riverbend, trying to put the pieces together. I've finally got all the proof you need to take Finley Cambridge to court and reclaim what's rightfully yours."

Max was too stunned to speak, but Len wasn't. She poked Adam in the arm with an angry finger. "All this time you were here to help Maxine and you didn't say a word to me?"

Adam tilted his head with an arrogant slant, his eyes distant. "As I recall, you said as long as I wasn't working for Finley Cambridge, we shouldn't get too personal. No questions asked. Your words. I obliged."

Max found her voice, stilted and clumsy as it was. "I need a second to—to, wait! The letter . . ."

"Letter?" Adam inquired.

Max grabbed his arm in her excitement. "Yes! Long story, which I'll let Len tell you about when you two go off to duke it out a couple of rounds. Dorothy sent me a letter from the nursing home she was in, but I didn't get it until a few weeks ago and long after her death. It all makes sense now." A rush of grateful tears welled in her eyes. Dorothy had taken it upon herself to look out for her and Connor, gambling someday her son wouldn't.

And Finley wasn't above stealing from even his mother.

Max's chin fell to her chest in sorrow. *I'm so sorry, Dorothy,* she said in silent prayer. *I'm so sorry Finley hurt you, and thank you. Thank you for an answer to my prayers.*

She opened her eyes to catch Adam's glossy business card under the light. Adam Baylor Crestwall, *Divorce Attorney.*

Bingo, bitch!

"You're a divorce attorney?" Max fought not to shout her excitement.

Len's face held what could only be described as shock. "I still don't get why you just didn't tell me, Adam."

He shot her a narrow gaze. "I had to make certain my ducks were in a row before I acted. I had to have the proof before I threw out potentially false hope and accusations." Adam turned back to Maxine with a brief smile. "I am a divorce attorney, and if you'll let me,

I'd like to help you. It'll be my way of trying to make up for this last year. I know about your situation with Mr. Cambridge. Nothing would please me more than to see him squirm. Pro bono, of course."

Max lunged for him, throwing her arms around his neck. "You're hired! And now, I have a man to nab. So forgive me for rushing off. Len has my number. You can call *her* for it when you're ready to begin the Third World War."

"Take no prisoners," Adam said with his first genuine smile of the night.

"Thank you, Adam. Thank you. *Thank you*. You have no idea what this will do for my son. And now, I'm out—wish me luck."

Len scooped her up in another hug. "Luck, honey," she whispered fiercely.

"You, too," Max whispered back, searching for Garner once more.

She found him flirting with the very cute, compact Leona. "Mr. Barker, can I have a minute?"

His smile was warm and so much like Campbell's it made her heart shift. "You can have two."

"Do you know where Campbell is?"

The playful expression on his face changed radically to concern. "Running some errands before packing for London. He leaves tonight."

Anxiety gripped her. "London?"

"He's considering a job there now that he's sold that web-whatever."

"But he's still here now?"

"He is."

"Can I ask a huge favor of you?"

Max sensed Garner's hesitance, saw it in the way he stiffened his shoulders. "As long as it doesn't involve hurting him any more. I don't want to mess in your private affairs, but he's hurtin'."

Max's heart throbbed with regret, and hope. There was always hope. "I promise you this—if you help me, I'll make it my mission to make him the happiest man alive." She'd never meant anything more. Ever.

"Your word, young lady?"

Gazing into his eyes, Max nodded solemnly. "*My word.*"

"Tell me what you need."

"Can you call Campbell and find out where he is?"

"I know where he is. He's at the Home Depot picking me up some PVC."

"Can you stall him by calling him and asking him to pick something else up? Like a lot of somethings so I can catch up with him?"

"I'm on it. Now get to gettin'!" he ordered with a smile, pulling his phone from his shirt pocket.

Max ran as fast as her heels could carry her to the mic by the bingo table. "Can I get some sound?" she asked Joe. She tapped the mic, drawing everyone's attention to her. "Everyone, listen up! First, thank you for this lovely party. I can't tell you how special and important it is to me that each of you is sharing this day with me. I *am* reborn, and that's thanks in part to you. Now as part of my rebirth, I have one thing left to do, and it means cutting out on you. I have a man to catch," she crowed into the mic.

Cheers once more erupted, followed by fists punctuating the air.

"So are you all with me? I need lots of good vibes!"

"Go get 'em!" someone shouted.

Max handed the mic to Joe Hodge, who gave her a quick squeeze of her hand before saying, "Don't take no for an answer."

She smiled, hoping it showed the confidence she wasn't feeling. "Show no mercy," she replied on a giggle.

Grabbing her purse, Max borrowed her mother's keys and zoomed out the rec center door.

With any luck, she was heading right toward a big chunk of her future.

At the Home Depot.

CHAPTER TWENTY-TWO

Note from Max Cambridge to all ex-trophy wives: Love the second time around doesn't come without its share of compromises, nor, when it happens, is it always in the ideal location. None of that matters when you're chasing down the love of your life. *Do not* be shy when it comes to going after what your heart truly wants. Use your outdoor voice if you have to to get your point across. If you must, bring heavy artillery to immobilize your intended. Wait. Forget I said that. Just wear comfortable sneakers, and remember, a princess in the process of sucking it up is a warrior princess!

"Divorce attorney. Care to explain?" Len spewed the moment she could catch up with Adam outside in the parking lot.

"About as much as you did," Adam shot back.

"Okay. Let's halt the back and forth and let me get this out before you rush off in an angry cloud of Mercedes. Which is quite an upgrade from the Ford Escort you were driving around a couple of weeks ago."

His grin was sheepish. "It was on order and didn't come in until just this week. I had to drive something. Nice, right?"

"How could you have never let something so important cross your lips, Adam? Maxine's my best friend. You might not have known a lot about me, but you knew what Finley was doing to her."

"I did."

"Then why didn't you go to Maxine to begin with?"

"I thought Lacey was *Maxine* when I came into the picture.

I couldn't figure out how a woman so young had a son Connor's age. The first time I saw her she was with you—at the mall. Then I thought you were Maxine—so I followed you around until I found out you weren't Maxine at all."

"And you kept following me," Len stated, hope rearing its head. There must have been a reason he kept following her, right? She burrowed deeper into her jacket. "So why did you keep following me?"

"You were a link to Maxine."

More hope crept in, and she fought a smile. "Okay, so why didn't you just tell me from the start you wanted to help Maxine?"

"At first I didn't tell you because you are Lacey's sister, Len. How was I to know you wouldn't tip her off and blow this before I had a chance to set things right? I didn't know about your disapproval until I heard you tell her to never call you again unless she got rid of Finley."

Len conceded with a sharp nod. "Okay, fair enough, but why not later on in the game?"

"Look, I'm a lawyer. I don't make a move without having my facts straight. It took some time and some digging to find the proof I needed to be sure Maxine wouldn't end up disappointed. I had to be sure before I went all bull in a china shop. Besides, if you'll recall, you barely let me speak two words to you before we were in bed. The only talking we did was of the dirty variety. That was your edict— your prereq for our meetings."

God, how she'd come to regret those rules. "I was a real bitch."

"You won't hear any denial from me."

As Len's mind raced, a fact Adam had revealed hit her with the sudden blunt force of a fist to her stomach. "Your father . . . I'm so sorry, Adam."

His eyes were clear of pain. "Don't be. He was a ruthless, cruel man. I came to terms with that a long time ago, Len. I had a terrific mother. One a lot like Maxine, who worked three jobs to support us. I became a divorce attorney because of what my father did to my mother and me in their divorce. My mother was a Vegas show-girl. He married her when she was twenty-two and he was forty, then divorced her when she was thirty-eight for another Vegas showgirl who was nineteen. He left us with nothing, too. I know where Max-ine is, but she won't be there for long when I get my hands on Finley Cambridge."

Len's sigh was riddled with sadness. "So you get it."

"Damn right I get it, and my goal is to clean up as much of the shady dealings he left as his legacy as possible."

"You have no idea what this means to my friend," she whispered. "You have no idea how much this will help Connor."

"I think I do." Adam turned to leave without looking back.

So it's now or never, sister. "You have no idea . . ." Len cleared her throat so her voice would be strong and sure. "You have no idea how sorry I am that I didn't let you in."

Adam stopped, but he didn't turn around, his back stiff in the glow of the full moon.

She moved closer, avoiding the patch of ice after last night's early frost. "You have no idea how sorry I am that I treated you so badly."

Still, Adam kept his back to her, but she reached a hand out, ignoring the tightening of his muscles. "I'm not pregnant." What a relief to say that out loud to the one person who deserved most to hear the truth.

She stepped in front of him, planting her feet firmly on the slip-pery pavement. "I'm premenopausal, and I had a mild case of food poisoning. It really was the tuna." She glanced up from beneath hooded lashes. "So no babies, just hot flashes, chin hair, and wild hormonal swings. Yay, right?"

"Yay," was his bland offering.

"My husband didn't just die either. But you know that, I'm sure. He was sick for a very long time. Cancer. Due to some bad financial investments, he was also broke when he . . . Gerald committed sui—suicide," she blurted. "And the one person in the world I always counted on, the man I thought was the strongest person I knew left me. Just like that."

Adam softened, cupping her chin. "And it hurt so much you decided you never wanted to do this again."

"I felt betrayed. I had no idea we had no money. I let Gerald handle everything. He did leave me a little something—in an offshore account. It was how I started Belle's Will Be Ringing. His suicide left me feeling out of control. Of my life, of my financial status—of everything. I promised myself that would never happen again."

"And I make you feel out of control."

She licked her lips. Just say it. "Ye—yes, and I began to feel things I thought I could only feel for Gerald. Then I began to feel things for you I never felt for Gerald. It was like betraying his memory."

"You felt guilty."

"I did."

"And you don't anymore?"

"No. Gerald was a kind man, a good man. He'd never approve of me letting an opportunity slip away if it involved a chance for my happiness. So, if you're still willing, I'd like to show you that."

"Would you show me over dinner? Like in a public place?"

Len grinned wide, the hard pounding of her heart easing. "Is this dutch or are you buying, Mr. Fancy Divorce Attorney?"

Adam pulled her into his arms, sending waves of thankful relief throughout her body. He smiled. "If you pay, you're in control," he teased, nipping her lips.

"Yeah, but if you pay, I'm facing my fears and letting go of that burdensome control," she whispered, kissing him back.

"So let's begin again. I'm Adam Baylor Crestwall and I think you're hot. Wanna have a meal with me I pay for?"

Her laughter filled the cold air. "I'm Lenore Erickson, and you're hot, too. So I definitely want to have a meal with you that *you* pay for."

Arm around her waist, Adam led her to his car.

Len let her head rest on his shoulder, broad and strong.

And it was good.

So good.

~ l ~

Max swung into a parking space so fast, all of NASCAR would be jealous. Slamming the car into park, she scanned the lot of Home Depot for Campbell's old truck.

The wind picked up in chilling gusts, sending orange carts in every direction. Christ, it was only early October. It was too early for it to be so damned cold.

She spotted Campbell at the exit, tall, huddling deeper into a goose-down black jacket and pushing a loaded cart.

On the other end of the parking lot.

"Campbell Barker!" she yelled as loud as she could over the wind.

His dark head, covered in a navy blue knit cap, turned then looked away.

Oh, if he'd seen her and was opting to ignore her because he was feeling spiteful when it was this cold out, she was going to throttle him—if she caught up with him.

She began a light jog toward him. "Campbell! Wait! Please! You listen to me, Campbell Barker!" Max shouted across the parking lot, ignoring the curious turn of heads. She'd humiliated herself publicly for something far less costly than the love of her life walking away forever.

Campbell's steps slowed, the rigid pull of his jacket across his back Max's sole focus. Yet he didn't stop. Grrrrr, if her foot wasn't now numb, she'd stomp it.

"Campbellllllllllllll!" she howled.

And still, he kept moving, head down against the wind.

So she ran—with the kind of determination she'd only reserved for stealing Candy Corwin's tiara from her at the Miss Rudniki's Deli and Twelve Pins pageant of 1982.

Like her life depended on it.

Because it did. Okay, dramatic. Her *future happiness* depended on it.

She lost a shoe in her trek. But no worries, it wasn't like it was a Louboutin.

She tripped on a pothole. Didn't Home Depot have cement to fill those things?

She avoided a careening shopping cart, tearing her nylons. Jesus, they just didn't make pantyhose like they used to.

She zigzagged in front of a car whose driver in turn furiously honked his ire. Well, for the love of—get some glasses. It wasn't like she was a size two. Surely he'd seen her ass from a mile away.

She fought for just one more gulp of air. Seriously? She was going to rethink Miss Kitty's Calisthenics on Thursdays.

Max sprinted the last one hundred feet until she thought she'd drop an ovary from the effort. Her hand grabbed at Campbell's arm, missing by but an inch and crashing into him instead.

He was there, like he always was, setting her upright, ensuring her safety.

God, please, let me get this right. If you're still on a Maxine hiatus, I hope you'll give me one encore performance. *Just one more.* "Wait," she heaved, her breathing ragged, bending at the waist, but clutching his arm like she'd never let go.

And she wouldn't. Not if someone held a gun to her head. "Wa—wait. Lemme—catch—my—breath." The parking lot spun and she wobbled, but she hung on.

"Max, why are you here?" was his gruff question.

She held up a hand and took another deep gulp of air. "To stop you."

"From buying PVC?"

"From making the biggest mistake of your life."

Campbell went silent.

She rose, facing him head-on—eyeball to eyeball. "That's right. You heard me. If you fly off to London or wherever you're going, and leave me, you'll be making the biggest mistake of your life."

His face didn't show an ounce of emotion. "I didn't leave you, Max. You left me. I just said it out loud."

Her hands, red and cold, flapped dismissively. "Technicalities. It's petty to place blame, don't you think?"

Campbell went all quiet again, but the flare of his nostrils said she'd better move along little doggie.

"Okay. Okay. I left you, but I made a huge mistake. A mistake I want to make right."

Campbell's hands jammed into the pockets of his jacket. "I can't do this with you, Max. Not anymore. We've gone back and forth about this, and as much as it hurts to let go, I have to. I told you once I wasn't going to chase you forever, and I meant it."

"That's why I'm chasing you!"

His expression was ironic. "Tell me something. What made you come after me tonight, Max?"

"Your father told me you were leaving for London tonight."

"Exactly. It was impulse. By tomorrow, you'll have changed that pretty mind of yours again—created some future disaster you're sure I'm going to spearhead to hurt you."

Max's smile was smug when she gazed up at him. "Ah, but I didn't make the decision to chase you tonight. I made it the night you slapped me in the head with the truth. That was *four* days ago. Ask Len if you don't believe me."

"How do I know that's true?"

Max read his doubt and owned that she deserved it. "You don't. I could be lying through my uninsured, capped teeth. You'll just have to *trust* me."

Campbell's head shook with firm skepticism, his face hard with frustration. "Right, and just when I get to the point where I think you're comfortable, where I'm actually starting to believe the effort I put into easing your mind has actually sunk in, you freak out again by clobbering me out of the blue with your two-by-four of insecurity? I'm not into that kind of masochistic repetitive shit, Max. I did everything I could think of to reassure you I'm not that prick Finley Cambridge. I was patient. I waited for you to see the effort I put into making you realize I'm a whole different breed of man. I didn't need a pat on the back. I didn't need an encouraging word from you. All I wanted was your trust—communication. But you never even noticed."

"But I'm noticing now."

"Until the next time. I'm tired of waiting for you to get it through your thick skull. I don't want to wait around so it can happen again. I've waited for you forever, but forever just ran out."

Forever? Her heart fluttered. "Wait, what?"

"What-what?"

Max latched on to his jacket. "What do you mean you've waited for me forever?"

Campbell's laughter was a cynical bark. "I've loved you since the first day I saw you in chemistry class. I had a crazy crush on you back then, and it all came back the day I saw you at the Cluck-Cluck Palace."

Max's heart tightened, so painfully it thrust against her chest like it would jump right out. He'd never said a single word in all this time, making every stupid mistake she'd made with him magnified to the nth degree.

She bracketed his face with her hands, forcing him to see her. Really see who was standing in front of him. "This isn't impulse talking because you're flying off to a place where they call the bathroom a loo. This isn't my fear of being left high and dry again, asking you to stay. No one can leave me high and dry ever again, Campbell. If you still decide to go, it'll make me really sad, but I won't die of it. So hear me when I tell you, *I've waited forever for you, too.* I didn't know it. I didn't want to admit it, and when it happened, I didn't see it clearly. I didn't understand it, but I do now." She knew.

She knew, she knew, she knew.

The shake of his head was followed by a wry grin. "If this is going to be followed by 'you complete me,' I have a plane to catch."

"Then you have a plane to catch," she whispered, keeping the tears she wanted to sob at bay. "You get me. You hear me. You want me despite the fact that I don't always get me. You ground me when I get too far ahead of myself. Those are all things I lack—deficits I don't always have control over. It completes who I am, rounds me out as a flawed human being, and if you go, I'll strive to handle those things all on my own. But I can tell you this: Trips to Home Depot just aren't going to be the same."

The subtle change in his expression, the life his blue eyes took on, spurred her on. "And you know what else, Campbell Barker?" she asked with a lighthearted grin.

The arm she clung to relaxed a fraction of an inch. "Do share."

"I'm going to make more mistakes. I just know I am, because that's *who* I am right now. This is me telling you I'll flub up some more. Maybe not as big, maybe not as dramatic, but flub I will. I don't know a healthy relationship from a pair of Payless shoes, but I'm sure gonna try to be an active participant in figuring it out. I can be a neurotic, paranoid loon, but from this moment on, no matter who I become involved with, I'm out in the open about it. Yes, I, Max Cambridge, can be infuriatingly difficult. There," she said with a jut of her chin.

"Now all I need is a strong, determined man who can handle a hot tamale like me." She let the challenge slip from her lips, daring him to take the bait. "So either it'll be you, or somewhere down the road, it'll be someone else. But I will move ahead, and I will have another relationship. A successful one."

The corner of Campbell's lips gave a slight turn upward. "You callin' me weak because I threw my hands up in the air?"

"Nope. I'm calling you misguided for dumping me—or letting me dump you."

Max watched the war in his head via his undecided blue eyes as they stared down at hers. It was time to bring out her last bit of artillery.

"And here's something else you might want to chew on while you sip high tea over there in London. I. Love. You. That's right. I said it. *I. Love. You.* I didn't want to. I was afraid to let it happen. But there it is. Do with it what you will." Letting go of his arm, Max turned to leave with one last thought. "I, on the other hand, am getting into my car before my teeth break from chattering and my feet get dry and cracked. I can't afford pedicures these days and no man—*no man*— is worth that kind of ugly."

"Did I just hear you right?"

Max stopped, her back to him, a chattering smile flitting across her lips. "You heard me. No man's worth ugly feet."

Campbell's hand clamped on to her shoulder, turning her around. "Did *you* just tell *me* you love me?"

Max's eyebrow rose. "Do you need to borrow Irene Riley's hearing aid?"

"Say it again. Go on. I dare you," he taunted.

She let go a mock sigh of irritation. "I love you, but my feet right now? Not so much. I'm missing a shoe."

Campbell was grinning, the biggest, widest grin she'd seen on his lips to date. "You said it first."

"Is there a rule that says I shouldn't?"

"You came all the way over here to tell me *you—love—me.*"

Max understood the huge step she'd taken, and now she recognized Campbell understood, too. She was putting herself out on a limb, whether it was comfortable or not, wobbling her way toward him with the best imitation of a tightrope walker she knew how to do. "Yeah, well, I'll be loving you from the afterlife if you keep me out here one more second."

Campbell hauled her into his arms, stopping her world when he drew her lips to his. They were warm despite the freezing temperature, warm and healing.

Max sighed into his mouth, soft, willing, pushing her hands under his jacket to wrap her arms around his lean waist.

Campbell pulled away first when she shivered. "You're freezing, honey, and you only have one shoe."

Max clung to his neck. "I'd have two if you didn't make me chase you down like Flo-Jo," she said with a smile against his neck.

"So I guess you don't want to push the cart?"

"I want to go home and bathe in the microwave."

Campbell suckled her bottom lip, sending hot waves of pleasure along her spine. "I can think of better ways to warm you up."

Her sigh was breathy, and she almost lost focus. "Yeah, me, too."

"*Reallllly?*" he drawled, low and sexy.

"Yep, and I'll show you all three and a half of them if you do the right thing here."

"In the parking lot? Wow, Max Henderson—give you four days of self-healing and you're an animal," he growled.

Letting her arms fall to her sides, Max penetrated his desire-filled gaze with serious eyes. "That's not what I mean, and you know it, and hurry it up before I have to have my foot amputated."

A lone snowflake fell, landing on her nose. Campbell brushed it away then cupped her chin, his eyes tender and so, so genuine. "I love you, Max Henderson. *Big.*"

A sting of pleasure punctured her heart. Perfect and pure, it settled in right where it should have always been. Exactly where it now belonged. Max pulled him down for a kiss. "Know what really says love?"

Scooping her up, he carried her toward his truck. "What's that, honey?" he grunted.

"A new pair of shoes."

"I'll scour Payless until its shelves are bare," Campbell teased, yanking open the door to his truck and tucking her inside.

"Promise?" she asked, dragging him to her lips for one more delicious kiss.

His blue eyes held hers for a long moment, solemn and honest in the intent she recognized he meant to convey. "That's definitely a *promise.*"

EPILOGUE

Note from Max Henderson-Barker to all ex-trophy wives and a final note on the art of sucking it up: When life sends you a monsoon, once the heavy rainfall has passed and you clear the debris, suck it up, Princess, and dance in the puddles. You *can* do this. You *will* do this—even if it blows big chunks. You will *not* give up. Nothing in life is worth having if it comes easy. Just ask me—I've got buttloads of worth.

"So now that you've heard my story, in closing, this is what I have to say to all of you. I know where you are. I lived where you are. I hated where you are," Max said, tacking on a knowing smile.

Her audience laughed. An audience that included Lacey Gleason. An audience of ten women or so, tired, alone, afraid.

But not for long. "But I can assure you, short of a natural disaster, I'm never going back to where you are again. And if I can prevent it, I promise you don't have to stay where you are either. Here at Trophy Jobs Employment Agency we provide job training, counseling, and the first of its kind Suck It Up, Princess, Boot Camp for the formerly privileged. It won't be easy for a lot of you. Adjusting to places like Walmart and Payless shoes will seem like a travesty. However, I need you to trust me when I tell you, Payless shoes are better than no shoes. Walmart might not employ personal shoppers, but it has a helluva deal on ramen noodles in bulk."

Each woman glanced around her, unsure, afraid, yet Max saw the determination to survive. It was only an ember, but who better than her to breathe life into that spark of a flame?

Her smile was warm when she concluded, "In closing, I'd just like to say that first, I'm so happy to have you all as employees. You each bring something unique to the Trophy Employment table, and I look forward to your input. And second, as we begin this venture together, one more bit of advice—no one but you can truly help yourself. It takes strength and the will to succeed—no whiners allowed. But if you heed my words when I say, 'Suck it up, Princess,' and get to the business of thriving, I promise you, you'll dance in the puddles of the monsoon responsible for washing away your former life."

From the back of the room, Campbell began to clap, joined by Len and Adam, who sat side by side, holding hands. Following suit were Connor, Mona, Mary, Gail, Mr. Hodge, Garner, and several of the seniors from the Village who'd offered their retired services in starting up Trophy Jobs Employment.

Max made her way around the tables in the coffee room, giving each woman a hug and a word of encouragement.

Campbell held out a hand to her, and she took it, still thrilled by the shot of happiness it sent to her heart. "So, how does it feel to be a business owner on her way to getting a fancy college degree, Max Barker?"

Max planted a kiss on his lips. "It feels pretty damn good."

Connor handed out paper cups filled with pink punch, nudging Max. "I have to hurry, Mom. I hate to trash your big day, but I gotta get back to study for my SAT."

Max tweaked his cheek. "I'm so proud of you, kiddo, and I'll miss you like crazy when you're off at college. Now, gimme a hug and beat feet." Connor obliged before thumping Campbell on the back and taking off.

"Wise investment you made with all that money Dorothy left you,

Maxine," Adam commented, tucking Len closer to him. Never once had Adam asked for payment of the debt Max owed him for not only helping her finally get divorced, but for recouping the money Dorothy had intended for her and Connor.

In turn, when Adam had come across two women so much like the person she once was, who needed representation but were penniless, she'd hired them. Skilless, clueless, and still sobbing over the loss of their private jets as they were.

"That's my girl," Mona bragged. "Finally landed on her feet. She's a slow learner, but when she gets it, she gets it."

Gail poked her head over Mona's shoulder. "I still say you should have shipped Penis-less off to jail for stealing your money."

Len's head nodded her agreement, running an affectionate hand over Adam's arm. "I'm with Gail. I rather liked the mental picture of him in orange."

Max shot Gail and Len an affectionate smile. "Oh, don't think for a second I wouldn't have, but he agreed to counseling with Connor and he shows up twice a week faithfully. If it mends their fences and teaches Fin to be a better parent, I'd rather see that than him end up Little Anthony's bitch."

Campbell pulled Max tight to his side, pressing a kiss to the top of her head. "So a toast—to sucking it up, and new beginnings!"

"Hear-hear!"

"Hear-hear," Max whispered up at him, wiping a drop of pink punch from the corner of his mouth.

Campbell nipped at her thumb. "So you suppose, being the boss, you can take *long* lunches?" He wiggled his eyebrows.

A thrill of warmth sizzled in her veins. "You just want to try out the new couch in the meditation room, don't you?"

"It is pretty comfortable," he whispered, nipping her ear.

"I guess I could be talked into it," she whispered back.

"Then I say we leave the celebrating to everyone else." Taking hold of her hand, Campbell led her out of the coffee room and down the small hallway to the infamous couch.

Max went instantly to the big window in the center of the room. The view from it never failed to thrill her. It was in a prime location, right in the center of busy downtown.

Campbell locked the door, coming up behind her to pop the button on her blazer and cup her breasts. "Have I told you I love you today?"

Arching back against him, Max shook her head. "Nope, but I have it covered. I love you, Campbell. You're the smartest choice I've ever made."

He walked her toward the couch, running his hot palms over her length. "You wanna show me how smart you are?"

Max chuckled, low, her throaty laugh filled with desire. "In spades."

Just as Campbell pulled her down to the couch and seconds before she let everything else go but the deliciously wicked things he'd do to her body, she caught one last glimpse of the view from the window.

Her window.

The one that overlooked downtown.

At a location that just happened to be right up the road from Cambridge Automobiles.

Didn't that put your seat in something sweet?